Wasteland

A Novel by Ann Bakshis

Published by Ponahakeola Press, 2015

Typeset in Garamond and Andale Mono

For my husband and kids. Thanks for putting up with my craziness through this journey.

TABLE OF CONTENTS

CHAPTER 1

My training today didn't go as expected. Neither did the screaming match I had with Devlan. He never wants to explain anything fully to me. No matter how many times I ask about my past, the nightmares I keep having, or my ability to heal from any injury in minutes, he skirts the topics. I know I'm not a typical person, but I'd at least like to know something about where I come from.

It's well past midnight when I finally walk through the door, returning after spending the last several hours cooling off. My temper can get the best of me. It can get to the point of pure rage, exploding, so much so that I could kill someone. This scares me as I don't know what causes such anger to develop.

I know Devlan isn't asleep, but working below the kitchen in his workshop. A pinch of light is visible between the floorboards under the kitchen table, so I stomp my foot three times, alerting him that I'm safely home.

"Come down here," he shouts in response.

I open the door to the pantry next to the stove, lift up the trap door, and climb down, making sure to close the pantry door behind me.

The workshop is a narrow rectangular room lined with shelves covered in pieces of scrap metal, soldering torches, wires, blades of varying lengths, remnants of battle droids I have destroyed in my training, and several Levin guns in various stages of repair. The entire room is lit by two rush lights, small boxes with outdated bulbs carelessly secured into an outlet and run on solar power because the generator is currently off.

Devlan is sitting on his workbench at the end of the room, hunched over the Levin gun I used earlier in the day.

"You keep frying the conductor nodules in the grip," he snarls at me, not bothering to look up.

"It's not my fault," I exclaim, annoyed by his continual harshness of my weapons use. "I can't get any power from this gun and when I do, it burns up. The Beta gun is a lot easier to use."

"The Beta gun is a child's toy. You need to figure out how to operate the Levin gun without destroying it." He sets down his tools, turns around in his seat raising his tired gray eyes to meet my gaze, and scratches his crinkly forehead. "I know how this is supposed to work… theoretically. We'll try again tomorrow." He sighs, gesturing that I'm dismissed.

I climb back up the ladder, closing both the trap door and pantry door behind me, then head into my room where I rummage through the dresser extracting clothes to wear, choosing items based on their texture. The clothes I finally pick feel soft against my skin. The sheets and blankets are not as comfortable, but I'm really too tired to care.

"You can't take her," my mother screams from somewhere outside my bedroom door.

I keep still, lying curled up under my blanket, eyes glued to the door. Shadows move between the floor and the threshold as the light in the hallway flickers on.

"We don't have a choice," a man shouts back. The voice is deep and rough. I don't recognize it.

"It's not safe anymore. I have to take her," he answers, this time a little more calmly.

"I thought we had more time," my mother cries, the sound of her voice getting closer, echoing those of the footsteps that approaches.

"You've had six and half years. I know you expected more time, as did I, but somehow they've found out. We're not safe anymore."

The hinges of my bedroom door creak as it swings open. The light from the hallway blinds me momentarily, but I don't shut my eyes. The older man and my mother stand in the doorframe, staring me.

"She's not ready," my mother whispers.

"She will be," the man says as he walks over to my bed, picking me up, blankets and all.

I wake up at my usual hour of five a.m., trying to shake my head free of the dream that continues to permeate my mind almost every night. I slide out of bed, throw my long auburn hair into a ponytail, then grab my running shoes and a clean pair of socks. As I lace up my shoes I can hear Devlan moving about in the living room, his footsteps causing the floorboards to creak as he goes through the kitchen and out the back door to start the generator. I follow in his steps and pause on the lower step of the back porch, waiting for him to begin my count.

"Five minutes," he says as he starts the timer.

I bolt off the step running my hardest, heart pumping in rhythm with my legs, reaching the first marker in about one minute. The second marker is over a mile away so getting there in two minutes is going to be tricky; however the real issue is getting back to the house in the remaining two minutes. I know the course by memory. I know exactly where every boulder, cactus, and animal burrow is. I can run it blindfolded, but run two and a quarter mile course in under five minutes?

That I don't know.

Rounding the second marker, I know I'm not going to make it back in the five minutes Devlan instructed me to. I always feel he asks too much of me, pushes me too hard, but I never argue since it won't do any good. He is never cruel when I can't meet his demands, he just simply makes me do it again until I learn the tricks, the methods needed to achieve my goals and exceed them. I have yet to figure out the trick to this course. It has to be on the route back to the house. The markers Devlan uses are sensors that record my time and speed. He knows exactly when I get to the two markers without me having to tell him. As I round the last boulder with the third marker, the house is barely in view, but as I get closer I see Devlan standing by the back door holding a pitcher of water and shaking his head.

"Again," he says when he hands me the pitcher.

I take small sips so not to cramp up my stomach, and take off again. For the next three hours Devlan makes me run the course, only allowing me to take the occasional break for water and crackers. After my last lap he goes inside and begins to cook breakfast while I hobble into my room. My feet hurt and I can feel blisters trying to form on the tops of my toes, but they never appear. I throw my sweat-drenched clothes into the hamper in my closet, wrap myself up in my robe, and head to the bathroom to take a shower.

The water is warm, not hot, but comfortable. I stay in long after the soap has gone down the drain not wanting to leave. My stomach begins to growl. I quickly dry off, put my robe back on, and join Devlan at the cracked, blue Formica dining table.

Breakfast this morning consists of dry wheat toast and oat squares.

"I need you to go to the Refuge for me and pick up something."

"You're kidding, right?" I snort as I place my spoon down and pick up a glass of powdered orange juice.

"No, I'm not." His tone is serious, as is his demeanor.

I stare at him for a moment, anxiety welling up, fear taking over. I see the face of the man, who kidnapped me all those years ago, which causes my pulse to increase. Sweat breaks out on my palms and forehead. My voice lost for moments as I tremble with panic.

"All right," I finally respond, my body shaking.

I don't bother to finish my meal since my appetite has vanished. I place my dishes in the sink after scraping off the remnants into the trashcan by the back door, and head to my room. An old hunting knife I found a while ago buried under years of mud and sand, sits idle on my nightstand, so I pick it up and throw it, watching as it slams into the chipped drywall above my bed, sinking to its hilt.

I feel angry and betrayed at Devlan's request.

He has always forbidden me to go to the Refuge when he makes his monthly trips. He has drilled into my head that it's a risky place for people of the Wasteland to travel. The name is polar opposite of its true nature.

I dress wearing nothing but black, including my calf high boots and leather jacket. This attire will cause me to burn up on my trip as the full sun will be blasting down on me, and the baked desert ground will radiate it back up, but it'll make me easily forgettable. I remove the knife from the wall, place it back into its sheath, and tuck it in my boot.

Devlan is out front, moving my motorbike out from the small shed a few yards from the makeshift driveway. His truck is still parked in front of the house from his visit to the Refuge two days before. This strikes me as being greatly out of character since he always keeps the truck a mile away.

Each city has their own spy satellites that sweep over the Wasteland looking for people to steal, so if we keep the truck away from the house it won't be associated with belonging to a specific residence. He doesn't want anyone to notice the house is inhabited, despite it falling apart in places. But he's drawing the cities to our home with his truck being left visible. *How can he be so careless?*

"Why am I going to the Refuge when you were just there the other day?" I ask, as I tie my hair back into a ponytail and don my helmet.

"I got a message that something I requested several weeks ago has come in, so I want you to go get it since the truck is not working properly and I can't ride your motorbike."

I question his excuse in not going. His truck has always run fine, and I find it odd that he is so willing to let me go.

I straddle the bike, turning the key in the ignition.

"Who do I ask for when I get there?"

"Go up to the bar and ask for Rena."

I acknowledge him with a nod, place my foot on the back bar by the rear wheel, roll the handle forward, and take off down the long dirt covered driveway. I turn right onto the crumbling asphalt of the highway long extinct and head north.

CHAPTER 2

The Refuge is known to be the most dangerous place to go in the Wasteland.

People have been known to disappear here or die here. It's a recognized hangout for the Collectors: bounty hunters who scour the Wasteland taking people to be sold to the cities or other unknown locations. Since no one is sure who is a Collector, everyone risks capture whenever they go to the Refuge, but it's the only place to get supplies in order to survive.

This fact is one of the reasons I'm so upset that Devlan commanded me to go. The thought of being collected sends shivers down my spine. The more I think about the possibility of being taken, the sicker I feel. I doubt my knife will be enough to fend off a Collector.

I approach the turn-off for the Refuge and spot another vehicle approaching from the opposite direction. The small car is caked in red dust. The windshield is missing, exposing the two passengers in the front seat to the harsh elements. I doubt they can see me as I'm over a mile away. My vision has always been exceptional, as are my reflexes and agility, though my speed, not so much. I know Devlan can explain these oddities, but he refuses to tell me anything whenever I've asked.

The car turns off towards the Refuge, so I reduce my speed, wanting to put more distance between myself and the strangers. They disappear over a ridge and I feel it's now safe to make the turn myself. I accelerate down the sand-covered road, then up and over the ridge, spotting the Refuge about a half-mile away. I take it slow, checking for any other vehicles or pedestrians making their way to the ramshackle remains of a ranch. The house itself is still standing, but several burnt-out structures lie yards away; wire fencing stands bent and twisted, rusting down to the same color as the sand that surrounds it.

I throttle back, turning off the engine to quiet my approach, and coast the remaining stretch of earth to the entrance. I dismount the motorbike at the rotted out gate and walk the rest of the way, pushing the bike alongside. The car is parked just outside the front door, its occupants nowhere in sight. I don't feel comfortable leaving the bike exposed, so I push it around behind the house, securing it by two dumpsters. Sweat is pouring down my face after I remove my helmet, so I wipe my brow with the sleeve of my jacket before I strap the helmet to one of the handlebars. Prior to entering the structure, I make one full lap around the building noting the position of the windows and doors.

The structure is only one level, with two windows in the back, three along each side, and two up front on either side of the front door. The only other entrance to the house is at the rear by the dumpsters. The demeanor of the area is unremarkable. The one other functioning building on the property is a barn to the east. The clapboard siding is crumbling and splitting, the roof sagging badly at the back, and all but two windows are missing panes of glass.

I hesitate briefly on the porch, debating whether I've made the right choice in doing what Devlan wanted. Drawing in a deep breath, I reach for the doorknob, turning it slowly and gently before stepping over the threshold.

The air inside is stuffy, and fans sway dangerously as they try to circulate the stagnant air through the large room. The interior doesn't resemble that of a home, as it's apparent several walls have been removed, some meticulously, others violently. Their jagged remains stand testament to their demise. The hardwood floors are beaten and scratched, flower wallpaper is peeling from the remaining walls. Not much light is entering the room due to the heavy drapes covering the windows. Several couches are pushed up against the far right wall, bunched around a broken table, probably smashed in a fight no one bothered to clean up after. To the left, a long bar runs from one wall to another, and stools in various stages of collapse are positioned along the tarnished brass rail. The wall behind the bar is lined with shelves housing various sized liquor bottles. I scan the room one more time, but don't see the couple that had driven the car.

"You look lost," a scratchy voice speaks from behind the bar. The woman the voice belongs to must've been stooped below when I first walked in. Her short red hair is streaked with white, her skin is as tan as the wood flooring, and also as worn. Her frame is tall and slender like mine, except for her arms, which are quite a lot more muscular.

"I'm looking for Rena."

"Well you found her," the woman says, sweeping her arms at her sides.

I walk over to the bar, leaning against the cracked grain, not daring to sit down on one of the stools. "Devlan sent me."

Rena scans me up and down before replying, "Did he now?"

I hear a click from behind me.

Moving sideways I side-kick the man standing behind me, grabbing the gun from his hands as he falls, and point it at Rena before either of them can blink. The man lunges for the gun, but I'm too fast and have him back on the floor in seconds; his face contorts in a silent scream as my knife lies cradled against his throat, all the while still aiming the gun at Rena.

She looks down at the man cowering on the floor.

"I like her," she says to him before reaching below the counter for a glass and filling it with Tequila from a bottle behind her. "All right, sweetheart, you can let Terrance go now, he won't bother you again."

I hesitate, but do eventually remove the knife and slowly stand, still keeping the gun on Rena. The man rolls over onto his stomach, gut touching the floorboards. He pushes himself into an upright position and goes through a door at the rear of the room where he must've come from.

"You still gonna shoot me, or do you want Devlan's order?" Rena asks, staring down the barrel of the gun clutched tightly in my hand.

I look at the weapon, noticing it's not one I'm familiar with, so I place the firearm down on the counter...but not too far out of reach.

"What is it?" I ask, nodding towards the weapon.

"It's an old .38 caliber Smith and Wesson. Those haven't been made in well over a century, not since the end of the last revolt one hundred and forty years ago. Terrance found it a few months back. There aren't any bullets in it. He'd have to make his own but the fucker's too lazy." Rena reaches below the counter and brings up a large plastic tumbler. "You thirsty?"

I nod and watch as she fills it up with water.

I down the first offering, then ask for a refill.

I hadn't realized how thirsty I was until Rena offered the drink. As I'm working on my third glass and Rena goes to the back to get Devlan's item, I notice the people who arrived right before me come out of the back door with Terrance behind, carrying two large boxes of groceries. Several of the items sticking out of the top have a strange red and black label on them, but the decal looks distorted. Minutes after the couple leaves, Rena comes out carrying a thin flat box.

"Here you go," she says, as she sets it on top of the counter.

"Thanks."

I finish my water and am about to leave when Rena offers me lunch, which I accept as my stomach is already growling. I sit down on one of the stools and am surprised at the sturdiness, but I can feel the iron bar supporting the seat poking me in the ass, something I can deal with for now.

Terrance comes back as Rena leaves to make the food. He goes behind the bar, pours himself a shot of Tequila, forgetting about the one that was already poured for him. He spots it just as he is about to take a swig and slides the shot glass over to me, gesturing for me to pick it up, which I do.

We drink the Tequila in unison.

Terrance has no reaction to the liquid; however I feel a fire going down my throat and into my stomach. I begin to cough as my eyes tear up. Terrance quietly chuckles to himself while I grope for my water to squelch the inferno. Rena reappears with a plate loaded down with sandwiches just as I get my coughing under control. She places the plate on the counter and refills my water.

"Terrance must like you. He doesn't share his Tequila with just anyone."

I give a half smile as I reach for a sandwich and begin to eat, downing two of the ham and cheese concoctions. I'd have more, but my stomach is so full of water I can't eat another bite.

The front door bursts open, causing me to jump and instinctively reach for the gun.

The young man almost fills the entire frame. He's wearing a sleeveless brown shirt, dirt-stained jeans, and brown leather boots with a matching holster strapped over his right shoulder, crossing his chest and down over to his hip. He enters the room as if he owns the place, slamming the door behind him to further emphasize his presence.

"Rena," he shouts, as he walks over to the bar.

He carries himself like an alpha male, only he can't be much older than me. His brown hair hangs loose around his ears at the front, but dusts his shirt collar at the back.

"Quin, I've told you time and time again not to do that," Rena reprimands him.

"I can't help it," he grins, plopping down on the stool next to mine. "Where's Terrance? I have goods for him."

"He's in the backroom," Rena says, nodding towards the back door.

Quin scopes out the room just like I had when I first entered. I feel his eyes settle on me and stay.

"Why does *she* get food and I don't?" Quin says in a pouty voice.

"I hate when you're in one of these moods." Rena slides the plate over to him, but he doesn't pick up a sandwich.

"Who is she?" Quin demands, still staring at me.

"You can ask her yourself, but if she's smart she'll continue to ignore you."

I crack a smile then ask Rena where the bathroom is since the water has finally moved from my stomach to my bladder. She points to the back door and tells me that it's down the hall between the storeroom and bedroom. I take Devlan's package with me, not trusting Quin, who continues to watch as I make my way through the door.

The hallway is in worse shape than the bar area.

Parts of the floor have been eaten away by some kind of animal; planks have been placed along joists to make a path to travel down. Terrance is busy rearranging boxes in the storeroom as I pass by, noticing that many of the boxes have the same strange red and black decal. I find the bathroom and use it quickly because it smells of decay, mildew, and vomit. As I go back, Quin is standing in front of the door, barring me from going any further.

"I've never seen you around here before," he begins, "and I know everyone who lives in the Wasteland."

"Apparently you don't," I reply, shoving him out of my way. "Rena, do you have something I can carry this in? I rode my bike here," I ask as I walk to the bar, placing the package on the counter.

"Sure just give me a second," she says, laughing as she goes past Quin and down the hall.

"So, where do you live?" he inquires after regaining his composure.

"Around."

He takes hold of my arm, spins me around, and grabs my face with his other hand forcing me to look up at him, my feet rising a few inches off the floor.

"Be careful, little girl, people have a way of disappearing around here."

I feel the anger in his eyes bore into me, the heat from his flesh burns.

"You should watch who you threaten."

I grab his fingers squeezing my face and bend them back until he relinquishes. He loosens his grip, but holds tightly onto my arm, so I plant my boot into his left knee, smiling as I hear the crack and he crumples to the floor.

My anger can be quite dangerous, but sometimes it comes in handy.

"Here you go," Rena says nonchalantly. She is holding out a black leather satchel to me, Devlan's package inside. "Come again, hon'." She gives me a big hug and waves to me as I exit the house, the satchel strung across my chest.

I wonder how long Rena was standing there watching Quin and I tussle.

I feel a grin spread across my face as I exit the door, walk down the porch, and head to the back.

A laugh catches in my throat as I replay the image of Quin crumpling under my boot, but my joy is short-lived. I find my motorbike gone. My helmet is lying a few yards away, with the visor cracked. Lifting the lid off of the dumpster, I toss the mangled item in, slamming the lid shut, trying to help vent my anger, but not fully vanquishing the rage building. The air is superheated and burns my skin the longer I stay in one spot, so the only thing left for me to do is to begin my long journey home on foot.

The sun rises higher in the sky, causing the temperature to increase, forcing me to remove my leather jacket and stuff it in the satchel. Sweat pours down my face right into my eyes, along with a river running into my boots from my legs. I have to suppress the strong desire to take off my boots and walk home barefoot.

All sorts of deadly creatures live in the desert and not all of them are visible.

As thirst and heat begin to get the better of me, I finally spot the turn off for home. I drag my sore hot body down the lone driveway, eyeing not the house, but the water barrel along the south side of the property.

Dropping the satchel to the ground, I open the spigot and drink as much as my stomach will hold, drenching my face and hair in an effort to cool the outer layer of skin. I shut off the flow, pick the satchel back up, and go inside the house, listening as Devlan putters around in his workroom below. I should go there first, but my clothes are soaking, which makes my first priority a change in attire. In the bathroom I discard every piece clinging to me then step quickly into the small hallway, diving into my room as I hear Devlan open the pantry door.

"Meg, is that you?"

"Yes. I'll be there in a minute."

"Okay."

I know the remainder of the day will be dedicated to my training, so I put on cotton shorts, a tank top, brush out my hair, secure it back into a ponytail, and slip on my running shoes. I go to fetch the satchel that I dropped on the couch in the living room, but it's not there. Devlan tosses me my jacket just as I'm entering the kitchen, the satchel resting in his lap.

"Go out back and start setting up, I'll be out there shortly," he says, standing up and heading to the pantry door.

I exit the back door, walk down the steps, and over to the clapboard storage shed that leans against the house. Inside sits one working battle droid, five ten-pound boulders, random scraps of metal, several detonators, and an arm brace for the Beta gun.

I set out the boulders in a semi-circle thirty yards from the house, placing a detonator on top of each. I head back to the shed and drag out the battle droid, along with my arm brace. I slide the sleeve of the brace up my right bicep, securing it in place by a thick black Velcro strap, making sure the rest of the brace, which is used to help steady my aim, is not too tight around my arm. Although the Beta gun is lightweight, the toll it takes on my body when using it causes muscle spasms, and the brace is there to prevent too much movement. The last strap I secure is the glove around the palm of my hand, into which I wiggle my fingers, checking my circulation.

As I begin to work the knobs on the battle droid to get it functioning, Devlan steps out with the Beta gun and a newly repaired Levin gun.

"Don't fuss with that," he says, as he swipes at the droid. "Let's see how this goes today before we bother with that junk."

I leave the droid and walk over to the small wicker table that sits on the edge of the cracked terra cotta patio. Devlan sets each gun down as well as a small first aid kit that he has tucked under his arm. I pick up the Beta gun and examine the energy chamber in the handle, but notice it's empty.

"Devlan, I can't use this," I say, as I hold up the gun for him to inspect. "It hasn't been charged."

"I know."

I look at him quizzically, trying to ascertain his motive for giving me an unloaded weapon. "What do you expect me to do with it?"

"Well, for starters, I want you to use the Levin gun." He picks it off of the table, handing it to me, and removes the Beta gun from my other hand. "After that we'll see what happens."

"Happens? Happens with what?"

"Oh, I removed all the safety features from the Levin gun."

"You did what?" I shout at him. "I'll blow my arm off if I try and use it without those."

"I have a theory."

"You and your theories! What makes you think any of your theories will work? When have they ever worked?"

Devlan looks genuinely pained at my comment.

I feel guilty for saying it, but it's the truth.

His theories have rarely worked. Sometimes I've felt like nothing more than his own personal experiment, watching, waiting to see how my body will respond to his various forms of torture. The removal of the safety attributes for the gun is most worrisome. The energy the gun produces is beyond destructive. The Beta gun will simply put small holes in the items it hits, but the Levin gun will create a much bigger blast hole, even with the safety features on. If they are off, it can cause its target to shatter, no matter the size.

The power is beyond control without the needed protections.

I reluctantly look at the gun in my hand, sigh in assent, and slide the handle of the weapon into the grip of my glove, listening for the click as the nodules on the grip sync with the ports in the glove.

With the safety features disabled, pressure begins to build in the palm of my hand and flow up my arm.

It's a sensation I've never felt before. It doesn't hurt, but I feel as if an electrical charge has begun to pulse through my body, slow at first, then faster. I'm not sure what to make of it.

Stepping closer to the boulders, I aim at the detonator blinking red on top of the rock to my right. I hesitate, not sure if I should squeeze the trigger, afraid of what might happen. Glancing over at Devlan, he nods with his arms crossed against his chest. I look back at the detonator, taking a deep breath as I pull the trigger.

An intense pain rushes up my arm, and my right shoulder blade explodes from the wave as it finds an exit out of my body.

A shrill scream fills the air—coming from me.

I drop the gun and crumple to the ground, feeling the warm flow of blood running down my back. I begin to rip at the arm brace that is holding my useless limb together, but Devlan grabs my hand, indicating for me to stop. My throat is raw from screaming, but I continue until no sound can come out. Devlan squats down with his first aid kit, rummaging around until he comes up with a syringe containing a creamy white liquid.

I begin to push him off of me as he advances with the needle.

For a man so old he is incredibly strong.

He subdues me, cradling me in a hug as he reaches over my right shoulder and injects the liquid into the mangled flesh that was my back. I begin to convulse as shock sets in; dry heaves take over and I shake uncontrollably. Devlan disappears from my view, but returns moments later with a thick wool blanket that he wraps around me. He sits back down next to me.

Why isn't he cleaning my wound? I wonder. *And what was that shot?*

As the minutes slowly pass I begin to feel better. The pain in my back is subsiding…I no longer shake. As I continue to stare at Devlan, he seems to be mentally assessing the situation. I try and find my voice to speak, but it's gone, only a whisper remains.

"What did you give me?" I finally croak.

"Quarum, it's to help with the healing."

The more time that passes, the better I feel.

Gingerly, I begin to remove the straps from the brace. Devlan helps to slowly pull down the sleeve, stopping every few moments as I wince at the residual discomfort. My eyes remain closed, afraid of what I might see. I no longer feel blood running down my back, but that appears to be the only good news so far. With one last gentle tug the brace is removed and I open my eyes to stare down at my arm.

Considering the agony I was in just minutes before, the damage is surprisingly minimal.

There are two small holes in the palm of my hand from the ports in the glove that are getting smaller and smaller. A thick blue line snakes around my forearm, through my elbow, and ensnaring my bicep, before disappearing just below my shoulder. This must be the place where the energy found the weakest point in my body and exited out my back.

"What the hell is this?" I cry, pointing to my arm.

"You'll be fine, Meg," Devlan says, as he tries to comfort me. "You're going to be okay. Why don't you go into the house and change?"

I'm shocked by Devlan's behavior. You would think he would be more concerned with the damage he has caused me, but he's taking it all in stride. I, on the other hand, am terrified by what has just happened.

What is this line? What does this mean? What has he done to me?

Still in shock, I reluctantly get up, almost losing my balance. Devlan catches me, helping to right me. I drop the blanket on the ground and retreat into the house where I begin to scour the rooms for a small hand mirror so I can check out the damage to my back. I finally locate one at the bottom drawer of my dresser, so I step into the bathroom, shutting the door and removing my blood-soaked shirt. I drop the garment into the sink, turn my back against the mirror, and lift the hand mirror to see the reflection.

The raw angry flesh pokes out in spots, but is healing rapidly. Several scars begin to form. Usually when I heal my skin heals smoothly, but this wound is too horrific to mend nicely. I continue to watch as the redness turns gradually lighter, then back to my normal skin color. Using my left hand, I try to reach over my shoulder and touch the area. Black charred spots flake off, replaced by clean pink skin. Twenty minutes after the Levin gun destroyed my shoulder blade, the only remnants of the mishap are four jagged scars around a small circular spot. I look down at my hand and I see two new freckles in my palm, but the blue line remains, diminished some in intensity.

I leave the bathroom, enter my room, and put on a clean shirt. Devlan is still sitting on the ground where I left him when I return. He looks up at me, the pained look has returned to his face.

"You all right?" he asks, as I reach down and pick up my arm brace, which is lying in his lap.

"I'm fine," I lie, not wanting to show how much I hate him right now.

I begin to put the brace back on, noticing it's undamaged, but Devlan places his hand on top of mine.

"I don't think you'll need that anymore." He takes the brace, walks over to the table, and picks up the Beta gun, handing it to me. "Try it now."

"There isn't any power in it," I remind him.

He thrusts the gun into my hand, almost hitting me in the stomach.

I shake my head, take the gun, aim, and fire at the detonator I'd been aiming at before. A small burst of blue energy leaves the muzzle, exploding the detonator on impact. I have to blink my eyes a couple of times to make sure I'm seeing correctly.

The energy for the gun came from me.

What the hell? I think. *How is that possible?*

What am I?

Somewhere inside, pleasure begins to grow. I fire at the remaining detonators with the same results. Devlan is beaming with joy. Apparently his theory, whatever it is, worked.

I spend the next several hours battling the droid, dodging its slashes and fire as I move from boulder to boulder, sometimes having to jump a gap of ten feet between rocks. I'm able to take out two of the droid's Pugio blades, long swords that have a thick blade with a curved tip, before I'm taken down by a Levin gun blast; another scar to live with. I heal shortly after the injury, but there isn't any mark remaining. My wound has healed a lot quicker this time than before.

What, exactly, was in that syringe Devlan injected me with? Did the Quarum speed up my healing ability even more?

The sun is setting, so I have to stop and help Devlan clean up the mess I made from the best training day I've had thus far. Scraps from the detonators are placed into a small tin trashcan, and the battle droid is shut down and stored back in the shed. Devlan takes the guns back into the house. I step inside the shed and turn off the generator.

When I get back to the house Devlan is cooking dinner on the gas stove, with several rush lights so he can see. I head to the bathroom to take a shower in the cold water, which feels good against my hot skin. Goosebumps form on my arms and legs, but I stay in anyway. When I hear Devlan call that dinner is ready, I step out and wrap myself up in a robe, putting my hair up in a towel. We can't keep fresh meat or vegetables in the fridge since it's not constantly running, so canned foods are our most common staple. I'm not much of a fan of canned stew, but I devour two hefty helpings.

As soon as the kitchen is cleaned up, I go to my room, rummaging in the dark for a clean pair of shorts and pajama top, but wind up putting on a pair of running shorts and a tank top since all my other clothes appear to be dirty. I know I should go to bed, but I'm too wired from the day. As I look down at my arm, I'm alarmed to see a slight blue glow radiating from my injury.

Great, and now I glow in the dark too, I think, shaking my head in disbelief.

I don't want the scar to be visible, but I really don't have any long sleeves to cover it up with except for my leather jacket, which I can't wear constantly in this heat. The sleeve part of the brace pops into my head. The material is thin but durable, and I didn't notice the wound in my arm until I took it off, so it should conceal the glow quite well. I exit the house, open up the storage shed, and locate the brace on the bottom shelf. I go back into the house, wondering where to work since I don't have rush lights in my room. Devlan is working down below, so I open up the pantry door and make my way into his workshop.

He doesn't look up as I pull a stool over and place the brace on a workbench next to him. Looking around at the tools, I reach for a pair of pliers to use to gently work the material free from its rough-sewn exterior. I try not to snag or tear the sleeve as I carefully labor the next hour extracting it, leaving the Velcro strap on for the bicep so I have a way to secure it. I slip the sleeve on, fastening it at the top most section of my arm. It looks a bit out of place with the rest of my clothing, but it covers every inch of the glowing line. I leave the brace section on the workbench and head upstairs to go to sleep.

CHAPTER 3

Acrid smoke fills my lungs.

I open my eyes, but only see orange flames flicker in the distance as ash thickens the air. The wailing of sirens is overpowered by the screams and cries of the children around me. The door into our bedroom is sealed. My bed is closest to the door, so I try to squint through the air to see if anyone is coming to our rescue. I notice a woman trying frantically to open the portal, screaming silently.

The windows inlayed in the door are blackening as I lose sight of her, so I slide down from my bed and onto the scalding hot floor, crawling my way over to the entrance, desperate for any fresh air that may be blowing through the gap in the floor, as my skin begins to blister from the heat.

The cries begin to diminish, but the screams beyond the walls of the bedchamber escalate. I place my small fingers into the opening between the door and the floor and feel a warm hand squeeze my fingers...and someone calls out my name.

"Meg."

A voice echoes in my nightmares. I feel my body rock back and forth, gently at first, then more violently as I try to shake off whoever is disturbing my sleep.

"Meg, get up NOW!"

The scream in my ears causes me to jump upright in bed, nearly colliding my face with Devlan's.

"What?"

"Get some shoes on and grab whatever clothes you can, then meet me down in the workshop. Do it now."

He leaves the room almost at a run. I sit disoriented from sleep for a few seconds before the anxiety in his voice registers. Diving into my closet, I grab a small duffle bag and begin to shove dirty clothes in, as well as my boots, leather jacket, and knife. I slip on my running shoes, tie my hair back, and dart out of the room. The pantry door is open, and the rush lights are blazing below as I enter the kitchen. I climb down, closing all doors behind me.

"What is it?" I ask, reaching the bottom and placing the duffle on the floor by my feet.

Devlan ignores my question, grabs the item I saw him working on earlier, and shoves it into the satchel from the Refuge. My ears register a low beeping noise that I've never heard before. Looking over to a panel on the far right wall I see a relay switch blinking in time with the sound. Devlan turns to me and pushes the satchel into my hands.

"That's marker number three," he says. "Two minutes before they reach marker number two."

I stare at him, puzzled.

Markers? I think, trying to make sense of what he is saying. *Markers? Mile markers...my mile markers...my racecourse.*

"They who? Who's coming?" I ask.

The second relay on the wall begins to blink, causing the noise to increase.

"Collectors...Collectors will be here. They must be in a vehicle to have reached the second marker already."

The message finally hits home.

The course was not just for me to train on, but to also see how long it would take someone to reach the house on foot. Devlan always knew where I was in the course because he had a relay system synced up to the markers, alerting him to my progress. If they have passed marker two it will take them one minute to get here, but that's on foot, so who knows how soon if they're in a vehicle.

Devlan sees that I understand the situation, and rushes past me to a heavy wooden dresser that he keeps his scraps in, next to the ladder. He shoves it with all his strength, sliding it along the wall, revealing a four-foot-high hole. He picks up my duffle bag, turns me around, and shoves me hard into the hole, tossing the duffle bag in behind me. I begin to protest, but he is already moving the dresser back into place. I begin to try to move it out of the way when I stop, hearing pounding from the floorboards above us.

Devlan didn't extinguish the rush lights, so the intruders will definitely know someone is below the kitchen. I hear shouts as wood is broken, furniture beginning to crash overhead. In the darkness, I turn around and notice the hole is actually a tunnel. I sit down on the red dirt, leaning against the dresser, trying to hear what is going on. There are more crashes and shouts followed by Devlan yelling. They appear to have made their way into the workshop.

I want to scream for them to leave when I glimpse small red lights beginning to blink around me in the tunnel.

Detonators.

The blinking means they have been activated, and the faster they blink, the closer they are to exploding. I grab my items and begin to crawl as fast as possible down the tunnel, but only make it twenty feet when the first of the detonators goes off, igniting the rest. I curl up in a ball, protecting my head from the debris raining down on me. The tunnel begins to collapse, so I sprint down the shaft, bent over, scraping my back against the ceiling as I go. The smell of fresh air begins to strengthen the farther I go, so I know I'm close to the exit.

I crawl up a slight incline to reach the surface, spotting my stolen motorbike parked a few feet away, as if expecting my arrival.

Before taking off, I strap the bags to the back of the bike. The urge to go back and help Devlan is strong, but my gut tells me to keep going, rather than look back to see what is happening to the place I have called home for the last ten years.

After going a mile, I reach a large mound of rocks. I park the bike at the bottom, rummage through the bag Devlan gave me, and find a pair of night vision goggles. Climbing the mound, I lie on my stomach at the top, and peer out at the landscape south of me.

The house is ablaze, fire licking every eave, as well as the shed. Three figures in dark clothing are rolling around on the ground, probably injured by the blast. I scan the yard and see two large vehicles parked by the boulders I use for target practice. Adjusting the setting on the goggles I zoom in for a closer look. Two people are standing by the vehicles, hands securely wrapped around weapons I don't recognize. The intruders are heavily protected, including face masks.

The house begins to collapse from the fire, but I don't see any sign of Devlan.

I know he is lost. My heart feels certain of it.

I stem the tears that try to escape my eyes. *Why should I mourn a man who denied me a childhood? A man who robbed me of my mother? I owe him nothing.*

My focus changes to the attackers and their mode of transportation.

The vehicles are large, dark, and without headlights; however they do have a bluish light emanating from the undercarriage. The wheels are thick rubber, attached by hefty suspensions to accommodate for the rocky desert terrain. One window at the front and four doors, two on either side of the vehicle, are open. I can't see inside as they are positioned perpendicular to me.

I've counted five people so far, and there are two more at the front of the house. Seven in total that I know of, but how many did they start out with? Their clothing is uniform; they're all wearing the same black armor, masks, and carrying the same weapons. I keep watching long after they leave, until the fire begins to die down to only smoldering wreckage. The sun will be up soon and I need to find shelter, but I don't dare move in the darkness, not with the remaining Collectors out there possibly looking for me.

I slide down to the bottom of the mound, sit in the sand, and lean my head against the cold rock.

What is wrong with me?

Anger is all I feel. Devlan was never mean or abusive to me. I should be torn-up inside as he was my only friend in this inhospitable land.

I'm not sure how long I sit there, but eventually the sun begins to creep over the horizon. Leaning over, I drag the satchel across the ground to assess what Devlan has given me. The first thing I pull out is a Beta gun, then the Levin gun that injured me. I set those aside and continue digging, pulling out a few detonators, one small metal canister, and something I recognize as a computer tablet, with a hand-written note taped to the screen.

Meg,

I have encoded your history into the memory of this device. It will only work if you place your right palm onto the screen. Anything you have ever questioned or wondered about is right here. Don't let anyone see you with this. Don't trust anyone you meet. Everyone in Sirain has their own agenda, even if they are from the Wasteland. No one can be trusted. I'm sorry I couldn't tell you in person. Everything I've done has been to protect you, please remember that. I've always thought of you as my daughter and I'm grateful for our time together.

—Devlan

My eyes finally begin to tear up then spill down my cheeks. He never told me how he felt about anything, especially me. I thought of him as my captor, and even jailer, not someone who genuinely had feelings. Let alone someone who cared about me.

I place the tablet back into the satchel, pick up the metal canister, and twist off the top. Inside are two syringes of Quarum. I seal the canister and shove everything back into the satchel then walk over to the bike, and dig in my duffle bag until I find my leather jacket, which I slip on. After strapping the satchel across my chest and secure the duffle to the back, I start the bike and head north.

I stay off of the main road and travel across the desert terrain. Luckily the monsoon season is months off, so the ground is hard and cracked, leaving perfect traction to ride on. I'm not sure where to go, but I keep heading north. Buildings are scarce so it will be hard to locate any useful shelter. The only place I can think of heading to is the Refuge.

I see the dilapidated roof of the barn about a half-mile away, so I throttle down and approach the area cautiously. There doesn't seem to be any sign of movement on the property so I turn off the engine, hop off the bike, and approach on foot, concealing my bike behind an enclave of rocks and tumbleweed several hundred feet south of the barn. I quicken my pace and sprint across the open expanse between the barn and the house, open the door, and then gently close it behind me, trying not to make any noise. The living room and bar are empty. I don't dare call out, just in case a Collector is hiding somewhere on the premises.

I walk over to the doorway at the back, looking through the small window in the door to see if anyone is in the hallway, but it's empty so I carefully step through and walk over the planks covering the basement. Rena is down below, going through crates with the red and black emblem. I begin to retreat backwards towards the door when the board I'm on begins to crack. Rena looks up when she hears it and sees me. At first she looks annoyed, but a smile slowly surfaces.

"I'll be up in a minute, hon," she calls out to me.

I exit into the living room, plopping myself down onto one of the broken couches. My eyes begin to get heavy, so I lay my head down onto the arm, falling asleep.

At some point I feel the weight of a blanket on me, so I wrap myself up further into it and lie fully extended on the couch, going back to sleep. My nap is restless, full of nightmares. Collectors oozing out of the walls, coming up through the floorboards, reaching for me, grabbing at my arms as I try to run. At last I'm caught, bound, and dragged through the desert. I lie there waiting for the inevitable. My heart pounds as I'm secured to a boulder, watching as a Collector stands feet in front of me, aims a Levin gun and fires, causing my body to explode into a dozen pieces.

I bolt upright, sweat drenching my clothes and the blanket. As I'm removing my jacket, I look around noticing that Rena is tending bar - though no one is around. I flop back down on the couch, rubbing my forehead as I try to erase the nightmare, along with the headache that is beginning to form.

"I wasn't sure you were ever going to open your eyes," Rena says as she walks over to me with a tall glass of liquid. I sit up as she hands it to me. The water is warm, but I don't mind. She sits on the couch opposite mine, watching me. "You look like hell, girl."

I try my best not to break down since Devlan warned me not to trust anyone. I do tell her my name as I didn't mention it on our first visit, then about Devlan's death, the Collectors, and that I didn't know where to go next. She gestures towards my right arm and the sleeve. I hesitate for only an instant, but explain that I was burned by the fire at the house. This seems to satisfy her, as that's the only question she asks.

"You can stay in the barn for now. There's a mattress up in the hayloft, a shower in one of the old horse stalls, and you can keep your bike in there as well. The barn is sturdier than it looks and no one ever goes in there."

I stand up, Rena does the same, and I walk out of the front door as she goes to the back room to make me something to eat after I tell her I can't remember when I last ate. I find my bike where I left it, walk it into the barn, and park it into one of the eight stalls that line the walls of the structure. I find the ladder for the loft, hoist both the duffle and satchel over my shoulders, then climb up.

The mattress Rena was referring to is just several blankets sewn together, with bits of tuft sticking out of the seams. I set my bags down and drag several hay bales over from the other side, lining them up between the mattress and wooden railing so I have some cover in case anyone decides to wander in. The position of the mattress allows me a perfect vantage point to see the drive into the Refuge. I will be able to see anyone who enters or exits, if they use the drive. I put the duffle bag at the head of the mattress to use as a pillow and remove both guns from the satchel, stashing them in-between the hay bales.

Hearing movement below me, I reach for one of the guns and look down to see Rena holding a plate of food in one hand, and blankets and towels in the other. I descend the ladder and meet her in the center of the building.

"The shower is over in that stall," she says, pointing to the last stall on the left. "It's not much, but the water runs. Here are a couple of towels and that blanket you used on the couch, along with an additional one. It can get cold out here at night. The only one here during the night-time is Terrance, and he sleeps in the bedroom at the northwest corner of the house. Let me know if you need anything else before I leave, which will be in about two hours."

She hands me the plate, blankets, and towels. As she turns to go I ask her about the mattress up in the loft and why it's there.

"My brother used to spend the night here. This is his place, but I haven't seen him in years. He went out on a raid...and never came back." Her face contorts as a memory takes hold.

I thank her as she quickly exits, holding back tears. Sitting down on the mattress and covering my lap with the blanket, I slowly eat my sandwiches - loaded with peanut butter. Once I have consumed about half of them, I grab a tank top and a pair of shorts then head back down the ladder to take a shower.

The floor of the stall is stained concrete, not hay like the rest of the barn. A makeshift shelf hangs precariously by the showerhead, with an old bar of soap and nothing else. There's no shower curtain, so anyone who walks in will see me naked, but I'm too ready for a shower to care. I spot a broken mirror on the opposite wall, and take a quick glimpse of myself in the reflection, noticing the black and brown smudges all over my face, and my hair sticking up in spots, with bits of debris clinging to my scalp.

I shed my clothes with the exception of the covering on my arm, place the towels I'd picked up from the floor over the railing of the stall, turn the knob, and wait several minutes until the brown water that first comes out turns clear. My head hangs down as I stand under the cold trickle with my eyes closed. I turn and reach for the bar of soap, washing the layers of crud off before using it, then clean every inch of my body several times over, causing my skin to turn pink and raw from the vigorous scrubbing. I use the soap on my hair since I don't have anything else, and pick out small bits of earth and wood. I even wash the covering on my arm, going gently over the area.

I shut off the tap, wrap myself up in the bath towel, and use my fingers to comb through my hair. After I'm dried off thoroughly, I put the newer clothes on even though they're dirty, drape the towels over the rail to dry, then wander from stall to stall, looking for whatever I can find that might be of some use. Several stalls have hay bales; in another I find a washboard and tub, which I drag over to the shower and then go rummaging for some soap to wash my clothes only to come up empty. I climb back up the ladder with the blanket that had fallen earlier and finish off my sandwiches.

When the food is all consumed, I take the plate and head back to the house. Terrance is standing behind the bar when I walk in. He downs a small shot of liquid before motioning me over. He pours me a shot of Tequila and another one for himself, picks up his glass gesturing for me to do the same, and we drink. He smiles at me, takes my plate, and goes out through the back door. Rena walks out a few minutes later with two crates. I grab one from her shaky grasp and place it on top of the bar as she sets hers down next to mine, plops down on a stool, and lets out a sigh.

"Thanks, that was heavy. So, you're settled in?"

"Yes, but I need to wash my clothes. I found a washboard and tub, but no laundry soap. Do you have any?"

"Let me go ask Terrance what we have in stock." Rena leaves, returning a few minutes later with a small box of powered detergent. "You're in luck, this is his last one."

"Thanks," I say, as I take the box from her. "How does he get more?"

"Oh, he has his ways," she replies with a sly smile and wink. "Well, I'm going to be heading out soon. Do you need anything before I go?"

I shake my head in reply.

"Well if you do, Terrance is here, but be careful not to startle him as he sleeps with a knife under his pillow."

"Thanks for the warning. Do you need help with these?" I ask, pointing to the two crates.

"No, those are for Quin. He'll be here in about an hour to pick them up."

I thank her again for the soap and leave since I don't want to be around when Quin shows up, especially if he is looking for payback from yesterday.

After scrubbing everything as best I can, I drag the few garments I managed to toss into my duffle bag over the railings to let them dry. Luckily, today is an exceptionally hot day so they dry rather quickly. I repack them, clean up my mess, and go back up to my little den to look at the tablet before it gets too dark outside.

I lean my back against the wall, bend my legs up so I can rest the tablet on my thighs, place my right palm on the screen, and watch as the screen turns blue to scan my print...then it goes black. I place my palm on the device again, but it remains off, so I toss it to the end of the mattress, frustrated. My instinct is to drop it over the rail and onto the barn floor below, but Devlan left it for me to use, so there has to be a reason behind it.

The puttering of an engine breaks the silence.

Rolling over, I crawl closer to the opening in order to see who's arrived. Quin jumps down from the driver's side of a large truck, moving a little too well for someone who had his knee blown out yesterday. He goes into the house and comes back out seconds later with both crates in one arm. He sets them down in the bed of the truck, then goes back inside for a much longer stint, finally emerging with Terrance in tow. The two hop into the cab of the truck and head out. I'm half tempted to jump on my bike and follow them, but just as I'm staring at my gear, thinking about getting dressed, the tablet begins to ping.

I crawl to the end of the mattress and lay on my stomach as the screen goes from blue to green to gray. On the side of the thin device a small port opens, revealing a pair of headphones. I pull them out and attach them to my ears. The voice starts speaking as a faded picture of a little girl appears on the screen.

The little girl is me.

"Meg, I'm sorry I'm not there to tell you in person. This tablet is programmed to activate every evening for five days just before dusk, but you must place your palm on the screen five minutes before or it will

not turn on until the following evening. This is a security precaution to protect the information on this device from being read by anyone other than you. Also, the messages will only last for ten minutes."

The screen moves from my picture to another of flags covered in stars, stripes and other insignia of various colors, burning.

"The country was at war with itself, class against class. The wars raged on for decades. Tens of thousands died. Those who survived were left without homes, food, or social structure. Many tried to take control, who then lost to others who had greater power or more influence. A century passed with more wars and lives lost. After a tumultuous battle, the decimated land of Sirain was divided up into three cities: Nuceira, Acheron, and Tyre."

The screen shifts to a map displaying each city in its own quadrant: Tyre past a ridge of mountains to the West, Acheron sitting amongst a chain of lakes to the Northeast, and Nuceira on a peninsula surrounded by a large mass of open water to the South. The Wasteland sits in the center, surrounded on all sides by the cities and their outlying Boroughs.

"Workers were scarce, so the cities used their armies to collect small towns that had escaped the carnage of battle. One particularly large tent city, called Asphodel, had the largest causalities from the cities' raids; the only recorded incident where Tyre infiltrated Acheron land. Each city sent in spies or hired criminals to cause chaos and unrest in the others' territory."

The map lights up, displaying different colors for each region, showing just how small the Wasteland actually is, and emphasizing that Tyre has the largest mass of land compared to Acheron and Nuceira.

"The only time the cities banded together was to protect the entire land from raiders determined to destroy Sirain; however the High Rulers in each city didn't relish the idea of having their own citizens going off to fight, so they decided to send workers who lived in the Boroughs and outlying villages off to battle. When the Rulers realized they were losing the conflict because of the inadequacy of their troops, they decided to design them instead. They wanted an army of super soldiers."

The image changes to a picture of a man and a woman wearing gray uniforms, their muscles bulging in the tight material.

"The cities knew they needed a defense against the hostile forces. At first they argued about who would donate the researchers to create the soldiers, then they argued about which city would house the facilities needed. It took years for a compromise to be reached."

The screen goes blank. I remove the headphones and they retract back into the tablet. Lying in my spot, I wonder what this could possibly have to do with me. My head begins to hurt and I grow tired, so I store the tablet between the two hay bales by my head, lie down, and watch through the large hole in the barn's roof as the sun sets and the stars start to shine. The temperature begins to drop, so I grab both blankets, wrap myself up, and fall asleep.

CHAPTER 4

My sleeping is restless.

The nightmares tonight contain people without faces falling dead in front of me as I dodge bombs that drop out of the sky. I'm glad it's not my usual reoccurring nightmare, but it still disturbs me. A bomb falls next to me, but doesn't detonate. Instead it makes a beeping sound that doesn't stop. Through the haze of waking up, I realize the beeping noise is coming from outside my dreams, so I open my eyes, seeing only darkness. The beeping sounds again, this time outside the barn. Crawling closer to the opening, I peer out of the corner looking for whatever is making the noise.

The car I encountered the other day is sitting just outside the house. One occupant, a male, is honking the horn of the car while another, a female, is banging frantically on the front door. Scanning the area, I don't see anyone else on the premises. I dig through the satchel and pull out the night vision goggles. As I slip them on, the darkness turns to daylight. I look far into the distance and see only desert. Terrance must not be back yet, or he is ignoring the pleas of the couple.

"Come on, let's get out of here," the driver pleads.

"No, we need help. Someone should be here," the woman cries.

The man gets out of the car, walks over to the young frightened woman, and drags her back inside. She is shrieking, fighting for her freedom, but eventually succumbs and crumples in the man's arms, whimpering. He holds her tightly, stroking her hair trying to comfort her. The two get back into the car and head up the road out of the Refuge.

They don't get far.

I lie there, too terrified to move, as two battered trucks cut-off the car, nearly causing it to crash into a tall cactus. The car backs up, but one of the trucks has anticipated the move and drives behind the vehicle, blocking all means of escape. Two men exit each truck, reaching the car at the same time. One set goes for the driver's door, the other for the passenger's. The driver is dragged out of the car and shoved to the ground. He stands up and tries to fight off his assailants while the woman is removed by her hair as she shouts, flailing her arms wildly, hitting one of the offenders in the nose.

"No!" she screams at the top of her lungs.

Her mate hears her, tries to dive over the hood of the car, but is immediately brought down with a kick to the knees. The woman is dragged around the vehicle to where her friend lies writhing on the ground. She tries to go to him, but the two holding her restrain her movements, forcing her to stay standing. The tall bulky man from the other group pulls a weapon from his waistband, aiming it at the driver's head. I notice it's a Levin gun, so I remove the goggles and crouch into a ball under the window as the man fires. The girl screams, an agonized sound that rips at my core.

I can only imagine the horror she is seeing. I'm too paralyzed to go to her aid.

I try and block the images from my mind as I hear her continued cries, which slowly fade. I get up and run quickly down the hay loft to the opposite corner and retch, not stopping until I have nothing left in my stomach. I walk back to the window, put the goggles back on, and see that the car and the body have been cleaned up.

Evidence of the incident no longer exists.

I store the goggles back into the satchel, crawl under my blankets, and try to block the world out a little longer, but instead I toss and turn. Sleep doesn't want to come. The woman's tormented cries still echo in my ears.

Nothing frightens me, except the idea of being taken. I guess it stems from when I was younger, but I can't be positive. I hate myself for not going out to help the woman, but at the same time I know that even with my training, with the odds against me like that, I probably couldn't have saved her or her friend.

Finally giving up on sleep after two hours, I walk down the ladder and close the doors to the barn since they had been left open, go back to the ladder, and begin doing pull-ups.

Feeling my muscles burn tells me I'm still alive.

Even as my biceps start aching after a half hour, I don't stop. A few splinters find their way into my palm, but I don't quit, not until my fingers begin to bleed.

I wash only my hands under the showerhead, splinters rising to the surface as my skin heals. I know the sun will be up soon, so I go back up to the loft and change into a pair of shorts, a t-shirt, and my running shoes. I leave through the back door of the barn, beginning a timer in my head: three miles, five minutes. However, not knowing the terrain makes my run harder. I get back to the barn after seven minutes and start the timer again. I continue to run doing a continuous loop until the sun has broken above the horizon, only stopping a little after dawn as I run up the porch of the Refuge, walk in, and see Rena counting boxes of goods on the counter of the bar.

"You had me a little worried," she says, as I walk towards her. "I went into the barn to check on you and you weren't there."

"Sorry," I reply, "old habits die hard."

"Terrance is looking for you. He's back in the kitchen. He made you breakfast."

I go through the back door and walk over the planks, the smell of cooking food wafting down the hall. The kitchen consists of a small wooden table, four identical chairs, each with a missing piece, and two large crates stacked on top of each other creating a makeshift counter. Terrance is currently bent over a hot plate.

He smiles when he sees me and gestures for me to sit down. I walk around to the other side of the table so I have a clear view of the entrance. He fills three plates with scrambled eggs, bacon, and almost burnt toast. He places a plate in front of me, reaches into one of the crates and removes silverware. He sets the other two plates down on the table, and as if on cue, Rena walks in and sits across from me.

"Terrance," she says, as she picks up her fork, "you have out-done yourself again."

He smiles, turning slightly pink, then takes a seat and we eat.

The eggs have to be fresh. I've never tasted anything so wonderful before. The bread is pretty fresh too, and the bacon is crisp. As we eat, I debate whether or not to mention the incident I had witnessed, but they haven't said anything. So I decide against it. I insist on cleaning up, and once Rena and Terrance are done I take their plates and utensils, walk down the hall, and wash them in the sink in the bathroom. It takes a while since the water coming out of the faucet is only a dribble. I go back to the kitchen and place the items in the open crate.

"Why don't you get changed and you can help me sort out the orders for the day," Rena says, as she wipes down the hot plate.

Back at the barn I take a quick shower, throw on a pair of denim shorts, and a black top with flames on the front. I put on my boots and slide the knife down inside, then return to the house just as Rena is coming out from the back. She asks me to pick up one of the boxes from the bar's counter and take it to the back for Terrance, who is in the storage room. I lift the box, expecting it to be light, when in fact it's quite heavy, forcing me to juggle it between my arms.

Terrance, clipboard in hand, is marking things down as he goes between the rows in the small room. Setting the clipboard down, he takes the box from my arms and points to the board, indicating for me to pick up where he left off. I look down at the laundry list of items, noticing that some of them are electronics such as bulbs, clocks, and small radios. Walking up and down the aisles, I check the quantities of each item, noticing no food items.

I hand the clipboard back to Terrance when I finish, only to be handed a pack of notecards, each containing a single name with a list. He points to a stack of empty boxes that have the bizarre red and black emblem, then motions for me to put the items listed into the boxes. It takes me about an hour to fill all orders I have in hand. Showing Terrance I'm done, he points down below his feet, indicating to take the cards and boxes down to the cellar.

I have no idea how to get down there, so Terrance guides me through the hall down to the kitchen, where he slides a stack of crates away from the far wall, revealing a door. I open it and see a staircase leading down. Instead of hauling every single box down with me, I stack them in the kitchen, take an empty crate that is hiding under the kitchen table, and head downstairs with my note cards. There isn't much light and I almost fall a couple of times since several of the steps are loose.

Rena has two strings of lights burning when I get down to the cellar, but they aren't very bright. We work as a team putting the rest of the orders together. A majority of the items have the red and black symbol, but a few have a blue and gold emblem. I can't make it out either as it blurs the way the other does, so I ask Rena if the symbols are supposed to be blurry.

"Yes, of course," she responds, seemingly puzzled by my question.

I continue to stare at her waiting for a further explanation.

She realizes I know nothing about these symbols, so she explains. "The red and black emblem is from the city Tyre. It's a black bull standing on a red cape that is still attached to his enslaver, who is being crushed under the bull's hooves. The blue and gold items are from Acheron. It's the symbol of a bird with gold feathers against a dark blue background."

Rena reaches into her pocket and extracts a small, round lens. She holds it over one of the crates and the image comes into focus.

"The cities do this to prevent counterfeiting, especially if it's a rival city trying to flood the Boroughs with rotten or worthless goods." Rena holds the glass over another symbol and it, too, jumps into focus.

"If all the cities use the same technique, couldn't they still counterfeit each other's items?"

"They've tried, but each city embeds their own code into the ink. Only a Regulator's glass can reveal the real merchandise. If the code is slightly off, the image will have blurry edges or lines, then they know it's counterfeit."

"Regulators?"

"They're in charge of law and order around the cities as well as the Boroughs. They make sure all goods going in and out of the cities are genuine, as well as enforce the laws."

Having never heard of such people, I begin to get concerned about what else Devlan didn't disclose to me.

Rena and I continue putting the orders together and when we're done with each box Terrance comes and removes it. We take a water break shortly after noon. The cellar is uncomfortably warm, so Rena brings us drinks down from the bar. Terrance doesn't seem to want to take a break, and continues to fill orders.

"Rena," I begin, just after Terrance scurries above our heads, "how come Terrance doesn't speak?"

A pained look crosses her face as she swallows the rest of her water. She looks at the planks above our heads, making sure Terrance isn't within earshot.

"He used to work in a paint factory in the Industrial Borough of Acheron. There was a huge fire there well over ten years ago. Hundreds perished. Those who survived were left scarred or deformed. Terrance's vocal chords were heavily singed, and his lungs polluted with chemicals. The doctors in Acheron left him for dead, but he's still here. He appeared in the Wasteland about a year after the fire. My brother found him wandering on the outskirts and brought him here. He's never left, except once."

"When was that?"

"To go look for my brother after he was taken by Collectors."

I'm regretting my questions, but Rena tells me not to worry about it.

We finish the orders around two. I carry the last of the boxes into the living room where Terrance has the rest stacked. He waves me over to the bar, pours out two shots of Tequila, and we drink in unison.

I'm beginning to like this ritual of ours.

Terrance is in the process of setting up another round of shots when Quin makes his very loud entrance. Our eyes meet and I can feel myself reaching down towards my boot for the knife. Quin must have sensed my motives since he also begins reaching for a weapon that he has holstered across his back.

"Quin," Rena says, trying to diffuse the sudden tension in the room. "These are ready to go into your truck for deliveries whenever you and Terrance are ready."

Quin smiles at me, but his eyes display hatred.

"Sure Rena. Come on, Terrance," he gestures towards the door. Terrance puts the bottle back on the shelf behind him and follows Quin out to the porch.

The two of them load the truck quickly and leave.

I excuse myself and walk out to the barn where I climb up the ladder, remove the Beta gun and place it into my waistband, hop on my motorbike, and drive down the path I ran in the morning. I go until the Refuge is well behind me. The anger in me seems to be propelling me forward. Stopping about an hour later I notice how exhausting the heat is and how I don't have anything to drink. The Tequila is playing havoc with my body as I become lightheaded, causing me to immediately sit down in the middle of nowhere.

I remove the sleeve from my arm, wanting another glimpse of the injury that I haven't fully looked at in two days. The stream up my arm has thinned, but is still bright and I'm able to make out small waves rolling back and forth colliding with each other, though I don't feel anything. Reaching behind me, I grab the gun, which seems to hum in the palm of my right hand. I clutch the grip, aiming it at a cactus twenty feet away, and watch as the energy that seems to be alive in my arm intensifies. A tingling sensation pulses up and down every ligament, muscle, blood vessel, and bone in my arm. I squeeze the trigger and put holes into the cactus till all that is left are several large lumps, then I strap the sleeve back onto my arm, re-secure the gun, and drive off going farther into the unknown.

I finally stop when I come upon a high wire fence with warning signs hanging precariously on the posts, warning of possible electrocution from high voltage. I stop the bike just a few feet away, hearing the hum of the current as it flows along the metal mesh. The barrier, which goes on for miles, stands twenty feet tall, with razor wire coiled several feet thick at the top. On the other side of the fence, about a hundred yards away, stand tall white support columns that are placed every ten feet down the length of the fence. I look up and see the supports are attached to a set of rails. A moment later, a shuttle speeds down the rail, probably loaded down with passengers. I want to sit longer and see if another one comes by, but my thirst returns, so I turn the bike around and head back to the Refuge.

Upon my return I notice that everyone has left and the building is locked. I park the bike back into its stall, drink water from the shower head to quench my thirst, crawl up the ladder to the loft, and see Quin sitting on my mattress. I grab my gun and aim at his face.

"What do you want?" I ask.

"Is this how you greet everyone?"

"Only those who have a death wish."

"Rena told me about what happened to you and your dad. Sorry," he says, with a quiet, somewhat reserved tone.

I stare at him waiting for the punch line, but he seems to be sincere.

"Did you know Devlan?" I ask, relaxing a bit.

"No not really. I would see him sometimes when he came here, but he was always very secretive." He clears his throat as if he had swallowed sand.

I sense he's hiding something. I'm not in the mood to ask, so I continue to stare at him, waiting for him to say something. Instead, he reaches under the blanket and pulls out a plate of sandwiches.

"Rena made these for you in case you returned."

I sit down opposite him and hesitantly begin eating. I only eat a couple then offer Quin the rest. He takes a sandwich, eyeing my right arm.

"What happened?"

"It was injured in the attack."

"Do you want me to take a look at it? I've mended plenty of wounds…mainly my own."

"No thanks, it's healing just fine."

I want to ask him about his knee, however I resist the urge in fear it will cause an angry response.

When I finish eating, he takes my plate, says goodnight, and leaves. I crawl over to the opening and watch as he goes into the house with a key, exits a few minutes later walking to the back of the house, and then leaves in his truck. I stuff the Beta gun back into its spot, remove the tablet from the hay bale, and press my palm onto the screen, which turns blue scanning my print while I sit with by back against the wall, my knees bent as I anxiously await five minutes until the tablet comes back on.

Devlan's voice begins to speak though the screen remains blank.

"Finally a compromise was reached that the Dormitories, as the settlement was to be called, would be constructed in the northern province of the Wasteland between Tyre and Acheron. Nuceira didn't want to contribute to the undertaking as they felt it was too dangerous, and they didn't have the wealth and resources that the other two cities had, but they eventually succumbed to pressure and allocated some of its people to work at the completed structure."

The screen finally comes alive with an aerial view of a large complex of buildings out in the middle of a vast forest valley floor. I'd always viewed the Wasteland as nothing but sand and heat, but now I'm wondering if the terrain varies depending upon which direction you go.

The campus of buildings is quite extensive, consisting of five large circular structures sitting in the center, encompassing a manmade pool with a fountain in the middle. There don't appear to be any roads except for one at the south end of the heavily guarded complex. The gate onto the grounds is a mile away, lined with large trees to obstruct the view of anyone that might be passing by. The rest of the land is covered in concrete sidewalks with a few trees and small ponds that look to have been created more for aesthetics, not utility. The remaining buildings on the grounds are smaller and grouped in threes, producing triangular patterns with spindle-like pathways to the larger buildings in the center.

"At first, the doctors at the Dormitories took volunteers, mainly Regulators, to test new weapons and experiment on to enhance their fighting ability. Many died, went mad, or were seriously deformed, so when the volunteers stopped coming, the cities resorted to using their convicts. Two came out of the initial project as super soldiers, however they reverted back to their criminal personalities and were executed. After several years, it was determined that to build a perfect warrior, they would need to start from scratch...the point before a human being is actually created."

The picture dissolves into another showing men and women huddled together over a large work table.

"Since childbirth is heavily regulated, the cities offered incentives to women who voluntarily underwent a procedure to remove their ovaries. They were paid handsomely, and the flyers they distributed touted the fact that they were contributing to the safety and security of Sirain. Many women took the cities up on their offer; Regulators were forced to contribute to the cause by donating their sperm. Out of the millions of embryos generated, only fifty thousand survived the regimen they were put through."

The image changes to a sizeable room containing shelves lined with thousands of vessels, all hooked up to machines feeding the embryos.

Then the screen goes black.

I place the tablet in the satchel, lie down, and clutch the blanket up to my chest. I'm beginning to understand where I may fit into this picture, and the thought sickens me.

CHAPTER 5

"Meg...Meg wake up," I hear someone shout off in the distance as the loft begins to shake. I reach into the space between the hay bales, remove the Beta gun, and aim it at Quin who has just reached the top of the ladder. "Well, good morning to you too," he says, with a half-smile on his face.

"Sorry, old habit," I say, as I put the gun back, sit up, and rub my eyes trying to remove the sleep that still sits behind them. "What time is it?"

"Five," he announces. "Feel like a run?"

I nod, then promptly kick him out of the barn so I can change my clothes.

We run three miles, then another five. On our third circuit, Quin decides to make it a competition. I win, but he says his knee is still bothering him. I roll my eyes and go to take a shower while he goes to help Terrance with breakfast. Rena comes by around seven and the four of us spend the day playing cards, drinking, and munching on scraps.

For someone who likes to get attention, Quin has barely spoken since earlier this morning. We need to keep bringing his focus back to the card game. His mind wanders a lot.

I wonder what his life has been like out here.

Around six, Terrance and Quin leave to handle an errand for Rena, who also departs a short time later. I head up the ladder to the loft and press my palm onto the tablet and wait.

A picture of the Dormitories fills the screen and Devlan begins where he left off.

> *"Training and conditioning was started as early as five years of age. The High Rulers wanted the soldiers to be prepared for combat as young as possible."*

The screen changes to images of babies growing into children then into adults; all muscular, agile, fast, and perfect.

"These soldiers were sent off to fight in remote areas of Sirain where pockets of resistance still lived. These men and women outperformed their predecessors, bringing adversaries to their knees in months instead of years. Then a new weapon was created by our enemies."

This is the first time I've heard Devlan refer to the opposition as 'our enemies'. I begin to wonder if he had anything to do with the Dormitories, and what went on there. More importantly, why he is suddenly siding with the cities? He drilled into my head that the cities are what we should fear, not that there was another adversary out there.

"This weapon had phenomenal power that would destroy our soldiers with one shot, causing immediate destruction of any body part that it encountered."

The Levin gun, that has to be what he's referring to.

"The Dormitories could not create soldiers fast enough to replenish the troops that were dying. One man risked his life to cross borders to bring back the technology and designs for our scientists to study to help create a defense against this destructive power."

The image shifts to a young man about my height, black hair cropped short, thin, and frail. I recognize the eyes set deep in the man's face. It's Devlan.

"I was hailed a hero by many, but I didn't see myself as one. I lost many friends to the wars our region fought, but I didn't know I was going to be bringing the conflict to our own front door."

The tablet shuts down.

This segment is a lot shorter than the others, only lasting five minutes.

I try to think if I've heard about any current fighting going on between the cities, but can't remember any. My eyes grow weary, so I slide the tablet back into the satchel as I contemplate Devlan's parting words.

I get up at five the following morning and do several three-mile runs, but this time I do them alone. Once back at the barn, I shower and change into a tank top, shorts, and my boots. When I enter the house, Rena is pacing back and forth, wringing her hands.

"Hi Rena," I say, as I walk up to her.

At first she doesn't appear to hear me, but as my voice registers with her mind she forcefully grabs my hands and starts panicking.

"Terrance and Quin didn't come back. Have you seen them?"

I think hard, but I don't remember hearing Quin's truck returning last night.

"Maybe they did come back, but left again," I lie, trying to calm her down.

She seems to consider my idea as her grip loosens. I guide her to the couch, get her a glass of water, and hand it to her as I kneel on the floor.

"What errand were they running for you?" I ask, as I help raise the glass to her lips.

"They were going to Oasis Eight to pick up a package for me. It should've only taken an hour at the most, but they've been gone all night," she blubbers after swallowing.

I help her take another sip. "How do I get to Oasis Eight?"

Terror enters her eyes. She grabs my shoulders, dumping the water all over herself and me. "You can't go there. No, I won't let you," she screams.

I gently remove her hands and place them onto her lap. "Rena, it'll be okay. I just need you to tell me how to get to Oasis Eight."

She slumps her shoulders, letting her depression take over. I leave her sitting on the couch while I head to the barn to retrieve my knife, motorbike, and satchel. I remove the contents except for the metal canisters with the Quarum and two detonators. I place the Beta gun in the satchel, but I leave the knife in my boot, put my hair up into a ponytail, pull the bike up to the porch, and go into the house to get a quick drink. Rena has moved from the couch and is now behind the bar drawing a map, along with directions on what to do once I get to Oasis Eight. Taking the paper, I study the map quickly and fold it, placing it into the satchel. Rena gives me a hard hug.

I head out of the Refuge and turn right at the abandoned highway.

According to the map, I will need to go thirty miles before I hit the security fence that surrounds Oasis Eight. The sky is overcast today, so I'm not competing with the heat from the sun, just the heat emanating from the ground. About a mile from the fence, I see an arrangement of boulders just off the left side of the road, so I slow down, pulling around the mound, and spot Quin's truck hiding amongst the rocks. I park my bike next to it, and peer into the cab and the bed, which are both empty. Rena's diagram indicates an entrance to a tunnel in the center of the boulders that will lead me to the other side of the fence and under Oasis Eight.

I see a crack between two of the stones and have to carefully squeeze myself through it, seeing the entrance exactly where it's supposed to be, at the base of the formation. As I enter, I remember the tunnel at the house and wonder if both were created by the same hands, as the structures are identical except in size. This tunnel is much taller than the other. Down the dark passageway, I walk slowly using my hand as a guide, sliding it along the wall. The buzz of electricity hums as I go under the fence and into Tyrean territory.

My pulse begins to race as I see daylight ahead, but don't know what awaits me on the other side. I try to mentally prepare myself for anything.

The tunnel ends, forcing me to climb up a ladder, but my path is blocked by a grate. I carefully look through the slates to see if there is anyone around, but the room it leads to is empty so I push up, quietly trying to remove the grate then pull myself up and out of the tunnel, replacing the grate before I have a look around.

I find myself a small utility closet. Light bulbs, electric brooms, and empty boxes lay scattered on the floor. Shelves lining the back wall contain toiletries, soaps, towels, and various scented lotions. I put my ear to the door and hear people walk by, announcements being made, and the low hiss of airbrakes of shuttles. I crack open the door and step out onto the bustling platform.

No one notices my sudden appearance as I walk with the flow of people who've exited one shuttle and are moving across the platform to another. I find a bench along the way and promptly sit down. Behind me the wall is paneled in glass, however the view behind it is a projection, not the real thing. Where I should see shrubs and desert, there is a lush landscape full of trees, glistening pools of water, and colorful birds flittering about.

The projected scenery is constant throughout the entire white metal structure. Wherever there's a window, the image is of a continuous flow of greenery. I wonder if the windows on the shuttles are the same. Looking up at the ceiling I notice it's as bright as the sun would be if it were out today.

The people walking by are in too much of a hurry to notice me. Many are smartly dressed in white linen suits, floral dresses, expensive furs, or blue uniforms with Regulator glasses hanging around their necks. Seeing the Regulators causes me to stand up and quickly rejoin the herd of people heading to the right. Halfway down the corridor I spot a large courtyard. I leave the pack and make my way to a large pool of water that is littered with coins of varying colors and sizes, some with the Tyre bull and others with the Acheron bird.

Large live palm trees line the square, jutting out from enclosed dirt mounds. The cities are creating a false outdoor setting to mask what the real world looks like, which makes me wonder what else they falsify to blind their people to reality. Sitting on the edge of the pool I pull out Rena's map to see what my next task is. I notice a pair of older women approach the water with coins in hand ready to throw until they spot me. At first they seem frightened of me, perhaps disgusted by my appearance, as I obviously don't belong there.

"Teenagers," one of them mumbles, as she tosses her coin into the pool. The other woman follows suit, and they head back down the corridor.

Returning my gaze to Rena's map, there is a circle indicated on the platform by the far end of the station. In small letters inside the circle is written *Max.* I walk to the other side of the courtyard to join the stream of people.

The corridor empties onto a large mezzanine full of shops, restaurants, and a brass door entrance to some condos that have For Sale signs next to empty nameplates. The smell of sweet-smelling pastries make me salivate and my stomach growl. I scan the restaurants to see if any of the staff have their names stitched onto their uniforms, but the outfits are too colorful to notice any identification.

I next move onto the shops that are loaded with expensive wares of varying size, color, and price. Glass baubles fill the windows, along with silk gowns and ornate jewelry.

How could anyone afford such things?

I feel completely out of my comfort zone in this area, but I need to find Max. I don't see any more useful information so I crumple up the map, and shove it back into the satchel. Suddenly I feel myself being propelled forward, hands firmly pressed into my back, shoving me down the platform and into a women's vanity room. I'm finally released after the door closes. Turning, I see a young girl behind me, finger to her lips indicating for me to stay quiet. She quickly moves from one stall to another, checking to see if anyone else is in here with us, then goes back to the door and locks it.

"What the hell is wrong with you?" she yells at me. "Are you trying to draw attention to yourself or are you just that stupid?"

"You must be Max," I say, my arms crossed over my chest.

"Rena sent you," Max says, more as a statement than a question.

I nod my head.

For the next minute, the two of us stand and stare at each other, taking in the other's appearance.

Max is a few inches shorter than me, choppy blond hair with purple streaks, and a few freckles crossing her nose. Her outfit is a pink and white striped smock covering a white dress shirt and dress pants. I'd spotted her restocking shelves in the candy store. She couldn't be more than fifteen.

"I'm looking for Quin and Terrance," I say, as the silence is beginning to bug me.

"They were supposed to meet me last night, but never showed up. You don't think they got taken, do you?" Her question seems more like a plea, but I pretend I didn't notice it.

"Do you still have the package for Rena?"

"Um...yeah." She reaches into the pocket of her smock and pulls out a small brown bundle.

I put the package into the satchel and leave her to her tears.

Unnecessary emotion is not something I'm used to, or know how to deal with.

I go back to the utility closet. After removing the grate, I slide through the opening, replace the grate, retreat down the tunnel, and squeeze myself through the crack in the rocks only to find Quin's truck and my motorbike gone, again.

I want to scream or blast something, but I stop myself when I notice tire tracks in the hard ground, headed west, and not east towards the road. The depth of the tracks tells me they put my bike in the truck bed.

I follow the marks in the dried sand for several miles before they make a sudden left turn down an embankment and across a dry riverbed to a small one-level house. Behind the house I see a smaller building with a door on the front and a smaller door on the side. There's no good place to sit and observe as the area is completely vacant of any vegetation and rock mounds. I decide to take my chances and hastily run up to the smaller building. As I'm half-way there, four men exit the front door of the house. I have nowhere to hide, so I quicken my pace and go behind the garage. They get into a truck idling a few feet away, and leave.

I wait until their taillights are gone before crouching down next to the side door where I listen for any signs of movement on the other side. There's only silence so I slowly turn the knob and slide into the room, shutting the door quietly behind me. I'm met by a foul odor, but it's one I've smelled before. Against the wall are rusty metal containers which I know hold gasoline, as Devlan had a couple in the shed to fill up his truck and my bike. The lone light in the room is coming in through several tiny windows lining the back wall above a work table. I recognize the brown truck sitting just a foot in front of me. It's one of the trucks I saw the other night outside the Refuge. I stand up and peer inside, noticing that it's empty, but through the passenger window I see a figure tied to a pole in the middle of the floor. Walking around the front of the truck, I bend down and lift Quin's face.

"I knew it was you," he says, in a tired voice.

"Liar," I say, with a half-smile. "Where's Terrance?"

"He's in the house." Quin nods with his head indicating the direction. "Get out of here before they see you."

"How many are there?"

"Six, but I think some just left."

"How did they get you?" I ask, as I move to his back where his hands are tied.

I notice the thick rope has been wound at least ten times around his wrists and the post.

"As I was entering the tunnel to go to the oasis, I heard a scuffling noise on the other side of the rocks. I'd left Terrance with the truck since he's too big to fit through that tiny crack. I don't normally take him with me when I'm going to Oasis Eight, but Rena insisted."

I take out my knife and begin cutting away the restraints. They're so tightly wound that I wind up cutting Quin's arms a couple of times. He winces, but doesn't complain.

"You could've taken all of them, what happened?"

"They used a couple of stun guns on me then struck me in the back of the head knocking me out. When I came to I was tied up in here. After I broke the restraints, they decided to wind the rope multiple times practically cutting off the circulation to my hands."

"What are they doing with Terrance?"

"Torturing him. They were going to kill him at the start, but when they realized he couldn't speak they thought they would have a little fun first at his expense." The last of the rope gives way and Quin is free from the pole. He rubs his hands, working the blood back through them. "Now, get out of here. I'll get Terrance."

"No," I say firmly. "I'll get Terrance, you get the truck ready."

"Are you nuts?" he says as he grabs my arm, turning me to face him. "They have a Levin gun."

"I know."

He looks at me, trying to figure out how I know this. He lets go of my left arm, but holds onto my right, rubbing the material covering it.

"This isn't a burn, is it?"

"No, it's not."

We exit out the side door, my gun in one hand and knife in the other. Quin goes over to his truck and joins me at the sliding glass door. His armament of choice is a crowbar. I'm guessing his real weapon is inside the house. I quickly peek inside to see where the targets are. Only two remain and they are both sitting on a couch with their backs to us, but I can't see Terrance.

I crouch down as Quin uses the crowbar on the door, sliding it open slowly so not to make any noise. I squirm into the small opening, Quin following close behind me. I stand up and see Terrance bent down, his back being used as a foot rest. He spots me and makes a little noise. It's enough to alert the other two of our presence. The first shot is fired by the man with the Levin gun. His aim is off so he winds up blasting the patio door sending glass shards flying. I fire my gun and hit him in the shoulder. The other one is on his feet fighting Quin with a Pugio blade. Terrance is curled up in a ball on the floor. I go over to him to help him up, but hear a noise from the man I just shot. He's up again, gun in hand, and I don't have time to jump out of the way. Quin, however, is already diving for the gun as the man fires.

The blast of energy hits Quin in the upper right part of his chest and exits out his back. Terrance tries to scream, but only gurgling noises come out. Quin goes down, blood pouring from his wound. I take my knife and throw it at the man, hitting him in the middle of the throat. He's dead before he hits the floor. The other one begins to retreat, but not after slashing at Terrance with the blade, cutting him badly down his left leg. I aim the Beta gun and fire, not stopping until there are several holes in the man's chest.

I crawl over to Quin, who's barely breathing.

I remove one of the canisters of Quarum, role up his sleeve, and inject it. Within seconds his breathing is returning to normal, the blood has stopped pooling under him. I go over to Terrance, remove another canister, and am about to inject him as well when Quin screams *no* behind me.

"He's injured, badly. He's going to bleed to death," I protest.

"You'll kill him instantly if you give him that stuff. His body can't handle the toxicity."

I look at Quin, puzzled that he knows what's in the syringe.

"How come I was able to give it to you?"

"I...don't know, maybe because I'm younger and healthier."

Quin's answer doesn't sound right, but I don't have time to waste. I put the syringe away while Quin looks around the house for something to stem the bleeding. He comes back with some towels that he rips into strips to wrap around Terrance's leg. I go over to the man with the Levin gun, remove my knife from his throat, clean the blood off by wiping it on his shirt, and re-sheath it in my boot.

"Get Terrance into your truck. I'm going to grab as many gas cans as I can and clean up our mess," I tell Quin as I'm heading out the back door.

He doesn't argue.

There's no room in the cab of the truck for Terrance, so Quin stretches him out in the bed next to my bike. I load the remainder of the truck up with as many gas cans as I can fit, some in the bed with

Terrance and the rest in the cab. Quin better secures my bike with some cord he finds in the house. I take the remainder of the gas cans, pouring their contents all over the truck in the garage, the bodies, and the furniture in the house. I leave two full cans in the middle of the living room and one in the other building, securing a detonator onto each and start the timers.

Quin has the truck idling when I run out of the house.

Terrance is covered in blankets; Quin has his blade holstered on his back. I jump into the passenger seat as Quin guns the engine. We're only a few yards away when the explosions go off. I watch the fires burn in the side mirror.

CHAPTER 6

Terrance continues to deteriorate as we make our way back to the Refuge. As soon as we pull up to the house, I jump out of the cab and run to get Rena. She and I help Quin gingerly carry Terrance down the hall and into his bedroom. Rena goes into the kitchen and comes back with some rubbing alcohol and a sewing kit, while Quin goes out to the bar for Terrance's Tequila bottle in case he begins to wake up. I go to the bathroom and fill a bowl with water and soap, making sure to grab the lone washcloth that is hanging from the towel rack behind the toilet. Quin rips open Terrance's pants while I wash away as much blood as possible, exposing the wound to the air so Rena can see what needs to be worked on.

The gash is about half an inch deep, and runs down the length of his thigh. Terrance's skin color has turned gray, and his breathing is labored. Rena sterilizes the needle, thread, and wound with rubbing alcohol, while Quin stands at the head of the bed, holding down Terrance's shoulders to prevent him from moving when Rena begins to sew him up. She is almost done when Terrance begins to rouse. He bolts upright, throwing Quin off his feet. Quin leans back down on him while I lie across his chest to help keep him still.

He resists us at first, but gives up the fight and falls unconscious. Rena finishes then leaves to clean herself up. Quin opens the Tequila bottle, takes a swig, and offers me a hit, which I take just as Rena comes back in the room with a glass of water and several pain relievers. We manage to wake Terrance long enough for him to take the pills and water. We know we can't leave him alone, so we decide to each take a shift. Rena says she will go first while Quin and I clean ourselves up. Before leaving, I reach into the satchel I'd dropped on the floor of the bedroom and remove the package. I hand it to Rena, pick the satchel up, and exit the room.

Quin moves his truck into the barn as I climb up the ladder to the loft to get some clean clothes. I see the tablet lying on the bed and begin to wonder if I have time to play the next recording. I shout down to Quin, asking for the time. He replies that it's nearly seven. I tell him to go ahead and take his shower first as I lie on the mattress and press my palm to the screen. I hear Quin turn on the water below and utter an expletive.

The headphones eject from the side as usual, but I decide not to put them on. The noise from the water should be enough to prevent Quin from hearing Devlan's voice and the volume is low enough not to travel far. The headphones retract and the screen begins to glow blue, followed by a picture of the Dormitories.

"Efforts to understand and replicate the Levin gun were now made the highest priority by the High Rulers. All resources that had once been solely dedicated to the Barracks, the training facility for the nation's army, was now dismantled, and diverted to the Dormitories. I myself was recruited in the effort since I'd witnessed the power the gun could produce first-hand. Two scientists from each city were relegated to create a specialized treatment to cure anyone unfortunate enough to be hit by the weapon. Over many months of research and testing, Quarum, the solution to healing the injuries was created. Testing was done again on the criminals of the cities, as well as the impaired, but the fluid proved to be too toxic. Many of the subjects died or went insane, which led to them having to be killed. The doctors returned to testing the solution on embryos to see if an undeveloped body would accept the poison. They began to see positive results, but only if they administered small doses at certain developmental cycles."

The scene dissolves to a picture of the embryos being soaked in the Quarum, then removed and placed into large glass containers where fluid feeds them through tubes. The whole process looks like an assembly line. Many of these containers encompass a large room, filled with embryos at various stages of development.

"The scientists decided to take their task one step further. They decided to replicate the energy produced by the Levin gun into a newer weapon, a human weapon. Researchers were able to duplicate the amount of energy needed to produce the destructive power, but it took several more years before they developed the Quantum Stream, a current of force embedded in every atom of the human body."

The next pictures show a group of scientists trying to map out the path of the Quantum Stream on a simulation of the human anatomy.

"They had to carefully choose the exact placement for this power. Too much in one area of the body led to the embryo bursting into blue flames, while placing the components of the stream too far apart caused the cells to collapse, deforming the subject, which then had to be killed. The first batch to be subjected to this experiment took to the Quantum Stream better than expected. A year after their birth they began military conditioning, cognitive realignment training, and emotional therapy, however word had leaked to the Nuceirans about what the other two cities had developed. They had been kept in the dark about the altered development of the soldiers since this was against their principles and beliefs. Nuceira sent their troops up to the Dormitories to destroy the installation, as they saw it as an insult to creation."

A burned-out complex appears on the screen; the once beautiful white buildings are destroyed to rubble.

"A warning had gone out to the complex after the first strike against the gates at the entrance. Of the two hundred children that had been successfully constructed, only four survived the assault. Four children who have been hidden from the world...thought to have perished in the flames."

"You're one of them, Meg," Quin says, appearing unexpectedly at the top of the ladder wrapped only in a towel. "Or should I call you Trea? That is your real name."

He climbs the rest of the way up, kneels down in front of me, and removes the tablet from my hands as the screen goes black.

"It's not true," I whimper, as his wet hair drips onto my legs. I suddenly feel chilled, even though the barn is stifling hot.

"I wasn't sure it was you until we were in Terrance's room. As you were lying across his chest and your ponytail flipped over. That's when I noticed the three small dots at the base of your hairline."

I instinctively reach around to my neck, searching for marks that I already know are there.

"I've had them forever...they're just birthmarks," I stammer, trying to think, trying to make sense of what I've just seen and heard.

Quin turns his back to me, lifts up his wet curling hair and points to his hairline at the base of his skull. There sit five identical marks, same width, same height, same placement, and same dark color. But Devlan said there were only four. How can I believe anything at this point?

I bolt from my spot, wanting to get as far away from him as possible, but he grabs my legs as I try to run past, bringing me down hard onto the loft floor. Flipping me over, he grabs my hands as I try to fight him off, but he is much stronger than I am. He places his weight onto my legs and eventually gets my arms pinned above my head. Tears are pouring down my face, and anger is surging through me. I feel my right arm heat up, acting as if a weapon will be thrust into my grasp.

"Stop, Meg, stop," Quin says to me in a calm voice. "I know how you must be feeling."

I don't stop wiggling my body as I try to dislodge his grip on me...on reality.

That's when I notice the wound in his chest, the hole that was blasted through his torso and out his back. The skin has sealed itself over the gash, scars stream outward in a radial pattern, but no blue light, no Quantum Stream like mine.

Quin follows my gaze to his chest. He takes his left hand and begins to remove the strap on my right arm. I fight some more as I don't want him to notice the difference between our scars, but I'm overpowered. He slides the sleeve off of my arm and examines the river of blue that courses down my arm to the two small entry points in the palm of my hand.

"How?"

"Levin gun backfired." My voice sounds shaky as I speak.

I'm both angry and scared, not sure which emotion I should allow to take over.

Quin looks back down at his chest.

"Then why doesn't my injury look like yours? That was a Levin gun he shot me with," Quin begins to protest, voice rising to the point of anger.

"Devlan removed the safety features on the gun I used. Those features must have been enabled on the one back at the house."

He releases me from his grip and hands me back the sleeve. I put it back on just as Rena calls from down below that dinner is ready.

"Whatever you do, don't say anything to anyone about what you are, or about what I am. People have been killed trying to find us," Quin whispers to me. "It's better if no one knows. You should die before telling anyone who you are."

Terrified by his last remark, I put the sleeve back on before we both descend down the ladder. Rena gives each of us a quizzical look as she notices my hair is full of hay and Quin is only wearing a towel. I go to take a shower while Quin follows Rena into the house for some clean clothes. Once I'm dry I put on my last clean pair of running shorts, a shirt, and a pair of flip flops that Rena found for me the other day.

The three of us sit silently in the kitchen eating lukewarm bowls of tomato soup. Quin cleans up the dishes while I tell Rena that I'll take the next shift, and send her to sleep on the couch in the front room.

Terrance hasn't improved much since I last saw him. His color is still terrible and the injury in his leg looks infected. Rena has placed an old folding chair next to the head of the bed so I sit down, pick up Terrance's hand, and hold it tightly in mine, willing him to get better. I can sense Quin standing in the doorway, but I don't acknowledge his presence until he sets his chair next to mine.

"Those Collectors," I begin, "they weren't the same ones that came after Devlan and me. How many kinds are there?"

"From what Rena told me about what happened to you, I'm guessing those were from one of the cities. The ones Terrance and I encountered are rogue Collectors, hired mercenaries kidnapping people for profit."

We sit in silence, waiting for the other to speak. I know the next question I want to ask, but for some reason I'm not sure I want to know the answer.

"Why did you call me that?" I finally ask, my curiosity winning out over my nervousness.

"You mean Trea?"

"Yes."

"That was the name you were given at birth. At least, that is what I remember from when we were kids. Devlan must have changed your name when he hid. You know it means three. My full name is Quintus, which means fifth."

Terrance stirs a little then begins to thrash around, obviously in the midst of a nightmare. I begin stroking his forehead telling him he is safe, he is protected. This seems to calm him down and he drifts back to oblivion.

"What happened to you?" I ask, as I lean farther forward in my chair, closer to Terrance, away from Quin.

"I lived with one of the researchers who fled the Dormitories. He was supposed to protect me, but left when I was younger. I eventually found my way out to the Wasteland a few years ago and live in an abandoned home several miles from here. I help Rena and Terrance, and they feed me in return."

"What do you help them with?"

"Terrance and I go out on raids to collect supplies. It used to be Mercer, Rena's brother, and Terrance. Mercer was taken several years ago."

"She told me a little about him, but I didn't push the subject."

More time passes in silence and my eyes begin to grow heavy. I must have fallen asleep because when I wake, I'm out in the front room on the couch with a blanket wrapped tightly around me. Light is filtering in through the windows. I rub my eyes, sit up, and swing my legs onto the floor. I make a quick stop in the bathroom then head back into Terrance's room. Rena is sitting in her chair playing cards with an awake, but groggy, Terrance.

He grins upon seeing me and waves me over. His coloring is looking better, as is the gash in his leg. Rena deals the cards, including me in the hand. I ask her where Quin is, and she says she sent him to sleep in the barn about three hours ago. We play a couple of rounds, each of us winning a hand. Rena goes into the kitchen to make breakfast while I wander out to the barn to brush my teeth, since I haven't done it in a while and can feel fur growing on them. Quin is not there from what I can tell, so I scrub until my gums are almost bleeding. When I return to the house, Quin is there in his old clothes, still damp from washing.

Breakfast today consists of oatmeal and canned peaches. We all sit and eat around Terrance's bed since he can't join us in the kitchen. I'm not that hungry, but I force myself to eat. The time goes by slowly; no one speaks, it appears we have run out of conversation. Rena and Quin take the dishes into the kitchen while I change Terrance's soaked bandages and give him more painkillers. He dozes off, so I leave the room and begin to go back down the hallway when I hear Rena and Quin arguing. I change direction and head to the kitchen.

"You're insane," Rena practically screams at Quin. "You can't go by yourself."

"We need supplies, Rena. The shipment tonight is the last one until next month, you know that."

"Then I'm going with you."

"Absolutely not," Quin yells back, poking his finger at her. "You need to stay here. I can do this by myself."

"A raid is a two person job, so I'm coming," Rena shouts, her face getting red with frustration.

"I can go," I chime in as I enter the room. They both turn and look at me. "If it takes two people I can go."

Rena seems to accept the idea, but Quin emphatically shakes his head.

"Why not?" I ask him.

"It's too dangerous, and you have no idea what needs to be done to pull off a raid," Quin says sternly, arms crossed over his chest.

"You're not leaving until later this afternoon, so you have plenty of time to go over the plan," Rena says, as she turns her attention back to cleaning the dishes.

Quin walks out of the kitchen in a huff, with me following.

We spend the next five hours going over the plan. There are three steps to retrieving the supplies, and Rena is correct, this *is* a two-person job. First, we will have to find a way to get onto the city's territory, subdue whatever security that may be guarding the supplies, and then make it back to the Wasteland without getting caught.

When it's closer to the time we need to leave, I change into my boots, a black tank top, and a pair of dirty black jeans while Quin gets the truck ready. I climb up into the loft, grab the satchel, which still contains the Beta gun, the night vision goggles, and then I throw in the last of the detonators and Quarum. I reach into the second hay bale for the Levin gun, but come up empty. I pull the bundles apart thinking it fell further in, but it's gone.

Quin is loading a crate of goods into the cab of his truck as I walk over to him, grab him by the arm, and spin him around.

"Where the hell is it?" I roar at him.

"Where's what?" He shakes me loose and begins to head back to the house.

"The Levin gun, Quin, what did you do with it?"

"I didn't do anything with it," he protests. "I didn't even know you had one."

As soon as he is inside I begin to rip apart the truck, but I can't find the weapon. Rena walks out with a sack full of sandwiches and two thermoses of water. Quin soon joins us, stuffing a Regulator's glass into his pocket. Rena hugs us each goodbye, tears in her eyes, and heads back into the house. I remember the tablet as we climb into the cab, but Quin says to leave it because if we get caught by any

Collectors or Regulators from the cities, we will certainly be executed simply for having it.

The building we are targeting tonight is the one farthest away, so the drive will take at least six hours. During our preparation, Quin said he hadn't been to the area for over a year. He's not a fan of this particular storage hangar, but the other ones have been raided too many times this year, so the odds of extra security on the others are extremely high. This facility is located on the outskirts of Tyre; one of the Boroughs lies a few miles on the other side of a large rock formation that lines its borders. The hangar is at the base of the formation, where security is not as tight.

The delivery is due at the storage hangar around midnight, so we will have about two hours to get set up. We travel in silence, munching on sandwiches and drinking our water sparingly. I ask Quin if he wants me to drive, but he waves me off so I decide to curl up in my seat and take a nap so I can be well rested for our incursion.

Some time later, Quin shakes me, indicating we have arrived at our destination. I open my eyes, which need to adjust to the darkness that now surrounds us, and scan the area, but can't locate any structures, even with the headlights of the truck on.

"Where is it?" I ask, as he shuts off the engine.

"We have to walk about a mile that way." Quin points directly in front of us.

We exit the truck, Quin grabbing the crate in the back. I take the sack of sandwiches and thermoses. In the crate are several flashlights, a role of adhesive tape, rope, and various pieces of scrap metal. Quin hands me a flashlight, takes the rope, loops it between the handles on the crate, and slings it on his back. We turn our torches on and head into the dark desert.

I can hear the hum of the electrical fence before I see it.

We stop and crouch right next to it. I dig in my satchel and pull out the night vision goggles. Quin doesn't seem surprised that I have them, which indicates that he has gone through my belongings, and reinforces my belief he knows where the Levin gun is, but I don't have time to confront him at the moment. I turn the goggles to full power to see past the fence and the rail supports for the shuttle.

The building is about fifty yards from a lone road that separates the building from the fence. The structure has two large warehouses at each end with a small delivery bay in the center. The hanger appears to be fully automated as I don't see any guards. There are cameras at each corner as well as spotlights that are dimly lit at present. Our target, however, is not the building, but the delivery truck. We are to take the truck before it gets into range of the security cameras and spotlights.

I hand Quin the goggles so he can take a look while I try to figure out how to get us over or through the fence.

The razor wire at the top will prevent us from climbing even if we are able to knock out the electricity, so the only option left is to cut through the chain metal. Quin hands me back the goggles and we proceed to go south along the fence until the hangar is behind us. The cameras and lights for the building will be triggered as soon as the truck hits the sensor pad in the road about a half mile from the building. We move another mile south of that to give us plenty of time to stop the truck before any alarms sound. Finding our spot, we settle in. Quin digs into the sack of sandwiches while I examine the fence a little more.

I remember Devlan telling me years ago that these fences travel the entire length of the cities' boundaries, and yet are able to carry so much electricity that it can light the entire city for days. The problem with this much power being generated is that it gets weaker the further away it is from its source. To keep the fence electrified along a massive span you need relay boxes to help carry the electricity across the great distance. If I can find the closest relay then I can knock out the power to this part of the fence. I tell Quin my plan, but he doesn't seem interested.

"How did you get in last time?" I ask, as I rummage through the crate Quin has set next to him.

"We had someone from the Farm Borough helping us. He and several others dug a tunnel under the fence."

"What happened to him?"

"He escaped to the Wasteland with us only to be caught and executed several months later."

"How are you planning to get in this time?"

"I'll think of something as soon as I'm done eating."

I manage to come up with a pair of wire cutters, so I leave the satchel behind, take out the goggles, remove the Beta gun, and begin my walk. My timing must be precise as I'm sure the power will be turned back on quickly after it's lost. Once I have the power down, my plan is to cut an opening wide enough to drive the truck through. Quin will need to drive the delivery truck back to the Refuge while I drive his vehicle.

I find what I'm looking for ten minutes later.

The relay is at the top of the fence, coiled amongst the razor wire. The box is approximately the size of a book, five inches by eight inches. I put the goggles on so I can see better, drop the wire cutters at my feet, aim the gun at the box, and fire. My hit is dead on and sparks shower down on me. I no longer hear the humming from the fence, so I begin cutting the large opening, hurrying so as not to get electrocuted when the power comes back on. If they're able to repair it, the electricity will be weak until they can replace the box, but will still cause massive injury.

I clip the last rung in the fence and yank the portion that is loose from the rest of the barrier just as the power kicks back on. Picking up my items, I walk back over to Quin, who is still sitting and eating.

"What was that?" he asks, as I drop the wire cutters back into the crate. "The power was off and then came back on, nearly shocking me." I notice the small hole he had managed to create in the links. "It would have been bigger, but someone ran off with my wire cutters," he says angrily.

"Relax and grab the crate," I say, as I pick up my satchel and thermoses.

We walk down to the hole in the fence then carefully make our way through it. Our next obstacle is overtaking the truck. I remove the detonators from the satchel and walk about a half mile down the road. The detonators can be set to be used as an explosive or signal. I flip the switch on the bottom of the device to indicate signal and place it in the center of the road, then walk back down to the opening in the fence where Quin is hunched behind one of the support columns for the shuttle.

"When the light begins to blink on the detonator," I state, as I point to where I'd just been, "we'll know the truck has passed that location. Between here and there it will only take them about five minutes." I point in the direction of the hangar, far off in the distance. "We should move farther down, closer to the hangar."

"All right, but we will need some kind of sign to indicate when the vehicle is approaching since we will be sitting on opposite sides of the road."

I think about it as we make our way down the road, stopping two hundred yards from the hangar, giving us an extra hundred yards before the movement of the truck activates the security cameras and lights. Digging in my satchel, I come up with the metal container holding the last of the Quarum and hand it to Quin. He doesn't ask, he just puts it in the front pocket of his pants. That's when I notice the Levin gun sticking out of the side of his waistband.

"Give me that," I scream at him, lunging for the weapon.

He grabs me by the shoulders, slamming me to the ground.

"No," he says angrily, face red with heat.

My head hurts from the impact with the ground, so I can't completely focus on his expression.

"You've been holding out on me. You've had this with you the whole time and never said anything. This is the gun that damaged your arm, isn't it?"

"Yes," I whimper.

His grip is so strong on my arms I can't feel my hands.

"Shoot me with it."

"What? Are you crazy?"

"Don't be stupid, I'm just like you, you already know that! I'm built like you except for the Quantum Stream. This is the weapon that gave it to you, that brought your body to life. If it worked on you it can work on me."

I stare at him, dumfounded at his request.

"You're mad," I mumble, unable to speak clearly due to the trembling in my body. "You don't mean it...you don't know what you are asking for."

"Yes, I do."

"I won't...I won't do it."

"Fine," he says, removing the gun from his waistband and aiming it at my head. "If all it takes is a simple pull of the trigger then that's what I'll do."

I try and move, but he has me pinned. My heart begins to pound even harder as I feel the energy coursing through my body. My right arm begins to tingle to the point of bursting open.

I hear the noise before seeing it.

The truck is barreling down on us as we lie in the middle of the road. Quin notices it as well, and gets off of me, muttering a few curses, still holding onto my Levin gun. I back up across the other side of the road, removing the Beta gun from my satchel. The idea is to blow out one of the tires to make the vehicle stop. When they get out of the cab to investigate, we jump. Rena insisted on placing a spare tire in the back of Quin's vehicle, so we can replace the one we damage on the truck, and make it drivable back to the Refuge.

I aim the Beta gun at the left rear tire, fire, and it goes instantly flat.

The truck slows to a stop, but only the driver gets out. I creep up to the vehicle, slinking low near the ground. When I'm close to the driver, I hear a struggle behind me. The driver turns as he hears the noise as well and I move, taking him down easily, binding his hands, feet, and mouth with adhesive.

I walk around the back to Quin's side, gun in hand. The security guard is halfway out of the vehicle. Quin pulling on the man's uniform as they fight over the Levin gun. I fire a warning shot, blasting out the passenger window. The security guard gives up the fight, letting me bind his legs and hands. Quin jumps into the driver's side, looking for the ignition switch. The guard begins to laugh as the vehicle apparently doesn't have one.

"How do you start the truck?" I ask, as I take the Beta gun and press it into his forehead.

"Go to hell," he says, spitting at me.

I stomp on his face with my shoe, breaking his nose, then tape shut his mouth, and walk over to where I left the driver. He cowers at my approach, curling into a tighter ball.

I'm kind of enjoying the viciousness that has come upon me.

"If you are nice to me I'll be nice to you, okay?"

He nods his head in compliance.

I remove the tape as carefully as possible, trying not to rip off the sparse black mustache that he's attempting to grow on his upper lip. "How do we turn on the vehicle?"

"I'll only tell you if you take me with you."

Somewhat taken aback by his response, as I was expecting a protest like that from the guard, I agree to the deal without consulting Quin. I use my knife to cut off the tape that I'd secured him with, and then tell Quin to scoot over. He stares at me, seeing the driver behind me.

"Are you fucking crazy?" he screams at me.

"He can start the truck and he wants to enter into the Wasteland, so what's the big deal?" I protest.

"What makes you think he isn't going to drive us into some kind of trap? You've gotten soft since Devlan died. If I had my way I'd leave your ass here, but seeing as Rena would kill me if I didn't come back with you I guess I don't have a choice."

After a brief standoff, Quin finally moves over. I climb in the middle and the driver gets behind the wheel.

"Since you blew out the back tire it'll be slow going, but I'm assuming you have a spare somewhere, otherwise why would you have blown it to begin with, correct?" the man asks, as he punches a code into the keypad on the steering wheel.

I nod as a screen rises up from the dashboard, requesting facial and voice recognition. He shifts his head directly in front of the screen and gives a password. The small camera built into the monitor scans his face and his voice is recorded.

The truck starts and I motion where to drive. He backs the truck up first so we don't run over the security guard, which disappoints Quin. As we make the turn and begin to drive, the truck wobbles as it slowly rolls forward on three good tires. We make it through the opening in the fence, but just by mere inches. It takes about a half hour to reach Quin's truck as the driver doesn't want to damage the other three tires.

The changing of the tire on the delivery truck goes faster than expected since we now have someone helping us out. Quin decides to ride with the driver so he can direct him where to go, while I follow in the other vehicle. The only danger we now face is the drive back to the Refuge, since we have to ride with the lights on. This will make us visible to any Collectors who might be out roaming at this time of night.

We barrel through the landscape, with no more than a foot gap between the two trucks. I feel my eyes getting heavy with tiredness, but we have only been driving for two hours, and there are four more to go. My head feels groggy and my body starts to ache as my eyes begin to close, but I'm jarred awake as something impacts the truck.

My eyes fly open, anticipating seeing the delivery truck against the hood, but it's not there. The vehicle is hit again, but this time it's behind me. Looking in the rearview mirror, I see only blackness so I keep driving thinking I must have hit a rock.

The truck jerks sideways as another impact jars the wheel from my hands. My head slams into the driver's side window, cracking it. I lift my head up as pain shoots down my spine, and notice my eyes are not focusing, so I force myself to blink several times until forms begin to take their shape. I see four small lights in the distance that are getting larger, rapidly. I have no time to move before the passenger side caves in, overturning the truck, and sending anything loose flying in all directions. I have the restraint on, so I remain in my seat, only now I dangle upside down.

I've lost sight of Quin, and panic. *What do I do? What do I do?*

I unbuckle myself and fall onto the ceiling. Someone smashes out the driver's side window, grabs my ponytail, and yanks me out of the vehicle, hard. I scream in pain, thrashing around in an effort to dislodge myself from the man's grip. Blood trickles down the side of my face from the head wound, but the pain begins to subside.

The wound is beginning to close.

"Look at what we have here, boys," the man who is holding me says, in a low, husky voice, his body smelling sour.

Three other men approach our location, two of which I recognize from the other night at the Refuge. However, the man holding me and his companion are new.

"She's sweet looking, Tank. She'll sell for a nice price," one of the men says.

My eyes begin to focus so I'm able to see my captors.

The three in front of me range in height from six foot to six foot four. One has a gut like Terrance's, while the other two are fit and muscular. I wriggle around to see what the fourth man looks like, noticing he is a twin to the one with the large gut.

"Hi, sweetheart, want to have some fun?" he asks, eyes examining me from head to toe.

"No," I spit back at him.

My knee nails him in the crotch, causing him to crumble. Two of the men charge as I reach for the knife in my boot and fling it at one of the brunettes, hitting him in the shoulder. I reach for the Beta gun, but it's not there. When the truck flipped it must have fallen out of my waistband. I dive back into the truck to locate the weapon. Someone grabs my feet, pulling me back outside, scraping my stomach against several pieces of shattered glass left in the window frame. I come out with the weapon drawn, pull the trigger, and hit the overweight ass in his thigh.

I try to fire again but off-balance, I miss, so I flip myself around and catch one of the men in the face with the heel of my boot. Three of the four are injured, but they're all still coming at me. I notice Quin coming up behind the last man standing, his blade in hand, charging through the two battering ram vehicles used to knock me off the road. I smile, as the man doesn't know he is about to die.

Quin raises his blade, but a blue flash from behind stops him dead in his tracks. He falls hard to the ground and doesn't move.

"Quin," I scream, as my stomach drops and I begin to convulse.

I know what hit him...I've seen that flash.

What have I done? I should've followed Quin's plan.

The driver of the delivery truck walks up from the same direction Quin had just come from holding the Levin gun in his hand, which he has covered in a thick black glove. He steps over Quin's body, past the blond who still hasn't moved, and over to me. He pulls me up by the front of my top so we are face to face.

"Should've listened to your friend," he says.

I shake him loose and run over to Quin.

His back is covered in blood and there are bits of flesh missing in spots around a hole that has penetrated through his ribcage and out the front of his torso. I bend down and begin to look for the metal container of Quarum I'd given him. I shove him onto his side and find it in his front pocket, but as soon as I have it in my hands I'm yanked hard from behind, causing me to drop it onto the ground. I scream as I'm being dragged away from him, trying to fight to free myself, but the blond who didn't fight has me secured tightly in his massive grip. Tears rolling down my face, I shriek Quin's name. As I'm being lifted into one of their trucks, I brace myself against the door frame, preventing my body from bending into the car. I feel metal being pressed against my neck and a current runs through my body as I go limp, and darkness takes over.

CHAPTER 7

Distant voices weave in and out of my consciousness.

At times I think I'm back at my house, with Devlan giving me instructions on training, then moments later I'm shifted to the Refuge where I watch Terrance die as I sit by helplessly, his tormentors ripping apart his flesh. I want to scream, but my mouth will not open. Eventually the nightmares fade and my head clears. I feel rough straw against my face, concrete under my feet, and smell foul air around me. A breeze blows in from somewhere behind me, warm and gentle. Words are spoken quietly at first, then louder as my hearing returns.

"What do you think Artemis will do with her?"

"Not sure."

"Do you think he'll sell her to one of the hatcheries? You know they like to take them young."

"Are you kidding me? Didn't you see how she fought out there, nailing James in the thigh without really aiming? She'll be too valuable to be sold to the hatcheries. If he's smart, he'll sell her as a fighter."

"I wonder if he'll let us have a go with this one."

"Are you stupid?" I hear one say, followed by a slap. "Now stop being an ass and wake her up."

Water is poured on me, soaking me from head to toe. I shake my head, trying to get my matted hair out of my face. My hands are bound behind my back, my feet chained to the floor. I roll onto my side and watch as one of the men walks over to me with a ring of keys, and unlocks my feet. As soon as they are loose from their bindings, I slam both of my boots into the man's stomach, sending him flying across the room. His companion laughs at his misery.

"See, I told you, she's a fighter, not a baby maker."

I wriggle my wrists, testing the bands. The rope is thin and not very well tied, so I easily snap them, pick up the bucket that was dropped on the floor, and swing it wide, hitting the man by the door in the side of the head, knocking him unconscious. I'm about to exit when three more men come in, all armed, followed by a fourth who is too well dressed to be from the Wasteland.

"I was told you were quite a handful," the man says to me, as his guards secure my hands behind my back again, this time with rope infused with steel thread. It begins to dig into my flesh as I twist my wrists to test its strength. "So, what do I call you?"

I keep my mouth closed, staring past him at the courtyard beyond, trying to plan my escape. One of the guards standing behind me hits me hard in the back, causing me to collapse onto my knees.

"The man asked you a question," he grunts.

"Meg," I whisper, as I have no wind in my lungs. "My name is Meg."

"Hello, Meg," the well-dressed man says to me, as he bends down gently gripping my arm to help me to my feet. "My name is Artemis Webb."

He holds onto me longer than necessary. He brushes the hair from my face, plucking out pieces of straw from my hair. I stare hard into his face, memorizing it. His eyes are deep green, almost emerald in color. His hair is sandy, slightly tousled, and just brushing the collar of his dress shirt. He appears to stand just under six foot, of slight build, but with hints of muscles tugging at the sleeves of his shirt. If I didn't know he was leading a bunch of killers and kidnappers, I'd almost say he was attractive.

"Are you hungry?"

I nod in acknowledgement.

He waves for me to follow him, and escorts follow on my tail. We walk along the wide brick courtyard that is in immaculate condition, lined with doors not unlike the one I just left. A small fountain sits in the center, crystal clear water pouring from the decorative spout at the top. We seem to be walking towards the main house at the end of the courtyard where we climb some steps before reaching the large, glass-inlayed doors.

The interior of the entryway is brightly lit, with skylights lining the ceiling. Pale sandy terracotta tiles cover the floor, and the walls are covered in a pale yellow finish. Decorations are minimal, just a few plants and a small wooden table in the center of the room with a large glass vase filled with roses. We turn to the right and walk down a small hallway, passing by a study filled with books and a lavish dining room that has a long dining table lined with fine China.

"How many people have you sold to buy all this?" I comment.

The only response I receive is a kick in the back.

We enter the kitchen at the far end, but the guards stay in the hallway, while Artemis walks me over to a barstool sitting in front of a large marble island. After removing eggs and what appears to be real butter from the refrigerator, he cooks them, along with some toast, then pours me a large glass of freshly squeezed orange juice. My restraints are removed so I can eat, which I do, slowly at first.

I'm unsure about how to interpret unexpected kindness from the man responsible for Quin's death, although I have to suspect there's some plan I have yet to hear about. Then my hunger takes over and I devour every bite.

As I work on my second helping, he walks over to the kitchen door, making sure it's closed before coming up behind me. He's almost right against my back, where I can feel his body heat, but he doesn't touch me.

"I know who you are, Meg," he whispers.

I put my fork slowly down onto the plate, but I don't let it go.

"I have no idea what you're talking about," I respond, as calmly as possible.

He gently brushes the hair off the back of my neck. My body tingles at his touch.

"I inspect everyone who comes to me, so of course I noticed the marks. The three dots you have here." His finger gently rubs the spot just below my hairline. "I recognize them. You're one of the four Antaean...soldiers built for fighting."

I'm reminded that like Artemis, Devlan mentioned only four, yet Quin is number five. I wonder how many really survived the destruction of the dormitories.

I grip the fork tighter, readying myself to attack. He doesn't move from his spot, but instead he continues to caress the back of my neck, to the point of annoyance.

"You're a very valuable asset, Trea. You're lucky that I found you before one of the cities' Collectors did. Who knows what could've happened to you if they caught you."

I think back to Devlan and the attack on my home. I'm not sure if Artemis' Collectors are any better than the cities'.

"What do you want?" I finally ask through clenched teeth.

"I want to help you, Trea." He walks around the island removing my plate, glass, and fork, setting them into the sink.

"I don't need your help."

"Of course you do." He leans over the counter staring hard into my eyes. "You just don't know it yet."

The door to the kitchen opens and the guards come in, binding my wrists together, and yanking me off of the stool. They propel me down the hallway, past the door we entered and to a small room at the back of the house. We march through the chamber, out a back door, and down a steep incline to five small buildings that sit along the edge of a large open area in the center. As we get closer, I notice several people in the open area fighting each other with Pugio blades. We walk past, but they ignore us since they're too intensely focused on injuring each other. One of my guards marches ahead, opening the door to a shack that is half the size of one horse stall in the barn at the Refuge. My restraints are removed and I'm shoved into the small room, the door slamming shut behind me.

I hear the lock click, and the sound of the guards' retreating feet.

The room is completely dark except for the errant streams of sunlight that are coming through slits in the wood. I wait a brief moment for my eyes to adjust before moving from my spot on the floor. The furnishings are identical to the ones of the room I was previously held in, and the odor is just as bad. I eye the hay with suspicion and decide to sit against the wall next to the door instead.

The heat in the room quickly climbs and I begin to sweat, drenching my clothes and hair. My head begins to ache as the moisture rapidly escapes my body. I contemplate testing the integrity of the walls, but I feel this move by Artemis is intentional.

I lean my head back and close my eyes, listening to the two men out in the ring battling. After several minutes one finally goes down, screaming from a wound his adversary has inflicted. The others clap and cheer the victor. From the voices, I can tell the audience consists of two women and one man. I sit and listen to the injured man's wails that slowly become whimpers, and then silence.

"Who's next?" One of the men holler, but no one volunteers.

I hear footsteps approach my door, but I'm too tired to move. After some fumbling with the lock, my door is opened and I'm dragged out into the sunlight. I wince at the sudden assault on my vision while I'm being pulled through the dirt into the makeshift ring.

"How about this one?" The man who seized me says to the others.

"Sweet," the victor says as he walks over to me. "Hey little girl, want to play?" He bends down to look into my face.

I don't acknowledge his presence, so he grabs my ponytail and hauls me to my feet.

"This should be easy," he says as he lets me go and walks to the others. "Choose a weapon." He nods his head to where several Pugio blades lean against the wood railing that encircles the area, along with a couple of Beta guns, but I don't move. "Have it your way, then."

He comes at me full speed, blade over his head. I wait until he is practically on top of me then simply step aside. He falters and slams into the railing, the blade of his weapon cutting his hand as he falls forward. The others break out into laughter, including the man he had wounded before, who is now resting in a far corner.

"Great job, Matt," one of the cheerers chuckles.

The man they call Matt gets up, wipes the blood from his hand onto his shorts, re-grips the blade, and changes his approach. Seems like he realizes there's more to me than he thought. He walks slowly around the outer rim while I walk in the opposite direction. This goes on for some time, neither of us giving in.

"This is ridiculous," Matt shouts at me. "Pick up a weapon and let's go."

"No," I shout back.

"Fine, then at least stand still so I can practice gutting you."

I reluctantly reach down and pick up one of the blades. I've never used them before, so I'm unsure of how to hold it correctly. Something Devlan didn't have me train with. It hits me again that I'll never that chance to learn from him again.

Thinking of Devlan makes me suddenly feel weak. My knees collapse, giving Matt an opportunity to attack. He seizes the moment to slash my back with the sword. The pain is something I've never felt before, my flesh ripping open with the sensation of thousands of pinpricks radiating down my spine. I scream and fall on my stomach as the ground begins to soak up the blood dripping from the wound, but the pain begins to subside as I begin to heal.

Matt lifts up his blade, readying himself to plunge it into my back. I grab the hilt of my blade, roll over, and slice open his thigh. He drops to the ground, and the others immediately run to his side, tending to his wound. Artemis walks into the arena, clapping. Another man follows, carrying a medical bag. He begins to attend to Matt's wounds.

Artemis walks up to me, lifting up my shirt to examine the slice in my back, which no longer exists. He doesn't say anything, just simply lets my shirt fall back into place. Matt and the man he defeated are carried from the ring and up the hill to the house to be tended to properly. Artemis motions towards several bodyguards that have joined the crowd. They walk over to me, take the blade I'm holding, and secure my hands behind my back. We walk back to the house, while Artemis instructs the other fighters to return to their quarters.

I'm led into a small but lavish bedroom off the stairs that rise to the second story. My restraints are removed, but I'm advised I can't leave my room. Of course the minute I'm left alone I try the doorknob but find it locked from the outside. My room has one window without any coverings, a large brass bed covered in a floral bedspread, a teak dresser and matching nightstand, and my own bathroom with both a shower and a deep-seated tub. I look out of the window and see the ring below. The backdrop behind the house consists of large snowcapped mountains and pine trees.

I miss the desert, the wide-open land.

These mountains feel confining and daunting.

I walk into the bathroom, turn the shower on, and then look under the cabinets, locating an extravagant variety of bath salts, lotions, shampoos, and conditioners. I locate a washcloth and towel under the vanity, along with soap. Placing the towel on the top of the toilet tank, I set the washcloth and soap on the floor of the shower stall, strip off all my clothes, and ease myself into the hot water. I stand under the deluge, letting the heat of the water ease the tension in my muscles. Then it hits me - my nightmare realized - I've been taken by Collectors. Sitting down on the tiles covering the stall floor, I hug my knees up to my chest, rocking back and forth as tears begin to spill down my cheeks. The hot water begins to run cold, but I continue to sit as my sobs subside into numbness.

How could I have let this happen?

Panic sets in. I shake in addition to the rocking, overwhelmed with all that has transpired.

How do I pull myself together? What can I do to get back to the Wasteland?

My first objective is to clear my head and come up with a plan of escape. After several more minutes, I take a couple deep breaths, stand up, and wash my body along with my hair, scrubbing everything off.

Stepping out, I wrap myself up in the towel, but leave my hair dripping down my back. I grab a second towel from under the sink to cover my head before walking back into the bedroom, where I rummage through the drawers in the dresser for something to wear, managing to find cotton shorts and a matching top. After I slip those one, I go into the bathroom, brush my hair, and hang up my towels. I wash the arm sleeve under the sink and slip it back on, even though it's still damp. The sun is still shining brightly outside, but I decide to crawl under the blankets and go to sleep, almost welcoming the nightmares that soon begin.

CHAPTER 8

My brothers and sisters thrash around me as they burn, heal, and burn again. The woman on the other side is trying desperately to open the door, but it's biometrically coded to open only for the instructors, and she appears to not have access. I cry out for the first time, my voice only a squeak. After sliding down onto the searing hot floor, I place my fingers beneath the threshold and feel her soothing touch as she grabs my fingers tightly, squeezing as if on a life line, but I feel her slipping away, leaving me alone to die.

Minutes seem to pass before I hear the popping noises of the metal door as it's forced open. Glass rains down as the window shatters from above. I'm yanked through the opening, my small body lifted into the air. The woman carrying me rushes down the dark hallway; blue lights flashing all around. I see others run down the same passageway, some in white uniforms, and others in orange, but I can't see the face of the woman carrying me as she has placed me up against her shoulder. I can only see the color of her white uniform, which comforts me.

The sheets are soaked in sweat when I awake. I don't get the chance to change out of my wet clothes before there is a knock on my door. Without answering, it flies open and is filled with Artemis' guards. They take hold of my arms, secure me in restraints, and escort me downstairs into the cellar.

To the left of the staircase lie several massive wine racks that extend along the entire length of the house; to the right is a maple door, partially open. My guards nudge me through the opening and into a very bright interior. Sitting in the center of the room is a black suede lounge chair. Next to that sit several small metal trays loaded down with instruments I've never seen before. A scale sits in the far left corner, next to a set of glass-inlaid cabinets. The man I saw yesterday with the medical bag is busy at his desk going over some paperwork. He looks up, glasses sliding down his long nose as we enter the room. He nods at the guards, who remove my restraints before leaving. He gestures for me to have a seat on the chair once the door is closed.

He carefully arranges his instruments on the trays then moves to the cabinets behind me and takes out a thin gown. From somewhere in my memory, he seems familiar. I recognize his elongated face, the slight hunch he has as he walks, and the short grayish hair that must once have been brown, though I'm still not sure how I know him.

He walks over to me, shines a small light into my eyes, and requests that I hold my head still while slowly moving the light from one eye to the next, perhaps watching for some kind of reaction. He changes instruments, coming up with a long cylinder with an eyepiece on the end. Switching on the tiny bulb inside, he leans close into my left eye, placing his hand on the top of my head to steady me.

"I know you," I state, while not looking away from the brightness that is temporarily blinding me.

"I was wondering if you might," he replies back in a soft voice moving to examine my right eye.

"How?"

"Not here," he whispers.

He hands me the gown and asks me to change into it, removing my clothing, including the covering on my arm. I hesitantly undress except for the sleeve. He doesn't say anything at my refusal to show my bare arm, but instead continues his examination of me. I've never been to a physician in my life, but his familiarity makes it easier. He has me dress, then walks me up the stairs and outside. The first building we come to at the bottom of the hill is full of exercise equipment. Two of the machines are currently in use, both by women. The physician has me move to a machine at the far end of the room, where I run for thirty minutes. He checks my pulse and heart rate as I go. The next machine he moves me to measures my leg and arm strength. After two hours, he escorts me back to my room where I'm locked away again.

The next day I'm brought down again in the same fashion for more tests, where I'm poked many times with several different syringes, all taking fluids, but none injecting any. I've not eaten in two days and according to the physician my nutrition levels are low, so he orders Artemis to provide me several meals a day. I have to eat in my room, leaving my tray at the foot of my bed when I'm finished. On my fourth day of confinement, my guards bring me down again to be examined. This time the physician doesn't hand me a gown. The instruments have been cleared from their metal trays, and only the lounge chair remains undisturbed. My restraints are removed and the guards leave as I sit on the chair, dreading what is planned for today.

"Meg, I need to look at your arm."

I grip my right arm with my left, afraid of what his reaction might be.

"Meg, I need you to trust me. Please."

His soft gray eyes are disarming.

I remove the Velcro straps and slide down the covering, laying it beside me. He slides his glasses closer to his eyes as they have slipped down, takes my arm gently in his hands, and begins to examine the wound. He concentrates mainly on the Quantum Stream running the length of my arm before scrutinizing the two tiny holes in my palm, followed by a look at the exit wound on my back. He walks over to one of the cabinets, opens a drawer, and removes a tiny syringe. Lifting my arm, he rests my palm against his shoulder. He takes the needle and attempts to insert it into the stream, which causes my arm to tingle, becoming extremely hot at the intrusion. The needle disintegrates and the plastic casing of the syringe melts in his hands. He goes over to the sink to wash the residue off while I secure the sleeve back on my arm.

"I should've expected that kind of reaction," he says as he returns, taking a seat next to me on the chair. "So, how do you like it here?"

"How do you think? I hate it. I can't stand being confined to that room."

He is about to respond when there is a knock at the door. He gets up and lets Artemis into the room, shaking the man's hand as he enters.

"So," Artemis begins, clapping his hands together, "how is our little warrior?"

I open my mouth to express my displeasure at the situation, but the physician quickly waves me down by placing his hand on my shoulder.

"She needs exercise, Artemis, lots of running. I suggest you let her wander the property, hike some of the trails. This isolation is not good for her."

"Okay," he says, nodding his head slightly, "I'll let her, on one condition. She wears a monitoring ring around both wrists."

The physician looks at me with a pleading expression.

"Fine," I reply, gritting my teeth.

"Now, about her arm," Artemis begins, walking over to me, picking up my arm as if to examine it.

"It's severely injured. No amount of Quarum could restore it, as the injury is too old. It must have happened as a child."

Artemis meditates a few moments with this news then summons the guards from the hallway into the room. Before I'm escorted out, I'm fitted with two thin black bracelets, one for each wrist. I'm warned not to wander past the boundary lines because if I do I will be brutally shocked, and locked away. Artemis does permit me to go up to my room and change my clothes before I go outside. I'm provided with a new pair of running shoes and socks, put my hair up into a ponytail, and leave the house.

After breakfast each morning, I spend most of my days jogging down hiking paths that lead up into the mountains. The air gets thinner the higher I go. I push farther up each day, looking to see where the property line ends, but the land seems to go on indefinitely. Besides running, I begin practicing climbing, first the trees, then the face of the mountain. I fall many times from small heights, but get right back up and continue. I also start to practice jumping from great distances, mainly from boulder to boulder at the base of the mountain.

At night the same dream haunts me. I can't seem to move past the scene of my rescue from the inferno. The screaming from the children invades my thoughts. I'm beginning to think these nightmares are my memories slowly restoring themselves, allowing me a glimpse into the horror of my childhood.

I no longer cry each night, but have chosen to accept my fate, at least for the moment. Anger is my driving force, the device that is keeping me alive.

A month into my imprisonment I find a nice outlook to rest on. My afternoons are spent perched up high, over-looking the ranch below and out into the unknown. Several times I stay until nightfall so I can watch the stars come out. The temperature drops, but I stay until the moon is almost directly overhead. I'm not only sightseeing from my vantage point, but I'm also studying the layout of Artemis' compound.

There is only one road in, and the whole complex is surrounded by sparse trees, lots of rocks, and tall grasses. I don't see any possible way of escape except through the mountain, but the air is too thin at the top to allow me to climb over to the other side.

One morning, in my second month of captivity, I run into the physician as I walk past the practice ring on the way to my favorite jogging path. He is busy getting the fighters prepared for their next contest, which they leave for the following morning. Of the five, only two have ever been to a contest, one of them is Matt. I do some stretching before I begin as I notice the physician walking over to me, so I prolong my warm-up to give him time to get to my location.

"Walk with me," he says, continuing down the path.

We walk together at a steady pace, waiting for the other one to speak.

"Have you figured out why I seem familiar to you yet?" he finally asks, breaking the long silence.

I shake my head, which causes him to frown.

"Antaeans have great memories," he begins. "It was known that an Antaean could begin collecting memories as early as three months. I know this because that is how I designed them."

"You're one of the researchers from the Dormitories," I say, more as an acknowledgement than a question.

"Yes, Meg, I was. I'm also one of the few researchers who made it out of there alive."

I think of Devlan's last comment. He would be very disappointed at the predicament I've gotten myself into.

I start to believe that his death was in vain.

"How did you know what would happen with my arm a while back?"

"I didn't actually, it was more of a hunch that I wanted to test. We knew how your body was supposed to behave when the stimulant was introduced, but we could never get it to work properly. Tell me, how did your stream come about?"

I explain to him some of the events that have transpired, including Devlan's death. He is saddened by the news. We change direction and begin heading back towards the house. As we get closer, the physician grabs my arm and spins me around to face him.

"Whatever you do, don't let Artemis see your arm. If he realizes your full abilities it will be disastrous and not just in regards to you. Many have died trying to locate the Antaeans and the cities will stop at nothing to find them all. You are a threat to them and they will do anything possible to either control you or eliminate you. Artemis is planning on taking you into Tyre tomorrow with the other fighters, so be careful. I won't be going, as there are physicians at the stadium where the contests are held, and Artemis has received word that new prospects have been acquired that need tending to."

He wraps his arms around me and hugs me tightly. We eventually part and he walks back to the fighters. I turn and run back down the path, trying to clear my head.

CHAPTER 9

The next morning, I'm greeted by a hot breakfast, and Artemis sitting at the foot of my bed.

"Morning, Trea," he smiles at me. "We'll be leaving for Tyre in an hour. Your clothing for the journey is hanging up in the bathroom, so eat up quickly and get dressed, and I will send someone to get you."

I place my tray of dirty dishes on top of the dresser after eating and go into the bathroom. The clothes Artemis has chosen for me are hanging on the back of the door; a pair of black leather shorts with a matching jacket, a black rayon tank, and a clean pair of socks. My footwear consists of knee high boots made of the same material as the jacket, and of the same color. I take a quick shower, put on clean under-garments then don my new apparel before brushing my hair and putting it up into my usual ponytail.

There is a knock at my door, but it's only a courtesy as my door opens before I respond. One of the bodyguards comes in announcing that it's time to leave. He removes my bracelets, escorts me down the stairs, out the front door, and through the courtyard to an awaiting transport. It resembles a smaller version of the shuttle, consisting of only one car that is not running on a rail but on wheels made of metal. I'm ordered to move all the way to the back where the others have already taken their seats.

As I sit in between two of the fighters, one named Corinna and the other named Raven, I notice the five fighters are dressed in brown cotton pants, beige twill shirts, and brown boots. Glancing around the small cabin I spy Matt glaring at me. I ignore him, focusing my attention on the window behind the fighter who is sitting directly in front of me.

As soon as Artemis boards, the engine starts and begins sending power down the length of the car switching the windows on. Transforming the scattered grasses and rocks that cover the front part of the property to a picturesque landscape of thick pine trees, blanketing a rugged mountainous backdrop, accompanied by sounds of chirping birds.

I wonder at the need for such deception. What are the High Rulers afraid of people seeing?

I have trouble telling which direction we are heading since I don't have a reference point to view outside. We're about three hours into our trip when we slow down and come to a halt. I hear the hiss of the doors as they open, sliding outside along the length of the vehicle and a man boards, dressed in a Regulator's uniform: a starched blue dress shirt, a heavy dark blue coat with an hour glass symbol sown onto each lapel, matching pants, a thick black belt with several holsters, a pair of shiny black shoes, and a blue semi-round hat that has a Tyrean bull and red cape badge attached to a small leather band just above the brim. The man paces the interior, scanning everything with a small device in his hand, touching nothing.

Artemis speaks to another person up front, addressing him by name, and inquiring about his family. The Regulator departs, the doors close, and we move forward then stop. There's a soft clicking sound, causing the car to vibrate faintly. The vehicle makes another slight jerk forward, settles downward, and begins to glide. We have now connected to a set of rails for the shuttle system.

The scenery on the windows slowly changes from mountains to lower highlands. I try to look out through the window in front of Artemis, but there is some sort of thin veil between him and us, preventing me from gaining any clear glimpses. Another hour passes before we come to a stop. The doors open and another Regulator boards. This time the power is shut down so they can inspect the undercarriage.

I look out of the windows and see we are in a transportation center. Many people are walking about the platform, with several shuttles loading and unloading passengers. The interior is constructed of the same white titanium as the oasis, including the ceiling with its artificial sunlight. No one pays much attention to us as the Regulators inspect every inch of the interior and exterior of our car. As soon as we are cleared, the car lowers back onto the rail and the engine turns on, however this time the windows don't change as we move forward, coasting past other shuttles, down the white interior, and out into the open.

I'm first struck by the brightness of the city as lights slowly turn on inside the tall structures that envelop us. The sun appears to be setting, as the sky above has a slight pink tint to the fading blue. We slide past buildings constructed of polished steel and blue tinted windows. Sidewalks scattered with residents sit along either side of us. Apparently the rail system in the city is not elevated like it is out in the Wasteland.

We come to an interchange, switch rails, and begin heading to our right, moving around the city instead of through it. Every inch is covered in concrete and skyscrapers. The only evidence of greenery consists of either large potted plants or sporadic palm trees strategically placed along the rail line. We pass through another interchange, then slow as we are diverted onto another rail that takes us underneath one of the high-rises, before coming to a stop. Artemis exits out of his door just as ours opens. Matt and the others get up, and I follow.

As we stand on the platform, our shuttle moves off down the rail. Artemis leads us to an elevator marked express. When the doors open, we step on board as Artemis pushes the last button at the top. Once the doors are closed we are quickly whisked skyward. The walls of the enclosure are glass, so we are able to observe the lobby briefly as we ascend. The floors fly past almost at a blur. There are several other elevator shafts surrounding ours, moving up and down in a bizarre dance in the center of the building. We soon reach the top level, popping up through the floor.

"Welcome to The Letchworth," Artemis announces, giving a mocking bow to us as we exit the elevator.

Matt lumbers past, knocking me slightly as he goes. He walks around the glass enclosure of the elevator towards a set of doors on the other side, and slams them loudly behind him. Corinna and Raven giggle as they prance over the hardwood floors to the living room, where they both lean against the windows, looking down at the scenery below. The other two fighters, Aidan and Wes, go off to another room at the far left of the entrance. I stay standing just outside the elevator, taking in the place.

The apartment is completely circular, the elevator shaft being the core. The living room lies in front of me, the kitchen and dining room are off to my left. The only walls are for room separation at the back of the apartment, where I assume the bedrooms and bathrooms are located. Thick white columns encircle the space, probably used more for support than aesthetics. The floor is light colored hardwood and the walls a pale rose. The apartment is furnished with overstuffed couches and chairs, many teak wood tables, and several marble statues.

Lights ensconced in the ceiling begin to come to life as the sun sets. I walk over to where Corinna and Raven had been standing, as they have now moved off to the kitchen. The windows in the living room are floor to ceiling in height. I've never been so high up before, so I hesitantly move closer to the windows, standing a few inches from the edge, making sure I'm not leaning against the glass before I look out.

Down below my feet is the rail system of the shuttle, bending slightly as it goes around the city. Several pedestrian bridges straddle the rails making it possible to move from one area to another without being electrocuted. The interchange is to the right of us, high-rises springing up across the street from the interchange as well as to the right and left of the Letchworth. The people roaming about the sidewalk look small and insignificant from this altitude.

My gaze moves outward to the large stadium directly in front of us. The arena is long, slightly bow-like. Seats encompass the inner walls, and only a few are blocked off by large chain metal links. The base of the arena itself looks to be metallic, spanning almost the entire length of the stadium. Reflective barriers encircle the arena floor, rising only a few feet, not giving much protection to the spectators. My eyes move over the stadium onto the mass of water behind it.

The waves lap slowly forward, breaking upon barriers I can't see. The color of the sea is blue with a hint of pink from the sun setting below the edge of the horizon. I've never seen such a vast amount of water. Water beds are dry in the Wasteland...no lakes...no rivers. I grew up hearing stories of the Great Seas, but had never seen anything but sand and dust, and thought that was how it was all over. Apparently I was mistaken.

"Beautiful isn't it," Artemis whispers over my shoulder.

I'm startled by his sudden appearance. "Yes, it is," I choke out.

"The ocean goes on forever, reaching lands that no one talks about anymore; republics that have fallen silent or are too terrified to speak; terrestrial beings no longer of any consequence to Sirain."

I feel his breath on my neck, warm on my skin. My heart rate rises as I begin to feel flush. *Why is he having such an effect on me?*

He moves closer to the window, smiling at the sight of the water, and nudges my arm, gesturing me to follow him as he guides me around the residence.

The room Aidan and Wes disappeared into is a game room full of all sorts of electronic gadgets, and several large view screens. It's the only room that has walls, other than the bedrooms and bathrooms. Artemis' room is right next to the game room, with a private bath and walk-in closet. My room is next to his, with a bathroom I'll be sharing with both Corinna and Raven, who are in the room on the other side.

Artemis leads me into the dining room, where everyone has assembled for a large gourmet dinner prepared for us by Artemis' private chef. The extravagant meal consists of a spinach salad mixed with fresh strawberries and a tangy dressing. For our main course we are served roast beef, mashed potatoes, rolls dipped in butter, and peas in garlic sauce. Matt and Aidan go back for seconds as I'm still working on my first helping. Artemis breaks out bottles of wine, giving everyone a healthy glass full. I only sip at mine as I don't like the taste.

The amount of food for such a small group surprises me. I feel guilty in eating this lavish food since those in the Wasteland are struggling to find their next meal. I place my fork down, unable to eat the rest.

The fighters laugh at each other's jokes, discuss strategies in regards to the opening battle sequence tomorrow, and make bets on who will come back a winner so they can advance to Round Two. Matt and Aidan have experience in this, and tell stories about their past battles. Matt retells more triumphs than Aidan as the latter has lost the last several times during the opening battle. Matt boasts about his many wins by showing off the tattoos he has on his right arm, each ring a different shape and color, indicating a win. Aidan tries to hide his left arm, but Matt grabs it before he can move, rolls up his sleeve, and shows the markings a loser receives.

Aidan's left arm is scarred, not by intricate scrolls like Matt's, but by raised burn marks, probably made by some kind of electrical bracelet placed around the bicep. Aidan shoves Matt away, who hits the table, knocking Raven's wine into her lap.

"Hey!" she screams as the liquid soaks into her clothes.

Matt shoves Aidan back and a fight breaks out. Artemis lets it go on for a bit before finally breaking it up, telling them to save it for the arena. Aidan shakes himself free of Artemis' grasp and stomps away to his room.

"Huh," Matt huffs as he retakes his seat, "the old man needs to take a joke."

Of all the fighters, Aidan is the oldest. He looks to be in his early thirties, a little overweight, and slightly balding on top. He's the man I saw Matt take out my first day at the ranch. I poke at the remainder of my food while the others return to their jokes, now mainly about Aidan.

Our dishes are cleared after the wine has run out and we each slowly wander off to bed. I lock my door before changing. My closet is full of dresses, silk tops, dress pants, several cotton tank tops, and a brand new pair of running shoes sits on the floor. The drawers in my dresser house lace thongs with matching bras, white cotton pajamas, running shorts, and socks.

Do all closets in Tyre look like this? This is too much. Why would you need so many items?

I put on the pajamas, brush my teeth, and crawl into bed.

I sleep very poorly, dreaming of Quin, his face plaguing my mind. He is yelling at me, blaming me for his death. I try and run from him, but am confronted by Terrance, who wears a mournful expression. He takes his old gun, aims it at my head, and pulls the trigger. I feel a projectile strike my forehead, shattering my skull.

I dart up in bed, pain radiating outward from between my eyes. Slipping out of bed, I go to check the medicine cabinet in the bathroom for painkillers, but can't find any, so I go looking for the next best thing...alcohol.

I remember seeing a bar in the game room, so I quietly exit my room and make my way through the dark. One of the large screens attached to the far left wall is on. Wes is sound asleep on one of the red covered couches. The program he had been watching is still running, something about Tyre's residents being more affluent than those of Acheron. I decide to leave it on as I walk over to the opposite wall and remove a bottle of Tequila from under the counter, along with a small glass to pour myself a shot, shaking my head at the irony of drinking Terrance's favorite beverage while trying to erase his image from my mind.

I drink it down and pour another before putting the bottle back under the counter, then pick up my glass while my eyes roam the room.

A large color photo hangs up on the wall behind the bar. It displays a large aerial view of Tyre that includes the Boroughs in the northeast and southeast corners, both outside the natural border of the city. Each Borough has its own shuttle rail entering into the main station, which seems to be the only entrance into the city; however from what I can tell, the rails don't actually enter into the station. The Boroughs are perfectly circular, surrounded by high fences with razor wire on top. Small brown buildings crammed together. There are no roads, either, only dirt paths that map the way around the buildings. In the center is a large circular concrete structure. There aren't any identifiable markings on the building to determine what exactly it is.

I move away from the Boroughs and exam the layout of the city itself.

The plan of the city is significant in scale. Each building is a high-rise, the smallest twenty stories high. The city is in the shape of an egg, oval, but elongated. The shuttle system outlines the border, encompassing the entire city. It also highlights the shape of the inner rings of the city, with an interchange at every crossing. Sidewalks hide all vegetation, no grass, and no trees except for those which have been planted by the city maintenance. Walking seems to be the only other mode of transportation, as the roads that I have traveled out in the Wasteland don't exist here. To the west of the city lies the Great Sea.

I finish my drink, setting the glass on the counter before I leave. Wes is still asleep, snoring lightly. As I step into the hallway, I see the elevator rising to our floor, with Matt and Raven inside. They step out as I step back into the game room, not wanting to be seen.

Raven is clinging tightly around Matt's waist, their lips pressed against each other's as they drip water onto the floor, towels wrapped around their bodies. Matt walks towards his room, Raven stumbles trying to catch up to his hurried pace. His door opens and closes loudly behind them. I quickly hurry back to my room, closing my door and crawling back into bed, but sleep doesn't come for me.

I finally decide to drag myself out of bed around five, dress in running shorts, a top, and my new shoes. The floor below us has a gym, indoor track, swimming pool, hot tub, and sauna. I first try to go down to the main floor, but it won't go any lower than the gym without an access code.

I go and run on the track, but it doesn't feel as refreshing as running on solid ground.

I do this for an hour then move to a slow jog for another half hour before returning upstairs. When I reach the top floor everyone is seated around the dining room table enjoying breakfast. I load my plate up with fresh fruit, eggs, buttered toast, and a large glass of orange juice.

"I need everyone dressed and ready at the elevator by eight o'clock," Artemis says, as he finishes his coffee. "The first battle is to begin promptly at ten."

"How many fighters will be competing this time?" Matt asks.

"There are forty this year. I think the High Ruler might enter his own this time, so the battles will go until every fighter has competed. I checked you five in this morning and have your times. Meg, you'll be sitting with me in the Possessor's box."

"Why isn't *she* fighting?" Matt demands, pointing his finger close to my face. "She's good enough."

"Don't worry, Matt. I have plans for Meg and they are of no concern to you."

I look at Artemis, trying to discern what he is planning, sensing Matt grinning and feeling a shudder come from Aidan. I lose my appetite, push my plate away, get up from the table, and go to my room. My head begins to pound and my right arm begins to tingle, but I'm not sure why.

The urge to destroy something surges through me. Taking deep breaths calms me down.

I find a new outfit hanging on the outside door of my closet. Red satin sleeveless blouse with a matching cover, charcoal colored twill pants, and red heels. I'm beginning to see the way Artemis thinks of me, and I'm not happy about it.

Going into the bathroom, I strip down and climb into the shower, then remove the covering on my arm to wash it as well. I hear Corinna and Raven move about in their room. One of them comes into the bathroom, rummages through some drawers, and leaves again. I rinse, dry off, and wring out excess water from the covering before I re-strap it onto my arm. I wrap the towel around me before stepping out onto the cold stone floor, step over to the vanity to brush my hair, and tie it up. Corinna walks in and promptly unties it, forcing me to sit down on the toilet seat so she can do my hair.

"Honey, you are in serious need of some style tips," she says to me, as she works on getting out the knots I missed.

I dismiss her comment, but allow her to do whatever she wants.

She manages to smooth out all of the kinks, making my hair stick straight. She applies some gel, coating any strand that moves out of place. She next finds a small pair of nail scissors and slowly cuts a few dead ends from the hair that surrounds my face, feathering it ever so slightly.

"You have great coloring, so no make-up for you," she says, as she applies a little hairspray.

I'm transformed before my own eyes, my hair perfectly framing my face. "How did you learn to do this?" I ask.

"I used to be a private beautician to one of the Tyre Superiors, until he caught me in bed with his wife." She smirks at the memory. "I had two options when I was detained. I could either go out and die in the Wasteland like the others, or become a fighter. I chose the latter, for obvious reasons."

"What others?"

"Those who defy the laws of the cities, of course. Some are condemned to die in the Wasteland of starvation or dehydration, others get sold to Collectors to be trained as fighters, and there are some that are forced to live and work in the Boroughs with the Laics. That by far is the worst punishment ever."

"Who are the Laics?"

"Honey, have you been living in a cave? The Laics are the working class, those who work for the cities. They do all the menial labor, crafting, anything the Tyreans or Acherons view as beneath their status. I wouldn't be caught dead being stuck as a Laic, horrible people."

"What happened to the wife?"

"She got a new lover last I heard, another Superior's wife. I guess it's safer to screw an equal than the hired help." She laughs and leaves the room.

I remain sitting, thinking about how Corinna referred to the Wasteland as a place to die. People flee to the Wasteland in order to survive, escape the hardships of the Boroughs. But it seems the cities are using it to threaten their own people into submission.

I go back to my room and dress.

Everyone is gathered at the elevator when I arrive, except for Raven. Apparently she is having issues with her footwear. The fighters are all dressed alike, in two-piece, long-sleeved outfits made of a black colored material that appears to be a blend of moleskin and an elastic textile that I don't recognize, with gray metal threads interwoven into the cloth. Their boots go up to just below the knee and are made of leather also black in color. Raven joins us five minutes late and receives an earful from Artemis.

We enter into the elevator and descend, passing the lobby, which is crowded with people all dressed in semi-formal attire. When we come to a stop at the garage level, our shuttle is waiting for us. Exiting the building, we go back the way we had come. At the interchange we make a left and veer north. I spot thousands of people gathering on the pavement outside, slowly making their way into the stadium. Our shuttle moves left and under the stadium where we stop and sit for some time. Ahead of us there are lines of shuttles also loaded with fighters waiting to exit.

All fighters are wearing the same outfit, which I guess must be a regulation by the High Ruler. We exit the shuttle and are immediately directed to our right. Artemis takes my hand and pulls me away from the others, who get in the queue for processing. A woman in a white uniform goes down the line of fighters, asking them questions, looking down at her tablet to verify the information, and then digitally stamps a code on the inside of each wrist. Another woman walks just behind, scanning the code, which appears on a large electronic screen, showing the fighters' name as well as the Possessor they belong to.

Artemis yanks on my hand, pulling me in the opposite direction. We wait in our own line to board the elevator that will take us to the seats above. Artemis greets people as we wait, some he calls by name. He is more relaxed now that we are here, but he continues to hold onto my hand, perhaps afraid I'll get lost in the crowd - or try running.

We get into the elevator, practically squeezed against the glass of the outer walls from the number of people riding. The ride, thankfully, is short. I trip on the shoe of the woman in front of me as I exit and she turns and leers at me in disgust. Artemis smiles at her, which causes her to blush and she quickly darts away into the crowd. The elevator lands us outside of the stadium, not inside like I'd thought. People are clamoring to get inside, anxious to get the best seats as they are not assigned.

Artemis lets go of my hand, only to bend his arm and insist I link my arm with his. I oblige and he escorts me down the sidewalk towards a mob of onlookers gathered by an entrance labeled *Elysium*. The closer we approach, the louder the mob becomes. They begin to shout Artemis' name, bombarding him with questions about his fighters.

"Artemis, which one of the five you have entered is your favorite?" One woman asks, recording device in hand, shoved close enough to us that I feel the electricity pulsing through its circuits.

"Well, my dear, I dare say they are all my favorites."

This generates a laugh among the crowd, smiles splash across plastic faces.

"But honestly I would have to say its number twenty. He's been undefeated in every battle he has participated in. Although don't count out my new-comer, number twenty-three. She has extreme potential."

I'm confused for a moment until I remember that the fighters are given numbers and not names when in battle. Matt is twenty and Raven is twenty-three. I look above us and spot an identical screen to the one in the lower level hanging over our heads, minus the fighters' names. I spot Corinna as number thirty-seven, Aidan is fifteen and Wes is four.

"Artemis, do you think fifteen will be able to win this time? He has been unable to get past the opening battle for the last four sessions. Do you think he will be able to overcome his shortfalls today?" a short man asks in the front row.

"I certainly hope so. If not, perhaps a turn in the Boroughs will straighten him out."

This produces another round of laughter and fake smiles.

"Artemis, who is your companion today? You normally come alone, so our readers will want to know who you're escorting," a large plump woman in the back hisses out.

All eyes are on me, searching every inch for a possible flaw or defect.

Artemis takes his arm and wraps it around my waist, pulling me in tightly against his hip.

"Ladies and Gentlemen of the Tyre Press Corp, may I introduce you to Ms. Meg Farland, my lover." He winks at the reporters, smiling at them like a true showman.

As the crowd stands up in applause, I can feel the ground spin.

He twirls me around, kissing me hard on the lips. I can feel my legs going out from under me, but his hands are on my back, propping me up. He thanks everyone just as we enter into the stadium. I try and pull away, but his grip tightens.

"Why did you say that?" I practically scream at him, but it only comes out as a whisper due to the volume of the audience in the stands.

"Who says it won't come true, Trea? I'm a man of influence and money. If I want something, nothing can stop me from getting it."

It is the first time in months that he uses my true name. I pull myself hard out of his grasp, almost knocking into the people entering in behind us.

"You're insane," I say, as I turn to walk away.

He reaches for me, grabbing the collar of my jacket, pulling me backwards. His hands close around my wrists, squeezing hard enough to halt the circulation. My right arm begins to tingle as my pulse pounds. I can hear the blood pumping through my ears.

"I own you," he spats at me, "and there's not a damn thing you can do about it."

Rage soars through my veins. I'm sickened at the thought of being his lover, yet the sensations I've felt when he has touched me have been uncomfortably pleasant.

Why am I so conflicted?

He pushes me in front of him, guiding me to our seats, five rows up from the arena floor, right in the center. The boxes are marked, so the general audience knows they're off limits. Each Possessor is given two seats as well as two monitors: a private monitor so they can view the fighters before they enter the ring, with a communicator in case there are any last-minute instructions that need to be given, and a second monitor focused on the arena itself, a full aerial view of the battleground. Artemis has me sit on his left. He enters in his code for the private monitor, which then displays five of his fighters sitting in the holding area. As he is talking to Matt about the other fighters, I look around at the stadium, trying to locate the nearest exit.

The interior of the arena is a harsh gray metal, polished, and no glass. The sky above is clear blue, but a retractable ceiling slowly closes, shutting it out. The seats are upholstered in crushed red velvet, which is very comfortable. The wall surrounding the arena is made of pressed metal sheets, perfectly melded into the base of the stadium, but only comes up waist high. The arena floor itself is sizeable. The same gray metal covers the ground with intricate lines and curves swirling back and forth along the floor, but I don't see any entryway for the fighters to access the arena.

I focus my attention to my task and scan for the exits, but the only ways in or out are through the entrances that are guarded by Regulators, and most of them are carrying Levin guns. I give up the idea for the moment, but know I need to get away from Artemis as soon as possible.

Time slowly ticks by as people try to find the last remaining seats available. Those who didn't come early enough are stuck watching the screens outside as they aren't allowing anyone to stand in the aisles, not even along the back wall behind the highest rows of seats. The lights dim as spotlights illuminate the arena floor.

CHAPTER 10

"Good morning, Tyreans," a man announces in a booming voice that emanates from speakers inside the chairs' headrests. "Make sure you have your favorite fighter picked for this opening battle day. In this series of battles we have forty contestants, the most we have had in two years. In addition, we have a special opening sequence for tomorrow's phase, so be sure to get here early to get a good seat. Now, please sit back, watch the monitors in front of you, and let the battles begin."

The crowd roars in applause and cheers. People begin to shout their favorite number, even though the arena floor is still empty.

A subtle whirring sound begins to my right. I look over and notice a section of the arena floor has given way, disappearing below. Seconds later it rises, carrying with it the first fighter. The section locks back into place with the rest of the floor, leaving the lone man standing amidst the harsh lights.

The fighter stands about six feet tall, dark, bushy hair covering parts of his arms and the majority of his head. His biceps are thick with muscles, and a Pugio blade at his side. He stands at the ready, waiting for his opponent to rise. The crowd grows silent at the anticipation of what is to happen next. The whirring noise begins again, this time from my left, as a piece of the floor drops away. I'm sitting at the edge of my seat just like the rest of the audience, waiting to see what will surface.

The clanking noise registers with me before I actual see what is coming, it's the sound of a battle droid springing to life, moving around down below. The fighter steps onto another section of the floor, moving closer to the gap. The clanking gets louder the closer the fighter gets to the hole. I look down at my hands and notice I'm clinging tightly to Artemis' arm, scared and thrilled with the expectation of what this fight might be like.

The piece that had fallen away rises up empty and settles back into place.

The fighter is cautious, leery of moving forward.

He takes a step back, almost falling through the hole that has suddenly appeared behind him, the cold black eyes of a battle droid staring up at him. The man whirls around, stumbling backward as the droid emerges from its crypt. The mechanical beast is the same size as the ones Devlan had me train with.

A blur rises from the wall surrounding the arena, a slight sheen between the audience and the battle. The droid shoots a ball of energy from a weapon connected to his hand, but the fighter is quick and dodges it. The energy ball hits the shield that has risen and is immediately absorbed.

The floor breaks apart, jigsaw puzzle pieces floating in every direction.

The fighter is forced to jump from one tile to another. He is able to force some to move downward and away from the massive arms of his opponent as it tries to crush him.

The crowd lets out oohs and ahhs at the sight, but no other sound is made.

I'm still gripping onto Artemis as I watch, trying to force myself to let go, but it's like I'm glued to him.

The fighter dodges more blows and shots. He appears to push a button on the blade, which brings the item to life; blue energy streams swim around the blade, dancing from the hilt to the tip. I watch as the fighter slashes at the droid, slicing through the metal as if it was paper. Within ten minutes of the battle beginning, it has ended with the droid being defeated and the fighter winning. Cheers and applause escalate as the droid is removed and the man is led back to the holding area.

The same types of battle play out for the next four hours before we are given our first break. Fighters two and three also win, as well as Wes. Fighter five is not so lucky. The droid crushes her within two minutes of entering the arena. The lights are dimmed as they clean her from the floor. With fighter number eleven we get to witness what happens when human flesh comes in contact with the shields around the arena. The droid tears through the protective material, exposing the man's arms, then the fighter is thrown at the shield, losing his right arm as the shield burns it cleanly off. His screams reverberate off the walls as he falls to the ground, and is eventually carted away.

Not all the losers are killed or seriously injured. Some admit defeat by laying their weapons down on the ground and kneeling. The droid is immediately stopped and the fighter escorted below to be branded.

Aidan finally wins his first match in a long time. I cheer loudly for him, but Artemis ignores his accomplishment. After a quick lunch of sautéed shrimp, garlic noodles, and wine, the battles resume. Both Matt and Raven are victorious. Matt sets a new record for the quickest win in history. It's close to ten o'clock in the evening when Corinna finally enters the arena. She has some stumbles, getting a bad scratch along her right thigh. Even though she's bleeding, she still manages to defeat the droid.

Since she is the last of Artemis' fighters, as soon as she is back down below we get up from our seats and exit the stadium. We're the only ones in the elevator going down to the garage. I stand outside the holding area, as only the Possessors are allowed inside. Looking up at the screen, I count how many are left for the second half of the battles tomorrow.

Of the forty fighters, eighteen are victorious, four are dead, nine seriously injured, six admitting defeat, and three who have not competed yet.

Artemis comes out and is immediately called over to a group of gentlemen who are congregating at the far end of the platform, out of earshot from me and the Regulators patrolling the area. He returns a few minutes later, grinning ear to ear, requesting his shuttle from one of the attendants. When it arrives, the five fighters join us, all with new victory tattoos they are showing off to each other. We climb into the vehicle and are quickly whisked away back to the Letchworth.

Corinna and Raven both decided to get identical markings, a thin red band around the upper part of the bicep with small diamond shapes dripping down along the length of the stripe. Wes is groggy and dangerously close to falling asleep on Matt's shoulder. Aidan sits quietly, a smile fastened to his tired face.

I can hear the screams from the crowd as the shuttle pulls out.

We enter under the Letchworth, exit the shuttle, and ride the elevator up to the top floor, everyone in good spirits. Bottles of champagne are lined up on the dining room table, each labeled to one of the fighters, and even one for me. Matt, Corinna, and Raven pop the cork on theirs and begin downing the contents, splashing each other occasionally. Aidan goes into the kitchen looking for food, while Wes takes his bottle into the game room. I follow Aidan into the kitchen and find completed meals in the fridge just needing to be heated up. He turns on the oven and pops the trays in.

"I was really cheering for you today," I say to him, as I look around for utensils.

"I could hear you. I think you were the only one shouting my number," he says with a grin.

"I heard some others chanting it," I lie.

He winks at me and I smile back.

The timer goes off on the oven. He finds mitts for his hands and removes the trays. I follow him back out into the dining room with the utensils I finally locate next to the sink. Matt and Raven are laughing loudly, legs draped over the arms of the dining chairs. Aidan sets down the trays and we all sit down to eat as Corinna goes to fetch Wes. We stuff ourselves with meatballs, spaghetti, various vegetables, and garlic bread. I finally crack open my bottle at the insistence of Corinna who has already finished hers.

The wrapping has been conveniently removed, and the cork is precariously sitting in the neck. Artemis steps off the elevator with a cart full of additional bottles a few moments later.

"To the winners," he shouts as he raises a toast.

They all hoist their bottles in unison; clinking them together. I too raise my bottle, nearly dropping it when Wes knocks his into mine.

I feel silly and light headed the more I drink, but I feel no pain and no worries at this moment. I spot Artemis watching me, grinning as I take another sip. His eyes sparkle more than when I first met him, hair tousled carelessly around his face. I feel a flush, a warmth building in me the longer I watch him then look around and realize we are the only ones left at the table.

"Where did everyone go?" I mumble, placing my bottle down.

"Wes and Aidan are in the game room, and I believe Corinna, Matt, and Raven went down to the hot tub." He picks up a glass of clear liquid and walks over to me, sitting in the chair next to mine. He gently rubs my right arm with his fingers, tugging slightly at the Velcro strap around my bicep. "How bad of an injury is this?"

My brain is fuzzy, so I can't formulate a lie too quickly. He notices the lengthy pause in my response, but doesn't push for an answer. I finally gather my thoughts enough to give a vague response.

"Mangled...it's a really bad injury...horrible accident."

He leans over, brushes his lips against the sleeve on my arm, kissing it gently as if to heal it. I want to push him away, but I can't. My body is hoping for something else.

"What was in that bottle?" I slur.

"Champagne, of course, why? Did it not taste right?"

I can't answer as he moves his lips up my arm, my neck, my cheek, and finally my lips. I resist for a moment, and then kiss him back. I feel the heat rise between us and find myself in his arms, lifting me out of the chair, and carrying me down the hall to his room. The little voice in the back of my head is pleading with me to stop, to run away, but my body wants differently.

His hands wander as they unfasten buttons and pull off my shirt. He leaves the sleeve on my arm untouched. The silk sheets on his bed feel cool against my hot skin. Eventually we tire, nestling together as we both drift off to sleep.

The pounding is what rouses me from my first pleasant dream in years.

At first it's in my head, but as I slowly open my eyes I notice the noise is coming from Artemis' bedroom door. He groans in annoyance as he gets up and puts a robe on.

"Artemis!" Raven is shouting, as she continues to pound on the door.

He ties the sash as he unlocks the door and opens it, allowing her to storm into the room.

"Where is she? What have you done with Corinna?" she screams, arms flailing about.

"I'm surprised it took you this long to notice your roommate is gone. Or perhaps you were sleeping elsewhere last night, Raven," he says in a controlled voice, though his tone is one of irritation. "I sold her last night." He turns around and begins to walk back to bed when Raven grabs him by the shoulder and whips him around.

"What do you mean you sold her? She won the battle yesterday, how could you do this?"

"It's very simple," he begins, as he sits down at the end of the bed. "I'm a business man and when a great deal comes along, I take it. I was offered a lot of money by the Superior of the Tyre hatcheries for her. It was an offer I couldn't pass up."

"You asshole," she says, as she slaps him hard across the face.

He grabs her wrist, almost bending it backwards.

"I'd be careful if I were you," he hisses harshly. "I would sell you also to the hatcheries if you had working parts, and there are other places to offload your kind."

He shoves her away, causing her to fall onto the floor, straightens his robe, and walks out of the room. As she stands up, our eyes lock. I lay there gripping the sheet tightly up under my chin covering my naked body.

"Well, sweetheart, you will never have to worry about your fate. Sleeping with the boss always keeps someone employed." With that, she walks out of the room.

I lean over, pick my clothes up off of the floor, dress, exit into the hallway, and enter my room. Disgusted with myself for allowing my hormones to overwhelm me, I force myself to throw up in the bathroom. Yet, I don't feel what happened was entirely in my control. The champagne did have a weird taste to it, different from that of the second bottle.

Taking a hot shower, I scrub myself until I'm raw then dry off quickly, brush my hair up into a ponytail, and brush my teeth. Upon reentering my room, I spot a new outfit laid out for me on the bed. Shiny metallic blue pants, white studded belt, blue sequin tank top, and white leather jacket. My footwear consists of matching white leather boots with blue trim.

I've decided now is the time to run, to leave Artemis and Tyre before something else happens. I rummage through the drawers in the dresser, looking for something else to wear, only managing to find a black tank top, which doesn't show up under the blue sequined one, as well as tight black leggings that hug my body so they aren't noticeable under the blue pants. I will just have to make do with the boots.

Everyone is gathered in the dining room, eating breakfast. I grab a plate, but only partially fill it, as I have no appetite. No one speaks as we eat. The absence of Corinna is palpable and appears to make everyone uncomfortable. When breakfast is over, we climb into the elevator, get into the shuttle, and head out to the stadium without anyone saying a word. The fighters get into their line and are assigned new numbers. There are nineteen competitors today and those who are triumphant will move to the final round tomorrow.

Artemis seizes my arm and walks me over to the elevators for our trip to the surface. When we are in front of the Tyre Press Corp, Artemis encourages everyone to choose number eight today… Matt. He squeezes me playfully in front of the crowd, but I try to ignore the attention. They ask me how I'm enjoying the battles so far, and though I'd love to say exactly what I think, but I don't want to put

Artemis on guard, so I lie and tell them it's absolutely thrilling and that I'm enjoying every moment of it, all with a fake smile plastered across my face. We wave goodbye to the crowd and make our way to the seats we occupied the day before.

While Artemis is talking with Matt over the monitor, I check out the stadium again to see if there is any possible escape route that I might have missed yesterday, but it's of no use; the place is packed to the brim and Regulators are everywhere. The roof is still closed as the lights begin to dim, and the spotlights engulf the arena as the announcer from yesterday begins to speak.

"Welcome, Tyreans, to the second day of competition. I hope you are all prepared for this most exciting day of events. As we promised you yesterday, there is a special opening act before beginning our second round of battles. Please help me welcome one of our most beloved and victorious past winners, Munera!"

The center tile of the arena rises. On top stands a very tall, dark woman wearing brown leather shorts and a matching single strapped shirt that barely covers her midriff. At a quick glance, I could've mistaken her for Raven until I spot the markings that cover her right arm and leg: winner's tattoos of all different colors and styles. Her frame is thin, but strong, and her hair is cut so short it curls up right against her scalp. The crowd is screaming louder than yesterday. She throws her arms up into the air and everyone loses control. The weapon she is carrying in her hand is one that I have only seen in photos Devlan has shown me.

The Dimachaerus is a dangerous weapon, a double-bladed sword able to cut a man in half without the user even really trying. Munera is wielding it like it's an old friend; her moves are graceful and soft, which is in stark contrast to the sharp and heavy blade.

"Munera will be battling ten brave souls at one time today," the announcer states as the crowd begins to settle down. "Men and women who have been selected to try and defeat this champion…a battle to the death."

The crowd erupts again as the far right section of the arena floor gives way, a platform rising in its place. Eight men and two women huddle together on the platform, shaking, eyes squinting in the harsh light that falls upon their faces. Their clothing consists of rags, torn pieces of brown cloth dangling from some of their thin frames. One woman sinks to the floor of the platform and begins to weep, while one of the others tries to pull her back onto her feet. They each carry various weapons, but it is clear they won't help...none of them have combat training.

I look hard at the faces and I know instantly that these people have been taken from the Wasteland. I lean over to Artemis and ask him if I'm right.

"Yes, they're the rejects the Collectors can't sell and the cities don't want. Some may have even been citizens at one time, but once you leave you are considered a law-breaker for life and there is no coming back." He kisses my lips and turns back to his monitor, not interested in the bloodbath that is about to begin as he's too focused on talking to his fighters.

The group is huddled together, afraid to move forward. Munera is thinking; I see the intense concentration in her eyes. She is looking for the weakest one to go after first. She crouches down, having chosen her target. I follow her line of sight and see her prey...and a shock of recognition runs through me. I can only hope Artemis doesn't notice.

Terrance is hiding in the center of the huddle, his clothes baggy and hanging off of his frame. His skin is pale and his eyes have sunken in slightly. He's thinner than before. I wonder how he could have gotten caught when Rena's words echo in my ears.

"He's never left, except once. To go look for my brother after he was taken by the Collectors."

He must have left to look for me. I'm the reason he is here to die today.

I want to scream out his name, tell him to fight, but he can't hear me over the noise from the crowd.

The electric barrier is not up, the arena is unprotected.

I know what I must do.

I don't even think...I just go.

I tear off my jacket as Artemis grabs for my leg, but I'm too fast. I hurdle over seats as if they were stairs. People yell at me as I fly past them, but I must get to Terrance. Munera starts to lunge forward towards the group. They begin to scatter, moving away from her. She ignores the others. Terrance is her target.

Munera pulls the Dimachaerus back, readying to plunge it into Terrance as I jump over the wall and onto the arena floor.

I see a Pugio blade lying on the ground, dropped by one of the men, so I pick it up, causing my arm to tingle. Grabbing the hilt tightly, I swing the weapon back and then forward as I come upon Munera, who is practically on top of Terrance.

Our blades meet, sending shock waves through both of us. The crowd goes silent. Munera looks at me, bewildered by my unexpected appearance. Her stunned look doesn't last long as her face grows red with rage. She raises the Dimachaerus again, this time trying to attack me. I jump back, push Terrance down, and come up with my blade, striking hers again.

I need to get him and the others out of the arena, but I'm not sure how. She strikes again and I counter, knocking her hard on her ass. The platform begins to vibrate slightly, then rises. I push Terrance off of it and I follow suit, both of us landing on the arena floor, only this time I can see the fighters' holding area. Aidan is running over to us, shouting at me.

"Meg, what are you doing?"

"We need to get them out of here, Aidan."

His face contorts as if he doesn't understand what I'm saying.

I look at Terrance who is clinging to me. "He's my friend, Aidan, I can't let him die. Please, you have to help me."

Aidan looks at me, his face softens. He nods his head, then disappears.

A group of fighters gather where Aidan had been standing and gesture for Terrance to jump, saying they will catch him. He looks up at me, tears in his eyes. I pat him on the shoulder, telling him it's okay.

Munera is back on her feet, her focus moving to the others that have scattered around the arena. I help Terrance ease his way down into the holding area. Once he is safe, I take off after Munera. As I run towards her, the floor begins to vibrate and I spot Aidan opening one of the floor tiles with another fighter at the opposite end. If I can distract Munera, he and the other fighter can get the rest out.

I run as fast as I can, the blade slung behind me. My best chance at the moment is to take out her feet. The floor has a nice sheen to it, so I kick off my boots as I run, slide on the metal in my socks, and ram into her legs. We both go down in a pile, legs entangled. Munera kicks my knee, sending waves of pain up my leg. I scream and she grins, as the crowd begins to get into the fight in front of them.

I keep an eye on Aidan as he is slowly getting the others down below.

Munera stands up, her blade high above her head, which she begins to thrust down into my direction, so I swing my legs wide and knock her down again. She hits the floor, splitting open her lip. I roll away, trying to get out of her reach. She grabs my ponytail, dragging me in closer. She pulls a small knife from inside her boot and plunges it into my chest, missing my heart by inches.

The crowd roars louder as I scream again in agony.

Munera gets up again, blood dripping from her lip onto the floor. She steps on my stomach to keep me from moving. I remove the blade and begin to heal. She raises the Dimachaerus up again, ready to finish me off, but I take her knife and thrust it into her upper thigh. This time she screams. I shove her off of me and stand up.

"You should be dead," she screams at me.

"I'm full of surprises," I respond as I pick up the Dimachaerus.

The weapon feels powerful in my hand. I imagine myself dissecting her, cutting her to pieces. My right arm radiates heat as it too is enjoying the power.

I raise the blade, but pause as I hear a voice in my ears.

An Antaean must kill the enemy. A soldier built for death leaves no one alive.

I shake myself and drop the blade.

Where did that come from?

Munera is crouched on the ground, blood pouring from her wound.

"Coward," she screams.

I turn my back and begin to walk away. Then the pain starts again, this time radiating from the old wound in my back. Falling forward, I extend my arms out to brace myself. As I hit the ground Munera comes at me again. I raise my right arm to shield her blow with the small knife, which causes her to slit my forearm, the blade slicing all the way down to my palm. I crawl around and reach for the Dimachaerus. She continues her assault on me as I pick up the weapon.

My arm is red hot, glowing brightly. The Dimachaerus becomes electrified the moment it's in my hand and I swing, not looking at my target. I hear the crowd gasp as I make contact with Munera, feeling the shudder in the blade, the electricity in the air. I open my eyes as they had been closed and look down at the mess in front of me.

Her torso is only hanging on to the rest of her by her spinal cord. The flesh is blistered and burned. She gasps several times, body involuntarily twitching, and then she stops moving. I look down at the blade still clutched in my hand. A thick band of blue encircles the blade, swimming around and coming to a point at the tip. I drop it to the ground and the light disappears. That's when I notice the protective sleeve is gone, the Quantum Stream pulsing brightly. Looking up into the crowd, they sit silently, watching me. Artemis is standing at the edge of the arena floor, beaming from ear to ear. I close my eyes and collapse to the floor, landing on my knees.

My life is over.

My secret exposed.

Meg is dead…Trea has been reborn.

CHAPTER 11

Artemis strolls out onto the arena floor. He brushes the hair that has fallen out of my ponytail back behind my ears.

"Welcome home, Trea," he says, as he helps me to my feet.

I look up at him, sorrow in my heart, pleasure in my soul.

I feel as if a switch has been turned on, a cloud lifted from my eyes.

"It's good to be home," I say in a voice I don't recognize.

He wraps his arms around me pulling me in tightly as several Regulators enter the arena. Numerous tiles in the center of the floor open, revealing a staircase. We walk down in silence while the announcer declares the events for today have been canceled and will resume tomorrow at noon. We walk through the holding area, passing fighters too stunned to speak. I glance around but don't see Aidan or the others.

We move through the expanse and further into the arena's sublevel, stopping outside an elevator that is encased in steel. One of the Regulators enters a code onto a screen by the door, which slides open upon acceptance. Artemis and I go inside alone and get out when we reach the top.

The room we enter is finely decorated in plush red carpeting, white wainscoting, deep cushioned couches, white granite support columns, and a window expanding the length of the room with a view of the entire stadium. The elevator door closes behind us, preventing our escape. I spot an older man in a tailored gray suit standing to the far right side of the windows overlooking the arena. He holds a small tumbler in his hand filled with ice and a caramel colored liquid. He doesn't turn to look at us, but I can sense his anger.

"You have been holding out on me, Artemis," the man says, sipping his drink.

"Being a business man, I must protect my own interests," Artemis responds, in a defiant tone.

"Indeed." The man turns around and approaches us. His face I recognize instantly, it hasn't aged in sixteen years, except his hair is a lot grayer now. The High Ruler of Tyre, Aldus Vladim, stops directly in front of us, one hand behind his back and the other holding his glass. "So, you have found one of the lost Antaeans. Which one is she?"

"This is Trea," Artemis says, as he places his hand on the small of my back, pushing me gently forward.

"Not that I don't believe you, Artemis, but I would like to check the young lady myself." Vladim focuses his attention towards me.

I shake slightly as I remember when he visited the Dormitories how powerful he seemed

"Trea, would you mind bending your head down?"

I obey, lowering my head till my chin rests against my chest. I feel him push aside my hair. The gentle touch of his fingers sends shivers down my spine and ice through my veins.

"Thank you, dear," he says, as he lifts my chin up. He reaches out and clasps Artemis' hand in his. "You have done well, son. As promised to anyone who brings me an Antaean, you can have anything you like."

Artemis smiles, and points to me. "I want her."

"Absolutely not, out of the question." Vladim dislodges himself from Artemis' grip, pushing the man's hand aside. "She is the property of Tyre and has been since birth. You can have any woman you want, just not this one."

"I see." Artemis steps forward, practically nose to nose with Vladim. "What if I tell you she isn't the first Antaean located, that she in fact is the second, what would you say then?"

"I would you say you are bluffing. No other Possessors have indicated they have found one, nor has any Collector come forward for the reward. No, Artemis, I'm sorry but you are lying."

"I never said the other one was here in Tyre. There are two other cities out there, all with their own Collectors looking for them."

"If Acheron had found one, they would have made it a public spectacle to rub it in our faces. The city of Nuceira would have destroyed it, as they see the Antaean as an abomination to their twisted ways of living. They would have made it a public execution. No, Artemis, you are lying." Vladim walks over to a small bar against the far left wall and refills his now empty drink.

"I know how to locate Kedua, but I need Trea to do it." I can sense Artemis grasping at straws, trying not to lose his prize possession.

"And how could you possibly know how to find this one?"

"Simple. I know the person who sold her."

"Someone sold Kedua? Did this idiot not know what they had?"

"Obviously not, but the good thing is, the city of Acheron doesn't know they have her in their midst. So it's imperative that I have Trea with me."

Vladim seems to be mulling it over, pacing back and forth for some time, his drink splashing onto the floor unnoticed. He finally stops, shaking his head.

"No, Artemis, Trea is too much of an asset to this city for me to just hand her over to you to go on some wild goose chase for Antaean number two, if indeed she has been located. You will be rewarded handsomely for your find, but that's all." Vladim places his hand on Artemis' shoulder after having set his glass down and escorts him back to the elevator. "Since I currently don't have a place to house Trea I will need to use your quarters, so I will need you to move your fighters as well as yourself to another floor for the duration of the battles."

Artemis looks back towards me as the door to the elevator opens. I want to wave a sarcastic goodbye, but I refrain. He's forced inside and the doors close on his stunned face. Vladim returns to me, hands clasped behind his back.

"Do you think he's telling the truth about Kedua?" I ask Vladim, as he stands silent by my side.

"Of course not my dear, Artemis' only concern is for himself and what will profit him. If he thinks telling me he knows where Kedua might be will get him more money, than that is what he will say."

"Why would he need me to find her?"

"Because you will know her the moment you see her."

"How do you know I will recognize her?"

"You'll know."

I doubt I will recognize her since I didn't recognize Quin, but decide to keep that information to myself.

Vladim steps over to an end table and begins to scroll through a small tablet screen. A few moments later a door down the hall to the right of me opens up, revealing another private elevator. Vladim walks down the hall greeting the person who just got off.

"Trea, I would you like you to meet the Superior of the Asphodel Clinic. Dr. Hersher." Vladim steps aside, but introductions are not required.

I know the man standing in front of me. He extends his hand out for me to shake. I hesitate, not sure of how to respond, wondering how much this person has told the High Ruler about me…about my past. I shake his hand gently, but I can tell he sees the tension in my face.

"It's nice to see you again, Trea," Dr. Hersher says to me. "That was quite a spectacle you gave today. Munera was one of my favorite fighters, but you bested her easily."

"You work for them?" I spit out in disgust, as I point towards Vladim,

"Of course. Did you think I actually worked just for Artemis?" He laughs loudly, swinging himself back and forth. "Remember, I told you I designed the Antaeans. Who do you think I designed them for?"

"So that warning at the ranch about not revealing my true self to Artemis was all crap."

"Not entirely. If Artemis had discovered your full abilities before I could relay to the High Ruler that an Antaean had been located, it would have destroyed my chances of claiming the…significant reward for your return."

I swing wide with my fist, but I'm grappled from behind, taken to the floor mid-punch. I try and throw off my assailants, rolling onto my side, kicking fiercely, but only manage to cock my head to the side, straining my neck to see who is standing on me. The only thing I'm able to ascertain is a Regulator's hat.

I'm hauled off of the carpeting with rug burns on my face from the tussle. The Regulators escort me over to one of the couches by the windows, each place a hand on my shoulder, and force me to sit down. Neither removes their hands once I'm properly seated.

Vladim remains standing while Dr. Hersher takes a seat on the sofa opposite me. Both looking pleased with themselves. I glower at them, imagining my hands snapping each of their necks, their tongues lolling to the sides of their mouths as their eyes go black.

I mentally shake my head before the images worsen as I'm itching to destroy these two. These thoughts must be coming from my programming, my design, as I don't normally feel this way.

"What do you want from me?"

"Well, first of all we will have a demonstration tomorrow." Vladim walks back over to the window, looking out at the now-empty seats. "Before the next round of battles, you will demonstrate your abilities to the entire country of Sirain. We will show the nation we are the first city to have successfully rescued one of the lost Antaeans, so we can show the public that all the time, money, and research our city put in to developing you wasn't wasted." He sits down next to Dr. Hersher, crossing his legs. "Then, we'll begin looking for the remaining three Antaeans. Dr. Hersher will now escort you below to evaluate you."

"He's already done that," I protest, trying in vain to stand up.

Dr. Hersher shakes his head. "Not completely, since I didn't have all of the necessary equipment at Artemis' ranch. The Care Room here at the stadium has all the items I need." He stands up, retrieving his bag from the floor.

I'm lifted up from my seat and ushered down the hall to the other elevator where we descend to the Care Room, under the holding area.

We exit into a vast space that runs the entire length of the stadium. Harsh lighting fills the massive area, casting odd shadows in corners too dark to see. Dense gray columns line the interior, creating chambers, each containing soiled cots lined in neat rows. Several cots have injured fighters moaning as women in orange uniforms attend to them. As we move to the left and begin to walk the length of the room, I look beyond the wounded and spot a metal cage holding the group of people I tried to rescue. Terrance is one of them, his face pressing against the iron bars. I turn my head away; trying to hide the tears I feel beginning.

I hear old voices echo in my head.

An Antaean should show no emotion, no attachment to others, as they can be taken quickly.

I begin to recall the hours of emotional detachment training we endured as children at the Dormitories. How so often we were given something and then having it taken away. We would cry for hours and then they would give the object back to us, wait for us to get attached again, and then remove it once more. This went on for months until we finally refused to take the object.

I lift my head back up to see where we are going and spot two boards propped up on wooden stands at the end of the rows of cots. One board contains the body of Munera, her naked body exposed brazenly. The other is that of Aidan, face up, arms dangling down off the board. Two Levin gun blasts have ripped open his chest, disintegrating everything inside.

I thrash myself around, trying to get free from the two Regulators gripping my arms. The loss of another friend is too much. It's my fault Aidan is dead.

Why does everyone around me die?

I want to break free and kill them all, but manage to only liberate myself from one as the other has a firmer grip on me. I look down at his hand and see an electronic pulse enveloping my left bicep. He is not physically holding me, but the small square device he's carrying is. The other Regulator stands up then proceeds to punch me in the face as he enables his holding device.

We stop in front of the door at the end. Dr. Hersher opens it and proceeds to turn on the lights as the rest of us step inside. The lighting in here is much brighter. A glass partition breaks up the room; two circular machines sit on one side, display screens on the other. Dr. Hersher and Vladim each take a seat on the chairs in front of the screens, while the Regulators escort me around the partition to the other side.

I'm stripped naked and placed onto a cold metal slab that sticks out from a machine that's labeled *NMR*. Thick leather straps are fastened to both my ankles and wrists. I surreptitiously test their strength, but I can't break through them.

The Regulators leave the room when the lights go off. The machine roars to life as I slide inside. I look at lights blinking above my head. The noise emanating from the device grows louder causing me to panic. I'm terrified I'll be crushed any moment. My heart races, my breathing quickens, and my arm tingles.

I'm going to die!

The Quantum Stream begins to glow brighter the louder the machine gets. I try and wriggle my right hand out of the restraints, but only manage to move the restraint further up my arm.

Twisting my arm backwards causes me great pain. I place my right hand onto the smooth metal of the machine and try to push the Quantum Stream out of my palm, but it doesn't work as I don't have any real connection to the instrument.

My arm is growing hotter, the light is almost blinding.

I'm going to explode!

I try and move my hand along the wall to see if I can locate some kind of flaw to exploit. My wrist cracks and my hand goes limp, but with adrenaline pumping I don't feel the pain. It begins to heal as the machine begins to wind down. The lights come back on in the room and I slide back out, unstrapped from the table, and handed a red robe. I tighten it around my waist as two Regulators lead me back around the partition.

"Trea, you're perfectly healthy for an eighteen year old," Dr. Hersher begins. "Your level of Quarum is higher than it should be, but that's okay as it will improve your healing ability. As for the Quantum Stream you have in your right arm, it appears to have latched onto every cell in your body, as it should have. It's probably only visible in your arm because of the accident you had with the Levin gun. This is most beneficial due to the design of the weapons Devlan has no doubt trained you on. With additional training and the proper device, I believe you should be able to manipulate and control the stream without any external prop needed."

"How?" I ask, as ideas flood my mind.

"You will be able to control the energy…have it work however you wish. Influence electrical barriers with a single touch, for example."

I smile inside, as they have just given me a way to escape.

CHAPTER 12

I'm taken back to Artemis' place. The whole floor is completely deserted and I'm warned by Vladim that the code on the elevator has been changed, so I won't be able to leave the top floor. Only he and Dr. Hersher know the code.

I go to my room, change out of the robe, and into blue shorts with a matching top. A fresh meal is sitting on the island in the kitchen for me, so I take the plate and go into the entertainment room to see what is on the displays.

"Tyreans, don't miss the exciting event tomorrow as we demonstrate to all of Sirain that we have successfully rescued an Antaean." The male announcer says on the screen directly in front of me. Flashes of me killing Munera run in a loop behind him. "Be there early as seats will fill up fast for this historic occasion."

I roll my eyes as I take a bite of the salmon filet.

The announcement is made every fifteen minutes on all channels. I scroll through the menu of available shows to watch, but nothing catches my eye, so I stay on the one I'm currently watching. Other announcements are made periodically throughout the evening including one warning the Tyreans that the Laics have a Work Free Day approaching.

"Be mindful of your children and belongings as the Laics will be free to travel between the Boroughs. If I were you, I'd stay home so not to be caught up in their crooked ways."

An hour later a bulletin comes across all three screens. The man perched in front of the camera is frazzled and slightly out of breath.

"We've just been notified that a Nuceiran has been apprehended this evening trying to sneak into Tyre by way of deception. The woman made it as far as the Superior Towers before finally being confronted by Regulators. She was killed on site clutching copies of the Nuceira treatise and photos of the Antaean known as Trea."

The screen switches to display the photos of me, one inscribed with *Death to the Abomination.*

"I didn't ask for this!" I scream, tears of frustration and pain falling.

I pick up the glass I had been drinking from and throw it, cracking the monitor glass.

"Regulators have stepped up security measures at the stadium as well as the exchanges. Many citizens are wondering how a Nuceiran made it that far into Tyre, as they are distinguishable due to the religious symbol emblazoned on their arms." Another photo flashes across the screen showing the top half of a cross with a point at the bottom, colored white and inlayed in a silver circle, white flames licking the bottom of the point. The marking on the woman was shimmering, almost alight even as she lay dead.

I switch off the screens, go into the kitchen to place my dishes in the sink, and get a drink of water. Walking into the front room, glass in hand, I pull one of the plush chairs closer to the windows, looking down at the stadium, its roof wide open. Workers are busy hanging colossal banners inside and out with the symbol of Tyre blazing across them. The sizeable monitors both inside and outside the stadium are also showing the symbol, but then cut away to my face showing my name and the time of the big demonstration tomorrow. My stomach begins to ache as the weight of what tomorrow means begins to sink in.

Gone are the days of running my course in the Wasteland, of sitting out in the desert just before dark watching the stars come out, of being no one.

Setting my glass down, I wander back to my room, crawl under the covers, and close my eyes.

I don't get much sleep, my nightmare from the Dormitories consume me.

The screaming in my head wakes me so I decide to go and watch as preparations continue at the stadium. Cameras are outfitted into every aisle, seat, and corner of each section. They test each angle of the cameras on the monitors dangling both inside the stadium as well as outside, making sure not one moment of action will be missed. Regulators stand guard at all the exchanges, pedestrian crossings, and stadium entrances. I find myself growing tired, and shut my eyes.

I wake up again around six and eat a small breakfast that I prepare myself. A young woman with pale hair and skin rises in the elevator, handing me my outfit for the demonstration, which is a standard fighter's uniform. She hesitates slightly in leaving, but the device on her wrist begins to beep loudly and rapidly, causing her to quickly run to the elevator and depart. I walk over to the windows and watch as lines begin to form outside the arena, winding over the bridges that cover the shuttle rails, down the concrete sidewalks, and around each building.

"You need to get ready," I hear Vladim say behind me. I didn't hear him come in.

I glare at him but swallow my pride, go to my room, don the outfit, and put my hair up before taking a hard look at myself in the mirror, not caring for the reflection. I put my fist through the glass, shattering it all around me, not bothering to pick up the pieces. The shards in my hand are forced violently from my flesh by my healing.

"Ready, Trea?" Vladim says to me as I rejoin him by the elevator.

"Yes," I say, as we step onto the lift and descend.

The High Ruler's shuttle is the only one currently in the garage. All other traffic has been diverted and no one is around except for his private security, who have a different uniform than the normal Regulators. As the shuttle pulls away from the Letchworth, Vladim hands me a red cloth bag. I reach inside and pull out a small black glove. I study the item and notice the covers for the fingers have been removed, and the center of the glove has a flat silver finish. The material looks metallic, but feels soft.

"What is it?" I ask, as I slip it onto my right hand.

"Our engineers have been up all night working on this. The silicone section in the middle of the glove will allow you to transmit the Quantum Stream to anything you touch. You no longer need a port to grip on to. The designers decided to go with silicone instead of metal due to the detectors that surround every building and entrance in Acheron, which will be our destination tomorrow."

I try and recall the layout of the holding area and the Care Room picturing the lifts as they are housed. I close my eyes to better concentrate, only vaguely recalling a door at the far right of the Care Room marked *Emergency Exit*. I don't know where it leads, but it seems the best chance I have.

We arrive under the stadium, but are directed to an alternate entrance, one only the High Ruler uses. The shuttle stops and I exit first, followed by Vladim. He leads me up his private elevator, to a special holding area, away from the rest of the fighters. He nods and returns to the lift, going up to his private box. Two attendants approach me, each holding various weapons. I attach a Levin gun to the right side of my belt and grip the Dimachaerus in my left hand. They step away as the announcer begins his speech about triumph over Acheron and Nuceira due to the fact that Tyre is the first to have located one of four Antaeans. The mystery of why they don't know about Quintus remains.

"Yes, we have been anticipating this moment for the last sixteen years and now we get to finally see what our many sacrifices have been made for. Ladies and Gentlemen, it's my honor to introduce you to Trea, Antaean Number Three."

The floor below me begins to rise as the ceiling above parts. The lights have been turned off, leaving only one spotlight shining on me as I emerge onto the arena floor. The applause is deafening. I don't wave, but stand poised for battle, which seems to excite the crowd, causing an uproar of triumphant, joyous shouts. I hop off the platform before it descends, the floor tiles moving back into position. The shields around the arena rise all the way up to the closed roof. This is something new, and I get the feeling I'm not going to like the reason for it.

The ground begins to tremble as a large section of the floor to my left lowers, then I hear the mechanisms of the floor groan as they attempt to lift the object. Since I'm standing in the center of the arena, I side step to the right and begin to walk backwards, not daring to turn my back on whatever is rising from beneath. The round metal top appears first, followed by huge red eyes. I know instantly what I'm fighting, but I'm overwhelmed by its size.

The battle droid in front of me is one I've never seen before. It stands several stories high, thick heavy metal encasing its body. The eyes are what I'm most concerned about. The eyes of a battle droid are usually black, devoid of color. This one has bright red eyes that dilate and contract as if it's thinking. I try to reflect back to Devlan's workshop and hazily remember seeing a set of these eyes lying around in the pieces of scrap.

I grip the Dimachaerus in both hands, feeling my arm begin to twinge and heat up. As I squeeze my right palm against the handle, a blue energy wraps around each blade, interlacing like a river. The droid stands there, staring at me, perhaps waiting for me to make the first move. The audience begins to chant my name. I decide to take the initiative and lunge at the monster, raising the Dimachaerus as I throw my body forward into the air. Its eyes narrow at my approach; it lifts its right arm and knocks me sideways into the barrier.

I scream at the pain I know is coming, but I'm not badly hurt. The clothing I'm wearing has deflected the energy. I shake my head and get back on my feet as the droid advances, a larger-than-life Dimachaerus high above its head.

I stand and wait until it's practically on top of me before I dive to the left. Its Dimachaerus slices into the barrier, radiating electricity up the weapon and into the droid. The metal beast shakes violently, but recovers.

The tiles around us begin to separate and we're both hoisted into midair, balancing precariously on the pieces. As I'm leaping from one tile to another the monster swings at me again, but I jump down to a section of tiles below just as the Dimachaerus hits the tile I'd just been on, splitting it into two. I continue skipping across tiles, then leap for one above my head as the droid comes around again. As I pull myself up, the machine hits the tile, sending it careening towards the barrier, forcing me to jump. It makes contact, but I land squarely on my feet. The tile I'm now on moves erratically, so I hop on over to another one.

An idea pops into my head, and I take the palm of my hand, laying it flat onto the surface of the tile, trying to push the energy through my arm and into the metal. I shove down with my feet and find myself surfing across the air. The crowd goes wild at my move. I dart between the droid's feet and come up alongside its back. Dimachaerus in hand, I vault myself onto the droid's back, slip slightly, but manage to grip the metal collar at the base of its neck. I take the Dimachaerus and shove it hard into the small gap between its head and shoulders. Sparks begin to fly as the energy from the weapon makes contact with the machinery inside. I shove harder, hear popping noises, and feel the metal head loosen from its spine.

I picture Vladim in my head and plunge the weapon further down, severing the spinal column.

The droid begins to drop to the ground. As the floor tiles begin to assemble to catch the mass as it falls, I dive below them, sliding down one tile as it's rising to floor level. I land in the holding area, slamming my back onto the concrete floor. I'm severely winded, and slowly roll over, pushing myself up into a stand. Fighters stare at me from closed cages and I hear feet approaching from my left. I drop the Dimachaerus and pull out the Levin gun, run to the lift and push the button to lower myself to the Care Room just as a handful of Regulators enter the holding area.

The Care Room is empty of people, except those in the cage. I make my way over to them and tell them to stand back as I shoot the lock. Pointing to the *Emergency Exit* that I see on my right, I yell at them to go through it. Terrance is the last one out of the cage. I put my arm around his waist and we run towards the exit as the elevator opens up and Regulators pour out. The other lift begins to descend, carrying another handful of Regulators. I start firing at them, striking two in the chest as I keep pushing Terrance to the exit. They fire back, forcing us to duck as bits of plaster are disintegrated by the Regulator's Levin guns' blasts. Two columns in front of me explode in half as weapons fire hits them.

All the others have made it through the exit except Terrance and me. We are forced to take cover in a small room just a few yards from the exit. I continue to fire, striking three more Regulators. I look at the pillars that have been damaged, and figure that if I can bring them down, the floor above will collapse on top of either the Regulators or Terrance and me.

I decide it's better than nothing.

I take two shots at each pillar, disintegrating the remaining plaster and metal rods supporting the floor above. Part of the ceiling begins to give way, but not enough to cause a full collapse. I turn and aim at the pillar by our door. Terrance grabs me, trying to stop me. I pull myself away and fire. It takes four rounds to do the job. I clutch Terrance by the collar and drag him along the floor as the ceiling above us begins to come down. I shove him through the exit as a blast from a Levin gun hits me in the back.

Pain radiates through my entire body. I try and catch my breath, but I can't seem to find my lungs. Terrance picks me up and carries me down a grassy hill away from the stadium as the brightness of the outside world encloses around me, blinding me.

CHAPTER 13

"Don't touch her," a far off voice shouts.

I know the voice…a familiar voice I haven't heard in months…a voice that belongs to the dead.

I want to see Quin's face when I open my eyes, but I'm afraid of what I will see, knowing he's dead, yet still able to hear him.

"Meg," Quin says to me. His voice is closer now, as if it was right next to me. "Meg, wake up."

I take a deep breath and open my eyes.

Quin's face looks down onto mine. His hair is slightly longer now, his eyes older. The sun is shining brightly behind him. Light cascades down between the leaves from branches that hang over us. I sit up, feeling grass and dried leaves under my palms. Terrance squats down next to Quin.

"I thought you were dead," I squeak out, as I stare at him.

"I almost was," he says, as he helps me lean myself against a trunk of a tree. "I managed to grab the syringe you had pulled out for me and inject myself before passing out. When I was well enough to walk, I made it back to the Refuge and told Terrance and Rena what had happened. It took some time to track you, and then Terrance wound up getting collected. I followed the people who took him and have been camping here on the outskirts of Tyre trying to figure out a way to get in."

I look around, but I don't see the city.

"Where are we?" I ask, as Quin hands me a roll to eat.

"We are about a day's hike north of Tyre. When the group of Laics came out of the door at the base of the stadium, I managed to cut away the wire fence surrounding the perimeter to allow them to escape. I waited to see if Terrance would come out, and he eventually did…carrying you."

"They were Laics? I thought they were rejects the Collectors couldn't sell."

"Not all of them. Terrance and one of the women were the only ones from the Collectors, the rest were Laics from the south Boroughs."

"Where are they now?"

"They've entered the Wasteland." Quin hands me some water to help me wash down the roll. "We should be heading back there as well."

"No."

"What do you mean 'no'?"

"We need to get to Acheron. I believe another Antaean is there."

"Hold on, wait. Let's think about this." Quin sits down next to me. "We can't just hop on a shuttle and waltz into Acheron. From what the Laics told me while they were fleeing was that your demonstration was broadcast all over Sirain, including Acheron. They're going to know what you look like, and since they will obviously know you escaped from Tyre, they're going to be looking for you."

"It's a chance I'm willing to take." I stand up, brush myself free of leaves, and look around for my Levin gun, noticing it's sticking out of Quin's rucksack. I reach inside and retrieve it. "Are you coming with me or not?"

Quin glances up at me with an apprehensive look. Terrance quickly springs to his feet and is at my side in seconds.

"No, Terrance," Quin begins, "it'll be too dangerous for you in your weakened condition. Go back to the Refuge."

Terrance looks pained, but he knows Quin is right. He will only slow us down.

I give him a hug, while Quin stuffs his pockets with goods for the trip home. He turns around and sets off down the hill, only turning back once.

"You're going to need a change of clothes," Quin says to me as soon as we've lost sight of Terrance.

We clean up Quin's make-shift campsite, leaving anything we don't really need, like the tent he constructed out of tree branches and vinyl sheets. I notice my motorbike buried under two feet of fallen leaves and unearth it. The wheels are flat, there's no fuel, and the engine is fried. I rebury it, making sure to say goodbye to my old friend. We have enough food to last us three days if we ration it out. I think about heading back towards Tyre, but Quin nixes the idea immediately. He says there is an Oasis about a two days hike to the east of us.

We begin our journey in the late afternoon.

The seasons are beginning to change so we have fewer daylight hours to work with. Rain pours down on us the closer we get to the mountains. Night falls fast, so we take shelter in a cave just before the mountain's height begins to dramatically rise. Quin collects firewood while I make bedrolls out of whatever I can find. The wood he brings back is hard to light as it's wet, but it dries enough to build a fire. We heat a can of baked beans with the Tyre logo on them, passing the one can between the two of us. I decide not to tell him about the extravagant meals I've been eating, though I have to admit, the beans are a sad substitute.

"I have something for you," Quin says, as he picks up his rucksack from the cave floor and extracts the tablet I left in the barn.

"What made you think to bring this?"

"It seemed important to you."

I take it from him, lean against the cave wall, and place my palm onto the screen, hoping there is still power. Quin sits next to me, resting partially on the wall, and partially on me. After the usual interval, the tablet comes to life.

"I went underground, as did many of the other survivors," Devlan's voice begins. No images this time. *"We were fearful of the cities because we thought they might hold us responsible for the deaths. The children were sent off with protectors - those we felt would make sure the safety of the children was their main priority.*

"You were sent off with one of the nurses, placed into her care until you were older. The High Rulers went scouting the country, looking for the Nuceiran troops that carried out the massacre. Their leader denied having any part in the destruction, but said he was glad it occurred. He stated that he wished he had thought of it himself, even though that would have meant the death of some of his own people, who had stayed to work on general research after the initial project was scrapped and the Antaeans created."

I feel Quin nuzzle closer to me, trying to help control the shaking from my fear.

"Six years after the event, I learned that you had been located. I came out of seclusion to go and retrieve you, to hide you again. I'm sorry I wasn't successful."

The tablet shuts down.

I hand the device back to Quin as tears stream down my cheeks. He stuffs the tablet into his rucksack and pulls me closer, wrapping his arms around me. We stay clutched together for quite a while before crawling under our bedrolls to try to get some sleep.

We start late the next morning as the sun begins to crest over the peaks. It takes us all day to maneuver over the jagged face. We locate a pass about two hundred feet up. Chunks of black rock line the wide trail.

"Looks like it was a road once," Quin says, as he examines the odd stones.

We continue down the path, keeping as close to the rock face as possible finally emerging several hours later where we begin our descent. As the sun fades, we huddle under an outcropping of trees close to the base of the mountain range. Rain begins to pour, and Quin wraps his arms around me to help warm me up. I nuzzle my head into his shoulder and fall asleep.

We reach the wire fencing surrounding Oasis Two in the late afternoon. Quin has me wait inside an abandoned home just a few yards from the fence. He takes my Levin gun and disappears. I wander around the house rummaging in cabinets looking for anything useful. From the looks of everything, this home was raided years ago. After I pilfer a few remaining supplies, I plop down on a sofa, curling myself into a ball.

I must have dozed off as I hear Quin whispering for me to wake up. The sun has just about set, so there is little light to see with, but I can make out his features. He hands me a pair of white linen pants and a long sleeved, thick black sweater. He has also snagged an outfit for himself. I look up at him and grumble at the selection of clothes he picked for me. I hate sweaters, but the long sleeve was a smart choice as it will hide my Quantum Stream.

I go into one of the bedrooms and change while he dresses in the front room. My socks are dirty, but he didn't provide me with a clean pair so I will have to put those back on as well as my boots. I decide to leave the top portion of the fighter's uniform on, as well as the glove Vladim had given me.

As I exit the bedroom, I notice Quin's back for the first time.

The Levin gun left a large hole between his shoulder blades and down to his lower back which glows a soft blue. Small lines of clinging flesh make a unique pattern, breaking up the Quantum Stream slightly. He puts on three layers in order to cover up the brightness. I walk across the hallway and go into the bathroom, closing the door silently behind me. Taking my sleeve, I try to rub off the dirt that is caked onto the mirror hanging over the cracked sink. I'm not sure it's worth the effort; the reflection is still me, only tired and worn, the effect being made dramatically worse by the fading light.

I begin to rethink my idea of going to Acheron.

Perhaps we should just rejoin those in the Wasteland. Go back to the Refuge and help Rena with supplies, and forget the other Antaeans. I think of Devlan and his sacrifice to keep me out of the hands of the cities. Flashes of my past dance behind my eyes. The Dormitories burning as I was carried away into the forest that surrounded the complex. People screaming and dying as the place crumbled. The four of us children clinging desperately to our rescuers as the others perished before our eyes; Devlan scooping me up and then handing me over to a woman. A woman I would call my mother for six years before he reclaimed me.

The knock at the bathroom door brings me back to reality.

I open it to find Quin is standing there, grinning at me. He looks more tired and worn out than I do. He gestures that it's time to leave, so I follow him into the living room. The light that had been filtering in through the holes in the roof is now completely gone; there is only darkness outside.

"What about my hair and face?" I ask him, as he picks up his rucksack.

"It'll be dark in the oasis. The shuttles don't run at night, so we will be able to sneak on board one as it sits parked. There will only be a couple of Regulators around, so we will need to keep an eye out for them."

I'm not thrilled with the idea, but what other option do we have?

Before we leave, however, I remove the Levin gun from the rucksack and disable the safety features. If we're to be caught, I'm not going down without a fight. I stick the gun into my waistband, covering the bulge with my sweater then leave the house and walk through the hole he made in the fence earlier.

We enter the oasis through an access door at the bottom of one of the support columns holding up the structure. After climbing, he pushes back a grate above us and we enter a janitor's closet. Quin cracks the door open just enough for him to see out into the hallway. He nods as he opens the door wider. We quickly exit and try to find the correct corridor that houses the shuttle that will take us to Acheron.

The lights are very dim down every passageway, including the main passenger loading platform. There are two shuttles sitting in the bay, one on either side of us, with a Regulator patrolling them. The platform is a wide-open space, ceiling darkened to give the effect of the current conditions outside. There is no place for us to hide, nothing to shield us from detection. I look carefully around the corners just to make sure there isn't another door or hallway we can use to get in a better position. The shuttle on our right is slated to leave for Acheron in one hour, according to the large monitor dangling in the center of the room.

"Okay, now what?" I whisper to Quin, as we slink back down the hallway.

"Let's try the cargo platform. It should be one level below us."

"How do we get to it?"

Quin goes past the closet, down a darker hallway, passing a lounge with a monolith-style fountain in the center, and comes to a stop just outside the edge of another concourse. He steps forward, gesturing for me to stay hidden against the wall, and then disappears around the corner. I can hear his footsteps echo faintly, then stop as he opens a door.

I begin to feel nervous, wondering if any Regulators might be coming down the corridor.

Quin returns several minutes later.

We scamper across the concourse, dodging between deserted shops and eateries that fill the space between the shuttles. The door Quin directs us to is situated between an upscale clothing store and a nondescript jewelry retailer. The silver knob turns easily in is hand, allowing the door to swing open silently. We amble into a narrow hallway that is lit from hidden lights below. I turn and see a set of stairs. Quin begins to head down after he has closed the door. I hesitate, standing still and listening.

If no one is supposed to be in the oasis at this hour besides Regulators I wonder where the light below me is coming from.

Muffled voices radiate beneath my feet. I hear wood scraping along concrete, so I take slow, gentle steps as I descend. Quin is standing at the bottom of the stairs, waiting as someone walks over to us.

I don't recognize the uniform the small man is wearing: gray coveralls, black belt cinched at his waist. His thick black hair looks slick and greasy. After removing his gloves he shakes Quin's hand.

"Come with me," he says. "The shuttle is about to leave, so we don't have much time."

We run across the platform towards an open door underneath the shuttle.

"You can hide amongst the cargo containers," he says, as we reach the door. "We've almost finished loading the crates that are to go to Acheron, so you will have supplies for the twelve hour journey. No one will be on board on the top level since the passenger compartments don't open until seven. They never have citizens ride on the same shuttles as the cargo, so you should be fine until you reach the inspection post just on the outskirts of the Boroughs of Acheron. There, Regulators will come on board to inspect the cargo to make sure it's genuine, but they shouldn't be on long, so you will need to find a good hiding place until then. The stop should last no more than ten minutes and then it will leave for the city itself. Once you get to the station, make sure the head handler sees you. I've sent him a message that you're coming."

I climb through the door, squeezing between crates to make my way towards the front of the shuttle. Quin joins me and we are soon in darkness as the outer door closes and the shuttle begins to move.

CHAPTER 14

There aren't any windows in the cargo area, so it's going to be hard to tell what time of day it is or even where we are in proximity to Acheron. Quin rummages in his rucksack while I decide to continue to move deeper into the shuttle.

A light flashes from behind me as Quin turns on the torch he must've been searching for. I look to my right, notice a ladder going upwards, and I begin to climb as Quin examines the crates to see what they contain.

The ladder brings me up to the passenger level. The seats lie in rows with an aisle down the center. The windows display tall grasses that bend from a non-existent breeze. I make my way down the aisle, moving smoothly between the partitions that divide the shuttle into individual compartments. Several have their own private rooms and full baths. I then pass an empty dining area and kitchen that sit behind the shuttle's front compartment.

I press my ear against the door, listening for any noises, but it's silent. I slide the door open, revealing two empty pilot chairs, an active instrument panel, and a large window displaying the true nature of the land we are speeding through.

Scorched earth is visible under bright green vines and grasses. Fragments of stoic metal structures rust and bend. Trees are trying to push their way up through ancient roads of concrete that are deteriorating back to rock and gravel. Sizeable regions are too damaged to ever recover. I sit down in one of the chairs and watch the chaos flash past us. The horrors that led to such destruction seem unbelievable to me.

What type of events have the High Rulers been hiding from their people?

"Shocking isn't it?" Quin says from behind me.

"What happened here?"

"No one knows for sure," he says as he sits in the other chair. "Any records of the event would have been altered by the High

Rulers and those who survived are long dead. We are only left with decaying reminders of those who once were. *This* is the true Wasteland."

We sit and watch the land as it goes by. I'm beginning to understand why they use imaginary landscapes, who would want to see this day after day? The shuttle approaches a long range of mountains capped with snow. We enter a tunnel and are thrown into darkness. This lasts only moments as we exit out the other side into a landscape similarly scarred and desolate. I've had my fill and leave, Quin following behind me.

We reenter the cargo hold and break open one of the crates holding crackers and nuts. It's not much, but it's easy to pilfer. We eat only enough to sustain us until we reach Acheron. Quin and I find nooks in which to conceal ourselves. He falls right to sleep, but I can't get comfortable, as the air is too stale and warm. I crawl out from my space and retreat to the passenger level and into one of the private bedrooms, where I plop myself down on the firm mattress and drift into oblivion.

```
Bodies lay scattered across the once pure granite
floors, some burned beyond recognition, others in
pools of their own blood. The walls begin to crack
from the heat, but the woman keeps running.
Cool, fresh air hits our faces as we reach the
outside. The building we exit is at the edge of a
large pool that sits in the center of the complex. We
move farther away from the building as the structure
begins to collapse. The night sky is alight with fire,
ash flakes float down from a cloudless sky.
```

The forward motion has stopped. My eyes fly open as I hear voices moving down the aisle towards my direction. I can't make out what they are saying, but the tone being used suggests they are Regulators.

The handler at Oasis Two said they would be boarding, but only to check the cargo, so why would they be up here on the passenger level?

The voices are just outside the door, moving towards the front of the shuttle. I let out my breath slowly, not realizing I'd been holding it. I wait for several minutes until I hear their footsteps retreating, then get up quietly and move over to the door, pressing my ear against it.

"All set?"

"Set."

They retreat further down the shuttle.

When I can't hear them any longer, I slowly open the door and peer out, staying low to the floor. No one is in sight. I open the door wider, leaning farther out. The aisle is empty as the shuttle begins moving again. I close the door and make my way back to the cargo area. I don't go more than two steps before noticing something flashing above my head. The object attached to the wall is about two feet above the windows.

My heart begins to race as I look around to see if there are any more similar items, which there are, about every five feet. I race back towards the ladder, counting the number of devices. There are forty blinking detonators, which means there have to be more than two hundred, covering the entire top deck of the shuttle.

"Quin," I shout before my feet even hit the floor of the cargo area. "Quin!"

He emerges from behind a stack of crates, looking puzzled.

"We have to get out of here," I say, as I frantically begin looking for the door that we entered through.

"We'll be in Acheron in ten minutes," Quin says, as he struggles to extract his rucksack, caught on the edge of a crate.

"We don't have ten minutes. The entire top floor is rigged with detonators, we need to go now." I find the door behind a crate that must have slid in transit. Shoving it away, I yank on the handle, but it doesn't give.

"It's pressure-sealed," Quin utters, as he slings his now freed rucksack over his shoulder. "We're moving too fast, there's no way for us to get off."

The shuttle jerks violently before coming to a complete stop as the first round of explosions go off. Crates topple onto us as we are thrown to the ground. Quin removes them as another set go off. We are at the back of the shuttle, so we only have a matter of moments before the set over our heads detonates. Quin grabs the Levin gun and shoots the handle on the door. We push the door open, nearly falling out of it. I thought we would be on the ground like the shuttles are in Tyre, but we're at least a hundred feet above a body of water.

"Now what, Meg?"

"We have to jump."

"Are you nuts? The fall will kill us!"
"We don't have any choice," I scream, as another round of explosions shake the cars. The air outside the door is acrid, large plumes of smoke pass by. I lean out the door to see where we are in comparison to the last set of detonators. "There is only one more section to go before we blow."

We're halfway out when the detonators go off. I see the blast before I hear it.

The heat ignites the air in my lungs as I'm thrown out the door. I tumble through the air, not able to tell which way is up, managing to swing my legs over my head as I see the water rushing towards me. I brace for the pain to come. At this height, the water will be like hitting cement. I brace for the impact—as well as I can—but the sheer force of the impact knocks me senseless, and causes me to immediately sink down into the cold. My head begins to cloud over with pain as I continue to descend. Somehow, I'm still conscious enough to strip off my sweater, socks and shoes, which cause me to rise.

I break the surface and see debris lay scattered all over the surface of the water. I find a crate top and cling to it in order to stay afloat, then look up to see the smoldering wreckage of the shuttle. Flames and smoke fill the sky as portions of the shuttle still cling to the rail. I look around for Quin, but all I see are chunks of metal and wood. I try to call out his name, but my voice is too dry from the heat and smoke to make a sound.

I kick through the water, holding onto the crate lid, and finally spot Quin a few feet to my right. He swims over to me, grabbing onto the crate. We float along the rail line, chasing it back from where we had come. It takes some time, but finally we see the shore. The lake bed meets our feet and we walk the remainder of the way onto land, then sit and take a moment, trying to determine our next move.

"What do we do now?" I ask.

"I don't know," Quin responds.

We move further down the beach, trying to put some distance between us and the shuttle. Quin plops down on the sand, too exhausted to move. I sit next to him, leaning my head against his shoulder. He puts his arm around me, holding me tightly.

A crunching noise behind us gets my attention. I look up and notice a pair of brown eyes staring at us from behind the foliage that lines the back of the beach. I jab Quin with my elbow, then point to the eyes, which blink once then disappear. We get up and walk over to where we saw them. I hear the buzzing of electricity as we get to the trees and bushes. Quin pushes back several of the branches, revealing a rusted metal fence, barely alive with energy. Much of the barrier has been swallowed up by the vegetation; pieces are embedded within tree trunks and limbs. The current is probably not as strong as it once was.

"How did you get on that side of the fence?" A small voice whispers.

I look down and see the brown eyes again.

"You need to get off the sand before the Regulators catch you. The beach is lined with sensors, so they're probably on their way."

"Can we climb over the fence?" Quin asks, bending down to be at level with the person.

"Yes. Go that way about ten feet. There is a large tree that has completely enveloped the barrier. Climb that and you can come over. I will meet you there."

The eyes vanish as quickly as they appeared.

We walk along the fence and find the tree. I go first as Quin stands below as a lookout. The branches of the tree are very thick and sturdy. I climb five feet up, swing my leg over onto a branch that is hanging on other side, and climb down. Quin joins me a minute later. The owner of the brown eyes is an elderly woman, severely hunched over. Her long white hair is unkempt, and pulled into a makeshift knot in the middle of her back. The few teeth she has are stained yellow, but she smiles at seeing us, lighting up her sunken face.

"Come with me," she whispers, waving her hand as she turns her back and scurries down the dirt path lining the wall.

She takes us to a small group of homes made of gray clapboard with sagging roofs. The homes are laid out in a circle around a fire pit full of charred logs and branches. Old men and women sit outside on broken concrete steps, some rocking in chairs that look ready to collapse from age. There are about a dozen of these homes, all the same size and in the same condition. I don't see any Regulators patrolling, and all paths around the area are made of either dirt or mud. Only one trail seems to lead out and down a small hill before disappearing.

"In here," she says, as she opens a door to one of the houses.

I follow, but Quin is hesitant. He seems focused on the people gathering around us, perhaps trying to determine if any of them are dangerous.

"Go inside, young man," an elderly fellow says in the same whispered tone. "You don't want to be caught outside with those things on." He points to Quin's clothing, tapping his pants with his stick for a cane. Quin enters the house closing the door behind him.

The dwelling is cool, and the smell of mildew permeates my nostrils. The room we're in has a table, two chairs, and a brick stove with burnt food stuck to the grill. Two other women are inside, sitting by the window towards the back of the room. Neither one gets up as we move about, following the old woman as she picks up scraps of rags lying on the floor.

"You, dear," the woman says pointing to me, "come with me. Young man, you can go into the back room and change. Darla, get him some clothes from Thomas' house." The woman with red hair gets up from her seat and exits while I follow the old woman up a narrow staircase.

The attic has a low ceiling, cracked flooring, and five mattresses spread out on the floor, three have quilted coverings while the other two are bare.

"Here," she says, as she thrusts the rags – remnants of clothing, as it turns out - into my hands. "You can change up here while I get some tea going." She heads back down the stairs, leaving me alone in the dusty space.

I take off my top and wring it dry, intending to put it back on later. Then I notice my glove has a nasty tear down the center of the palm. I remove it and stuff it into the pocket of my discarded pants. The material of the rags feels like sackcloth: rough and itchy. I pull the shirt over my head, don the pants, and take down my ponytail using my fingers as a comb to brush through the knots, removing debris as I go. I decide to leave my hair down so it can dry, then head back down stairs.

Quin is wearing the same type of clothing as I am, and looks just as uncomfortable. We are both instructed to take a seat at the table while Darla brings us cups of warm liquid that looks like tea, but upon first taste makes my stomach immediately hurt. She along with the other two women drags over the chairs that were sitting by the window and join us. I sip the drink sparingly and notice Quin is doing the same. The old woman seems to have remembered something, gets up, goes towards a cabinet above the sink next to the stove, and returns with a small plate filled with brown wafers. I take one and bite into it, almost chipping my tooth.

It's difficult to choke the stuff down, but it's clear, though, that these people are living on very little, so I thank them for the tea and biscuits, watching their faces light up in happiness.

"What is this place?" Quin asks, after having finished eating one of the biscuits.

"We live in a Bejaardes Camp, one mile north of the Factory Borough of Acheron," Darla answers.

"What is a Bejaardes Camp?" I ask, setting down my teacup, not being able to swallow any more of the tepid, bitter liquid.

"It's housing for the elders of the Boroughs," the other woman responds in a whisper.

"Yes, where the High Ruler places us to die." The anger in Darla's voice is thick as she pounds the table, causing the cups to rattle.

"Now, dear, you just need to get used to it here. It's not so bad." The old woman gets up and opens the window to let some fresh air in.

"I don't want to get used to it, Claire. You and Helen have been here too long; you have forgotten what life is like."

"We didn't have the same upbringing as you did, Darla. It's not our fault you were banished to the Boroughs from the city all those years ago. This is where people our age live until it's our time to pass." Helen gets up from the table and climbs the stairs to the attic. Darla storms out of the house, leaving us with only Claire for company.

"You will have to forgive Darla; she's only been with us for a month. She's not used to the boredom and isolation."

"If you don't mind me asking, how old is Darla?"

"I don't mind at all, dear, but she might," Claire answers with a smile on her face. "She must be approximately fifty or so, which is pretty old for the Boroughs, but young for the residents of this camp." Claire pours herself a cup of tea. "Now, let me ask you two a question. Where did you come from?"

Quin tells her we stowed away on the cargo shuttle to escape the Wasteland and were washed up on the beach after it had exploded. She takes the tale in stride, but I can tell she isn't completely buying it.

"Well, it sounds like you two have had one rough day. There is someone I would like you to meet, but first we need to eat. Young man, go outside and see Thomas. He will have you help him prepare the meat for roasting. Young lady, you come with me and we will go out into the garden for some vegetables."

Before we leave the house, Claire gives us each a pair of handmade sandals to wear, just like the pair she has on. Once they're on our feet, Quin goes to the house across the way, while Claire and I walk to the back of the camp and pick food from their garden for supper.

The meat is barely enough to feed four people, let alone the twenty that live in the camp. Quin and I are each given an extra helping of meat despite our protests, but each resident proudly gives up their portion. We all sit around the fire pit eating and telling stories. No one seems too afraid that Regulators will show up.

"They don't bother with us," Thomas says, putting another log on the fire. "We only see them once a month for our food rations. They don't consider us much of a threat." He begins to laugh, which causes the others to laugh too.

The sun has fully set and the temperature has dropped when everyone begins to wander back to their homes. Quin goes to stay the night with Thomas, while I take one of the empty mattresses in Claire's house. Helen gives me her quilt to sleep with since she says she is warm, but I see her shake from the dampness that has settled in the attic. I'm about to give the blanket back to her when Claire lies down next to Helen, wrapping her blanket around the both of them. I don't sleep well, but it's not due to my surroundings. Helen's quilt is soft and warm; the mattress is comfortable. The nightmares that keep coming leave me feeling unsettled and disturbed.

How I long for a night where I don't dream.

The following morning, Claire cuts up fruit for us to put in our bowls of oatmeal for breakfast. The stuff tastes like paste, but I know it's all they have, and we need the sustenance, so Quin and I eat every bite.

Thomas is to take us into the Boroughs today to meet his friends, Naomi and Jagger. Claire gives me the sack of apples we had picked the day before. I give her a hug; she grips me hard in return.

"Good luck, Trea."

I pull my head up in surprise, as I'd never told her my name.

I don't see any monitors around the house, so I doubt they saw the spectacle from Tyre. *How did she know?*

I catch up to Quin and Thomas at the edge of the camp. We have to walk slowly due to Thomas' sluggish pace. It takes us a better part of an hour before we are near the gated entrance of the Boroughs. I halt, fearing I will be recognized the minute we're near the Regulators. Thomas has come prepared. He removes a pair of broken glasses from the inside pocket of his coat. The frames are bent, the lenses chipped, and I can't see anything properly through them, so Quin props me up against him and I begin to walk with a limp at Thomas' suggestion, using his cane for emphasis.

We stop in front of the Regulator's tower, waiting to be allowed entrance into the Boroughs. The rectangular stone structure rises up three stories, towering over the electric fence that emerges from the wings that extend out in the distance on either side. A gravel road beyond the gate stretches down past lines of broken-down buildings, some spewing black smoke into the air. Several people are walking up the road, some entering the buildings, others continuing on.

Thomas rings a bell on the gate then stands back as it swings open.

No one comes out of the tower to greet us, but the gate slowly closes the farther we walk in. I turn back around and see Thomas standing on the other side, tears in his eyes. He smiles, turns around, and begins to walk back to the camp.

"He's not coming with us?" I whisper to Quin, as we continue to walk.

"He can't, but he'll be back for us in three days."

"How are we going to meet him? They're not going to let us out." I say, as we pass under part of the structure connecting the two halves of the tower.

"He told me where we need to go. It'll be all right, Meg."

I hear voices coming from above us as we walk past the building, so I turn my head skyward.

Two large screens are affixed on either side of the post, displaying a blurry image. I slide the glasses down my nose so I can see what is being shown. The image is of a shuttle ablaze, smoke billowing skyward as flames shoot out in all directions. In the right hand corner of the screens is a smaller display of a man sitting at a desk, addressing the bystanders who have gathered beside us to watch.

"As we have reported throughout the night, searchers have only recovered a few remains from the attack on Shuttle Six. This shuttle left Oasis Two early yesterday morning with approximately two hundred Acherons on board. It passed through the checkpoint around two yesterday afternoon with a dozen or so passengers disembarking."

The larger image changes to security footage from the checkpoint showing people getting off of a shuttle, as well as several Regulators inspecting the undercarriage and interior.

"The Superior of Transportation and the Superior of Safety met with the High Ruler late last night to discuss possible motives behind this attack. It's believed this act of violence was orchestrated by none other than Aldus Vladim, High Ruler of Tyre."

"They're nuts!" I practically scream.

People turn to look at me, surprised by my outburst. Quin drags me away as the story begins to repeat and the images flash back to the smoldering wreckage.

"Don't say stuff like that too loudly," he says, scolding me.

"There was no one on that shuttle except for us and it was their own Regulators that placed the detonators inside. Why would they lie about their own people being killed when they weren't even there?"

"Easy, Meg, Acheron is trying to start a war with Tyre."

"Why? What could that possibly gain for them?"

"Us," he whispers.

He side-steps and guides me between two warehouses. I hear machines inside, creating what, I don't know.

"Think about it…Vladim broadcasted to Acheron the existence of the Antaeans. When you escaped, Acheron saw it as an opportunity."

"An opportunity for what?"

"Hey…you two. Get a move on back to your homes." We turn and see a Regulator standing a few feet away, his hands on his hips. "No work today, so go back to your homes."

"Yes, sir, we were just heading that way." Quin replies, as I push the glasses back up my nose and lean on Thomas' cane.

"Get going then."

We walk past the Regulator and continue on down the road, under another Regulator building expanse, turn right, and start to head towards what looks to be a ravine. As we get closer, I notice a small wooden bridge spanning the gully. It doesn't look sturdy enough to hold a great deal of weight. I look down into the chasm as we slowly cross the bridge and notice it's partly full of water; the channel's edges have been carved out by a great force. This must have been a river at one time, feeding whatever city once stood here.

The water looks slightly green in color and is moving sluggishly north. Three boats move against the current, determined to make their destination. One boat floats under us, then begins to veer to the left and down another smaller channel, metal doors sealing the boat into a box. It begins to rise as water passes from one part of the channel to another. Slowly the boat is moved forward, eventually exiting out onto the lake, where I lose sight of it.

Quin shakes my arm and we continue across the bridge.

The lane we step onto is covered in broken red brick, grass sporadically trying to reach for the sun through the pavers. A stone wall about four feet high lines one side of the lane, with the river running along the other. We walk south along the wall, only spotting the occasional person scurrying down the path, avoiding all eye contact, heads bent down, feet shuffling as he or she goes. We turn right, following the wall. Three story dwellings are crammed together along the lane. I hear voices next to us and look up to see a Regulator's tower standing in the middle of the field the stone wall has surrounded, with a monitor affixed to the side of the structure displaying the same scenes we saw earlier.

Quin and I continue to walk; I'm watching the screen while he seems to be counting the doors of the houses.

"This one," he says, as he pulls me around the corner and up to a glass door.

He goes right in without knocking, and walks up the set of stairs in the front entranceway. We climb to the top floor, go down a dank, narrow hallway and stop in front of room 313. Quin knocks once, then twice, then three times. I hear movement on the other side of the door, which opens, revealing a tiny room with five people sitting around a table, playing cards. I hear the same voice from the screen outside echoing from somewhere beyond the door.

"Can I help you?" A young woman with long red hair, thin fingers, and slight build says after she opens the door only part way.

"Thomas sent us," Quin says to the woman, while watching the people at the table. They seem to be too wrapped up in their card game to notice us.

"Come in," the woman says, as she opens the door wider, allowing us entry. She gestures for us to have a seat on a pale orange couch that looks like it could double as a bed. She sits on a small chair opposite us, her gray clothing bunching around her waist and ankles as she sits down. "What can I help you with?"

"We need passage to Acheron," Quin says, as he leans forward, arms resting on his knees.

"That's a pretty serious request," the young woman proclaims, as she stands up and begins to pace behind her chair.

The group playing cards begin to argue over the number of cards that have been dealt.

"Why would you want to go to Acheron?"

"That is a private matter," Quin states, shortly.

I can feel the agitation building in his body as he stiffens, balling his hands into fists that still rest upon his knees.

"Well, if I'm to risk my life for the two of you I certainly want to know why."

"Let's go, Quin, this is a waste of time." I stand up and head for the door.

"You're not going anywhere," one of the men at the table says, as he rises out of his seat and lunges for me.

I whip the cane around and crack him in the jaw, knocking him to the ground. Another card player grabs the arm with the cane, and twists. I take my free hand and grab him around the throat, squeezing until his eyes roll into the back of his head, watching with a grin as he falls to the floor.

Finally, some real action. Let's see who I can kill today.

The lone female player jumps on my back, driving something sharp in between my shoulder blades. I reach over my shoulder, grab her by the hair, and throw her across the room, into the cabinets. After removing the knife sticking out of my shoulder, I seize our hostess and fling her to the floor, putting the knife to her throat.

"Now, are you going to help us or not?" I say through gritted teeth, sweat dripping down my face.

The woman is crying as I continue to press the knife into her throat, cutting her. A hand touches my shoulder and I watch as Quin reaches for the knife. I look up at him, watching his mouth move, but I don't hear the words that he's speaking.

"Meg," he says to me.

Meg? My name is Trea.

"Meg snap out of it."

I look at him for a moment then down at my hands and recoil in horror as I see the knife covered in blood, a terrified look upon the woman's face. I drop the weapon and slink back against the wall, knees up to my face. Quin tends to the injured as I try to secure Trea back into the recesses of my mind.

What causes me to lash out so much? The littlest thing seems to set me off now.

I stay in my little spot for some time, afraid to talk or move, as the small apartment is placed back into order. The card game resumes while dinner is prepared. Quin is talking with our hostess and making plans for our trip. They decide it will happen the day after tomorrow, though I catch only snippets of the conversation.

Room is made for us at the table when dinner is ready. The man I choked kneels down in front of me, offering his hands to assist me in standing. I shake my head no, as I'm too embarrassed about my earlier actions.

"Don't worry about it," he says in a sweet voice. "We've gotten worse from the Regulators."

I smile slightly and take his hands as he introduces himself to me as Jagger, then brings me over to the rest of his housemates: Naomi, Bea, Karl, Faber, and Cass.

We eat watered-down mushroom soup amid casual conversation. Naomi seems eager in learn all about Quin. She is practically glued to his side, much to my displeasure. I turn my attention to Jagger, who is sitting next to me.

"How do you know Thomas?" I ask him after swallowing some soup.

"He was my trainer at the machinist plant from when I was thirteen. When he was forced to leave, I made it a point to do whatever I could for him."

"Like what?"

"At the back of the Borough, part of the fencing is bent, so we can crawl through it, but only a little way. It's enough to get extra supplies down to the camp so they don't starve."

Talk slowly winds down as the evening approaches. The dishes are cleared and the men, along with Quin, adjourn to the bedroom for the night while the remainder of us stay and sleep on the small foldout bed in the front room.

Naomi takes the left side, while Bea takes the middle, and I cling to the right edge of the thin mattress. I try to fall asleep, but the constant droning from the monitor is making it virtually impossible. I nudge Bea lightly, rousing her from sleep to ask if there is a way to turn it off.

"No, it's always on. It's controlled by the Regulators. We can't even adjust the volume." She falls back to sleep with ease, though I remain wide awake, watching and listening.

The supposed death toll from the shuttle disaster rises when the announcer claims that more bodies have been located floating among the wreckage. I close my eyes and try to will myself asleep only to be jarred by a sudden high-pitched whistle coming from the screen. The words *Special Announcement* scroll in bold red type across the top. I look over at Bea and Naomi, but neither has stirred.

"We have just received word that High Ruler Aldus Vladim of Tyre has announced he will send forces to Acheron and attempt to seize the city."

I sit fully upright in bed, listening to every word the announcer is saying.

"Our Superior of Communication was able to intercept the broadcast High Ruler Vladim sent out to his people today."

The screen changes to Vladim standing on a balcony on one of the many high rises in Tyre, gesturing to the crowd that has gathered below him.

"My fellow Tyreans, the High Ruler of Acheron sent thieves into Tyre to rob the Antaean known as Trea from us. He carefully orchestrated her removal from our city, but we have located those responsible." The picture changes to five men and women lined up in the center of one of the Boroughs. "I have no doubt that he has taken her to Acheron where she will be tortured and eventually killed. I have called on my security forces from the Boroughs in the north to form a recovery team and enter Acheron to take back our most prized possession."

"When this was brought to High Ruler Hayden's attention," the announcer breaks in, "he had the following comment."

The screen changes to the symbol of Acheron.

A new voice, presumably Hayden's, begins to speak. "We have always known the people of Tyre could not be trusted. Ever since the destruction of the Dormitories, our relationship with them has been severely strained. If this war is to happen, Acheron will prepare itself, and we will prevail."

I climb out of bed and head to the bedroom to get Quin.

CHAPTER 15

Quin is lying on the floor, covered in thin blankets. The other men lay on small cots spread throughout the tiny dark space. I kneel beside him, place my hand on his shoulder and shake him. He stirs slightly, but doesn't wake. I shake him a little harder causing him to open his eyes and look up at me.

"What?" he asks, eyelids still half-closed.

"We need to get to Acheron today."

"What...why?"

I tell him about the announcement I saw on the monitor.

"He'll do anything to find all of the Antaeans, which is why we need to get to Acheron before he does."

"I understand your concern, but there's nothing we can do at the moment. Naomi and the others are not scheduled to depart until the day after tomorrow." He grabs my arm and pulls me down next to him, draping one of his blankets over me. "Now try and get some sleep." He pulls me into his chest, resting his chin on the top of my head.

I know he's right, but my anxiety is getting the best of me. I try to mimic my breathing with his to calm myself down and it begins to work as I slowly feel my eyes begin to close.

"Meg."

I hear my name uttered from a far off location. I begin to rock along with the violent waves in my dream. My stomach turns as the motion becomes more vicious.

"Meg."

My eyes shoot open and I see Quin bending down over me.

"You need to get up, now."

I toss the blanket off, get up, and follow him into the living room. The monitor is displaying work orders for the day, showing Naomi and her roommates as last minute add-ons to the rotation.

"Looks like you're going to get your wish," Quin says at my back.

"We need to get a move on if we're to get you two on board the ferry," Jagger says, as he lays out tools on the top of the dining table. He picks up a thin metal thread, which he inserts into a menacing-looking device that is clutched tightly in his hand.

"What is that?" I ask.

"It's an encoder. I need to program Bea and Karl's details into these threads and then implant them into your wrists. Everyone is scanned before they are allowed onto the ferries." Jagger rolls up his sleeve, revealing a bar code just under the surface of the skin on the inside of his wrist.

"Won't the Regulators know we aren't Bea and Karl?" I ask, as I sit down across from him.

"They don't look at faces, only the bar codes."

The lights that had been flashing red on the encoder are now bright green. Jagger takes my left wrist, sets the mouth of the encoder against my skin, and squeezes the trigger on the handle. My flesh begins to burn and I'm forced to bite my lower lip to keep from screaming. I feel the thin metal slide under my skin, snaking its way along my wrist. Jagger removes the encoder and motions for Quin to take a seat.

I look down at my wrist as I stand; the flesh is bright red, slowly changing to pink. The bar code is just beneath the epidermis. I wonder how easy it is to pull out.

Bea and Karl hand us their uniforms, which consist of gray twill pants, matching long sleeve tops and black boots. I pull my hair up after running a brush through it. Faber and Cass each fill a sack with food, handing it to us, as we won't be returning for a few days. Then we leave the apartment with the others. The six of us exit the housing unit and walk straight towards the Regulator's building in the center of the square. Jagger and Quin take the lead, with Naomi and me in the middle. We line up behind several other groups of workers and walk through the thick barbed wire gate.

The building we enter is comprised of gray cinder blocks stacked two stories high, topped with a once-copper roof. We are directed down a flight of stairs to our left as soon as we walk into the structure. The air smells more and more sour the further down we go. I'm practically choking back bile as we reach the bottom, where I notice several Regulators are wearing air purifier masks over their faces. They scan each worker's wrist before letting them pass into the ferry terminal behind them.

Jagger is right; they don't look at my face, but only scan the code and then let me pass when the lights on their reader turn green.

We walk down the damp cement sidewalk and break off to the right after passing five ferry slots. I follow Naomi as she descends a small flight of stairs leading toward a wide metal boat. I nearly fall the moment I step on, due to a slimy film covering much of the floorboards. Faber and Cass head below deck to get the engines started while the rest of us untie the vessel from its moorings. We shove off and join the parade of boats as we make our way out into the canal.

We are seventh in line to go through the locks leading into the lake. As we wait our turn, I watch people walk along the canal's edge and over the bridges on their way to the factories that have started jettisoning black steam into the air. Every ten feet or so along the bridges and paths stands a Regulator, more today than yesterday. I sense someone is watching me, so I turn my head around to see Jagger staring at me intently. He motions with his head towards a monitor we are about to pass under. I turn my attention back around and observe as Acheron's emblem blazes across the screen: a large golden hawk, its wings wide open against a dark blue background.

We sail under the bridge and come out the other side to an identical screen, and I watch as the bird vanishes, replaced by large red letters: WAR. As the word spins slowly around on an invisible axis, an announcer comes on over the speakers, his voice harsh and deep.

"Laics of Acheron," a voice begins, "our fears have come to pass. As your leader, I appeal to you to assist us in our time of need. With the violent attack several days ago, and by the proclamation made by High Ruler Vladim of Tyre our city will soon be at war. We must do whatever it takes to secure the safety and well-being of Acheron and of its people. Supply shipments from the outlying Oases will soon stop, so all food reserves will need to be moved to the city itself; rationing will begin immediately. Each household will be given enough supplies to last them for several months as winter is approaching, and this will cause supply runs from the city to the Boroughs to be slower due to the inclement weather. Be ever ready for the new challenges that are approaching."

The word dissolves from the screen and is replaced with the emblem. I notice Quin is now standing next to me, resting his hand on top of mine as I grip the side of the boat.

"The quicker we find Kedua the better," I whisper to him.

The boat turns into the first lock, and the metal gates close behind us as the greenish water is slowly piped out and replaced with clearer liquid. We continue through another set of locks and the same process continues until all of the green water is left behind and we sail out onto the clean clear lake.

We travel slowly for two hours, heading south along the coast before finally coming to a stop about one hundred yards from a large dune. Jagger and Quin secure the boat to an iron supply depot that stands thirty feet high, fastened to the lake floor with large mooring clamps. Faber and Cass come up from below and enter the building. We begin to load steel canisters onto the boat, stacking them ten high below deck. I notice the boat beginning to ride lower in the water due to the weight, but Naomi assures me we will be fine. We're back underway an hour later, heading north towards Acheron.

A perimeter has been established a mile outside the city's edges. Our boat is searched and we are scanned again before being allowed passage. The platform we pull alongside juts out from a barrier wall. There appears to be a total of six such platforms, extending outward in a star-like formation, all radiating from the city itself. Skyscrapers shoot upward, leaving long shadows against the cold waves. The reflective material everything is constructed out of is not a metal I've ever seen before. The waves are cold and the air crisp, yet the deeper we sail into the platform, the warmer the atmosphere becomes.

Our boat slides into dock number three, locking into place. Naomi and Jagger motion for us to follow them below deck. As we enter the holding chamber, I watch as Faber and Cass turn off the engines and open the large door at the far end. A Regulator is standing on the opposite side, waiting for us to begin unloading our supplies onto the conveyor belt next to him. After I lift a canister onto the belt, Jagger pokes my shoulder and motions me to follow him. We head back towards the front of the boat and into a small bedchamber. Quin changes into a Regulator's uniform that had been concealed in one of the canisters. Jagger reaches down to another canister, opening the lid to reveal the cache of weapons inside.

"We've been waiting for our moment," he says, as he removes a Levin gun and hands it to me. "Now's our chance."

I take the gun and slip it into an empty sack. I hear Faber calling the Regulator back into the boat, saying that he needs assistance with one of the canisters, then a small scuffle occurs just on the other side of the closed door to the bed chamber. There is a soft knock on the door, which Jagger opens, and Cass shoves the dead man into the room. His head is at a grotesque angle due to his neck being broken. Quin exits the room to take the Regulator's position while the rest of us change clothes. I put on a pair of tight black pants, a silver belt that hangs loosely from my waist, a long sleeve purple Lycra top, and a pair of black leather gloves with the fingers cut off. I decide to keep the boots, as the shoes they had acquired don't look comfortable.

As soon as I'm dressed, Naomi grabs my arm and pulls me across the hall to a tiny bathroom. We both barely fit inside. I look at the bathroom sink in front of me and spot a small bottle filled with a black liquid and a pair of scissors.

"The minute you exit the docking area you will be recognized," she says, shoving me down onto the toilet, grabbing the bottle, and squeezing the liquid into my hair.

She soaks my hair thoroughly after placing a filthy towel around my neck and back to keep the dye off my clothes. She leaves me to let the dye do its work while she makes sure everyone is ready to leave. As soon as Naomi returns, she rinses out my hair in the sink and begins to chop it off. She cuts my hair to the length of my earlobes, parting it on the left side.

I look in the tiny mirror hanging over the sink when she is done. I don't recognize myself.

"How do we get out of the docking area? There are cameras and Regulators stationed all over," I inquire, as we head back across the hall to the bedchamber.

"Faber and Cass are going to cause a distraction, which will allow the rest of us to escape. Quin will stay behind to arrest Faber and Cass. They will meet up with us in an hour."

My nerves begin to fray. I know this plan is not a solid one; too many variables can go wrong, but they put it together, so I just have to see how it plays out. I wait in the room with Jagger and Naomi as Faber and Cass leave, heading for the docking area, their voices already rising in anger.

Canisters begin to clank onto the cement floor. I peek my head around the doorframe and see Faber push Cass hard into the conveyor belt, knocking the steel containers onto the ground, some spilling open from the force. Three Regulators are immediately there to break them up, but I can't tell which one is Quin as they're wearing the same outfits. Cass gets up and jumps in-between Faber and the Regulators, giving us our chance to escape.

The three of us go past them, running along the undercarriage of the conveyor belt to stay out of sight of the cameras that hang down from the ceiling. I hear shouting behind us, more scuffling. The conveyor belt takes a violent jar to the right, spilling everything onto the floor next to us. Jagger and Naomi are far ahead of me, almost out of the docking area. I turn back to look for Quin, but all I see is Faber lying on the ground with his neck torn open, blood pouring out of his wound.

I knew the plan wasn't going to work. Too bad about Faber. What will the others say? How will they react? As long as there are no hysterics. I can't stand overly emotional people.

I turn around and catch up to Jagger and Naomi. We exit the area through a small ventilation shaft, crawling on our hands and knees through dust for about twenty minutes. Naomi stops ahead of me, reaches into her pocket, and removes a small screwdriver, using it to remove the bolts of the screen covering our exit. Once the screen is removed, we step out into a small alleyway, and Jagger quickly replaces the screen as Naomi and I step out into the main thoroughfare.

The temperature is quite cold, and the air stale. We walk past others dressed like us, shivering from the chill. We stroll by small shops filled with smoke, simple food, and laughter. We keep heading towards what appears to be the center of the place. A large blue energy field at the heart of the city cascades skyward, disappearing into a reflective metallic ceiling.

"What is that?" I ask, as we move around it.

"It's an energy core. The heart of Acheron. It's what keeps the city alive," Naomi responds, as we turn a corner and walk down another alleyway.

We enter a door on our right, walk towards the back of the establishment, and sit down at a small booth. A young woman with bright yellow hair, facial piercings, silver bracelets down one arm, and carrying a green glowing tray, asks us what we would like to drink. Jagger and Naomi both order a Cloud Tea. As I'm not sure what to have, I ask for the same.

We sit in silence, waiting for the others to join us.

The woman returns with our drinks in tin cups, steam billowing from the brims. I take a small sip of mine, enjoying the flavors of cinnamon, nutmeg, and warm milk with something else in the mixture, but I can't quite tell what it is. I take a bigger sip and begin to feel my insides warming up, my head getting a little lighter. I'm in the process of taking another mouthful when Jagger places his hand on the top of my cup.

"You're going to want to drink this stuff slowly," he says, as he guides my cup back to the table's surface. "It tastes good now, but you'll be floating later if you drink it too fast."

I smile at him in thanks and put down my cup.

We keep an eye on the entrance, waiting for the others to walk through. I see a couple of Regulators walk in, sit down and order drinks. Many other people in the place look run-down, and worn out. Some remind me of the occupants of the Wasteland, others look like Laics who left the Boroughs a long time ago. There are a few individuals who are finely dressed in silk suits, freshly pressed linens, and wool coats.

"What is this place?" I ask.

"This is the Underground. It's like a waste disposal for people. Those fortunate enough to have escaped the Boroughs, or vile enough to mingle down here with those they can't control, live down here," Naomi replies quietly, as if she is afraid someone will overhear her.

"The Superiors and High Ruler know this place exists, but they don't dare do anything about it since most of them come down here to have a temporary escape from their lives above the surface," Jagger adds.

He points skyward.

"See that man over there," he begins, pointing to an older gentleman wearing a gray silk suit and tie. "He is the Superior of Education, but the woman he is fondling is not his wife."

The man gropes the woman's breast, then nuzzles her neck as his other hand slides up her short skirt. She squeals with delight and the two soon part, his communicator beeping incessantly, though he pays no attention to it.

We sit there for half an hour before Quin and Cass walk in. Quin has disposed of the uniform and is wearing dark blue pants, black shirt and jacket. The two sit down with us and order Cloud Teas.

"Where's Faber?" Naomi asks, as she finishes her drink.

"He's not coming," Cass says, as he begins to sip his drink as soon as the waitress sets it down.

"What do you mean he's not coming?" Naomi's voice rises, "where is he?"

"Dead," I utter, before anyone can stop me.

Naomi stops and stares at me, shocked, before she bursts into tears, her body heaving uncontrollably. Cass puts his arm around her and rocks her back and forth while Jagger gives me a nasty look.

I'm shocked at my candor about the matter.

How could I just blurt something like that out? Why am I not that upset about it?

I determine it's my detachment training kicking in. Trea responding, not Meg.

Quin leans over and whispers in my ear.

"You might have tried a little discretion. Faber was her twin brother."

I sit quietly and drink my tea while the others try to console Naomi.

I notice that the monitors down in the Underground don't display any of the cities emblems or news flashes, but instead show snippets of women dancing provocatively, men drinking excessively, and couples in the throes of passion. Each segment lasts five minutes before moving on to a new one. The display currently on screen is of a man lying face down on a mat, two women massaging his back with oil. The caption at the bottom reads *Acheron Baths*, as soft music plays and candles burn in the background.

The screen changes to a semi-dressed woman clinging to a pole, her body moving with the chaotic sounds from behind her. The woman's long auburn hair is pulled behind her in a braid, and the harsh spotlights bounce off her dark skin. The camera changes to show a face with deep brown sad eyes, bony cheeks, and no smile.

Kedua.

"Where is that place?" I ask, pointing to the monitor. My arm jerks so fast I nearly knock Quin's cup from his hands.

Everyone follows my hand and stares at the screen. In the bottom right hand corner the words *Club Alasti* flash then the scene changes again to men drinking.

"You don't want to go there," Cass states.

"Why not?"

"You'd have to be depraved to go there," Jagger says, as he orders another round of Cloud Tea.

"How depraved?"

"Meg, you're insane. First off, you're a female so they'll never let you in. Second, it's strictly for the Superiors and those who work for them. Laics like us are not welcome."

I look around at all the concerned faces, but I've made up my mind.

"We're getting inside...tonight."

Cass and Naomi try to argue, but Jagger seems to be thrilled with the idea and begins to hash out a plan. Quin looks at me and mouths Kedua's name, to which I nod.

"It'll be best if we go in during a shift change. Quin, do you still have the Regulator's uniform?" Jagger asks, as he pushes away his tea and begins to map out our next move.

"Yes, I stashed it in a waste bin around the corner."

"What do you plan on doing once you get inside?" Naomi asks, having regained some of her composure.

"I haven't thought that far ahead."

Cass and Naomi continue to argue about going, but Jagger has it all worked out. He seems very interested in getting into Club Alasti, even though I haven't said why, since they'd be tortured if caught.

Once I get Kedua out of there, we'll need to get out of Acheron quickly, so we'll need to use the boat again, which means getting back into the docking area. I'm sure their boat has been seized, so how we get off this floating city to me is the real challenge.

CHAPTER 16

Naomi and Cass decide to stay at the bar while Jagger, Quin, and I go to the club. Quin goes and gets the uniform he stashed, while Jagger and I wait over by the energy core. I finally tell Jagger why I want to get into the club. He seems skeptical at first, but then I show him the marks on the back of my neck. It's easier to see now that more than half of my hair is missing.

Jagger seems unsure of how to react.

Quin nudges me as he walks past.

Since Regulators don't socialize with Laics unless it's for work, Quin has to keep his distance from us. We follow him around the core and towards a crowded alleyway. He manages to get through the crowd easily, but Jagger and I are not so fortunate. I'm stuck standing behind two men in blue silk suits complaining to a Regulator about how they've been denied entrance to the club.

"Yes, Superior, I understand your frustration, but we have our orders. No one is permitted into the club tonight as it has been reserved by the High Ruler himself."

Jagger pulls me back and we step over to the side.

"There's another way we can get in."

He takes my hand and we go back to the core, around another corner, and down a walkway between the club and another establishment. There's a back entrance guarded by one Regulator. Jagger approaches the man and easily overpowers him. He strips the man of his uniform and begins to put it on while I work the lock on the door. It breaks easily in my grip, and the door swings open. I drag the man inside and shove him into the first room I see, which, unfortunately, is a broom closet. Jagger closes the door behind me and stands guard outside.

The hallway I'm in is dark, but I can see light shining from beneath a curtain at the end. The scent of sex and sweat fill the air, almost choking out any oxygen that is pumping through the vents overhead.

I hear voices echoing through closed doors barely discernable in the darkness. Distracted by the noise, I don't notice anyone around until someone grabs my arm, halting my forward motion.

"You're too dressed up to be working here," the woman with smoke on her breath says. Her grip is light, but her manner is acidic. "What are you doing here?"

"I'm looking for someone."

"Aren't we all?" she says, winking at me. "What's her name?"

I'm about to say Kedua, but if her protector changed her name like Devlan changed mine I won't have a way of knowing what it is.

"I've forgotten her name, but she has long auburn hair, kept in a braid."

The woman looks at me with a suspicious sparkle in her eye, but releases her grip and holds out her hand for me to shake it.

"You want Deanna. And you are?"

"Ash," I say quickly, taking her hand and shaking it.

"Well, Ash, I don't know if you're going to get a chance to talk to your friend, but you can watch her from backstage. She is giving a special performance tonight to the High Ruler himself."

The woman shows me to a small stool to the left of the stage where Kedua is dancing. I watch her move gracefully with the music that is blaring around us. She straddles a pole that stands in the center of the theater and begins to twirl her body around it like a snake. I peek around the curtains that are blocking me from the audience and see the place is more than half empty. A man in black robes is sitting at a table at the end of the stage, surrounded by personal bodyguards in blue and gold uniforms, with the city's emblem blazoned across their lapels.

The man in the robes appears to be in his seventies, with short white hair, cruel eyes, shallow features, and long thin arms. The voice heard over the loud speakers earlier doesn't match the man sitting there. I scan the area one more time and notice a figure standing in the shadows.

"Who's that man?" I ask the woman, as she is still standing by my side.

"That's Deanna's owner. He owns several of the young women who work here. She, however, is his favorite."

I continue to watch Kedua dance, her movements changing in perfect time with the music. The man remains standing in the shadows as Kedua steps down from the stage and begins to seduce the High Ruler. She pushes his head back as she begins to remove his robes. He closes his eyes, a smile growing on his face. She works her way down to his waist. He moans in delight.

Kedua's owner, unnoticed by anyone else but me, sidles behind the High Ruler.

The blade in his hand slices so quickly the High Ruler doesn't have time to utter a cry. Blood pours down his chest, spattering Kedua. She rises from the chair, holds her owner's face in her hands, and begins to kiss him passionately as the spot-light cascades onto them.

I bolt upright from the chair and am instantly struck in the face, feeling my jawbone crack, blood trickling down my lips. I grab the woman's hands before she can cast a second blow and close my hands tightly, her brittle bones crunching in my grasp. She lets out a shriek from the pain. I know Kedua and the man are coming, but I don't move.

Trea wants to play.

"Midge, are you...?" The words trail off as he sees her down on her knees, with me holding her there.

"Hello, Artemis, nice to see you again." I smile wickedly.

"Trea."

I hear my name but it's not spoken by Artemis, but by Kedua, standing to his left.

"Hello, Kedua. Long time no see."

Tension begins to build between us. I feel electricity flowing through the air, though nowhere more so than in my right arm. The Quantum Stream is boiling under the surface of my skin, looking for a weapon to hold. I remember the Levin gun in the sack around my shoulder and begin to reach for it, but am stopped by Artemis.

"Why don't we find a better place to talk," he says, as he holds my hand against the strap of the bag. "Somewhere a little more private," he whispers into my ear, practically biting it in affection. "Midge," he turns to the woman who cowers at my feet, "please make sure the mess out there gets cleaned up, and then reopen in a half hour so the gentlemen can have some entertainment."

Midge nods and steps through the curtain onto the stage, walking with her arms in front of her. The High Ruler's bodyguards have already begun to remove the man's body and wrap it in black tar paper.

"I take it the guards knew you planned this?" I probe, as we head towards the back exit.

"Of course, why do you think it was so easy? Money can buy you anything, including a position of power. After all, they report directly to the High Ruler, which is now me." He smirks, winking at me.

I swing wide, nailing him in the temple. Kedua is on top of me in an instant, banging my head on the wooden floorboards. Artemis pulls her off and helps me up.

"Now, now, ladies, there is plenty to go around." He leans over, wraps his arm around my waist to pull me closer. "Try that again and I will have Kedua here make sure you don't self-heal," he says through clenched teeth, snatching the sack from my shoulder after kissing me on the cheek.

Kedua grabs a long fur coat that hangs from a hook by the door before we step out. She's covered in blood and manages to wipe most of it from her face, but she'll still need to bathe in order to remove the rest of it. She wraps herself tightly in her coat.

Jagger is still standing guard when we exit. He looks at Kedua, who is walking in front of me, and Artemis, who is holding onto my hand, caressing my palm with his fingers. I make brief eye contact with him, but not enough to draw attention to him.

"So, High Ruler," I say, a little louder than I should. "Where are we going?"

He simply smiles at me, tightens his grip, and pulls me along the alleyway to the other end. As we turn the corner, I catch Jagger hastening to catch up to us, joining the rest of our entourage.

We stop in front of a set of large steel doors, which open as we approach. The interior is decorated in plush gold walls and flooring; ornate wall sconces encapsulate soft glowing light bulbs as violin music fills the air from well-hidden speakers. Jagger tries to step on board, but is immediately reprimanded.

"Did you forget your place, Regulator?" Kedua hisses at him. "Use the service elevators."

The doors close, we quietly but rapidly rise, then the doors open onto a sun filled sky. The temperature difference between the Underground and the surface is a good twenty degrees. Tall buildings shimmer in the sunlight, reflecting the heat from the sun's rays.

A small transport car sits waiting for us a few yards from the lift. It is ornately decorated, with gold seat coverings, and the city's emblem is inscribed on the ceiling. I see Jagger step off of a service elevator fifty feet away and jog over to a waiting transport, which falls in line behind us. We skirt along the outer rim of the city on a rail embedded into the surface of the base of the floating metropolis. The car winds around to the opposite side, stopping only momentarily at a guard post sitting at the entrance to one of the extended platforms. We quickly pass through security and slow down.

A hawk with gold wings is embroidered in tile on the surface of the center of the platform, with large fountains of water erupting from its talons. The building on our right is only two stories high, columns extending the height of the building on all sides. An identical structure sits on the opposite side of the fountain. I notice men in blue robes exiting and entering these buildings, and figure this must be where the Superiors meet.

The car turns and stops in front of a four-story structure in the same design as the other two buildings. Artemis exits the vehicle, followed by Kedua, then myself. Jagger and several bodyguards exit their transports and follow us. We walk up a small flight of steps and into a grand foyer with blue marble flooring, a gold encased chandelier hanging from the ceiling four stories high, and an oak table in the center of the floor with several granite statues from a time long since passed.

Artemis clutches my arm and escorts me up many flights of stairs till we are on the fourth floor, our entourage in tow. I try not to look over the railing for fear of getting dizzy from the height. He shoves me into an expansive sitting room at the back of the palace, shutting the door, and locking me in. I hear him instruct the bodyguards to stay at my door. Kedua advises Jagger, who she apparently thinks is her personal protector, that he is relieved for the evening and she will call for him if he's needed. Then she retreats down the hall and enters another room.

Like Artemis' penthouse at the Letchworth, the entire back wall has floor-to-ceiling windows. I walk over to them trying to see how far down the water actually is, noticing what appears to be a barrier just below the surface that seems to circumscribe the whole platform. Four large boats filled with a mixture of bodyguards and Regulators also patrol the area.

Clouds slowly roll in as rain gently hits the panes. I case the room for an hour, looking for a way out, or something I can use as a weapon. The marble statues that adorn the bookshelves are cemented into place; nothing in the room can be moved except the furniture. From what I can tell the only way out is through the door, or the windows. I press up against the glass, testing its tension. It doesn't give, no matter how much weight I push against it, so I decide to pick up one of the fabric covered footstools to test the window. As I'm about to throw it Artemis clears his throat from the doorway. I turn and look at him, then proceed to heave the stool against the glass anyway, a small crack appearing and beginning to extend outward in a spider web pattern.

"If you're hoping to escape out the window, that will be a very painful way to go, Meg." He strolls into the room, hands behind his back. The look on his face is one of triumph. "How foolish your escape attempt was…trying to get to Kedua before me, how laughable. I told you I knew who sold her. What I neglected to mention was that person sold her to me," he smirks, as he begins to move about the room, walking slowly, hands behind his back.

"Did you know who she was when you purchased her?"

"Of course I did. Remember, I inspect everything I buy or collect, so when I saw the two small markings on the back of her neck I knew exactly who she was."

"Did she know?"

"Yes. You see the person who sold her to me was her protector from the Dormitories. My men had collected her and Kedua in the Wasteland. She made a deal with me that if I didn't send her to the hatcheries or enslave her as a fighter I could keep Kedua. Of course I didn't believe the woman at first, until I inspected Kedua, saw the markings, and knew she was telling the truth."

"Where is this woman now?" I ask, moving away from the windows.

"You met her earlier. Poor Midge will probably never heal from the injuries you inflicted upon her frail body."

"Why kill the High Ruler?"

"I didn't kill anyone. Very few people outside of his guards have ever actually seen what the High Ruler of Acheron looks like. The person in that position is constantly being altered. It's easier for the people not to know who really is in power."

"Why?"

"Why take power? Why not? Being the leader of a city is very profitable."

"And the war that Vladim is about to start?"

"How naïve you are, Meg. There is no war coming. My Superior of Communication is very skilled at distorting the truth. Vladim only gave part of that speech; the rest of it was added by Hayden, my predecessor. Fear is what keeps the people in line, and how we make a profit. The Laics will need to work harder to provide for the increase of supplies that will be demanded by the citizens of Acheron."

"This, in turn, will generate more profit for you."

"Now you're catching on," he says, winking at me.

"What do you want me for?" I ask, as I fold my arms against my chest.

"You will help me obtain everything Sirain holds," he replies, as he walks up to me, pushing a loose strand of hair behind my ear. "Remember what I told you in Tyre? If I want something, nothing can stop me from getting it." He kisses me hard on the lips.

My hand flies across his face, striking him hard. He hits back, harder, splitting my lip.

"Don't you ever raise a hand to me again," he spits at me. "You enjoyed our moments together in Tyre. What happened to you, Meg?"

"Trea happened. She's not a fan of you."

"I can get her to like me," he sneers, letting go of me. "But before that, I need your assistance." He gestures over to the doorway where Kedua now stands, freshly bathed, and wearing a sheer pink gown.

Artemis removes a Levin gun from under his shirt. "It wasn't until your encounter with Munera that I realized the true potential the Antaeans have. What power you contain, what force you have when yielding the appropriate weapon. When I came back to Acheron, I had Kedua here try and mimic your ability, but she failed."

She rolls her eyes at his comment.

"I requested the test that had been performed on you back in Tyre to be done on Kedua. And that's when I saw it. The Quantum Stream needs a catalyst in order to become activated." Artemis takes my right hand, removes the glove, and rolls up my sleeve, revealing the snake on my arm.

"I saw the blast wound on your back, the entry wound in your palm. I knew it had been caused by a Levin gun, and reasoned that it was the catalyst the stream needs to become functioning." He places the Levin gun into Kedua's hand.

She aims it at me, but I notice all the safety devices are still enabled. Still, it's a Levin gun, and it's going to hurt.

She fires, striking me in the right shoulder. I scream as my shoulder blade fragments from the energy pulse, causing me to drop onto the floor. Blood gushes down my arm, staining the gold leafed carpet below my feet. I begin to heal, the pain slowly subsiding as I stand back up, anger flushing my face. Artemis examines Kedua's hand. The look of confusion on his face tells me he doesn't understand why it didn't work. Before he can question me, the building's alarms begin to ring.

Bodyguards rush inside moments later, and inform Artemis that there has been a breach in the outer rim security.

"How could this have happened?" Artemis demands.

"Midge found the body of Kedua's guard in the broom closet at the club. Someone has been masquerading as her Regulator. He's been spotted with several others who were involved in a disturbance earlier today. They've managed to retrieve their boat from the lock-up and are attempting to breach the perimeter."

I move back towards the window, my eyes glancing down to the water below to see where the security boats are currently located, noticing several are engaged in a fire-fight with another vessel. The long metal craft has managed to penetrate the security shield around the platform and has destroyed one of the patrol boats.

I smile inside, figuring it was Jagger who alerted the others about where I was.

I look over at Artemis and Kedua, then begin to move. He grabs the gun from Kedua, and fires at me, hitting me in the leg and torso. Even with the injuries, I manage to throw my entire weight against the fractured window. The glass breaks and I plummet the four stories into the icy water beneath.

The impact feels like it did when the shuttle exploded.

My head is aching as I sink deeper into the water's depths, but this time I feel arms around my shoulders, pulling me skyward. Jagger reaches his hands over the side of the boat as Quin jumps into the water to push me up. Cass and Naomi are firing propellant rounds at the security boats, aiming at the hulls in order to rupture them. As I collapse onto the boat's deck, Quin climbs aboard right behind me. Jagger heads below and guns the engines, moving us out of the perimeter, and into open water.

CHAPTER 17

"How do you feel?" Quin asks, as he lies on the deck next to me.

"Like a human target."

He looks over my almost-healed wounds.

"What went wrong?" he asks, as he sets my arm gently down by my side.

"Artemis was there," I squeeze out of my lungs, coughing up water. "After having the High Ruler assassinated, he caught me and forced me back to the palace, where he had Kedua shoot me with a Levin gun. But the safety devices were still on."

"Why did she shoot you?"

"To get this," I say, rolling up my sleeve and pointing to the serpent crawling up my arm. "He thought he'd figured it all out. You should've seen the look on their faces when it didn't work." I begin to laugh, trying to make light of the situation I'd found myself in, then cough up a little blood.

That's concerning. What long lasting internal injuries will I have? How much more punishment can my body take before it stops healing?

I sit up and watch as Acheron fades away behind us, the rain coming down in a steady pour. Their timing for the rescue was perfect, but....

"How did you know which building to be under? How did you get past the perimeter?"

"Jagger found us and told us what had happened. He described the building and its location, so we knew right where you were. We took out the timing switch to get past the blockade," Cass says, as he helps me to my feet. "The barrier won't operate without the timing switch."

I look to see if any vessels are chasing us, but I see none.

"Won't they follow us?"

"No, their boats are pretty damaged and they don't travel any further than one mile from the city."

We move below deck to get out of the rain.

Naomi hands me a blanket to wrap myself up in as Quin goes into the engine room to assist Jagger. I notice as I stand in the doorway of one of the cabins that several of the steel canisters are still on board. I walk over to one and open it, seeing cans of preserved fruit sitting inside. Naomi locates a can opener and we begin to eat. I look through the other containers as I slowly eat my peaches. Two hold more cans of food, a few sealed pouches of dried meat, crackers, and some nuts. The final container has four Beta guns, two Levin guns, a Pugio blade, and about a dozen detonators. This doesn't include the two Dorongan weapons that Cass and Naomi were using on the other boats.

I've never actually used a Dorongan, a weapon that shoots propellant rounds, though Devlan did keep a couple in his workshop.

The boat begins to decelerate as a chill cascades down the steps. Quin walks past me, heading up top. He shouts down to Jagger to go ahead and shut off the engines. I walk up the steps, still wrapped in my blanket, to see where we are.

Snow is falling gently from the cold gray sky above. Several inches cover the land we are now anchoring to. Dense forest blocks us from seeing past the shoreline. Naomi calls for me to come back down below as the engine goes silent. She hands me two satchels to fill with food. We empty the canisters of their contents while Quin and Jagger handle the weapons container, hoisting it onto their shoulders and walking up to the deck. Jagger jumps over the side of the boat and Quin lowers the canister to him. I grab as many blankets as I can before abandoning the boat.

The snow crunches under our feet as we walk along the shore, up a steep dune, and into the forest. Tree roots jut out from the frozen ground causing me to stumble a few times. We walk for about an hour, our hands and feet frozen. Cass finds a spot with little snow due to the thick canopy above. Naomi gathers firewood, while Jagger and Quin set up a makeshift shelter with the blankets. Naomi uses a short blast from the Beta gun to get a fire going once the wood is set for burning. We all sit as close to the fire as possible, freezing from the dropping temperature.

Jagger opens one of the sealed packages of dried meat then passes it around for all of us to take some.

The meat is soft and salty. Cass opens a bottle with some red wine inside and we all drink from it. I sit with my knees up to my chin, rocking slightly in the cold breeze. Quin sits down next to me, puts an arm around me, and pulls me close. As I stare at the flames, I remember the bar code in my wrist. I reach into my satchel, extract a small carving knife I'd grabbed from the bedchamber, make a small incision in my wrist, and pull out the coiled wire. Quin takes the blade from my hand and does the same.

Jagger is too restless to stay in one spot.

He advises us that he is going to go explore the woods to see if he can find us better shelter. I offer to go along, but he declines and we watch as he disappears into the brush. Cass and Naomi cling tightly to each other, trying to ward off the cold that is quickly enveloping us.

Jagger returns almost an hour later and motions for us to follow.

Naomi and I grab the satchels of food and take down the blankets while Cass and Quin carry the weapons container.

Several miles from where we stopped is a clearing with two long wooden structures, their roofs sagging from age. A circular stone building sits in the center with a cement house just a few feet away. Small lights attached outside each door on the wooden structures give off a soft glow no more than a few feet. Snow covers much of the ground, and continues to fall. I hear low mewing and clucking noises coming from the northern end of the encampment, so I follow them and come upon a fenced-in yard where several chickens are pecking away at the snow. I can make out another building in the distance where the mewing is emanating from.

"Hello," Cass calls out before we can stop him.

His voice doesn't travel far, muffled by the mounds of snow. We stand still, waiting for any sign of movement.

"There has to be someone living here," Jagger says. "The livestock appear well fed and the lights are still working."

"There are only a few of us left," a small voice says behind me. A small old woman carries a lantern making her way out of the animal paddock, a shawl clenched tightly under her chin, an empty pail at her side. "You all look frozen. Come on let's get you warmed up." She walks past me towards the stone building.

A fire is burning hot in the hearth in the center of the large single room. Crates sit stacked ceiling high against a far wall, barrels of grain next to them. A worn cot rests cozily next to the hearth. Cass and Jagger take down a few of the crates for us to sit on. The woman puts a kettle on a hook and swings it onto the fire, warming up the liquid inside. She fetches tin cups for each of us and pours the hot fluid into them. My hands warm instantly from the heat, but I take small sips so as not to burn my throat.

"What is this place?" Naomi asks, sipping from her cup.

"Siedler Village," the woman says, as she sits down on her cot, throwing the blanket over her lap.

Her face crinkles from a smile. Her long gray hair is matted in spots and it looks like she hasn't bathed in weeks, but her clothes appear to be nicely kept, no holes or tears.

"How many people live here?" Naomi asks.

"Well besides myself there is Henry, Magda, and Andrew. So only four, no more, no less," she says with a smile, displaying only a handful of teeth.

"There's a power plant a few miles south of here, right?" I ask, without thinking about it.

The woman looks startled at my remark, but she recovers quickly.

"Yes, there is. How do you know about it?"

"I remember...my mother working there when I was little."

The words are out before I grasp what I'm saying.

"That's not possible, dear. No children have ever lived in this village." The woman refills our cups and settles herself back down onto her cot.

Uneasiness settles around me. *The woman is lying, but why? And how do I know it?*

I set my cup down onto the bricks of the hearth, as no amount of heat from the tea is going to warm my insides.

"Would it be possible if we could stay the night?" Jagger asks, diverting everyone from the change in my demeanor.

"Of course, the people of Siedler are always very hospitable."

She picks up the lantern by her feet and walks us back outside, showing us to one of the small houses, insisting we can stay in there for the night. There are three bedrooms and plenty of heat as the furnace is working. We say our thank yous, closing the door behind us.

The living room is sparsely furnished, with only one badly moth eaten couch sitting on top of a braided rug in front of a dingy fireplace. The kitchen is separated by only a half wall. Down a small hall sits two bedrooms along the left side of the hallway, a small bathroom across the way, and another bedroom at the far end.

Jagger and Cass take the first bedroom, while Naomi takes the one next to it. Quin decides to sleep on the couch. I walk towards the far bedroom, listening as the floorboards creak under my feet. I close my eyes and remember the warm glow of the light radiating from the fixture above even though it isn't presently on

The hallway echoes, even though there's no one in the hall but me. I hear my mother talking to me, telling me it's all going to be all right. She says the man who is carrying me is a friend who's going to take me someplace to be safe. I open my eyes, the soft light vanishes, and I see a closed door in front of me. The doorknob turns easily in my hand and I let the door swing open of its own accord.

The purple flowered wallpaper is just how I left it.

Crude sketches hang waist-high along two of the walls. I bend down and recognize the images in the drawings from the nightmares

I had as a child. They match the ones on the tablet that Devlan left me all those months ago: a bright white campus of large buildings, some seemingly flowing into one another. Several other drawings show those same buildings on fire or in some stage of collapse - horrifying drawings, that shouldn't be made by a child.

I don't know what to feel.

My emotions are so mixed up that I can't tell what the right one is. Meg wants to sit in the corner and cry, while Trea wants to become violent. If only I could get these two merged somehow, with a common goal or feeling, something to rid myself of this constant turmoil rolling around my head.

I want to go back outside and confront the woman about the lie she told, and to ask her why she placed us into this specific house, especially considering there are at least a dozen others that are empty, but sleep draws me in. I pick up a discarded blanket from the floor. It too is familiar. It's the one that fell off after Devlan picked me up from my bed. No one has been in this room since that night.

More mysteries.

I shake the dust off of my pillow, wrap myself up in the blanket, which still smells of lilac, my mother's favorite flower, and promptly fall asleep after lying down on the familiar lumpy mattress.

Breakfast is waiting for me when I arise.

Cass is busy cooking while Naomi is cleaning cobwebs from the table and chairs. I go into the bathroom to wash my face and run wet fingers through my hair, noticing that I've seemingly aged ten years in only a few days. I join the others and thoroughly enjoy the hot meal. Naomi takes it upon herself to clean the entire house, while Jagger and Quin work on fixing the wiring in some of the fixtures. Cass has met Henry and the two of them have gone off to the small farm and garden that sits in the far north corner of the village, to tend to the animals.

I go off on my own, knocking on the door to the stone building, waiting for the woman inside to answer.

"She's not there," a soft wispy voice says behind me. "She's gone off to collect fire wood."

The woman standing behind me has aged gracefully since the last time I saw her. Tears fill my eyes, then slowly run down my cheeks.

"Hello, Meg," she says to me, hugging me tightly.

I soak her shoulder with tears of joy.

"How did you know?"

She holds my face in the palm of her hands, wiping away my tears with the tips of her fingers.

"Hannah told me. She woke me up in the middle of the night and said some strangers had stumbled into the village. She recognized you immediately, even with your odd hair."

I smile as she tousles a few strands at the back of my neck.

"I was wondering if you'd ever find your way back here." She takes my hand and walks me into the stone building. We both sit down on Hannah's cot next to the fire. "Where's Devlan? Is he with you?"

"No," I answer, as my voice chokes back a lump.

She puts her arm around my shoulder to comfort me.

"He was a good man," she says.

"Where are the others?" I ask, turning my face to look into hers.

Pain seeps into the corners of her mouth as she squeezes my hand tightly.

"Devlan was right," she begins. "They did find out about you." She lets go of my hand and stares into the fire. "It was only a few days after Devlan came and took you away that they showed up."

"Who are *they*?"

"Soldiers from Nuceira. They're called the Morrigan. Somehow they learned that children had survived the devastation at the Dormitories, and went looking for them. How they found out, I don't know." She shudders at the memory, but continues to talk. "They came in the middle of the night, dressed in black armor of some kind. We could hear the engines of their vehicles off in the distance, but only after they came into the village did we know what they were looking for. They pulled everyone out of bed and held us in front of this building while they collected the children. The Morrigan took a small blade and pierced every child on the back of the hand, looking for the one that would self-heal. Some of the children became ill from the injury and died months later. It was rumored that the blade had been impregnated with some kind of poison, so that when they did find the right child, that child would self-heal, leaving the poison inside their system causing them pain and eventually death." Tears begin to stream down her face.

It's my turn to put my arm around her shoulder to comfort her.

I remember a comment she made when I was younger that she had wished I was her real child. I know I'm not her child, I don't know whose child I am, but I call her my mother all the same.

The thought of losing the other children, causes anger to rise. I feel heat growing from my arm from the thought of innocent lives taken because of me, but I conceal it behind my mother's back.

We sit in silence, not knowing what to say next. Hannah walks in with Quin behind her. I hear him explain to her that he's in need of some tools since they've decided to fix everyone's homes. She says the only tools are down at the power plant, which is an hour's long hike.

"Is it guarded?" he asks, as he continues to follow her around the room, while she fills small bowls with grain from the barrels.

"Not since Acheron abandoned it when they became self-sustaining with that energy core of theirs." She hands the bowls to Quin, picks up others, and begins to fill them as well.

"How does it stay functioning?"

She looks at him with a funny expression. "Where do you think we get our electricity from, young man? Why do you think we keep the tools down there?" She loads his arms with more bowls and then promptly exits the building, Quin following closely behind.

I smile at the exchange but stop when my mother's face falls, and a concerned expression appears. She waits until Quin and Hannah are out of earshot then turns to me.

"How well do you know the people you're traveling with?"

I feel my nerves beginning to fray.

"What do you mean?"

"Quintus is with you," she says, more as a statement than a question.

"We met in the Wasteland. Why, Mother, what's got you so frightened?"

"Quintus never came out of the Dormitories with us. Thatcher went back for him, but the housing unit he'd been living in was obliterated, so he couldn't get to him. As far as we know, the only children who made it out were Kedua, Lehen, Vier, and you. If someone helped him escape, who was it? Or even how, or why?" She takes my hands, grasping them tightly. "Promise me you'll be careful?"

"Of course I will."

I stay sitting on the cot as my mother gets up to help Hannah who has returned with an arm full of eggs. I think about what my next move should be and shudder at what I come up with.

I think I may need to get rid of Quin.

More questions come up from what my mother has said.

If only four are accounted for in the escape, and Quintus was not one of them, then where are the other two? Where has Quintus been if they didn't save him? Who has he been with? Did Devlan ever recognize Quin?

I pull my feet up to my chest, hugging them. My instinct is to run, but there's nowhere to go. I don't want to leave my mother. It's been over twelve years since I saw her. She and Devlan are the only family I really every had. Magda calls to me to assist her and Hannah with the chores. I nod my head, more to clear it than acknowledge her request.

The remainder of my day is spent working around the village. Jagger and Quin spend the day down at the power plant, doing maintenance, and picking up tools and any other items they may need to fix up the houses. I spend my time in the stone building, which is the dispensary, with Hannah and my mother. We bake bread, tell stories, and get a large feast ready for the evening.

I'm happy to be here, but at the same time, my fears about Quin and my questions about what I must do next are eating away at me. I don't feel like celebrating anyway.

Snow continues to fall over the next several days. Jagger and Quin have moved into the house next to my old home that I now live in with my mother, while Naomi and Cass stay in a house across the way. They seem quite happy here and have made it known they're intent on staying when the rest of us are ready to continue on.

I'm restless, and can't sleep the fifth night.

What my mother told me about Quin has left a sour taste in my mouth. I wish it were warm outside so I could go running and burn off some of this tension. Donning a used wool coat Henry found for me, and putting my boots on, I wrap myself up tight and exit the warmth of the dwelling. I go over to the barn to check on the animals. Several are snuggled in their beds of hay, so I go and sit next to a calf that is only a few hours old. Its mother died during labor, so Andrew has placed it in the icehouse for food. I stroke the head while the calf sleeps, and she sighs softly with each caress. From where I'm sitting in the barn I can see the entrances to all the houses.

The cold starts to seep into my bones after sitting for almost an hour. I'm nuzzling myself closer to the calf when Quin steps out onto the small wood porch, furtively heading toward the path to the power plant. He doesn't appear to be carrying any kind of torch to light his way through the dark, which strikes me as odd.

I pat the animal's head, get up, and begin to follow him making sure the Levin gun I keep tucked in the small of my back has not slipped out of place. I don't go anywhere without it now. Since the ground is covered in fresh powder, I try to walk in Quin's footsteps so not to leave any trace of my own. His stride is much wider than mine, which makes it more difficult.

My feet and hands are getting colder the longer I stay outside, but I keep pressing on.

An hour seems to pass before we reach our destination. I walk past several trees with bits of razor wire poking out from under a few layers of bark, then notice a clearing up ahead beyond another grid of fencing. The area is dark, with no lights around the perimeter of the plant. I can hear waves crashing, so we must be close to the shoreline. I stop short of the clearing and listen to my surroundings.

I hear the hum of electricity from the power plant, but there is an underlying growl somewhere further south of me, so I step off the path and walk a little deeper into the woods staying along the fence line now impregnated with the tree trunks and branches. The further south I move the louder the growling noise becomes. A broken road appears on the other side of the fence with two large black vehicles parked on top. I listen as the distinct sounds of closing doors echo in the darkness, and move silently closer, until I see them and can hear their voices.

"Hello, Rabaan," Quin says firmly.

"Quintus," the man says and gives Quin a hug. "Glad to see you're all right. Hope Trea hasn't been too difficult to catch."

"No, at least not after her escape from Tyre," he responds with a laugh. "She's back up in the village."

"Good, it will make the capture easier."

I see a grin form on Rabaan's face.

"What about the other one?" he asks.

"Kedua is heavily protected in Acheron. We will need to draw her out of the city if you are to seize her."

"That will prove challenging, but not impossible."

I tilt my head slightly to see what Rabaan looks like, but his face is hidden in the darkness. The man next to Rabaan is a little shorter.

But I have seen their clothes before. They are wearing the same uniform as the men that raided my home in the Wasteland.

So they were Morrigan.

"Is Lehen still not talking?" Quin asks, crossing his arms.

"No, he's being awfully stubborn. He takes torture well, but of course he heals from it. I want to burn him, but Parson Mathan wants to keep him alive until we have all the remaining Antaeans so we can destroy them all together…with the exception of you of course."

"Of course," Quin says. "So when will you come to the village?"

"Tomorrow night. It will give us time to surround the area and take her by surprise."

I begin to slink backwards away from the area, having heard enough of the conversation.

I'm sickened by the betrayal.

Tears cascade down my cheeks, but freeze to my skin. My stomach tightens up as the full impact of what I just witnessed dawns on me. My feet stop moving as I'm momentarily paralyzed with fear. I try to pull Trea up from her hiding spot, willing her to surface, but she doesn't react to fear, only anger.

How could he do this to me? How long have they been tracking us? What is Quin really?

I hasten back to the village, but make sure not to take the path back. Instead I hug the tree line next to it. As soon as I'm back, I go into my house, pack some of my items into a satchel, and kiss my mother gently on the forehead, trying not to rouse her.

I don't leave her a note as I don't want Quin to know what I'm up to. I'm not proud of myself for running out on her, but I need to protect her like she protected me, and this is the only way I know how.

Hearing his footsteps on the planks outside, I wait to hear his door open and then close.

I exit my house and stand outside his front door, making sure he's gone to his room, then wait a few more minutes before letting myself in. The house is identical to mine, all the homes are, so I turn right and walk down the small dark hallway. I open the door to the room on the left, tip toe in, walk over to Jagger's sleeping body, and place my hand gently over his mouth before nudging him. He startles slightly, but relaxes when he realizes it's me.

"Meg, what time is it?" he asks, through a deep yawn.

"Almost two," I whisper, as I take a step back from his bed.

He swings his legs over the edge, but doesn't stand.

"I need your help. You need to show me how to operate the boat."

"What?" he asks, again through another deep yawn, rubbing the sleep from his eyes.

"You need to get dressed and go with me back to the lake to show me how to operate the boat."

"You want me to show you now? Can't it wait until morning?"

"No, it can't," I whisper in a hoarse voice.

Jagger looks up at me with a concerned look on his face.

"Please?"

He grabs his clothes that are hanging over the back of the chair next to his bed, puts on his boots, and grabs a Dorongan, slipping it over his shoulders.

He doesn't ask me any more questions as we step out into the cold and head back to the lake.

Why is he so trusting?

CHAPTER 18

The boat is exactly where we left it, although now it's buried in snow.

Jagger climbs aboard to get the engines warmed up while I clean off the deck. The engine is cold, so it turns over several times before it will fire up properly. I go below deck and into the engine room where he is checking the monitors to make sure the boat has enough power for long-distance travel.

He shows me the control buttons and the small steering wheel, but says all I have to do is punch in my coordinates and the boat can guide itself. I thank him with a hug before he climbs the ladder, then I check the previous logs to get the exact coordinates for Acheron. After I feel him cast off the moorings and push the boat into the water, I enter in my destination.

The boat backs up slowly and begins to turn itself around just as I hear footsteps coming down the ladder. I poke my head out into the gangway and see Jagger standing on the bottom rung.

"Where you go, I go," he says.

I try to protest, but he won't hear any of it.

"I trust you, Meg, and I'm not letting you go by yourself."

"You could get killed," I warn him.

"So be it...I'm protecting you no matter what it takes. Thomas spoke about your kind when I was younger. He told me the Antaeans are our only hope for freeing us from the High Rulers, so I made a promise to myself that if I ever had the luck of meeting one of you, I would do everything I can to protect you. I trust you have a valid reason to go back to Acheron, so I'm going with you."

I decide not to pursue the argument any further.

We stay in the engine room, slowly making our way through the cold choppy waters.

"They'll try to destroy us once we are within a mile of them," Jagger finally says, after a long respite.

"I know. That's why I'm going to go on deck and signal our surrender."

I wait for him to balk, but he just nods his head in agreement.

I climb the ladder, hugging my wool coat as the wind lashes at my skin. The silhouette of the city can be seen through the haze that has settled over the lake. I hear motors revving just ahead of us, approaching fast.

"Turn away or prepare to be fired upon," a voice booms through the ether.

"My name is Trea, and I have come to see the High Ruler," I shout into the air around me.

I hear more boats approaching, some beginning to slow. Our boat jerks as it hits metal. A man in a guard uniform climbs aboard, making sure I am who I claim to be. He calls over to his crew to tow us in and radio the High Ruler as we begin to pick up speed. Jagger reaches the deck and stands with me as we approach the same platform I escaped off of just a few days ago.

Our boat is secured to the moorings along the east wall of the platform. Two Regulators search us and remove our weapons. Jagger is placed into binders, but they don't bother with me since they know I can easily break them.

We walk through a back entry to the High Ruler's palace and head down to the floor below. The air is moist and cold; mold covers much of the walls. Jagger is secured to a notch in the cement blocks while I'm left standing between two Regulators and two palace guards.

Artemis saunters over, grinning ear to ear.

"I see you just couldn't stay away," he says, as he motions for the men to step back. "If only all women felt this compelled to return to me as often as you do, I would never be lonely. Then again, you did make a fool of me."

He punches me hard in the face.

"You son of a bitch, don't you fucking touch her like that again. I'll kill you if you do that again." Jagger screams, pulling hard on the chains.

"Stepping out on me, Trea?" Artemis smirks, sizing Jagger up. "My, my, you have been a busy girl."

"Artemis, please, you need to listen to me."

"Why should I? You've caused me nothing but grief. Killing you would be counterproductive, so perhaps a more fitting punishment would be to punish your friend here instead. Watch as he is slowly ripped apart."

"No," I shout, realizing the sincerity in his threat. "I have a proposition for you."

"I don't take proposals, especially from someone who has caused me so much frustration." He begins to walk back towards the doorway, gesturing to the guards. "Kill him slowly, make sure she watches, then bring her upstairs."

Two of the guards force me down onto my knees, holding my head up by my throat as the Regulators approach Jagger, knives drawn. He screams as the first wound is inflicted on his exposed arms. Blood runs down onto the floor as they begin slicing away.

Anger triggers my actions. Trea finally emerges.

Snapping my head back, I roll over, twisting out of the guards' hands. I grab the guard on my right, plant my foot into his lower back, and shove him across the room, taking out two more guards. The other guard is on me the moment I attack the Regulators. I try and fight him off as others approach, but there are too many now as more come down the steps, past Artemis, and into the room. I can't fight them all, but I have to help Jagger somehow.

"I'll make a deal with you!" I shout to be heard over the ruckus.

Artemis turns around, snaps his fingers, which causes everyone to stop moving.

"And what, my dear Trea, could you possibly have to make a deal with?

"You let Jagger live and I'll tell you where you can find another Antaean."

His face takes on a serious tone as he narrows his eyes, trying to determine if I'm lying. He walks over to me as I hang between the arms of two guards.

"Where is he?"

"Ha. You think I'm going to tell you now? You let Jagger go free and then we'll talk."

Artemis hesitates in responding, a single finger bouncing off of his lips as he ponders the exchange.

"Nope, forget it, keep going. Make sure you spill all his blood."

"No, Artemis, please. I'm begging you, I'll do anything, just leave Jagger alone."

"Now that's more like it. Begging looks good on you, Meg." He walks over to me, kisses me on the cheek. "Take Jagger here back to the Boroughs. We'll find some use for him."

I twist myself free from of the guards' grips, remove one of their blades from a holster inside one of their coats, knock Artemis to the ground and nestle the sharp edge against his pale-skinned neck. "No, Artemis, that's not the deal. The deal is Jagger goes free and I tell you where to find an Antaean. If you don't accept, I will open your neck from ear to ear."

"Neither you nor Jagger will make it out of this room alive," he whispers.

"You'll go first."

I take the tip of the knife and begin to slowly cut him under his right ear. He screams, swearing for me to stop.

"All right," he shouts, "but you have to do everything I ask, no matter what."

"Fine," I consent, as I step off of him, placing the blade in my belt for safekeeping.

He signals the guards to release Jagger while a Regulator helps Artemis to his feet and places pressure on his wound to stem the bleeding. Jagger's wounds are hastily cleaned and stitched before we walk back up to the surface. Sweat pours from my body. The guards begin to escort Jagger around to the front of the palace, but he stops.

"If it's all the same to you," he says to me, "I'd prefer to stay."

"Why?" I ask, wondering why he's giving up the freedom I've gained him.

"To protect you, Meg. Like I said before, I made a promise. "

I feel for the first time in months that I have a true ally.

Artemis rolls his eyes, turns to his lead guard, and tells him to escort Jagger to their quarters to get properly mended and fitted for a uniform. The Regulators return to their post out on the jetty while Artemis takes me inside the palace and up to the top floor where I'm shown to a suite next to Kedua's. Once the door is closed and I'm alone, I walk into the marble-covered bathroom, turn on the hot water in the enormous bathtub, strip down and slide into the warm embrace. I lay there, eyes closed, trying to drown my mind of all that has previously happened, and focus on a plan I need to put together fast.

If Artemis is thinking I'll do whatever he asks, he's sorely mistaken.

My intention is to use Artemis to free Lehen, but it's after the rescue that I need to plan for.

I stay in the water much too long and it becomes cold, so I drain the tub then refill it again so I can properly wash up.

I'm so covered in filth and my hair is so exceptionally tangled that it takes five washings to rinse clean, only then do I begin to feel human again, skin freshly cleansed, and pink from stringent scrubbing. I wrap myself up into a thick towel before stepping onto the cool blue floor where I search the cabinets under the dual vanity for nail clippers and a comb. Suitably groomed, I finally exit the bathroom and find an identical outfit to the one I'd worn in Tyre when I fought the droid, lying on the gray comforter of my bed. I place it on the dresser, don a plush blue robe, and crawl under the inviting covers, falling deeply asleep.

I don't stir until I hear a knock at my door. The room is dark, so as the door opens I'm slightly blinded by the intense light from the hallway. Jagger pokes his head in, blue and gold uniform fastened tightly to his fit body. He tells me he wants to make sure I'm all right and that he'll be standing outside my door all night. Then he quietly closes it and I go back to sleep.

There are no nightmares this night, just sound restful sleep.

I feel like I haven't been able to properly maintain the training that Devlan had me doing, and I know I'll need it, so it's just as well I'm supposed to start training Kedua. It's one of Artemis' demands in exchange for saving Jagger, and as it happens it also fits into my plans, so I agree.

Artemis places Kedua and I in the Regulator's housing complex on the northern platform. The top three floors are dedicated to weight training, an indoor climbing wall, a five-lane track, and a substantially large swimming pool. Kedua isn't too thrilled about being removed from her luxurious suite, but Artemis wants to make sure she has the same abilities as I do.

I spend the next week working on her strength and endurance. She fights me every step of the way, so I eventually stop telling her what to do and just concentrate on getting myself into shape, spending about eight hours a day between the track and the climbing wall.

Jagger is in charge of my protection, so he makes it a point to train with me. I out-pace him at every turn, but he never gives up. He's well-trained and very fit, for a Laic. We spend many nights staying up late talking. I hesitate to discuss anything I've been through with him at first, but after a while I do let him in on some of my fears.

"Why don't you like being called Trea?" he asks, as we sit in my room watching some endless propaganda video on the large monitor over my dresser.

The video continually states that the war with Tyre is approaching and everyone must be prepared, however from what I have seen and heard, Tyre has made no move to invade Acheron. We keep the monitor on since it also provides some white noise in case anyone is trying to listen in on us.

"I don't like losing control," I say. "Trea is unpredictable and I can understand why Devlan did whatever it was to keep her quiet all these years. She's dangerous. And I don't want Meg to be lost, possibly forever."

He doesn't press the topic even though I can sense he wants to ask more questions.

The second week begins with me showing Kedua how the Quantum Stream works while Artemis is finalizing our plans with his Royal Guards to enter Nuceira.

First, I demonstrate using a Pugio blade. Her eyes light up upon seeing the energy stream wrap itself around the metal of the blade, almost causing it to sing. I take the blade and spar with Jagger, showing her how to properly hold the weapon, wielding it in a slow rhythmic dance. After several hours of practice, Kedua picks up one of the Levin guns lying on the table by the windows.

"Show me how to use this," she says to me, placing the gun in my hands.

"I would prefer you to have more experience with the other weapons before we move onto this one."

"You're kidding, right? I already know how to shoot the damn thing. The only thing I need from you is your power," she says, as she gestures to the blue line meandering up and down my arm, all the while her tone threatening.

"You're not ready for it," I grumble back at her, placing the gun back and walking away.

"*Meg!*" Jagger screams from behind me.

I turn around in time to see the Pugio blade coming at me, so I'm forced to dive to the floor, rolling away from Kedua as she tries to plunge the weapon into my chest. Jagger picks up the Levin gun I'd been holding and aims it Kedua, but he doesn't get a chance to fire as several guards grab him, shoving him down on his knees. They restrain him, forcing him to watch Kedua try to kill me.

"You don't want to do this," I tell her, as I try and make my way back around to the weapons table.

"Come on, Trea, I know you're in there," Kedua taunts me.

It sounds like she's been eavesdropping on my conversations. The annoying thing is, it works.

My mind begins to distort the images around me.

I feel heat growing inside, pulsating through my veins. My right arm burns red hot, searching for a weapon to manipulate. A smile grows on Kedua's face as she sees Trea escaping from her lair. I fight myself to keep her hidden, but I'm losing control every second. Kedua jabs at me, grazing my thigh.

I reach the table, grabbing a hold of whatever enters my grasp first. Looking down at my fingers, I notice I'm gripping a simple Beta gun, but I don't have time to choose an alternate weapon as Kedua comes at me again. I fire the gun, hitting her in the arm and shoulder. She drops the blade to cover her wounds with her working arm. I walk over, pick up the blade as the heat grows; bright blue beams intertwine around the weapon, wrapping tightly around the metal causing it to glow intensely.

"You want this power," I hiss at Kedua who is now crouching on the floor, "you can have it."

I thrust the blade deep into her left arm, almost severing it. She screams in pain…a noise I'm very familiar with. I pull the blade out, drop it to the ground, and walk away, as the guards drop Jagger and immediately rush to tend to Kedua's multiple gashes. I go back to my room and stay there for the remainder of the day.

The only person who comes to check on me is Jagger as he carries a dinner tray filled with pasta noodles covered in a thick red sauce. He sets the tray down on the small end table by my bed before he pulls the black plastic chair he normally sits on over to the bed where I currently lay.

"Artemis is restricting you to your room for the time being," he says quietly, hands folded together as he leans forward.

I don't say anything. I only remain laying there, staring up into the blue painted ceiling.

"Kedua won't be released from the hospital for a couple of days. They had to amputate her arm just below the elbow and are fitting her with an artificial one." He pauses, waiting for me to respond, but I don't. "She didn't heal quickly from her injuries...not as fast as you do."

This surprises me for a moment, but the more I think about it, the more I understand our differences. Devlan injected me with Quarum after my injury from the Levin gun. Quin did the same after he was severely hurt, so he heals faster as well. But there isn't any Quarum left. The formula for it would have been destroyed in the Dormitories, and only Devlan had some left over, so unless Artemis finds a way to synthesize it, Kedua will never heal as quickly as Quin and me.

I wait for Jagger to leave before I get up to eat my food, but he stays. I look over at him, his face drawn down.

"What's wrong?"

"Meg," he stammers, "I need to tell you something."

I continue to look at him, but he doesn't raise his eyes to meet mine. I'm not sure I'm going to like what he has to say.

"One night when Quin and I were down at the power plant, I did something." He wipes his brow with the back of his hand as he begins to perspire. "While we were looking for some parts to repair the electrical outlets, I came across a couple of lead wires with nodules at the ends. Quin asked me to do it, and I didn't see the harm in it at the time."

"Do what?" I ask, sitting up.

"I connected them to the Quantum Stream in his back, then laced them just under the skin of both biceps and down to the tips of his fingers where I created tiny ports. All he has to do is touch anything now and he can transmit the energy." He lifts his eyes, guilt etched on his face. "I didn't see the harm in it at the time," he repeats.

I'm too shocked to speak.

"Say something."

I continue to stare at him, anger building inside. *How could Jagger have been so foolish? What was he thinking? Quin now has an ability I don't.*

"Please," he begs, "say something…anything."

I simply fold my arms and turn my attention to the monitor as a new propaganda video starts.

Jagger gets the hint, stands up, and leaves back hunched over, head down.

I've lost my appetite, so I place the tray on the floor outside my door.

I lock my door, crawl under the sheets, and try to sleep even though it's early in the evening, but I wind up tossing and turning for hours, my body aching. I give up and sneak out to the training room where I spend the entire night working my frustrations out on the track. When I tire of running, I find a couple of sparring dummies in one of the weapons closets, drag them out, placing them at equal distances apart, pick up the Pugio blade that still has spots of Kedua's blood on it, and use it to slice up the dummies, all the while picturing Artemis as one and Quin as the other.

CHAPTER 19

The plans for getting into Nuceira have been made without me.

Even Jagger is left out of the preparations, so I've no way of knowing exactly what Artemis has in mind. I sit by my door daily, hoping to hear anything about the trip since I'm not allowed to leave, and the housing complex has been jammed with people for the last several days. I'm finally lucky today as I overhear someone walking past advise the guard outside my door that they're leaving for Nuceira early in the morning. I crack open my door to get a better listen, pressing my face against the small opening.

"Braxton has ordered twenty guards to begin preparations for leaving from the south platform before first light. He wants you to stay here and make sure *she* doesn't leave." The man points to my door. "He doesn't want her to move from that room until we get back, understood?"

"Yes, sir," the guard says, standing a little straighter.

The man walks away just as Jagger approaches with my lunch tray. I quietly close the door and go sit down on my bed. A few moments later my door opens, Jagger walking inside. The guard closes the door. Jagger places the tray on the dresser instead of handing it to me. He lifts the silver cover from the plate and hands me what is hiding under it - a Levin gun.

"I'll bring you a change of clothes at dinner time," he says, as I stare at the gun. "We'll leave through the service doors at the bottom of the rear stairs. I'll have a transport car waiting to take us to the southern platform."

"How long have you known?"

"Since last week when I overheard Braxton telling his second in command that you and Kedua are to be kept here while Artemis monitors the incursion from the Overseer's office in the city. I figured your main goal has been to get to Lehen using Artemis, so let's use him."

I smile as he leaves the room. Jagger's made some mistakes, but all in all he's a valuable ally.

Dinnertime rolls around a few hours later, but no Jagger.

I begin to pace the room wondering what might have happened as the hours tick by slowly. I eventually tire and resign myself to go to bed as it appears he's not coming.

At some point later on, my door bangs open, startling me out of a fitful sleep. Artemis's head guard, Braxton, marches into my room, the light from the hallway cascading onto his grimaced face.

"Here," he says, as he throws articles of clothing at me, "put these on and be downstairs in five minutes." He goes back out the door, slamming it loudly as he leaves.

I turn on the light by the side of my bed and look at the items that have been given to me: black form-fitting pants, a long sleeve shirt, and a belt with a holster for the Levin gun. The material is thin, which will allow the Quantum Stream on my arm to be visible even through the dark color. I get up and dig around the dresser drawers, looking for a thicker top to wear underneath, which I eventually find, slipping it on. Before I don the pants, I strap the knife onto my inner thigh with a brown leather sheath, grab the pair of boots that I've been wearing, and make my way downstairs. As I reach the bottom step, I spot Jagger talking to Braxton. They are both wearing a similar outfit to mine, but are carrying more weapons.

"Your friend here is very persuasive," Braxton says to me, as I join them.

"What Artemis doesn't know won't hurt him," Jagger says authoritatively.

The three of us, along with two other guards, pile into a small transport car. I become cold quickly as the weather is freezing and the material of the clothing is not retaining heat. We move about the platform then onto the city proper. I watch as tall metal skyscrapers go whizzing by. We wander through the city and exit onto the southern platform where a lone shuttle rail juts out of the station.

The transport car slows down as we approach the interior of the structure, then stops alongside the shuttle that currently sits idling. As I exit the vehicle I see more than two dozen guards and Regulators step onboard. We join them in the lounge section towards the front, leaving the station moments after our arrival.

It'll take us a full day to reach Nuceira. Our shuttle changes tracks once we reach the station just outside the Boroughs. The windows of the shuttle change from the hard landscape of the Boroughs to a lush evergreen forest as we begin our journey south. We eat a small meal after four hours into our trip.

"How'd you get Braxton to agree to this?" I ask Jagger, as we sit next to each other munching on our sandwiches.

"I'll tell you later when there aren't so many people around," he replies.

After eating, I get up to go wander down the shuttle, Jagger right behind me. The first two compartments we enter are sleeping quarters, ten rooms total between the two cars. I try the door at the end of the second car, but it won't open. I know this should lead down to the cargo hold, so I'm not quite sure why it's locked. I place my ear against the door, but don't hear anything from the other side.

Jagger and I go back to the lounge where we stare out the windows at the imaginary landscape as it passes us by. As night approaches, I go to one of the bedrooms to sleep; Jagger takes the room next to mine. I get very little sleep, but stay under the soft blankets anyway.

The shuttle begins to slow as the evening grows darker. The windows turn off and I can see real stars in the sky. The environment outside is dense forest, and no man-made structures are currently visible. We slow down even more, passing under a metal awning with the letters *N.S. 7* painted faintly along the outer rim. The only light being cast onto the platform that glides next to us is emanating from the shuttle's interior fixtures. We finally come to a stop; a hissing noise breaks the silence.

I exit my room and walk back to the lounge, but no one is there. Heading back down the corridor, I run into Jagger exiting his compartment. We walk towards the back of the shuttle and notice the door we couldn't get open earlier yawning wide. Voices radiate off the metal interior, growing louder the closer we get. I pass through the opening and into a control room. Large plasma screens hang down from the ceiling along the sides and far back wall. Control panels line the wall to my left.

"Do you have the satellite in position yet?" Braxton asks, as he notices me standing in the doorway.

I walk over to a long glass table in the center of the room where many of the guards and Regulators are standing.

"It's almost in position," the man operating the controls answers.

Jagger comes up behind me as I nudge my way to the front, wanting to know what they are all looking at. The table is an enormous display screen, showing a view of what appears to be the forest outside, but from miles above.

"Go two degrees north," Braxton says, as the motion of the satellite begins to slow. A thin outline begins to appear at the top of the screen, sliding south until it encompasses the entire monitor. "Stop!" Braxton shouts when he has the image in place. From the satellite's current vantage point, the outline of a large cross is visible among the thin trees.

I notice that the trees there are quite different than the ones outside.

"Magnify twenty percent." This makes the outline thicker and more defined.

Braxton pushes a button, and the image rises from the table into the air. He presses more buttons and the foliage surrounding the city disappears. A clear picture of Nuceira's boundaries becomes visible.

The city is surrounded by a twenty-foot-high wall made of limestone, topped with razor wire. A scan is conducted from the satellite, which bounces back an overlay of electrical markers hidden inside the wall every two feet. The picture rotates ninety degrees, laying the city on its side. I hear Braxton talking about their strategy to penetrate the city, but I continue to stare at the image.

There appears to be five miles of forest between the exterior walls, which are also in the cross configuration, and the city itself. In the center is a circular building with a domed roof. On the left arm of the cross there look to be farmland and gardens, on the right arm, wooden structures with smoke stacks, most likely housing. To the south there's a thin building with a metal roof. A large two-story structure stands farther down, almost at the bottom of the layout.

"Everyone understand what needs to be done?" I hear Braxton say, as I focus back on what is happening around me.

We leave the control room and walk back up the corridor to the shuttle's entrance in the lounge.

Braxton and his second in command open the door, warm sticky air filtering in from outside. One of the Regulators adjusts the thermostat inside the shuttle, changing the air inside from hot to cool. As the atmosphere changes, condensation begins to build on the outside of the windows. I follow as they step out onto the metal platform that extends the length of the shuttle. There are railings along the farthest edges with a single staircase as the only exit. There's no structure encasing the station, only the trees and sky for cover. The light from the shuttle doesn't travel any further than the top two steps of the staircase.

Braxton takes my arm and escorts me back inside. He tells me to sit down on one of the couches in the lounge as he removes the Levin gun from my waist.

"You won't need this because you are staying here. Jagger will stay with you while the rest of us make our way to Nuceira."

"Why am I being kept behind?"

"Because, Meg, you'll be recognized," Jagger says as he takes a seat next to me, pain etched on his face. "Braxton spoke to me about the plan while you were sleeping."

I begin to protest, but Jagger takes my hand in his, squeezing it gently.

"If Quin is there, he'll give you away."

"I don't care. I didn't come all this way just to be kept out of it."

"Enough," Braxton says to me. "I was foolish enough to let you on board in the first place, but this is as far as you're going."

Moments later, Jagger and I are locked in, stranded in the darkness.

We watch as the troops descend the stairs and disappear into oblivion.

The sun has risen, set, and risen again.

I'm going stir crazy being locked inside this tin can, and Jagger isn't faring much better. We've spent our time rummaging through every bit of the shuttle, looking for something that will open the doors and let us out. I have tested several of the windows with a few of the end tables, but they're shatterproof. The power is still on, but this shuttle is different than the other one. This must be the High Ruler's private carriage, so the normal handles or keypads to allow access to the driver's compartment are missing. We've gone back into the control room several times, but can't get the satellite to operate so we don't even know if they were able to successfully get into Nuceira or not.

Sitting down on a lounge, I hang my head back in frustration. Jagger sits down opposite me.

"How did you convince Braxton?"

"Huh?" Jagger responds, not hearing me initially.

"What did you say to convince Braxton to let me come along?"

His face turns sorrowful. "About a week ago, I overheard one of the High Ruler's guards sending a communication to someone in Tyre. He was providing the man with tactical information on how to breach the security around Acheron. I told Braxton this, but of course he didn't believe me. Then a few days ago, Braxton located a transmission that was sent from the High Ruler's office to the High Ruler of Tyre. He thought it suspicious and confronted the High Ruler about it. Artemis laughed at him. Apparently he said 'can't a son talk to his father'."

"Wait, what? Vladim is Artemis' father?" I ask interrupting him.

"It appears that way. It also sounds like they're planning an invasion. Braxton pulled me aside to admit he was wrong. I talked about the need to protect you from the High Rulers if there was to be an attack and the only sure way to do it was to bring you along to Nuceira."

"He's protecting me? But why?"

"He's fed up with Artemis, and Acheron. He wants change, and we all know you're the one who can bring that change." He stands and heads down the corridor, away from me.

I feel a great weight being placed upon my shoulders that I don't think I can carry.

A storm kicks up outside, heavy rain, lightning. Winds pummel the exterior of the shuttle, but we don't hear anything inside, nor does the vehicle sway in any way. Lightning strikes close by, causing the power in the shuttle to flicker then go out. I look out the window to watch the storm as it grows fiercer.

I catch movement off to my right, just along the tree line about fifty yards from the platform, but can't see if it's anything important as the wind is thrashing the trees about. Another bright flash erupts, allowing the image to remain in focus longer.

Quin.

"Jagger," I shout.

"What?" he inquires, as I hear him race towards me.

"Quin's outside," I say, pointing to where I last saw him.

"Braxton underestimated him." Jagger walks over to a cabinet behind the sofa on the right and extracts two Levin guns.

"Why didn't you tell me about these earlier?" I demand, as he hands me one.

"These won't work against the windows or the door...I already tried it."

Lightning flashes again, briefly showing Quin's outline still lurking in the shadows.

I lower myself so that only the top of my head and eyes are exposed. The storm grows again, rain falling heavier still. As the sky lights up, I watch Quin slowly make his way towards the platform. Jagger pokes my shoulder then points to an area on our left.

Four Morrigan in full armor gear, including masks, are approaching from the opposite side. They're moving faster than Quin so I estimate they'll be at the shuttle in a matter of minutes.

"Go hide," I tell Jagger, pushing him away from me.

"No, I need to protect you."

"I know, but right now I need to protect *you*."

He stares into my eyes, sorrow and pain filling his. I imagine the truth is uncomfortable for a warrior such as Jagger, but I don't have time to sugar-coat this.

"You'll be no match against Quin and the Morrigan will kill you the minute they see you. You need to trust me on this, Jagger, you need to go hide."

I take his hand and give him my Levin gun then kiss him gently on the cheek, brushing the blonde tresses away from his blue eyes. I smile at him, trying to mask the fear that has violently begun to rise in me and watch as he disappears into the shadows.

I go over to the couch to the left of the door, and back in to the shadows to give myself a little cover. Faces appear in the windows, looking inside. It's at this moment I pray for Trea to appear, but I still can't just call her from the recesses of my mind. Fear has driven her into disappearing; only anger will make her materialize.

I take a deep breath as the door slides open, metal being forced to part. Quin stands in the doorway, drenched. He takes a step in, raising a Levin gun in front of him.

"I know you're here, Trea. This will all be easier if you come out of the shuttle willingly," he says, puddles forming around his feet.

"Why, Quin?" I ask, still sitting in my spot, "Why would you do this to your own kind?"

"We're not the same, Trea. You and the others were created for destruction. I was designed for protection. I was redeemed from the hell that was the Dormitories, and the bastard scientists who felt like playing God. I was saved by the Morrigan and Parson Mathan. And so shall you be."

He fires the gun in my direction, but misses. I jump to my feet, looking for any venue of escape, but I'm trapped. He fires again, missing my head by mere inches.

"All right," I shout, raising my hands above my head and stepping out into view. "You win."

He smiles as he places his gun into his holster. He grabs my arms, forcing them down along my sides before escorting me out of the shuttle and into the rain. Binders are secured to my wrists behind my back. I can easily break them, but choose not to. I feel defeated and weak. He escorts me down the stairs, rain pelting every inch of me while two of the Morrigan have gone inside. I pray that Jagger has found a safe hiding place.

A black armored vehicle is waiting for us about a mile from the platform. Quin shoves me inside, not bothering to protect my head as I smack it on the hard metal. I take a seat between him and the Morrigan he called Rabaan back at the power plant. The others join us several minutes later. We only move a few feet when the sky behind us lights up. I turn around to look out the window behind me to see the shuttle disintegrate into ash.

My heart screams as Jagger is killed.

Everyone I try to protect dies. Everyone.

Tears start to roll down my cheeks. I've let everyone down. I can't take any more. I wish they would just kill me. I no longer care what happens. I'm dead inside.

CHAPTER 20

The trip is quiet.

Quin continues to grip my arm, perhaps fearful I will slip my restraints. Hours pass by slowly. The forest begins to thin out slightly as the trees begin to change from evergreens to large ficus covered in Spanish moss.

A headache begins to build behind my eyes and I'm growing restless from the long ride. I start to fidget with the binders since they are now cutting into my skin. Quin tightens his grip, almost cutting off the circulation in my arm but I manage to slide the binders off.

More hours pass as we drive, and now the sun is bright over our heads. Cool air filters through the vents along the roof, but it doesn't help with the stagnant feel inside the car. My headache grows, moving from behind my eyes to my temples. I ask for some water, so Quin places a cup to my lips in order for me to drink. The water helps my headache, but only a bit.

We approach a tall stone archway with a closed iron gate. The driver pushes a button on the console, causing the huge gates to swing open, shaking from their size and weight. We pass through, the gate closing behind us. We go by four cinderblock buildings, all with small windows and metal doors. Men sit perched atop rooftops, two sets on either side. Behind the buildings is thick forest, tall canopies that cast great shadows onto the earth below.

The vehicle begins to slow as we come upon people walking about the area. Men and women run around the barren ground, going from one building to another. We go about a mile before stopping in front of the tall round structure with the domed roof; ornate columns and stained glass windows complete the picture.

Quin yanks me out of my seat. I step out into the humid air and squint in the bright sunlight, but no one pays much attention to us. Rabaan takes my other arm as he notices I'm no longer wearing the binders, and I am escorted up a small flight of marble stairs, under an elaborately decorated archway, and inside.

Long wooden pews cover much of the floor, candles burn in the corners, and paintings and sculptures of ancient religions hang on every wall. The fragrance lingering in the air is one I haven't smelt before and it's increasing the pain in my head. The three of us, along with two heavily armed Morrigan, walk up the red-carpeted aisle towards a man preaching to rows of pews filled with young children.

He is yelling about the evils of the world, and how humanity can only truly continue if they believe in him. He stands tall and straight, holding a worn leather-bound book in his arthritic hand, shaking it above his head, thinning hair as white as snow. His slender stature makes him look frail, but from the vibrato in his voice, he is far from it.

"Here children," the man says, as we march down the center. "Look at this young woman being brought before you. She was created by the devil's hands." He points towards me, book shaking in his grasp. "She must be punished for the sins of the men and women who created her, as she's not of human flesh. We must seek these demons out and cast them back to hell."

The children turn and stare. The man approaches me, brushing my cheek with his cold bony fingers.

"Trea, I presume." He pushes my head down to check the marks on the back of my neck. He places his hand under my chin, bringing my face up to meet his. "How long I've been waiting to see you."

He gestures to Rabaan and Quin and I'm dragged out the back door behind the altar. We pass a small ring with a tall pole in the center, charred wood and cloth scattered beneath it. Approximately a hundred yards away is another cinder building with a tin roof, bars on the windows, and two guards outside. One unlocks the bolt as he sees us approach. Rabaan and Quin walk me through the door, down a small hallway, and into a cell. I'm secured to the wall by heavy metal chains, one around each ankle and wrist, as well as my neck. Rabaan steps away as Quin finishes fastening me in place.

"It will be okay," Quin says to me. "You'll see." He kisses me and leaves.

As soon as the cell is closed and locked I try and break free of the chains. The moment I move my arm, the restraint around my neck tightens. The same goes if I move either of my legs.

Great, I think to myself, *I'll wind up choking myself to death.*

Nothing is coming to mind at the moment as I try to think of a way out of this. I begin to wonder if Lehen is being held in the same building, so I decide against better judgment and call to him.

"Lehen?"

No response.

"Lehen, its Trea."

Still no response.

I hear the front door open and shuffling steps heading in my direction as a light turns on in the hallway outside my chamber.

Rabaan unlocks my cell door, allowing the old man from earlier to enter. He wears a ragged brown suit and tie, and is still clutching his brown leather book in his right hand.

"Trea," he says to me, getting really close to my face, "I'm Parson Mathan. Rabaan, would you mind releasing this young woman from her binds?"

Rabaan unlocks my chains, removing them from my aching body. I rub my wrists and then my head as the pain has increased again. Parson Mathan takes my hand and escorts me to a chair where I'm made to sit down.

"Let's see it," he says, more to Rabaan than me.

Rabaan walks over and pulls up my right sleeve, revealing the Quantum Stream. Parson Mathan's eyes grow large at the sight. Rabaan forces my hand palm side up to show the port marks.

"Interesting," the Parson says. "I want to see the full extent of her powers. Quin has advised me they're far more advanced than

Lehen's." He calls to one of the guards and asks that the prisoner be brought inside.

"Where's Lehen?" I ask them.

"Don't worry, my dear, he's in good health. You'll see him shortly," Parson Mathan replies.

A young man, who looks to be my age, is dragged down the hall, the tops of his feet scraping against the concrete. He's carried by two guards who affix him to the wall using the chains I'd been held with.

"Kill him," Parson Mathan says, pointing to the young man as the guard fastens the last lock.

The man begins to scream, thrashing his body violently. The restraints around his neck pulling tighter with every movement. Rabaan offers me a Levin gun, but I refuse to take it, so he forces it into my grip. I feel heat begin to rise in my arm. He holds my hand tightly around the grip of the gun, but I still refuse to pull the trigger.

"Fine, have it your way," he says and lets go.

He escorts Parson Mathan out through the cell, locking the door behind them. I place the gun down onto a small wooden table next to the chair and walk over to the young man, who's finally stopped screeching. He looks at me with terrified eyes as I begin to unchain him. As I bend down to release his right foot a force pulls me up off my feet and into the air. I hit the far wall hard, cracking my nose against the dusty cement block. Shaking my head free from stars, the man frees himself from the rest of his bindings.

It seems the guards didn't secure the man as tightly as I'd thought.

Why am I not thinking clearly? I'm being set up, but I can't grasp on the reality around me. *Is Trea messing with my mind?*

I begin to scour the room for a weapon other than the gun, but I waste too much time and he's now freed himself, charging at me. We both go down violently, smashing the table into shards. He reaches under his shirt and comes up with a knife that was hidden in his waistband. I block the blows that he swings at my face, managing to only get nicked in a few spots before I use my legs to propel him off me, but I can't get the correct leverage. I twist my body to better my position and wind up taking the blade in the left shoulder. I cry out, but secure my feet against his stomach and push him up and backwards. He slams into the wall, knocking him out.

Looking over to the large mass on the floor, I slowly stand. His eyes begin to flutter slightly then open wide, he lunges at me again. I have little time to react as he drives the knife deep into my chest. The steel penetrates my heart. The electrical current making it pump stops. He removes the blade; blood begins to pour down my chest.

I fall to my knees. Inhalation has become very difficult, my breaths becoming shorter.

My hands reach out to the ground in front of me as I fall forward. I notice out of the corner of my eye the Levin gun as it lays just a few inches away amongst the broken shards of table. The ground before me is thickening in a pool of blood as it continues to pour from the gaping wound, my heart pumping again.

I reach cautiously for the weapon as I feel myself beginning to heal, my breathing restoring to normal. The young man thrusts himself forward, determined to finish the job. I grab the handle of the gun, firing multiple times into his upper body. He falls onto his back, dropping the knife. I stand, completely healed, and kick the knife into a corner.

I hear applause behind me as my cell door swings open. Parson Mathan's huge grin tells me he's satisfied with the outcome. It's only at this moment that I realize why I've been set up.

The intention wasn't to demonstrate my abilities with the Quantum Stream, but how I heal.

I'm still holding the Levin gun, but before I can take aim at the Parson, Rabaan removes it. The young man's body is carried away by the two guards. One of Rabaan's men enters the cell with a smaller man in bent wire-framed glasses, wearing a white coat covered in red spots, and carrying a heavy black leather bag. The man sets the bag down between his feet, reaches inside, and removes a small syringe. Rabaan grabs my arms, pinning them to my side.

"Now my dear," the man says, as he approaches me, "this won't hurt a bit."

I try to shake off Rabaan by thrashing my body around, kicking around me, but his grip is surprisingly strong. The other man grabs my legs and I'm hoisted into the air, held firm between them.

The needle stings as it enters my arm. The pain is so intense I begin to lose consciousness.

CHAPTER 21

Scorched, cracked granite falls from the sky as the woman in orange runs down the smoke-filled hallway. I turn my head slightly to the right; soot covers Magda's face as she runs out into the night. The air is cool, steam rising from our hot skin as we go uphill and away from the fire. I can still hear the screams of my friends as they burn alive. Magda turns to her left, heading towards the forest that flanks the east side of the complex.

A few others have escaped as well; we find them huddled together to keep warm. Claire is cradling Kedua as she screams from a burn on her face, Midge standing behind them. Kedua continues the noise long after she's healed. Several men I don't recognize stand guard outside our hideout. Three other men, including Dr. Hersher and two little boys, scurry up the ridge. Magda sets me down on a rock to tend to one of the men, who's cut his leg badly.

The boys flock over to Kedua, who's still crying, watching her in rapt silence.

"Devlan," I hear Dr. Hersher call out, as a tall thin man runs up to the group. "Where's Eunice? I thought she was with you."

Devlan pants, bent over, trying to catch his breath.

"She went back for Trea. The building collapsed just as she entered," he spits out.

"I have Trea," Magda says, pointing over to me.

His face grows pale; he ages twenty years in a matter of seconds. He slowly walks over, dropping to his knees in front of me. Tears well in his eyes and spill over as he brushes my check with his rough hand.

"Meg," he whispers, as his body is overcome with emotion, "remember that your mother will always love you."

"My name is Trea," my young voice squeaks out.

"Not anymore."

I awake bent over and strapped to a thick stone table. My tops have been removed and my flesh is pressed against the cold stone. My arms are tied along the side of the table, dangling downward while my legs remain standing. I try to move my head, but my neck won't rotate so my face remains pointing to the wall on my left. The air around me feels cool and damp; the only light is from the fixture above the table.

"Hold still please," I hear the little man say to me, as he stands to my right.

My skin begins to burn ferociously as something is slid under the flesh on my back. I try to scream, but Rabaan is there and shoves a leather strap into my mouth. Spasms begin to take over my muscles as my body tries to heal itself, but the multiple devices being inserted are preventing it. I watch out of the corner of my eye as Parson Mathan walks around me placing small clay pots on the floor around the table. Liquid begins to roll down both of my sides. I hear my blood hit the bottom of the pots.

I scream with the strap in my mouth, tears streaming down my face as a total of five implants are placed. Parson Mathan walks around me one more time, then everyone leaves.

It seems like hours pass by as I lay in the dim light with no one coming to check on me. The pain is so intense I'm on the verge of passing out. The hard surface of the table continues to dig into my abdomen as my legs grow strained from standing, my neck muscles growing tighter.

I cry softly until thin rays of sunshine begin to peek through a small window near the top of the wall. Parson Mathan is the first to enter my cell as soon as the streams of light touch the floor. He hums to himself as he walks around the table, checking the pots. He seems satisfied, and calls for Rabaan and the doctor to come in and remove the implants.

I'd spit the strap out at some point during the night, so Rabaan places the strap back into my mouth. The doctor begins to remove his gruesome contraptions. Rabaan smiles deeply, taking great pleasure in watching me flinch. The doctor is taking slow and methodical steps to ensure he inflicts the most pain. I feel myself beginning to heal once the metal has been removed, but still ache all over. Parson Mathan gathers the pots as Quin enters. Once the room is clear, Quin frees me from my restraints and hands me one of my tops. I feign being much weaker than I am, and slip halfway to the floor as if exhausted. I feel my fury building inside at what has been done to me.

I welcome Trea.

Moving slowly, I slip my arm through the sleeve of my black top, draping it over my head as I place my other arm through. When my face emerges I lean towards Quin as if still weak, and he comes closer to help. I take hold of his shirt and slam his head onto the stone table. He crumples to the ground. I know he won't be out long, so I quickly exit the room and go down the hall on my left. As I round a corner I hear shouting behind me, so I quicken my pace, although I have no idea where I'm heading.

I turn my head to see if anyone is directly behind me when I run into a Morrigan. Trea is about to break his neck but stops when his face is revealed in the light. I know him.

"This way," the man whispers, pushing me further down the corridor and through an opening that hides among the paneled walls.

As the door slides back into place, he presses me hard against the wall on the other side, his gritty hand covering my mouth. He places a finger in front of his lips. We stand there quietly, listening as heavy steps fall along the wall opposite us.

Once they pass, he removes his hand and mask.

"How did you know where I was?" I ask Braxton, as he wipes the sweat from his brow.

"I saw them carry you down here, but I wasn't able to get to you sooner because these tunnels are crawling with Morrigan. I've been hiding in here, checking every couple of minutes to see if anyone was coming, then I saw you."

"Where are the others?"

"Let's not talk here. Come on, follow me."

The walls of the tunnel we're in are covered in sheetrock, and dusty wood floorboards creak beneath our feet. We walk for several miles before coming upon a set of granite stairs that lead up to a small oblong room, with two caskets sitting on either side of the arched doorway.

"What is this place?" I ask, walking slowly through the room.

"It's a mausoleum. The previous society used them to bury their dead, from what I understand. According to the names etched on the stone coverings, these appear to be Parson Mathan's parents."

The tomb smells of death and decay. Petrified flowers lay scattered atop the windowsill by the woman's resting place. Two stained glass windows depicting ancient beliefs adorn that side of the wall.

We exit the building into overcast skies. As we walk towards a small wooden house, I turn back and see thousands of tiny flagstones lining the ground. The nuggets are no bigger than my palm, but are precisely placed in perfect alignment behind the crypt.

Braxton knocks on the door three times before opening it.

The door opens to reveal the last person I ever expected to see...Jagger, alive and well. I'm overwhelmed with emotion. At last I can start to believe that things might actually work out somehow. He stands, beaming, and we rush together, wrapping our arms around each other in an embrace that I'd rather never end. It feels good to be there, secure and safe, if only for a moment.

He gives me some food before he goes back to help tend to two of the four guards that have minor wounds. After taking off the uniform, Braxton removes a small kit from a rucksack at his feet and applies ointment to his wounds; his face and arms are blackened and bloody. I sit down on the floor close to his feet.

"What happened?" I ask, after finishing a tin of pears.

"They were waiting for us," Braxton begins, wincing. "We made if about twenty miles before they attacked. They were waiting in the trees. The skies rained propellant rounds at first, then conflagration slugs. They took out a good portion of my men, then captured the rest of us."

Jagger comes over and sits next to me. I lean on him as he wraps an arm around my shoulders.

"How'd you all escape?"

"There are tunnels underneath the city," Braxton begins. "The city seems to have been built one story off the ground. The other night when they were transferring us from the interrogation room under the chapel to the prison, Jagger showed up dressed as one of the Morrigan, and managed to overpower the guards. We followed the tunnels that seem to wind in all directions under the city. They finally led us out here."

I look up at Jagger, quizzical expression on my face.

"How did I escape the blast? Yeah, good question. When those two came on board the shuttle, they separated. One went to the front, while the other one headed towards the back. I was able to corner the one in the control room, snapping his neck, then stripped off his clothes and put them on. The other one didn't even notice the difference."

"The High Ruler isn't going to be happy about this," one of the guards states as he puts his boots back on.

"That's an understatement," another replies. "When are we leaving, Braxton?"

"As soon as you all have your strength, we'll go."

"I'm not leaving without Lehen," I voice, rising to my feet.

Braxton frowns. "Fine, then you're on your own. We're going to hike to the nearest hatchery and call for a transport as soon as we locate a passageway out of here."

"What will the High Ruler think if you come back without me? I'm not even supposed to have left Acheron."

"Then what do *you* suggest, Trea? We don't even know where he's being held," Braxton says with contempt in his voice.

At the mention of her name, I feel Trea fully emerging, as anger and rage begin to build up.

"Let's obliterate the city," I say with a grin on my face.

"You can't be serious, Meg," Jagger says standing. "How does that help find Lehen? That was the main reason for coming here."

"If they don't want him killed, they'll have to move him, giving us a chance to rescue him amid all the chaos."

"And how do you propose we do that?" Braxton asks, as he stands.

"Jagger can do it. He can put on the uniform, go into the city and retrieve supplies and weapons that we can use to take down this monolith." I point to the discarded clothing on the floor.

"No," Jagger replies walking out the door into the small forest outside.

"Fine," I say turning my focus on Braxton. "Perhaps one of your men will volunteer to go."

"I'll do it myself," Braxton retorts. "Nuceira has always been an adversary of Acheron, so seeing this place fall will please the High Ruler. I'll also try to locate Lehen while I'm in there." He puts the outfit back on and heads out.

Rain begins to pour as I close the door behind him. I'm not able to see Jagger any more even though he was just there a moment ago. I could follow him, but perhaps he'd rather be alone with his thoughts, so I decide to leave him be.

Tobin, Braxton's second in command, goes and stands outside to keep the first watch. While the rest of the guards get comfortable for our temporary stay, I take some time to examine the interior of the house. It's well kept, not a speck of dust or cobwebs anywhere. The walls are lined with built-in bookshelves bursting at the seams with manuscripts of every size and thickness.

Many of the books are bound in leather, cracked, and the pages are yellow from age. I don't know any of the writers' names: William Shakespeare, Sinclair Lewis, and Edgar Allan Poe. I pluck a book off the shelf, sit on the couch, and flip through it. Several of the margins are covered in tiny handprint. Some of the notes have lines directed towards a word or phrase that is circled. One particular phrase in a book titled *Julius Caesar* catches my eye:

"Cowards die many times before their deaths;
The valiant never taste death but once."

I put the book back, pick up another one, then another. I spend the remainder of the day going through the manuscripts. Not all have notes written in them. One of Braxton's men finds some candles to light as the darkness grows, and another locates stale crackers and a small can of tuna. He divides the items among the other guards and himself.

The leather band around my thigh is starting to irritate my skin, so I go through the bedroom, which has the lone bathroom, close the bathroom door, and slip my pants down to remove it. I wash my face and use the toilet, then tuck the knife into my waistband before exiting. I look around the bedroom to see who may live here, since it's obvious this house is still in use. The only pictures hanging up are landscapes: there are no portraits anywhere. The walls are covered in the same paneling as the corridor.

As I walk around the bed, the floorboard under my left foot creaks loudly as it bends, causing a section of the wall in front of me to pop slightly out of place.

I take hold of the piece to shove it back into place when I notice it has hinges. Swinging it wide, I see a small room. There aren't any windows, so I grope in the dark looking for a light source. I find a small knob on the wall next to the door and turn it. Lights come on over my head, illuminating a workbench against the wall to the right, a few shelves covered with odd trinkets, and a large drawing hanging on the wall to the left. I go in further to examine the illustration. A rough sketch of Nuceira takes up most of the top half of the page. The small house we're in isn't present, but there are a lot of little squares with initials lining practically the entire bottom half of the page.

"Meg, where are you?" I hear Tobin call from somewhere in the house.

"I'm in here."

He joins me a few minutes later, squeezing himself carefully through the tiny opening. He looks over the picture, noticing the markings at the bottom. I change my focus to the workbench as he moves behind me to get a better look at the sketch. Lined against the back wall on top of the bench are clay pots stained in blood, but the markings are old and brown. Their contents empty. Small stains cover the workbench, outlining whatever containers the blood had been poured into.

From outside the room we hear Gage, another lieutenant, call out. "Tobin, come out here."

We exit the room, turning the light off, and closing the door behind us. As we leave the bedroom and enter the front room, I see Jagger standing in the entrance to the house, soaking wet, a sack flung over his shoulder. His face and arms are gouged with blast marks, and there's a deep cut on his forehead. Keller and Gage remove the sack of clothing from Jagger's shoulder and place it on the couch.

"You said you wouldn't leave without him so I came up with my own plan," Jagger says to me. He gives me a wan smile, then collapses onto the floor. Meg is disappointed Jagger did this on his own—for me—while Trea applauds his spirit.

Gage goes outside while Tobin and another guard named Rey help Jagger back onto his feet, half dragging him into the bedroom. I walk over to the couch, staring at the mound of rags. Keller goes into the kitchen and brings back a cup of water. The lump begins to shift, slowly pulling itself into a sitting position. The man brushes the hair from his eyes and accepts the cup in shaky dirty hands. His cheeks are shallow, his torn filthy clothes sagging off of his bony frame. Is the brown color of his hair natural, or dirt? I'm not sure if Lehen is exactly what I expected, or the opposite.

CHAPTER 22

Lehen takes slow, methodical sips, a few drops running down his parched, cracked lips. Keller leaves us as Tobin calls for him.

"How long have you been here, Lehen?" I ask, after bringing him a fresh cup of water.

"I think almost a year, but I'm not sure." He stares at me, seemingly puzzled by what he sees. "Who are you?"

"Trea."

He struggles to smile.

I go into the kitchen and locate a bowl, an old worn towel, and a mangled bar of soap. I fill the bowl with warm water and carry my items back to the front room. I soak the towel in the water then scrub the soap bar, trying to get a lather.

"Tell me what happened," I whisper, as I begin to wash the grime from his face.

"My protector told me if anything were ever to happen to him that I should try and make my way back to the Dormitories. He made me memorize the location, as well as a way to get there." He winces slightly as I touch a tender spot on his forehead.

"Why did he tell you to go back to the Dormitories?"

"He said the protectors had made a pact that the Antaeans would return to the place where it all started once we had turned eighteen. He told me the Antaeans were designed to have reached their full abilities at that age. That is how Dr. Hersher designed us."

"Devlan never mentioned any of this to me. He never divulged my true self until after his death." I walk into the kitchen to refill the bowl with fresh water. I look up at the window above the sink and catch a glimpse of Lehen in the reflection, an evasive look upon his face.

I kneel back down in front of him, lathering the towel once again.

"What went wrong?" I ask, as I begin working the damp cloth on his hands.

"My protector was killed during a raid on one of the storage areas Acheron uses for their medical supplies. I barely escaped with my life."

I stop midway up his arm as Jagger begins to scream. I close my eyes, trying to block out the world around me, as he howls in agony.

Fear of his pain and the possibility of losing him again, this time for real, freezes me.

I feel Lehen take my hand, removing the cloth from my clenched fingers. He squeezes as the volume intensifies inside my head.

"Tell me how you got here," I inquire through gritted teeth, my eyes still clamped shut.

"I found the Dormitories. It took me several months to get there, and I wasn't the first one to come home." I open my eyes and look into Lehen's pink scrubbed face.

"Quin."

He nods his head.

"It was almost like he was expecting me. I came up a ridge that flanks the south side of the complex and there he was, standing under a lone oak tree. He was leaning against the trunk, bending a blade of grass in his fingers. He told me I was the second one to come home, that the others hadn't shown up yet. I looked past him, spying the remains of the Dormitories, which appeared to be about a mile north and below the ridge. I swore I could still see smoke rising from the blackened granite. Screams seemed to drift along the breeze as it floated past." He gets a distant look in his eyes

I shake his hand, trying to get him to focus back on the present. "Is that when they took you?"

"No," he says faintly. "They came the night Vier arrived."

The screaming stops. Keller walks out of the bedroom, his hands covered in blood. He goes to the kitchen sink and tries to scrub it off. Gage enters, with Braxton following. Slung over Braxton's shoulder is a large burlap sack, which he sets gently down onto an armchair by the couch.

"What's going on here?" he asks, after he removes the Morrigan head armor from his face.

"It's Jagger, sir," Keller begins, as he dries his hands on his clothes. "He's more injured than we thought. He may not make it through the night."

Braxton tells Keller and Gage to take turns keeping watch, while he goes into the bedroom.

"Tell me about Vier." I want Lehen to continue talking, as it's a distraction for me.

"Quin and I'd spent most of our time scavenging through the old buildings looking for whatever we could find. We camped out at night in the woods to the east, never wanting to be near the Dormitories when it was dark. One day, two months after my arrival, Quin left the camp. It had to have been during the night because he was gone by the time I woke up. We were almost out of firewood, so after a quick meal of canned fruit that we had taken from a transport who was delivering supplies to a hatchery, I headed deeper into the woods, making several trips back to the campsite with heavy bundles."

He sighs deeply, almost as if trying to catch his breath.

"My fourth trip back, I found Vier sitting next to a freshly made fire. Winter was starting to approach, but Quin and I only built a fire at night to keep warm."

Lehen shivers, pulling his feet up under him on the couch. I leave my perch on the floor and sit next to him.

"He asked me if I knew where Quintus was. I said I didn't, but he wouldn't accept that, even though that's all I could tell him. I asked him how long he'd been in the area...did he just arrive...if he knew where the others were. He simply told me it would be best if I left the place. I asked him why, but he only repeated that I should leave. As he got up to go, I noticed he was carrying one of the satchels of food that we had stolen, along with a Pugio blade slung over his back. But what made the biggest impression was when he pulled off the hood that had been covering his face. When he was sitting down I only saw the left side of his face. After he removed the hood, he brought his full face into view."

Lehen closes his eyes, either trying to focus on the image or block it out.

"A bright blue, jagged scar snaked down from his right eye, across his cheek, and around his neck, ending at his collar bone. Pieces of brown flesh poked out in spots along the scar. His right eye appeared to be dead with the exception of the iris, which was bright blue." Lehen reopens his eyes, and looks down.

He strokes my arm, following the path of the Quantum Stream shining under my shirt.

I feel sickened by his touch. I carefully remove his hand, placing it back down at his side.

"Did Vier ever tell you how he got the scar?"

"No, he just turned around and walked away. The Morrigan came that night."

"Trea!"

My name echoes through the house.

I get up from the couch and rush back towards the bedroom. Braxton meets me at the door, blocking my view into the room.

"Trea!"

At first I thought it was Braxton who summoned me, but it's Jagger. I know this is going to be bad, as he's never called me by my real name before.

"Let me pass," I say to Braxton, who continues to block my way.

"You don't want to go in there," he replies, stepping closer.

Jagger lets out another howl. Braxton sees I'm not backing down, so he steps aside to let me by.

The sheets of the bed that were once white are now deep crimson. Jagger's many wounds continue to bleed no matter how much pressure is placed upon them. He thrashes as pain spasms seize his body. Tobin steps aside, allowing me to pass so I can be by Jagger's side. I brush the blonde tresses that keep falling into his face. He turns his head towards me, tears welling in his eyes.

"Trea," he whispers, a small smile forming on his tight face.

I feel my shoulder being bumped and look over to see Tobin tapping the handle of a Levin gun against my back.

"Jagger wants you to do it," he says to me, voice cracking with emotion.

"No. I won't." I turn my head away.

"Please," Jagger gasps, gripping my arm, leaving behind bloody impressions.

"He's dying, Trea." Braxton states in a matter of fact manner. "This is the only way to ease his suffering."

"I won't do it," I protest, tears welling in my eyes.

I try to move away, but Jagger is in the middle of a seizure causing his muscles to contract, tightening his grip on my arm.

"Trea, I'm ordering you to do this," Braxton shouts at me. "As a soldier you have an obligation to follow orders."

Anger begins to build inside.

My right arm is on fire with delight.

I take the gun from Tobin and aim it at Jagger's chest while the others begin to recede to the other end of the room.

"I'm sorry," I whisper to him, as my finger begins to tighten on the trigger.

I begin to sweat as the air around me dramatically increases in temperature.

"No, wait," I hear Lehen shout from the doorway.

I barely hear him through the pulse of blood coursing through my veins. His sudden appearance causes me to hesitate, as if I'm waiting for an absolution.

"There's another way," Lehen says, as his hand guides the gun down to my side.

He removes the gun from my hand, giving it back to Tobin.

"Keep him comfortable. Trea, come with me," Lehen says, as he takes my hand, escorting me out of the room.

Braxton follows the two of us out.

"We're going to need that," Lehen says, as he points to the Morrigan uniform Braxton is still wearing.

"What for?" he asks, walking closer to Lehen, whose energy has surged.

"To get into the city. Specifically, the healer's den."

"You're not going back in there, and neither is she," Braxton shouts, pointing at me. "Now let's calm down and discuss this."

"No. The longer we wait the less time we have to save Jagger."

"What's in the healer's den?" I ask, trying to get Lehen and Braxton to back off from each other.

"You were taken down to the chamber, like me, correct? They drained you too, right?"

"If you mean the room with the stone table and the bloodletting, then yes."

"The doctor who collected your blood has refined a process to remove the Quarum and synthesize it. Anyone who injects the substance, Antaean or not, will experience our advanced healing ability...the body will self-repair."

Realization dawns on me. *The hypocritical coward!* "That's the real reason the Parson wants the Antaeans, isn't it? So he can save himself from ever dying?"

"Yes. The supply they harvested from me only lasted a few months each time, and then the Parson's body started to break down, so he had to keep injecting himself. However with your blood, he won't have to replenish every couple of months. The supply he took from you will last years. It will work the same on Jagger."

"Braxton, give Lehen the uniform," I say forcefully.

"Trea, let's think about this." Braxton walks over to me, placing himself between Lehen and I. "I know you care for Jagger, but you don't know what that stuff will do to him…if it will even work at all."

"It works on Parson Mathan. And anyway, I have to try."

"Then I'm going with you. But Lehen is staying here."

"Why?" he protests.

"Because you're not well enough. You'll only slow us down."

"Captain," Keller calls from the doorway. "What if we all go? I don't relish the idea of staying here, and we should all stick together."

"Carrying Jagger will only slow us down," Braxton retorts. "Besides, moving him might kill him. No, we'll stick with just the two of us going in. If you run into any trouble while you are out here, head for the woods."

"You'll only be able to go two miles into the forest before a trap is set off," Lehen chimes in. "No one has ever reached the boundary."

The group agrees not to venture far from the house even if they are forced to leave. Braxton makes sure the weapons he has confiscated are fully functional. I'm outfitted with a Morrigan uniform that he brought back with him in the sack.

Lehen gives us directions on finding the healer's den. Before leaving I secure my knife into a hilt attached to my belt, along with a Levin gun. I say a silent goodbye to Jagger, who has passed out from the pain. Braxton and I leave the small house then enter the tunnel just as the sun is rising.

The battered body of a Morrigan lies between the caskets as we enter the tomb. His body is clothed only in an undershirt and shorts.

"You're wearing his uniform," Braxton says to me, as we step over the corpse's outstretched legs.

I'm a little uncomfortable with the thought, but Trea just shrugs.

We retreat down the stairs, reach the hidden door, and listen for sounds on the other side. Feet run past, then there's silence. Braxton begins to lean on the door to open it, but I stop him. My hearing is better than his and I hear someone else approaching. Another set of pounding feet hurry by, then I nod that it's safe. We quickly step inside, carefully closing the door behind us. Braxton picks up the pace as we head north.

We enter the portion of the tunnel that runs under the prison in about ten minutes. Several Morrigan pass us as we go, but don't stop us as they believe we're on patrol. I catch my breath as one asks Braxton if he's seen any more disturbances, but Braxton answers no and the other man leaves down another hallway.

We continue our way past the prison, still heading north. The tunnel divides into three branches and we take the path on the far left, as Lehen instructed. It curves in accordance with the circular structure of the chapel above. We enter into an anteroom that has a set of stone steps leading up to the surface, along with a door on our right. We try the door, but it's locked. Braxton uses his shoulder against the door, and after some effort, the door finally gives way.

Braxton closes the door behind us and we proceed with caution down the narrow hall. I remove my gun from its holster, side-stepping my way through the dim light of the flickering sconces on the walls. Faint music begins to permeate the air, a haunting melody that grows louder the closer we get to its source. A wooden door stands slightly ajar at the end of the hall, bright light pulsating through the opening. The music is now almost deafening.

We peek through and see the doctor hunched over his workstation, hands floating in the air as if he were conducting the music himself. The room is a small round chamber. Flasks line most of the shelves along the wall on my right; chemicals perfuming the air. I spot the clay pots that had been used to collect my blood sitting empty on a table against the far wall. I draw my gun as we approach, removing my mask for better visibility. Braxton on my left draws his as well, but leaves his mask on.

The doctor begins to pour a clear liquid from one large beaker into smaller vials. Braxton and I remain standing behind him, not saying a word until he's finished.

"How does that work?" I ask once I'm sure he won't drop the vial.

He turns around on his stool, face pale with fright.

"One shout from me and security will be here in moments," he stammers.

"Not with that racket playing," Braxton says with a smirk.

"It's not racket, it's a classic," the doctor hisses, sounding offended. "Beethoven's Symphony Number Seven is not a racket."

My memory drifts back to my time at the Dormitories. I remember myself as a toddler watching war films with this song playing in the background. Then I realize where I know this man from.

"Dr. Baccus."

"Hello Trea…I was wondering when you would remember me. Music has a profound impact on the memory. It can help us recall the minutest details," he begins, climbing down from his stool and walking over to the device that is blasting the noise. "Obviously you remember this from battle conditioning." He goes to turn down the music, but Braxton points his weapon, stopping him.

"Why would you help someone like Parson Mathan?"

"Why? Because I'm a Nuceiran." He rolls up the sleeve on his right arm, revealing the light tattoo of the city's emblem that all Nuceirans have. "Why wouldn't I help him?"

"Did Lehen ever recognize you?"

"No, I kept my face out of his view."

"What about Quin?"

"Quintus and I were saved together. He came back to Nuceira with me."

"Where you twisted his mind?"

"If you think that. But we just opened him up to the concept of redemption. That if he served Parson Mathan he could be forgiven for the sins of his makers."

"You tortured him?" Braxton asks, moving closer to the table with the vials. "He was only a child."

"He had to be cleansed, cleansed of the evil within him."

"And that's when the Parson discovered the Antaeans' healing ability?" I ask, as I place my gun back into its holster.

"Yes."

"So you had kept that part secret from the Parson after his Morrigan rescued you?"

"I never believed it would actually work, so I was just as shocked as he was when Quintus healed from his wounds."

"Where is Quin now?"

"He's probably in his room at the estate."

Braxton takes the vials and their matching syringes from the table, and pockets them. I remove my knife and approach Dr. Baccus, who pales as I draw near.

"You kill me and you'll never know the truth about the Antaeans," he stutters.

"Sorry, Dr. Baccus, I've had all the truth I can handle."

I grab him by the shoulders, spin him around, and slice his throat.

CHAPTER 23

Jagger is barely breathing when we return. Rey fits a vial into one of the syringes and injects the fluid into Jagger's bicep. His respirations stop immediately. His body goes into one final seizure before relaxing. I look over at Lehen, but he tells me to wait. Minutes seem to pass slowly, but Jagger remains still, no rising in his chest. As I continue to wait for him to start breathing again, I notice the deep gash above his right eye begin to heal.

"Look," I say, pointing to his face.

Jagger gasps. His injuries heal as he begins to breathe again, shallow at first then stronger. After a few minutes, his eyes flutter open.

"What happened?" he asks, voice cracking slightly.

"You got a little banged up, but you're fine now," Rey answers, returning the used vial and syringe to Braxton.

"What did you do to me?"

"Nothing," I say, cautiously approaching his bed, noticing the anger in his eyes, which fades upon seeing me. "We just took care of your wounds. You'll be fine now."

"Meg," he begins, but I place my finger on his lips quieting him.

"Get some rest."

We all leave the room except for Rey, who wants to monitor him.

"He's going to be different now," Lehen announces, once we are back in the front room.

"Different how?" Tobin asks, as he removes the sack from the chair so he can sit down.

"His strength will be intensified, and he will be quick to anger. These are the side effects of the Quarum."

"Will he self-heal like we do?" I inquire, sitting back on the couch.

"Not for much longer, this is only a temporary fix. He will need to be given another injection if he gets severely injured again. How many vials were you able to collect?"

Braxton begins to empty out the contents of the sack. "Five total."

"As long as he doesn't sustain any critical injury, he should be fine for about a year. He'll need another injection at that time as he's now dependent upon the Quarum to survive. With only five vials, Jagger will only live for five years, and if he does get badly hurt the more Quarum we put into his system before the year us up, the harsher the effects. He could lose himself in a fit of rage, for example."

"So, in saving him, we may have just woken a dangerous monster?" Keller asks, pounding his fist on the small kitchen table.

"He'll be fine," I stammer, hoping I'm correct in my belief.

"He'll be your problem if you are wrong, Trea," Braxton says.

I know he's right. Why did I do it? Why did I act so rashly? I've condemned Jagger to death. Maybe not now, but definitely in five years.

"Well," Braxton begins, tossing the now-empty sack into the corner of the room, "how do you want to do this?"

"Did you grab a master control for the detonators?"

He reaches into his pocket and pulls out a small, thin black device, handing it to me. I touch the darkened screen, which lights up, activating all the detonators.

"Just program in the time you want them to explode, or manually select them to detonate."

I smile at the pile of red flickering lights as they dance before my eyes. A vision of Nuceira imploding tantalizes my brain.

Braxton locates some parchment and starts to outline the tunnel system from memory.

"Hang on," Tobin starts, "I've got something better to use." He disappears for a moment then reemerges with the map from the hidden room, spreading it out on the table. "This whole place is filled with secret passageways and rooms." He points to broken black lines that run the length of the city, including several that lead out beyond the borders.

"Why would someone have something like this?" Gage asks.

"To keep secrets," Lehen answers. "And the Parson has many."

We all huddle around the kitchen table, including Jagger who looks fully rejuvenated. Since it's my plan, I will carry the master control. Every person will be in charge of placing ten detonators in the tunnels, and on any buildings on the surface they can get to. Morrigan are to be shot on sight.

"The Parson is mine," I state, cleaning my knife of dried blood.

"Fine," Braxton agrees, as he flattens the map at the corners. "We'll meet by the front gate. Rey and Tobin will secure our transportation once their detonators are set. Try and get two of their vehicles," he tells them. They nod in compliance. "Once we have set off the detonators, we will make our way back to Acheron."

We decide to wait until nightfall to breach Nuceira. I remove the uniform I'm wearing and hand it to Keller. I keep my Levin gun secured to my belt, along with my nicely polished blade.

As the sun begins to set, we each take our allotment of detonators, making sure they are synched with the master control. Jagger and I enter the tunnel through the mausoleum, the others break off into groups of two, and Braxton is alone. Tobin and Gage enter using the tunnel hidden in the farm fields to our north; Keller and Rey are using the tunnel on the other side of the cemetery that leads straight to the housing units. Braxton will be sweeping the grounds for Morrigan. Jagger opens the tunnel door after a group of Morrigan march past. We decide to secure the detonators to the ceiling of the tunnels. That way they won't be noticeable. Jagger and I are tasked with placing our detonators in the tunnels under the Parson's estate.

We begin moving north, placing the devices every twenty feet. We duck into a small alcove as a group of Morrigan go by. In the alcove is a small staircase leading up to a place near the Parson's compound. I give my remaining detonators to Jagger.

"I'm going to look for Quin."

"Meg, he's not worth saving."

"He's done bad things, but I think that somewhere inside is someone worth saving."

I head up the stairs while Jagger continues on as planned.

The treads lead up to the main entryway of the Parson's home. Tall columns line the interior walls, soaring skyward into the story above. White marble with flecks of gold cover the floor. Paintings depicting antiquated stories line the walls, some displaying naked beings floating on white fluffy clouds. I quietly cross towards the far end, making for the grand staircase.

The carpeting on the second floor landing is plush, concealing my footsteps as I slowly creep down the hall looking for Quin's room. I try several of the doors, but all of them are locked. I hear whimpering coming from the other side of the next door I try. The knob gives easily in my hand.

The interior is cast in shadows, lights flickering in each corner throwing shadows at odd angles. I hesitate, cautious about stepping inside, so I decide against it and close the door.

The ground beneath my feet starts to shake as the columns begin to crumble. I haven't activated the detonators, so I'm not sure what's going on. I'm thrown off my feet, the floor tilting towards the opening that's been created by the collapse of the pillars. I slide across the carpet, desperately grasping at anything to arrest my fall.

Someone grabs my wrist, pulling me up. Above my head I see Quin standing in the doorway I'd just opened.

"Give me your other hand," he screams at me, as the building collapses around us.

I throw my arm up. He catches hold of my fingers, gets a better grip, and pulls me up to him, holding me tight against his chest. Then, off-balance, we begin to fall into the abyss.

I close my eyes, not wanting to see the upcoming impact, but it doesn't come. Instead, I feel a jerk, and heat hits my face. I open my eyes to find the room around us engulfed in flames. Quin is keeping us alive by holding onto a cable that must have come loose.

He has his legs wrapped around me to secure me in place while his one hand is coiled around my shoulders, the other attached to our lifeline. I look down and watch as the main floor collapses into the tunnels. Smoke and dust shoot heavenward as the debris hits an air pocket below. I can hear screams shattering the night air, but I can't tell from which direction they're coming from.

"Hang on," someone from above shouts to us.

Jagger and Braxton take hold of the cable and begin to pull us up. It's at this point I realize we have fallen below ground level. Quin has me climb up him and into Braxton's arms. Jagger grabs Quin by the collar, extracting him from the inferno that now rages beneath.

"What happened?" I shout to be heard over the roar of destruction.

"I don't know. Jagger caught up with me by the prison and said you had gone looking for Quin. Then all hell broke loose."

"Where are the others?"

"Following orders. Do you still have the master control?"

I pull it out of my pocket. The screen is badly scratched, but it still turns on.

"Check to see how many detonators are still on-line."

I tap the screen, sliding my finger over the corner to pull up the information.

"Sixty still haven't ignited."

"Let's head up to the gate. Jagger, take Quin."

"I still have to deal with Parson Mathan."

"Trea, it's over. Let's get out while we still can."

"Here," I say to Braxton, handing the master control to him, "I'm not leaving till I'm certain the Parson is dead. Do what you have to."

I run in the direction of the chapel as Braxton calls after me, but I have a mission and I'm determined to see it finished.

The distance between the estate and the chapel is approximately a mile. Smoke chases after me, the smell of burning wood floating along the air. Nuceirans slowly begin to emerge from their homes to see what's happened. I pull out my Levin gun as I approach the prison. Two guards come around the corner, their weapons drawn. I fire, dropping them. I climb up the back steps of the chapel, lights ablaze inside.

I enter quietly, shutting the door slowly behind me, hearing voices radiating in song from the main room. I step through the entryway behind the altar, gun raised. The singing continues as I come out from behind the altar, gun aimed at Parson Mathan. A woman finally looks up from her songbook. She doesn't scream, but instead goes silent and nudges the man next to her. This causes a ripple effect through the small audience. The Parson lifts his head to see why everyone has ceased. He turns around and flinches at the sight of me.

"Trea," he stammers, "welcome to the house of forgiveness. We're all just praying for your soul."

"Are you now?" My right arm begins to tingle, warmth growing from my shoulder down to the port in my hand. "Who's going to pray for yours?"

I fire one shot, hitting him just below his left knee. The congregation begins to scatter, running towards the front entrance.

Parson Mathan falls to the ground, his frail body quickly weakening. Taking him by the collar, I drag him down the aisle. The world outside erupts. The ground rumbles below my feet. As we step down the last stair the chapel implodes. Parson Mathan writhes in my grasp like a snake, hissing as we move towards a large group of people, many of them his followers. Morrigan lie dead nearby; the survivors are restrained by Lehen, Braxton, and his men. Jagger has Quin secured tightly in his grasp.

The group opens up, allowing me to drag the Parson into the center of the crowd.

"Was it worth it?" I scream so everyone can hear. "Was your life worth all those who perished in the Dormitories?"

A laugh catches in his throat. His breathing becomes labored, but has enough breath left to chuckle.

I place the nozzle of the gun against his forehead.

"Answer me!" I shout.

"You will only bring destruction, not redemption. Look around at what you have done to Nuceira. You did this, not I."

"It began with you, it will end with you."

"That's what you think." He smiles wide as his skin grows paler from the blood loss. "Your creators were wrong to believe you would defend the cities from our enemies. You bring the enemies with you. You will fail."

"I don't believe in failure."

"Go to hell."

"You first."

The flash is bright.

I turn and watch as the city burns around me. Chaos now reigns.

Trea smiles as homes go up in flames, and people scream from either terror or pain. This is her world, the place she feels most at home.

Families flee past us, escaping the carnage and out the open gates as others wail and moan for those that have already perished before their eyes. Explosions continue to fill the night sky as the once bright stars become invisible from the smoke.

Keller hands me two Pugio blades as I step over the Parson's body. Rabaan is made to sit on his knees in front of me while the remaining fifteen or so of his men await their fate. I look down at him, crossing the two weapons before his throat. He understands that with one motion from my wrists he'll be no more.

"Tell me why I shouldn't kill you."

"I know the truth about the Dormitories."

"You lie," I spit at him. "You murdered my family. You traveled into the Wasteland to destroy everything I held dear to me."

"Not true. Devlan's death was an accident. We were supposed to bring him back with us. And I'm telling you the truth when I say it wasn't the Morrigan who attacked the Dormitories."

"Keep talking. You'll live until I hear something I don't like."

Sweat begins to cascade down his brow. "One of our spies got word to us that plans were being made to annihilate the Dormitories, as a way to destroy the cities. Since Nuceira helped build the facility, I felt a need to protect it. It was the one and only time I went against the Parson. The sun hadn't yet risen when we arrived, but we could see our way in the dark from the flames. We searched for survivors, but only found Dr. Baccus and Quintus." He gestures towards Quin, a look of defeat upon his face. "They were sitting in one of the pools in the center of the complex."

I look over at Quin, his body sagging in Jagger's arms. He lifts his head and nods at me. I turn my attention back to Rabaan.

"If the Morrigan didn't attack us, who did?"

"The same consortium that developed the Levin gun: the Hostem. And I hear they're mobilizing again, preparing to strike the cities, and anything affiliated to them."

"Like a hatchery?" Braxton asks in an alarmed voice.

"Yes. The Hostem camps were destroyed after the Dormitories. It's believed many went into hiding in the Wasteland."

"Where's the closest hatchery?" I ask Braxton.

"Acheron Hatchery Nine. It's the one we were planning to go to before your plan."

"What's there?" Lehen asks.

"Children."

I cautiously ponder what Rabaan is telling me. I don't want to believe him, but I feel somewhere inside he's telling the truth. And Quin did confirm his story about the Dormitories.

"How many men will you need to defeat this horde?"

"If we can get to the resources the cities have off site, no more than ten."

"Then you have determined your own punishment." I look over at Braxton and Lehen, and nod to them.

Within moments, only ten Morrigan remain.

"What about the Nuceirans?" Lehen asks me as he wipes his blade.

"They embraced the poison that Parson Mathan spewed. They're on their own."

CHAPTER 24

We grab as many supplies from the Morrigan quarters as we can move, loading three armored vehicles with both weapons and food. Keller, Gage and four Morrigan take the first vehicle; Rey, Tobin, and another four Morrigan are in the second; the rest of us ride in the third.

People are still pouring out of the gates as we make our way forward, Braxton driving. We make our way around the crowds, ignoring those who try to flag us down for help.

The hatchery is fifteen hundred miles north of Nuceira and since there aren't any direct routes or roads, it'll take us several days. No time to help the refugees, even if I had the inclination.

The fuel cells operating the vehicles are solar powered, so we don't have to worry about being short on power, but the air inside becomes stagnant after a couple of hours so Rabaan flips a control switch on the front dash opening a panel in the roof allowing fresh air to flow in. I close my eyes, lean against Jagger, and drift off to sleep.

My nightmares resume the moment my eyes close.

My friends perishing around me…the buildings collapsing…Magda rescuing me.

Sometime later, I sense the vehicle is no longer moving, and open my eyes.

I'm alone inside, the sun radiating through a group of trees just above the roof. I sit up and exit the vehicle. Everyone is gathered on a small patch of open land. Some appear to be sleeping while others are stretching or eating. Jagger and Lehen are sound asleep under a large elm tree. Quin is off to the left of the group, sitting alone, and reading. I walk up to him, sit down, and remove the worn leather bound book from his hands.

I recognize the book as belonging to Parson Mathan. "Where did you get this?"

"I took it from his study early yesterday."

I hand the book back to him, but he doesn't reopen it.

"I followed you and Braxton into the healer's dean and stood out in the hall when you two were talking to him. I knew they were all lies...the same that they'd been telling me."

"What did they say to you?"

"That I was wicked, crafted to lead the destruction of man. In order to save myself from death, I was told that I would need to befriend the other Antaeans. It would make their capturing easier. I had no idea what Parson Mathan's real plan was. They never tried to harm me like they did Lehen and you. I think that's because Rabaan prevented it."

"How long had it been going on?"

"The torture?"

I nod.

"Since I was ten. I just accepted it after a while. I was taught to never question anything the Parson or Dr. Baccus did, or wanted. When I heard what Dr. Baccus told you and Braxton, I knew I had to find out more. I went to confront the Parson, but he wasn't in his study. I found this instead." Quin holds up the book. "The lives he destroyed, all captured in his little ledger. People he murdered, including his own father, women he raped, and children he sacrificed, all for the name of some deity he didn't even believe in. He would carry this around, claiming it was scripture when in reality it was a log of atrocities he committed against his own people...against me...against you."

Tears begin to well up in his eyes. Quin tries to choke them back before they spill over. "I'm sorry," he says to me after a long pause.

I hold him tight and begin rocking him, my own tears falling. My life in the Wasteland was trouble-free compared to the cruelty Quin suffered. He wraps his arms around me, weeping softly. We stay there, holding each other for over an hour, afraid to let go.

Quintus has returned.

After another hour of rest, we climb back into the vehicles, and continue our journey. We traverse over small foothills, past dried-up lake beds, and watch as the moon shines brightly overhead. The next day we make another two hour long stop. I elect to stay inside the vehicle and sleep. Quin stays with me.

The next morning, just as the sun is rising over the cracked ridge, we come across a transport road that should take us right into the hatchery. The vehicles pick up speed now that the terrain has leveled out. Thin pine trees line the left side of the narrow road as the right side cascades down, jagged red and brown rocks leading the way. We wind our way up the elevation, making a sharp right once we're at the top. Another hour passes before we reach the outskirts of Hatchery Nine.

The road is blocked by a heavy metal gate, coated white. When our convoy stops at the entrance, Braxton exits the vehicle walking towards the front. The post on the right side of the entrance that holds that side of the gate in place, slides open at his approach. He steps inside the opening and a few moments later the gate opens. He climbs back into our vehicle before we pass through, the gate closing quietly behind us. About a half-mile later we're at another gate identical to the first. This time Rey gets out and approaches. I can't see what security device he needs to trigger, but within moments the gate swings wide allowing us to pass.

We travel only twenty miles per hour for the next half hour, even though the road is straight and flat. I look over at Braxton who is continually monitoring our speed on the digital dashboard. Looking out the window on my right, I notice conflagration artillery hidden amongst the trees.

"The road is speed sensitive," Braxton says, now keeping his eyes on the vehicle in front of us. "If anyone goes over twenty miles per hour, the vehicle is showered with artillery fire."

"What about the other security devices we passed?"

"The first gate is a full body scan. The biometric scanner inside the post maps out the person's structure. If you're in the data banks, the gate will open."

"And if you're not?"

"You're incinerated."

Jagger grunts at Braxton's comment.

"Gate two is triggered by weight. The person needs to be between two hundred to two hundred and forty pounds. The sensor is directly in front of the gate. If you're over or under by a quarter of a pound, you're electrocuted by a pulse from the gate."

"How many more gates do we have to go through?"

"Just one more…and you're going to have open it."

"Why me?"

"You'll see." He looks at me with a large grin on his face.

Another half hour passes before the convoy stops again.

Braxton gestures for me to exit the vehicle. I hesitate and he doesn't rush me, but waits patiently as I contemplate what might be waiting for me at the head of the line. I open the door, carefully placing my feet down onto the asphalt, and make my way slowly up to the gate, all eyes on me from every passenger in the first two vehicles.

The gate is a simple archway, nothing visible blocking our procession. I stand in front of the first vehicle, staring up at the white granite keystone perfectly centered in the arch. Focusing my gaze forward, beyond the haze that has settled over the landscape, I slowly advance, aligning myself directly under the keystone.

A red veil drops down on me, my skin prickling hot from the waves of energy bombarding it. The heat begins to increase; I feel my molecules accelerate, colliding into each other. I close my eyes, not wanting to see my flesh break apart, but just as the sensation reaches the level of pain I can barely tolerate, it stops. I open my eyes. The red veil is gone, and the haze lifted. Moving beyond the keystone, I step off to the side to let the vehicles pass. Braxton stops to allow me back inside.

"Even though I'm whole, a part of me feels as if I've been ripped into pieces and hastily reassembled," I comment as I secure myself into my seat.

"That's a side effect of the gene decoder."

"What was it looking for?"

"It was looking for your X chromosomes. In order to unlock the last gate, you have to be female."

"Why go to such lengths to protect the hatcheries?"

"You'll see."

We maneuver around a tight ridge, and a large, white square building comes into view. The drive circles in front of the building; a group of short pine trees adorns the center. The structure stands two stories high. It's long, with precise ninety-degree angles at the corners. It appears to be sitting on the edge of the rock face, and I guess there are more stories below the surface.

Braxton is first to the door, placing his right palm over a scanner next to the entrance. A small bulb above the scanner goes from red to green, but the door doesn't open.

"Welcome Captain Braxton," a high-pitched female voice announces from hidden speakers. "What can we assist you with today?"

"Our communications with Acheron have been lost and we desperately need to contact the High Ruler."

"Only five of you may enter the Intake Facility. Please advise the remainder of your party to stay with their vehicles. Remove all weapons from your persons before entering the building."

Braxton walks over to Keller and Rey who've exited the trucks, and speaks quietly with them. I place my Levin gun and knife on the front seat of the last vehicle. The two Morrigan who've been riding with us are divided between the other two vehicles, which leaves Jagger, Quin, Rabaan, Lehen, Braxton, and I. Jagger elects to stay behind with the others as we line up in front of the door, which hisses open and then quickly closes behind us.

No one is there to meet us.

The entryway is flanked on both sides by glass inlayed doors. The glass is clouded over by a white film. I step out of the group, walk to the far side of the room, to a large window, which allows me to see into several rooms on the other side of the building. There are a couple of women sitting in chairs, their legs elevated as they're being examined. I look away, my eyes drifting down through the whole in the center of the structure to the rust colored rocks below where massive sturdy columns extend out from the cliff face, holding the building into place.

I return to the group just as the door to the right opens. A tall woman wearing dark red slacks with a matching blazer walks out. Her red hair is pulled tightly back into a ponytail at the nape of her neck. She doesn't extend her hand as she introduces herself, but rather keeps her hands firmly clasped together behind her back.

"Captain Braxton, I'm Superior Hersher. What can I assist you with?"

"Hersher?" I question, making sure I'd heard her clearly.

"Yes, Diana Hersher, and you are?"

"You wouldn't happen to be related to Dr. Hersher?" My voice raises an octave. I can tell I'm startling this woman, which makes me smile inside.

"He's my father. Why...has something happened to him?"

"No, Superior Hersher," Braxton begins, as he gestures for me to keep quiet. "I'm sure your father is quite fine. We're in need of your security and communications room. We've not been able to contact Acheron for a few days and we need to radio for assistance."

"I'm sorry, Captain, but our link to Acheron seems to have failed as of this morning. I was in the middle of a video conference with the High Ruler when our system went into emergency shutdown. I haven't been able to raise them since."

"That means it's begun," Rabaan says from the back.

"Superior, please excuse me for being so abrupt, but it's imperative that you take me to your security and communications room."

She hesitates briefly, but upon hearing the urgency in his voice she nods and signals for us to follow her back through the door she'd entered through.

The corridor is brightly lit from the windows that line the wall on our left. We turn the corner, rushing down the passage at a quickened pace. A few pictures hang between closed doors, which slowly begin to open as we go past. Half-way down the hall we turn left and begin descending a flight of stairs. We pass two additional floors before coming to the bottom level. The Superior makes an immediate right, opening the door after she inputs a code on the keypad embedded in the handle.

Several of the monitors hanging on the wall are black, but a faint humming noise filtering through the speakers indicates the screens are still on. The remaining monitors show changing scenes of the complex from outside, including the front entrance. A couple of workers in gray uniforms are busy working the controls, probably attempting to reestablish the connection with Acheron.

"Security footage from the Centurion satellite is usually displayed on these screens," the Superior states, as she gestures to the blackened monitors. "We also control all Acheron broadcasts through those monitors to the other buildings in the complex."

"What does the satellite take pictures of?" Rabaan asks.

I image he's probably curious about whether it was ever directed over Nuceira.

"It sweeps about one hundred miles around the hatchery checking for any people from the Wasteland or Nuceira who might be trying to enter restricted territory. The satellite is controlled from Acheron's main security building."

"Is there any way to get the satellite back online?" I inquire, trying to make myself useful.

"It'll take us a while to reroute the connections between here and Acheron," Braxton answers, voice tense with fear.

The two workers look up, finally noticing our presence. Superior Hersher introduces them as Duren and Hera, the security officers of Hatchery Nine. Hera is the voice we heard at the entrance. They, along with Braxton and Rabaan, try to work on reconnecting the complex with Acheron.

"Should I be concerned?" Superior Hersher pipes in from the doorway.

"What kind of defenses does this facility have, other than the gates?" Lehen asks, as he begins to assist Braxton who has now crawled under the main console.

"We have an armory in our emergency bunker."

"Where's that?"

"It's off the connecting bridge between the housing unit and the Predestination Center."

"Superior, we'll need you to allow those other men into the complex," Braxton demands, as he slides out from his corner.

"Is that really necessary? Having so many guards inside this facility could be worrisome to the children."

Braxton doesn't back down in his persistence, and indicates they may be crucial to helping the children.

She purses her thin red lips at him, but concedes to his request with one rule; that no guards be allowed beyond the emergency bunker, and no entering the Predestination Center or the Developmental Quad.

Quin and I follow Superior Hersher back up the stairs and to the entrance. He goes outside to collect the others while the Superior and I wait in the entryway.

"I know who you are," she says to me, hands still clasped behind her.

I look over at her, watching as her face darkens, a wrinkle forming between her perfect brows.

"You're my father's creation. A perfect soldier for times of chaos...for a reckoning that never came."

"It's coming now," I whisper, not really sure that she hears me.

Jagger is first to enter, with Quin at the end. Superior Hersher leads us through the opposite set of doors, down another corridor, and around the corner on our right. Women in light orange uniforms exit from small, closet-sized rooms, standing in awe of the parade of men going by. At the end of the hall is a set of double doors that seem out of place. Upon our approach, the doors quietly slide open, leading us to a metal-framed walkway with floor-to-ceiling glass panes as walls, and bright incandescent lights flooding the area with a soft yellow glow. The walkway makes a sharp left, taking us to the housing unit.

The passageway seems to float in midair, with slate covered hills to our left, and a deep slope to our right.

We enter the next building, which is identical to the first, turn right after entering, then turn left. Halfway down this corridor sits another set of double doors off to our right. We pass through them and walk onto another connection bridge. This one cuts into the cliff at an angle, probably to allow access to the emergency bunker.

Before the corridor breaks right towards the Predestination Center, the Superior stops at a small portal on our left and hurriedly provides a palm and retinal scan. When the door opens, she instructs Jagger and Keller on where the armory is located as well as the passcodes needed to gain entry. She doesn't allow me to enter, but instead insists I accompany her back to the Intake Facility.

"If I'm to understand, you all will be here for some time," she begins, as we reach the housing building, "we'll need to arrange sleeping quarters. As I don't want any of my women disturbed, the nurses and instructors will be moved from their usual sleeping quarters in the Intake Facility. The nurses will stay with the women, while the instructors will stay with the children."

She quickens her pace as a thought enters my mind.

"How were you able to conference with the High Ruler of Acheron if no one ever sees him?"

"The Superiors are always informed as to who's in charge. It's the Laics that are kept from knowing. If they knew how many times the High Ruler position has changed hands, they would find a way to exploit it and rebel."

Once we're back at the Intake Facility, Superior Hersher pages Dr. Werner, Ms. Amara who is in charge of the nurses, and Ms. Eryn, into her office.

The office, one floor below the main level, affords a view of the entire layout of the hatchery. The other buildings have two additional floors below the initial first floor, for a total of four floors. Each building is identical in shape, design, and color.

The interior of the office is decorated in Acheron colors, and the city's emblem emblazoned on a monitor sitting on the Superior's desk as well as the carpet on her floor. Few personal items take up some of the empty spaces on bookshelves that line one wall. The only other furniture is a coffee table that sits before a blue leather couch and matching side chairs. Clearly the Superior enjoys all the privileges that can be afforded her.

A soft knock on the office door breaks the uncomfortable silence. A heavy-set man in white dress clothes with thinning brown hair enters, along with a mouse of a woman in an orange cotton uniform, her graying hair cropped short, and glasses tucked too tightly against her bony face. Ms. Eryn, it seems, has yet to arrive.

"Dr. Werner, Ms. Amara, this young woman and a number of guards will be spending a few days with us. The High Ruler has sent them to do a security check on our facility due to the lingering threat Tyre poses on the city of Acheron and its people. We must make them feel welcome and be of any assistance to them if needed."

She's already told us she doesn't want us here, but I'd never know it from what she's just told her inferiors. The lies seem to come naturally to the Superior, as if she tells them every day.

"Dr. Werner, you, Ms. Amara and the medical staff will be temporarily moved into the housing unit with the women. I know this is a great inconvenience, but an unfortunate necessity." She looks over at me, trying to pass the fault of this arrangement onto me. "Your daily routines will continue. Ms. Amara, would you mind advising the kitchen staff about our extra guests? Their meals are to be served after the rest of the facility has eaten. I want to avoid as much socializing between the staff and children and our guests, as possible. If any issues arise, call for me immediately."

As if on cue, they both rise from their seats and leave.

Superior Hersher pages Ms. Eryn again, her tone bordering on hostile at having to repeat her demands. A few more minutes slowly tick by, agitation growing on the Superior's face. Ms. Eryn practically falls into the room just as the Superior is about to call for her again.

"Sorry, Diana," Eryn gasps, as she places herself gently down onto the couch. "Several of the young children were fighting after being sorted. Saree and I were trying to calm them down when you first called. I had to have several of the instructors assist so I could leave." Eryn's pale checks are flushed a bright pink, probably due to her rush when called. Even sitting on the couch, Eryn is tall in stature, lean build. She straightens out her khaki skirt, adjusts her blue dress shirt, and crosses her ankles.

"That's quite alright, Eryn. I'd forgotten that you were sorting the children today for their final predestination coding tomorrow." Superior Hersher relaxes, sitting down in her office chair, leaning back in comfort. "Those can be trying affairs."

The Superior tells the same story to Eryn as she did the other staff.

"I'll move the instructors' belongings to some of the children's rooms and recode the entrance to the Predestination Center to prevent any of the instructors from accidentally exiting our section of the complex. When the meals are ready for the children, I'll open the doors for the kitchen staff."

"Excellent," the Superior says, beaming at Eryn.

"You're going to imprison your staff? What if something happens and the children need to get out?" I protest.

Eryn turns her head, looking at me as if I'm something to be discarded, a blemish in the Superior's room.

"This is a secure facility, Miss. Besides, there aren't any threats to this hatchery. No one would purposefully harm children."

I think back to the Dormitories…the pictures from my nightmares…my past.

"You're wrong," I reply, focusing my attention away from her and out towards the window as a light snow begins to fall quietly outside.

"That'll be all, Eryn." The young woman leaves the room, but not before taking a second glance at me, confusion in her eyes.

"Why do you lie to them?" I inquire, as soon as the door closes.

"Believe it or not, Trea, it's to protect them." Superior Hersher stands, walking up beside me as I continue to watch the snow fall out her window. "If these people knew about the true monsters that lurk outside the boundaries of Sirain, they'd be mortified."

I notice fine gray hairs peeking out from the bright red of her mane, wrinkles beginning to form around her mouth and eyes. Perhaps there's more to her than I first believed.

"My father was devastated by the attack on the Dormitories. He looked at all of you as his children, never realizing the evil intent the world held for them. He was never the same after that. He was a broken man…who sunk below human."

Her voice quivers, choking back a wall of emotion that has probably been caged for years. We stand in silence for a little while, watching as the clouds grow thicker, the snow starting to stick to the pine trees below us.

"Let's go check on Captain Braxton and get the rest of the group situated into their sleeping quarters."

We go back down to the security and communication's room, hoping that some progress has been made.

"Any luck?" Superior Hersher questions, as we enter.

"Unfortunately no. This room doesn't have the proper equipment to access the satellite." Braxton grumbles, pulling wires out of panels.

"Can you try to contact Tyre?"

"I'm trying, Superior, but they appear to be on permanent black out. With your permission, I'd like to use some of the equipment we have in our vehicles to try and get us back on-line with Acheron."

"Do it. I'll make sure your biometrics is upgraded to allow full access into the facility. I've made arrangements with my staff for your group to have full use of the living quarters. Meals will also be made available to you, but only after the facility has eaten. Is there anything else you may need?"

"Not at this time, Superior."

"Very well. Trea will show you to the armory, where your men are currently located." She smiles tentatively and then retreats up the stairwell.

The rest of the day is spent on moving equipment from two of the vehicles outside, mapping out a defensive strategy, and trying to establish a connection to the outside world.

Quin, Lehen, and I are sent to check around outside, looking for possible vulnerabilities of the complex from the cliff side. The Morrigan are tasked to hold our rappelling cords, making sure we don't fall to our deaths as we survey the land.

The rocks are cold and slippery from the still falling snow, and make climbing treacherous.

The three of us are wearing only a few additional layers over our clothes to keep the plummeting temperatures at bay. The farthest we can climb down is about ten feet below the structures. I can't see the ground beneath me due to the thick foliage. Many of the rocks are smooth, but a few jut out, creating a ledge for me to stand on. The supports holding up each building and connecting bridge are bolted into the side of the cliff face, but it's hard to judge how deeply they are anchored.

Gage calls over the small listening device sitting uncomfortably inside my ear canal. "Have you placed your cameras yet?"

"I'm about to place the first one," I respond into the tiny microphone attached to my jacket.

"Well, hurry up. Quin and Lehen are about done with theirs."

I swing to my right and choose an edge to place my first camera on. The adhesive being used to secure the cameras doesn't like the dampness, so I have to dry the spot before sticking it into position.

"How's the view?"

"Tilt the lens a little farther down and it'll be fine."

I adjust the camera and then move on.

Quin and Lehen begin to ascend to the surface. I hesitate, enjoying the quiet of the landscape. The air feels calm and peaceful, cool and crisp. I close my eyes and just listen to the falling snow. But a few moments later my line is violently tugged, breaking the serenity of the moment, so I begin my climb back to the surface.

CHAPTER 25

We eat dinner after everyone else has gone to bed. The food is lukewarm and a little tough, but it's better than what we're used to, and we clean our plates. Some even go back for seconds. I retreat to my room for the rest of the evening while Rabaan and five of his men take the first patrol. Keller, Rey and Tobin will relieve them around two in the morning. Braxton and Jagger elect to forgo sleep and work in the security and communications room, allowing Duren and Hera to get some rest. Lehen, Quin, and the remaining five Morrigan will patrol the grounds during the day. I'm being made to stay inside, much to my unhappiness.

Since I'm the only female in our little entourage, I'm allotted an entire living quarter to myself. I have four bedrooms, a sitting area, and a large bathroom all to myself. The room I'm occupying belongs to Saree, who works with the newborns-to-six-year-old age group. Her room is small, one window just above her built-in bed. The bed linens and furniture are uniform, probably issued by Acheron to keep conformity. Shelves cascade down on the wall next to her closet, covered in hand-made art pieces obviously done by the children, unlike the Superior's office, which contained no personal items or mementos.

I'm in desperate need of a shower, so I discard my filthy clothes and pull on a blue cotton robe. The bathroom is blue in color much like the bedroom and sitting area. Every fifth tile has the emblem of Acheron etched in the center. I find toiletry items in one of the shower stalls, as well as a freshly laundered towel. I take the center stall, and stay in the hot water for almost an hour, letting it rain down on me as I try to cleanse every cell of my being. After drying off, I wash my clothes in the sink and then return to my room, where I exchange the robe for a pair of satin blue pajamas. I turn off the light and crawl under the soft gold blankets, burrowing myself as far down as possible.

```
Devlan hastily leaves, followed by Dr. Hersher. I walk
over to Magda, take her hand, and stand to watch as
the complex continues to implode. Another man
approaches us from the inferno.
"Thatcher," Magda calls out, "Did you find him?"
"No, the housing units are gone. I'm afraid these four
are all that remain."
```

A pounding outside my dream world rouses me back to reality.

I push the covers back, step out of bed, and grope my way in the dark as I haven't turned the light back on. Shielding my eyes in preparation for blinding light from the sitting area, I open the door, but am met by a soft yellow glow instead, and Quin standing before me.

"Are you all right?" he asks, standing arm's length away from the threshold.

"I'm fine," I lie, "why?"

"I was coming to check on you when I heard you crying, so I wanted to make sure you were okay."

I want to turn him away, but loneliness and loss has crept inside, so I step aside leaving the door open. I walk back over to the bed while Quin flips on the lights and closes the door.

I sit at the head of the bed, pulling my knees up tight against my chest. "What do you remember from that night at the Dormitories?"

"I was sitting in the medical wing, being treated by one of the nurses. I'd been feeling ill all day, so they kept me separated from the other boys as a precaution. The nurse was running tests on me to see why I was feeling very ill, because Antaeans are not supposed to get sick."

Quin sits down at the foot of my bed, feet resting on the floor.

"The perimeter alarms started to sound, so the nurse told me to stay where I was while she went to see what was going on." His gaze is unfocused as he thinks back to that night.

"I heard screaming from down the hall, so I crawled off the work bench she had me propped on and wriggled under a set of cabinets against the far wall. The screams became louder when I saw bright blue flashes erupt beyond the window of the door to the room. The nurse came stumbling in, her right side badly singed, and bleeding at the shoulder. I was about to come out from my hiding place when a man in black clothing came in and shot her in the back with a Levin gun. I watched as she fell to the floor, eyes wide open, but lifeless. I couldn't move from that spot until the fire was practically on top of me."

"That's why you weren't with Lehen and Vier when they were saved," I say.

I let the silence settle between us, turn my head, and look out into the darkness. The snow has stopped falling, but the clouds remain as the stars are blacked out.

"Is that what you were dreaming about?" Quin finally asks, breaking the quiet.

"Yes," I say relaxing a bit, settling my legs down onto the bed. "I've no real recollection of that night except in the nightmares that come to me. I doubt I'll ever be able to remember everything."

"I think that's a blessing."

I smile at his remark as my eyes begin to grow heavy. Quin gives me a hug just as he gets up to leave. I hang onto him for longer than is required, but it's nice to see the Quin I grew to love. I crawl under the covers as the light in the room is extinguished, but I don't hear my door open, instead I feel Quin lie down next to me, wrapping his body around me as if encasing me in a cocoon to keep the nightmares at bay.

I sleep well past sunrise, but Quin doesn't leave until I'm fully awake. He waits for me in the sitting room while I change from my pajamas into the damp clothes. We've missed breakfast, so all that's left is some dry cereal. After we finish eating, Quin decides to go and check on the guards outside as he was supposed to relieve them this morning with Lehen. I go to see how Braxton is faring with the satellite.

All but one of the monitors is displaying a live feed from the cameras that we placed yesterday. Braxton is sitting at a control panel while Jagger is hunched down in the back connecting wires together, Duren kneeling by his side helping. Neither notices my appearance until I ask how they're doing.

"We have intermittent control of one of Acheron's satellites. This room isn't meant to handle this function, so the link is spotty at times." Braxton answers through gritted teeth, frustration weighing heavy in his voice. "We don't have a...wait," he shouts. "Hold it right there."

The picture on the monitor is grainy, but outlines of the city are visible.

"It looks okay to me," I comment, as I sit down next to him on one of the stools.

"No...it's not." Braxton tries to pan out further from the city. "See...there." He points to a white line in the lower right section of the screen.

It takes me a moment to focus in on what he's pointing to, so I take a step closer to the screen and see the shuttle rail. Whole sections are missing.

"What would've caused that?" I question, as I notice areas about a mile wide crumbling into the lake water below.

"It's a failsafe for the city," Braxton replies, as he continues to try and move the satellite view. "The shuttle rail is designed to break apart if the city is attacked. The only way to get close enough now would be by boat, but if you don't know the correct paths through the water you'll hit detonators just below the surface. They should've been released from the lake bed when the failsafe was put into action."

He focuses briefly on a metal wreck in the water, just off shore. A small boat sits tangled in the shallows, with several bodies floating next to it. Other boats sit idle, waiting to be launched.

"What about the Laics in the Boroughs?" Jagger asks, as he crawls out from his spot, wires in both hands.

"There's nothing that can be done."

The image moves to the left; smoke and flames reaching high into the sky. Buildings have disintegrated into dust, a river of fire flowing into the lake.

"What about the defenses? The Regulators? Don't they have anything that will help defend the Boroughs?"

"The Regulators aren't trained for battle; they're only a control force for the Laics. The cities dismantled all of their aircraft and defensive armory long ago."

"Why would they do that?"

"Because that was what the Antaeans were supposed to be for!" Braxton barks. "After the destruction of the Dormitories, Tyre and Acheron located the individual responsible and eliminated him, along with his faction. That was supposed to be the end of it."

"It appears the High Rulers were wrong about that."

Braxton scowls at Jagger's comment before returning to the monitor.

"You can't just leave them to die!" Jagger exclaims, coming around to our side of the room, knocking Duren down in the process. "They're defenseless because of you and the city, so you're just going to let them be slaughtered?"

"They can be replaced," Braxton snaps back. "What do you think the Hatcheries are for? You were born in one. I was born in one." He rises out of his seat, veins pulsing in his neck.

Jagger surprises everyone by gripping Braxton around the throat. Braxton tries to free himself from the vice-like grasp, and I stand and watch Braxton's face turn purple from lack of oxygen. A smile grows on my face. Trea is enjoying the spectacle.

Rabaan steps into the room, pulling Jagger off Braxton, who's gasping for air.

"How can you defend him?" Jagger shouts.

"Now is not the time."

"He's letting all those people die!"

"More will die if we don't stop the Hostem."

Jagger steps back, still enraged. He storms out of the room, hands balled into fists. I get down from the stool and chase after him. He's in the process of going up the stairs when I stop him.

"We'll get our chance, Jagger. Just give me time and we'll take care of them all at once."

He turns to look at me, rage in his eyes.

"Them? You're no different!"

He plants his fist into my chest, sending me sailing across the hall, landing hard against the far wall. I slide to the floor, stunned more by his remark than his blow. It takes me a few seconds to regain my composure...as well as my footing. I stand up, walk up one flight, and hide myself in my room for the remainder of the day.

Quin comes to check on me in the late afternoon, but I don't answer his knocks. I miss lunch and dinner, so my stomach is growling from emptiness. Normally I'd do something physically challenging to drive off tension, but there's nowhere to go in the hatchery, and venturing outside isn't an option. A headache begins to grow behind my eyes from being inactive, so I turn off the lights and curl up under the covers, falling asleep.

CHAPTER 26

Shouting rouses me. As the voices grow in pitch and in number, I roll over onto my left side, opening my eyes just a little.

A large figure looms in the doorway; light from the hallway casts his shadow deep into the bedchamber. I see a woman in orange charging up behind him, but in one smooth motion he turns and snaps her neck.

The man steps back into the light, placing an object he has clutched in his hand onto the biometric pad outside the entrance. The door begins to slowly close, light from the hallway ebbing backwards out of the chamber. A series of explosions echo through the room. The face I see on the opposite side of the door is one I recognize...a face of kindness...the face of a friend.

I bolt upright in bed, screaming.

Quin is in my room in a matter of seconds. He must've been sleeping in the sitting area.

I'm drenched in sweat and tears. I begin to retch as Terrance's face floats back into my mind. Of all the people I've met in the past few months, for it to come down to Terrance....

Quin clutches me tightly, trying to get me to settle down.

I hear feet pounding down the hallway; Braxton and Rabaan are next to enter.

"What happened?" Braxton shouts.

"She's had a nightmare," Quin answers, brushing my wet hair from my face.

I hang onto him as a life-line, fearing if I let go I'll be sucked back in, to the vision of Terrance murdering my family and friends....

"That must've been some nightmare," Rabaan adds. "We heard her all the way downstairs."

Sobs shake my body and I'm suddenly chilled to the bone. Quin wraps me up in my blanket as Braxton and Rabaan leave. He cradles me, rocking me gently.

"It was Terrance," I whisper to him. "He did it. Terrance he killed them."

"It was just a nightmare," Quin tries to reassure me.

"No, it wasn't." I gently pull myself away from his hold. "I remember it all now. He tossed detonators into one of the girls' bedchambers, then closed the door just before they ignited."

"How would he have gotten the door open, Trea? He would've needed access to the biometrics reader in order to do that."

"He did. He had a severed hand in his palm, which is how he opened and closed the door."

"Are you sure?"

I take a deep sigh before answering.

"Yes."

Quin gets up from the bed, hands rubbing the side of his head. He puts his arms around me again and holds me tightly. I feel warmth grow between us, which I haven't felt in a while. We stand there for several minutes, neither of us wanting to move. Eventually sleep overtakes us. I crawl under my blankets, Quin by my side.

When I wake in the morning he's gone.

I don't leave my room at all the next day. Even when Jagger makes the effort to check on me, I turn him away. Quin brings me my meals, but I hardly eat. I feel myself wasting away. Knowing the truth behind who destroyed the Dormitories has taken its toll on me.

How could this be? He was my friend. I trusted him. I risked my life for him.

The next morning a constant pounding on my door rouses me from bed. I try to ignore the noise by putting the pillow over my head, but the banging won't stop. I drag myself out of bed to go yell at the person disturbing me.

"Good morning, Trea," Superior Hersher announces, looking severe in a crisp blue suit, hair tightly pulled back into a chignon. "Captain Braxton has informed me that you're not feeling too well. Is there anything I can do to assist you?" Her manner is cool and matter of fact, not at all comforting.

"No, I'm fine."

She hesitates a few moments to take stock of my appearance and demeanor. "Come with me please," she demands more than requests. I get dressed and reluctantly follow.

We take the stairs up to the main floor, and walk over the connection bridges to the Predestination Center's entrance. Eryn is waiting for us, a bland expression on her pristine face. She enters in a code on her side of the door, which quietly slides open. We pass through, after which the door closes and locks behind us.

"Newborns to six year olds live and learn in this building," the Superior explains. "Each child has a purpose. Some will become teachers, doctors and nurses, others will be trained as Regulators and guards for the High Ruler and Superiors. The remaining children are coded to be Laics, to live and work in the Boroughs."

She pauses briefly, making sure I'm paying close attention.

"The room directly in front of us is the Destiny room. Infants and toddlers up to age two are monitored and observed here to see what qualities they may exhibit."

We cross the hall and enter into a large room segregated into smaller areas by half walls. Each section has several children of one particular age group. "When the children are close to turning three years old, a code is embedded into their wrists, which marks them for life. This code tells the instructors what purpose the child will have for the rest of their existence."

"Why?"

"Why? To assist in population control and to keep the Laics in their place, of course. Tyre does the same thing. They have several of their own hatcheries, as does Acheron."

"What about children who are born in the Boroughs? You can't predestine them."

"There's no breeding in the Boroughs," Eryn states, grimacing at the idea. "We take measures early in a child's life to ensure this doesn't occur. There are incentives given to women who feel an obligation to assist in the creation of children. They're sent to live in a hatchery for several years, giving birth to four or five children, after which they are sterilized and sent back to the Boroughs."

It's my turn to grimace. The idea of using people as breeding machines repels me.

"It's not as horrible as it sounds," Superior Hersher says in reaction to the face I make. "Many of the women are happy to do this, as they know they're contributing to the wellness of society."

"What about the citizens of Acheron and Tyre?"

"They are limited to only two or three children. That's to prevent overcrowding, since the cities' limits are very confined."

"There's plenty of space out in the Wasteland," I remark, trying to suggest its better there than in the cities.

"That land, my dear, is contaminated from the many wars fought on this soil over the last century and a half. Those who decide to live out in the Wasteland are doomed to have short lives. The cities could only clean up so much of Sirain to make it inhabitable."

Knowing the Wasteland as I do, I have sincere doubts about what the Superior is telling me. Perhaps it's a story that was passed down from generations to keep those in the cities and Boroughs from leaving.

I turn my attention away from Superior Hersher and watch as one little curly-blond-haired girl tries to pull herself up into a standing position using a small chair. The nurse is monitoring her progress very carefully. She is the smallest in her group, yet appears to be far more advanced than her peers. After several minutes of effort, she accomplishes her goal. The nurse takes down some notes on an electronic pad and moves onto another group of children.

"What happens after they're coded?"

"The children are moved down to their respective rooms below the main level. Every day they are brought up to this floor and conditioned in the rooms designated for their occupation. When they reach the age of seven, they're transferred to the Developmental Quad, where they're trained until the age of thirteen. From there, they are moved to their permanent dwellings where they'll live and work for the remainder of their life."

"And you don't think there is anything wrong with this?"

"Really, Miss," Eryn begins, huffing away, "what kind of society do you want to have? How else will we survive if we don't have order?"

Superior Hersher places her hand gingerly onto Eryn's shoulder, calming the woman. She thanks Eryn for her time and we leave the room. Before we exit the building, the Superior places her hand on my arm, turning me to face her.

"I know it's hard and it doesn't seem fair, but Trea, you must remember everyone has a purpose. Whether it's a destination we accept or not, we all have a purpose...even you. You need to determine what that purpose is."

We return to the Intake Facility in silence. I go back to my room and watch the snow begin to fall again, harder with every passing hour. Quin brings me dinner after he's done with his turn at patrol. I finish my plate, but still feel weighted down with what the Superior said.

My original purpose was to protect the cities, but from what I've seen, the cities don't need protecting as much as their people do. I need to decide where my loyalties lie.

Quin lies next to me, falling asleep the moment his head hits the pillow. I, however, am feeling fitful and decide to take a walk, closing my bedroom door quietly as I leave.

Gage, Keller, and Hera are trying different frequencies in the communications room in an effort to reach someone in Acheron. I stand silently in the back of the room, listening as they tirelessly attempt to contact someone.

"Regulator Tower 1, do you read? This is Hatchery Nine, please advise," Keller calls, his voice heavy with exhaustion. "Regulator Tower 2, is anyone there?"

"Still can't reach anyone?"

Gage turns around on his stool to look at me.

"What're you doing out of your room? I thought you'd permanently retreated into your cave."

"I'm tired of being useless. I need something to do."

"Go outside and see Rabaan, he could use some help with the patrol for tonight with all the snow that's falling."

I leave and head to the main floor. As I approach the entrance, Lehen comes in covered in snow, looking frozen to the bone.

"Hey stranger, I thought I was never going to see you again."

"I'm jumping out of my skin from boredom. Gage told me Rabaan needs help with the patrol tonight."

"Yes, he does. Let me go find you some protective gear."

He disappears for a few moments, returning with a thick fur-lined white coat, matching pants, gloves, and boots. I cinch the hood around my head and pull on the gloves. The outfit makes me feel bulky and awkward, and Lehen says he feels the same way. We step outside into the snow.

Rabaan is surprised to see me, but hands me a Levin gun and a Beta rifle, and tells me to proceed north through the trees. He hands me a communications earpiece, which I place in my ear, and I head off down a small slope through ankle-deep snow, into the forest.

I walk with the Beta rifle pointing forward as the Levin gun bangs against my thigh. I reach the edge of the cliff to the north and look over. It drops straight down a good mile before hitting a plateau. There isn't much to see in the dark, just pure white snow falling noiselessly to the ground.

My feet begin to get cold standing, so I walk along the rim going east. Off to my right in the distance I can see the lights from the housing unit. I continue my journey, passing the Predestination Center and the Developmental Quad, where I reach the edge of the cliff and double back. This is my routine for about an hour, then I retreat inside to get warm. The biometrics for the front entrance has been deactivated in order to allow those on patrol access in and out of the facility.

Once I'm inside, I remove my jacket, gloves, and boots, then place the Beta rifle up against the far wall. I pace back and forth in the foyer as there isn't any place to sit down.

Ten minutes later, an ear-piercing alarm shatters the silence.

The lights above my head change from a soft white to a harsh red and begin to flash. After several seconds, the alarm decreases in volume, as a message is broadcast.

"Captain Braxton," Hera announces, "please report to the security and communications room." The message repeats several more times.

I run through the doors in my sock-covered feet, turn the corner, and head down the stairs. Braxton reaches the room just as I do.

"What is it?" he asks, as Hera gets up from her stool.

"The perimeter alarm by the first gate has been tripped," she says in a surprisingly calm voice. "Nothing is appearing on the cameras, but we thought you should be notified."

The panel in front of Gage displays the layout of the complex, as well as the location of all perimeter alarms. The alarm indicator to the top right of the panel is glowing red. A few seconds later another one illuminates on the top left of the panel. Although the cameras are in night mode, nothing is displaying on the monitors as yet.

I step closer to the screens, scanning every inch.

As the camera by the Developmental Quad rotates, I see my footprints, almost buried under the new layer of snow, along with a second set of fresh tracks.

"Rabaan," I call through the device still in my ear.

"Yes, Trea?"

"Is anyone patrolling the far east perimeter past the Developmental Quad?"

"No, why?"

"We've got company."

At that moment, the cameras that we had planted go dark. Hera pushes an emergency button on the panel in front of Gage. We watch on our screens as all windows and doors are coated with some type of film.

"What did you do?" I shout at her.

"Emergency protocol states that if there's a breach of the complex, all windows and doors will be automatically coated with impenetrable film."

"You've just locked out the guards on patrol!"

"Rabaan," Braxton calls to him by pushing a button on the panel that controls the front entrance. "Rabaan, can you hear me?"

"Braxton, what happened? The door is sealed and we can't get in."

Braxton shoots Hera a dirty look. "Gather your men and try to find another way into the complex. The buildings are on lock down, but there might be another way for you to get in."

Braxton turns to me. "Where's Quintus?"

"He might be in my room."

"Go get him and see if you two can get that front door open in case the patrol can't find another way in."

I leave, go up to the floor above, and run down the hall to my little section of the living quarters, slipping occasionally in my socked feet.

Quin is exiting my room when I enter.

"What's going on?"

"The perimeter has been breached," I say, as I sit down just long enough to remove the socks. "Hera placed the complex on lockdown, so Rabaan and the others on patrol outside can't get back inside. You and I need to get up to the front entrance to try and open it."

I strip off the pants, removing the Levin gun from the front pocket and tucking it into my waistband. We rush up to the main level, taking two steps at a time. As we exit through the doors into the entryway, we see bright blue flashes outside. Quin picks up the Beta rifle from where I left it. We take our places in front of the glass doors, weapons raised.

Rabaan is firing into the woods as he crouches behind one of the vehicles off to the right. Two Morrigan lay motionless on the ground a few meters to the left. I can't tell if they're dead or simply wounded. Lehen and three other Morrigan are standing their ground just a few feet from the bodies.

A deflagration round detonates in front of the entrance. Quin and I both duck, but the device doesn't penetrate the glass. Another round hits one of the vehicles, sending shrapnel flying. Rabaan shrinks back against the building after taking a hit in the shoulder. Frustrated, I raise the Levin gun at the door and fire. The energy blast is absorbed by the film, a blue wave rippling through the clear coating, dissipating away from the initial hit.

Another explosion radiates a few feet away, shaking the building slightly.

I get close up to the glass to see where it hit, when I spot Rabaan dragging himself over to the door, legs badly wounded. Quin tries his turn at blasting the glass with the Beta rifle, but it has no effect. He drops the weapon and tries to manually force open the door. I drop down to my knees and try to assist by pushing on the lower half. From the corner of my eye, I see a bright blue glow begin to radiate from Quin. It pours into the doorframe as he applies more pressure.

The film begins to quiver, pieces fragmenting slightly. I look out and see Rabaan watching, his battered body leaning against the glass. His focus changes to my face, an expression of sadness on his. He places his right palm onto the glass. I mirror him, my hand pressing against his.

He might not have always been on the right side of this struggle, but he did what he could when asked. I can think of worse people in the world.

A burst of brightness causes my vision to momentarily falter.

Rabaan sinks to the ground as a hole is opened in his chest.

"No!" I scream, as the protective film on the entrance shatters.

Quin pushes the doors open. I pull Rabaan's body in as Quin shouts for the others.

Two of the Morrigan take Rabaan from me as they enter, dragging him further in. I fire my Levin gun at the Hostem outside, trying to provide cover for Lehen as he and another wounded Morrigan limp their way towards us.

Once everyone is safe, Quin closes the door. The protective film for the entrance doesn't reappear.

"Everyone to the emergency bunker," I hear Superior Hersher announce over the speakers. "This is not a drill. Everyone must evacuate to the emergency bunker."

"You heard the lady," Lehen says.

He and Quin practically carry the Morrigan through the doors and down the hall to the connection bridge, but I linger behind, watching the door close behind the group.

I kneel next to Rabaan, closing his eyes, check his uniform, and locate a dozen detonators secured to a sash around his waist. Dark figures on my right slowly move forward from the shadows. Glass from the doors fragments as it's hit. Another blast sprays the shards into the room, covering me.

I remove two detonators from Rabaan's waist and set one for fifteen seconds. I throw the detonator out the door, and watch it land a few inches from a small group of Hostem. They are blown into pieces from the ensuing blast. I set the second one to twenty seconds and toss it outside as well, towards what remains of the vehicles. I remove the sash from Rabaan's waist as the vehicles ignite.

"I'm sorry," I whisper to him.

I sprint off through the door, ignoring the cuts on my feet from glass shards that litter the tile, sling the belt around my shoulders, and secure the Levin gun in my waistband. As I pass through the set of doors for the connection bridge, I see children pouring from the Predestination Center, hurrying toward the emergency bunker's entrance.

Shots are being fired at the glass of the bridge, but the protective film is preventing any real damage. With the lights of the complex shining brightly, I can see the full assault being led from the cliffs below. At least a hundred people are scaling the cliff face.

I bolt down the bridge, through the housing unit, and onto the other bridge. Women in various stages of pregnancy are shuffling as fast as they can towards the emergency bunker. I push my way past them. One of the windows on the bridge has been blown out, probably before the emergency protocol was put into place. Jagger, Keller, and Gage are rapidly firing down at the climbers below. I remove a detonator, set the time to ten seconds, and drop it out the window.

"Get down," I shout.

Everyone crouches down as the device ignites below causing the bridge to shake slightly. The women stand back up, hurrying even faster down the walkway. I look down and see a number of the climbers have either fallen or are dangling from their ropes.

"Where are Quin and Lehen?" I ask Jagger, as he picks his Beta rifle back up, firing down at those who continue to climb.

"They went to the Developmental Quad," he says between bursts of fire. "The building was breached just before lockdown."

I hand him and Keller three detonators, leaving me with four.

I squeeze past the mass of people rushing into the emergency bunker while Tobin and two Morrigan direct everyone. Children and instructors continue to exit the Predestination Center as I make my way in. I follow the line of kids, hoping they will lead me to the connecting bridge to the Developmental Quad.

I find the entrance and bolt down the walkway.

Smoke empties from the building, floating along the ceiling of the bridge. I can hear shouting and screaming echoing through the halls as I gingerly step inside, remove the gun from my waistband, and hold it up in front of me.

Two children round the corner to my left, blood and ash covering their faces. I point them towards the door, practically shoving them through, as a tall figure in black follows from behind them, firing in our direction. I shove the kids to the ground and lie on top of them as I fire at him, hitting him in the leg just above the knee, then in the stomach. I pull myself off of the children, shouting at them to run.

I walk over to the moaning lump on the floor and remove his hood.

Terrance looks up with anger in his eyes that changes to sorrow when he sees who I am.

"How could you be mixed up in this?" I shout. "I trusted you." Tears stream down my face. "I thought you were my friend. You murdered my family...my friends," I whimper.

His hand reaches up, fingers brush my face. *I'm sorry*, he mouths, then goes limp.

I stand and walk away, leaving Terrance to die alone.

A moment later, Quin and Lehen drag Rey around the opposite corner from where the kids came from. He is badly injured, his shin bone shattered beyond repair. I cover them as they drag Rey down the bridge. Braxton and three Morrigan meet them halfway. Two of the Morrigan take Rey and carry him into the Predestination Center.

"How many are in there?" Braxton asks, as he comes up to me.

"I'm not sure," I answer, smoke around us getting thicker.

"Almost all of the children got out," Lehen says, as he, Quin, and the remaining Morrigan join us. "The building is crawling with Hostem."

"We can't let them get any farther."

"I've got an idea," I say removing one of the detonators from Rabaan's sash.

"The glass is impenetrable," Lehen says. "How are the detonators going to help?"

"I'm not going to use them on the glass." I look over at Quin, who smiles as he senses what I'm planning.

He places his palm onto the film covering the window closest to the entrance on the right. His back begins to glow as his Quantum Stream pulses through his system. The coating cracks under his palm, radiating outwards, before finally shattering. I fire the Levin gun at the window, disintegrating the glass.

"Cover me," I say, handing Braxton my gun before jumping out.

I aim for a thick pile of snow just a few feet below, so I don't have to jump far. Energy blasts shoot over my head at the intruders down below.

I lower myself slowly from one ledge to another. A Hostem swings up next to me, but a shot from above kills her within seconds of reaching my ledge. I remove the rope from the woman's harness, watch as her body plummets to the valley below, then secure myself and push off of the rocks, swinging hard to the right, aiming for the farthest support column. I secure the detonator by one of the column's joints, setting the timer for five minutes, swing back around to my left, and place another detonator on the middle column at the same joint, this one set for four minutes. For the final column, I set the timer to three minutes, untie myself from the rope, and begin my climb back up.

Quin reaches down from the walkway, grabbing my arm to help pull me up, but a moment later he is shot in the arm, dropping me. I begin to fall, and am just barely able to grab hold of the rope I'd been tied to. I pull myself back up to the ledge and Quin grabs my arm again, and pulls me up. We run down the connection bridge as Hostem begin to make their way through the smoke filled entrance of the Developmental Quad.

Energy blasts ricochet around us. Lehen and Braxton return fire.

The walkway sways mildly when the first detonator goes off.

We turn the bend in the bridge as the second one ignites, fiercely shaking the metallic structure. I turn my head and see the Developmental Quad bending, buckling under its weight.

Lehen goes down from a shot to his thigh. He's never been injured before, and buckles, slow to heal. I crouch in front of him to give him time to recover, taking several shots to my side and back.

The bridge shakes violently as the final detonator ignites. The Developmental Quad collapses with a great roar and shriek of metal, sliding down the cliff into the snowy darkness below. Those still standing are knocked to their feet as the connection bridge begins to slide, the glass walls cracking from the pressure exerted by the supports failing. The Hostem in the walkway try to retreat, but fall out of the broken window as the bridge twists to the right; Braxton and the Morrigan make it into the Predestination Center; Lehen, Quin, and I slide down the metal flooring.

The bridge collapses, folding at the doorway seam. The rest of the building has been lost, eliminating the protective film, and the three of us fall through the glass. Lehen and I manage to grab hold of the metal window casing. I grab Quin as he falls past, just moments before he's out of reach.

"Quin, you're slipping," I shout, as my hold begins to loosen. "Grab my arm with your other hand!"

Energy blasts fly at us from below. Lehen is hit in the back, but manages to keep his hold. Quin is also hit, his body swaying from the blast.

"Let go, Meg," he says to me.

"No, you need to hold on."

"Meg, it'll be all right. You have to let go."

I shake my head and try to pull him up. He uncurls his free hand, showing me an activated detonator, counting down brightly in the darkness.

A moment later he lets go of me, falling into the abyss below.

I scream his name, my wounded voice resonating off the rocks.

The detonation is bright blue, and powerful. The remaining glass in the bridge rains down on us. The shock wave radiates skyward then all is quiet.

Tears pour from my eyes. My heart breaks, mourning another loss of someone I love.

"Trea," I hear Lehen say, as if from somewhere off in a distance.

I look over at him, his face emotionless.

"We have to climb."

He pulls himself up and begins to ascend the window frames like a ladder.

I look down one last time, rage beginning to build.

CHAPTER 27

Braxton reaches down to me as I make it onto the last metal frame. I place my hand in his and he pulls me up to the doorway.

"It's not over," he announces, as more blasts can be heard from the other connection bridge. "We need your help."

Just what I need to take out some of the frustration I'm feeling right now. "How many do you think remain?"

"Just about a handful. They shouldn't be too much trouble." He smiles at me as he places his Levin gun in one hand and the Levin gun Quin dropped in my other.

Trea grins back.

I take off down the hall of the main level of the Predestination Center leaving Lehen, Braxton, and the Morrigan behind.

I enter the walkway, firing at anything that moves, taking down three Hostem before I reach the entrance to the emergency bunker, which is sealed shut. I come upon four more as I make the bend in the walkway and cut my way through them, leaving nothing alive behind me. I kill two more as I enter the housing unit. The remaining Hostem is at the far end, firing at me, but missing. The Hostem turns to run, but a well-aimed shot shatters a femur, and the Hostem falls.

I walk slowly down the length of the hall as the fighter tries to crawl around the corner, but the person doesn't get far and I'm there in seconds.

"Why?" I ask, pointing the gun at the Hostem's back.

"To bring an end to Sirain," a familiar voice answers. She rolls over onto her back, breathing labored due to blood loss. Her face is covered in dirt and sweat, but the white-streaked red hair is very recognizable.

"Rena?"

"Hello, Meg." She tries to push herself up into a sitting position. "I imagine you're as surprised to see me as I am to see you." She shakes her head. "If Terrance had known the truth about you, he never would have left to go looking for you."

I take the butt of the Levin gun and hit her across the face. A cut above her eyebrow forms deep and red. "What truth? What did I ever do to you or Terrance? You're the monsters here, and I'm going to stop you."

"You can never stop this, Meg. Acheron is lost and Tyre soon will be. You've failed." She taunts me, a smile growing on her face.

I kneel, bringing myself down to her level.

"Why do you care so much about destroying the cities?"

"They obliterated everything…murdered hundreds when Asphodel fell…they're the reason why the Wasteland exists. They manipulate and control those they feel are beneath them. Destroy anyone who thinks differently."

"Your brother was the one who planned the attack on the Dormitories," I state, finally starting to figure out the story behind the story.

"And for his efforts to cleanse us of the abominations, the High Ruler of Tyre had him executed in that arena of theirs, in front of the whole country. He was sliced to pieces by a battle droid, as if it was a game." A brief smile crosses her lips then quickly fades. "Those of us who'd escaped the collection migrated into the Wasteland, away from the moral decay of the cities."

"So why come back?"

"To finish what my brother started. We thought all the Antaeans had died that night. It wasn't until your display in Tyre that we all realized we were wrong."

She moans from pain as her blood loss continues, her breathing becoming labored.

"You'll never win, Meg. Sirain's enemies are too great. This is only the beginning."

I hear feet approach from behind me. Lehen and Braxton are at my side, weapons drawn.

Rena's focus shifts from me to them. "Sirain will fall. You all will burn…murderers, all of you."

"You're no different," I say, as I stand up, aiming the barrel at her heart. "Tell your brother hello for me when you see him."

The wall behind Rena singes as her chest opens upon my firing. I turn to Lehen and Braxton. Both still have their weapons pointed at the body.

"Let's end this."

A roll call is taken after the fighting ends. Thankfully, casualties from the hatchery are low: four children from the Developmental Quad, two instructors, two Morrigan, Rabaan, Rey who bled out from his leg wound…and Quin.

Tobin, Keller, and Gage are tasked with collecting the bodies and disposing of them. The Superior doesn't want the children seeing them when she allows everyone to leave the bunker. I sit in the security and communications room, my head resting on my hands, while Braxton takes inventory of the working weapons and vehicles. Jagger and Lehen do several sweeps of the complex, making sure all the Hostem are gone or dead; occasionally a short blast of a gun rings out when they find one still alive.

"Well," Braxton says upon entering the room. "I can get at least one of the vehicles to run. It'll take a few days because of all the damage, but I can make it work." He wipes his hands on a greasy towel before sitting on one of the stools next to me. "What's the plan?"

"I don't know," I answer after taking in a deep breath. I glance over at him, dirt covering most of his face. "We need to draw the Hostem away from the cities, Boroughs, and hatcheries."

"I can try and reestablish communications with Tyre and Acheron to see what resources they may have. Our weapons are almost out of power, and Lehen isn't as strong as you are, so using him as a weapon isn't going to work. If the Hostem attack the hatchery again, we may not be so fortunate next time."

"Losing Quin…was not fortunate." Tears spill down my cheeks.

I suddenly feel very alone, my body aching from a pain I can't see.

"You know I didn't mean it that way," Braxton's voice quivers.

I do know what he means, but it hurts all the same.

He sits with me in silence for some time. Occasionally he looks down at the panel in front of him, turning some of the dials, attempting to make some kind of connection with the outside world. A few of the monitors go from black to a gray haze, but no one answers. He continues to play with the various settings as Jagger and Lehen join us.

"Hello…?" A faint female voice is heard through one of the monitors to my left. "Hello…can anyone hear me? This is Superior Gatlen of Hatchery Seven, is anyone there?"

"This is Hatchery Nine, Superior Gatlen," Braxton responds after pressing a sensor on the panel to his right.

"Is Superior Hersher there? We're in urgent need of assistance."

"This is Captain Braxton of the High Ruler guard, Superior. Can I be of some help?"

"Our complex is under attack," she says.

I close my eyes and strain my hearing to see if I can pick up any background noise. Shots are being fired, followed by minor rumblings from possible explosions.

"Captain Braxton, we have no defenses. We can't raise anyone in Acheron." Her voice resonates with urgency and confusion.

"Move everyone into your emergency bunker as quickly as you can."

"We are trying, but the pathways between buildings have collapsed and many of my staff and children are trapped."

Braxton points down to the screen in front of me, and tells me which controls to work. The screen on our lower left turns on. He tells me coordinates to plug into the panel, and the screen quickly changes from a dense gray to white snow. I focus the satellite until the image comes into frame.

Hatchery Seven is made of four buildings just like Hatchery Nine, but the complex is located on the floor of a valley, making it an easy target. Smoke and flames are eating up the ground around the structures. There are large holes between each building, and metal beams are poking up out of the soil.

Their walkways must have been underground.

Small flashes of light emanate from each corner of all four buildings.

Superior Gatlen screams on the other side of our connection, which is soon lost. We watch as the entire complex erupts into flames, every inch engulfed in orange and red.

"They'll destroy all the hatcheries if they can. How do we stop them?" Lehen asks.

"By giving them what they want. Us." I reply.

"We need to get to the Dormitories," Lehen responds. "We can set up defenses there."

"How do we find it?" Braxton asks.

"It's about a day north of Oasis One. We need to follow the old shuttle line from the Trade Borough north."

"That's three days northwest of here," Braxton says. "The old shuttle line Lehen is talking about was supposed to connect the Trade Borough with Nuceira, before the relationship with the city deteriorated."

"Is the place occupied?" I ask.

"Yes, if it's still standing. It's five miles north of Hatchery Seven."

"So even if we make it to the Dormitories, it'll probably be too late," Jagger states, as he slumps against the wall by the door.

"We have to try," I say.

Braxton and Jagger work non-stop for a day and a half on getting one of the vehicles operational, while Keller, Gage, and Tobin set up a perimeter around what remains of the hatchery in case it's attacked again. I work with Lehen on getting his skills sharpened. He and I stay away from the functional buildings and train around the destroyed Developmental Quad.

During our scarce breaks, I try and think of a way to trigger Lehen's Quantum Stream. He's the only Antaean left without it. Lehen seems reluctant, almost to the point of being defiant, to take the necessary steps. I drop the topic, but I continue to think of my options.

Three days after the attack on Hatchery Nine, we're finally ready to leave.

The eight remaining Morrigan elect to stay behind and defend the complex if it's attacked again. Superior Hersher allocates some food rations for us, though it's not too much as she needs it for the women, children, and staff. Communications are still down with Tyre and sketchy with some of the outlying Boroughs.

Braxton instructs Hera and Duren to keep attempting to contact Tyre. In five days, when we're near the Dormitories, Duren is to send out a transmission stating that the city's forces are mobilizing for an assault on the Hostem from the Dormitories.

Braxton is hoping this will compel the Hostem to pull out of Acheron and the Boroughs. Of course this is a very tenuous plan.

We're still unsure of where Tyre stands.

As I climb into the front seat of the vehicle, I notice my Levin gun and knife sitting on the floor under the dashboard, so I place my knife in my back pocket and leave the gun by my feet. Braxton takes the wheel and begins to drive us slowly down the battered road. We pass under what remains of the keystone dangling over the third gate, its stone pillars reduced to rubble. Gates two and one are almost impassable. Jagger and Gage have to leave the vehicle in order to clear a path for us. Occasionally through the trees I catch a glimpse of several metallic objects with reflective panels on their roofs.

The carriages the Hostem used aren't big, but there are a lot of them, and they're in good working order.

I tell Braxton to stop. He is reluctant at first, but does finally comply.

I pick the Levin gun up from the floor and exit. Jagger and Gage join me and we make our way to one of the carriages. We approach cautiously, weapons drawn in case there are any Hostem around. I peer into the window, but no one is inside. Jagger and Gage stand behind me, facing the road as I open the driver's side door to take a better look inside.

The interior is cramped, loaded down with communication equipment, conflagration slugs, Levin guns, detonators, and a great number of other weapons I don't recognize. I sit in the driver's seat and flip on the monitor just above the gearshift. The screen hisses at first, then I hear voices in the background. The screen is damaged so I can't see who the voices belong to, but it's just as well, since it might be a two-way screen. I switch it off and exit the vehicle. We examine several other carriages and find the same equipment, along with provisions that should last us a couple of days.

I take a closer look at the crates holding the food and notice a blurry image on the bottom right corner of all the boxes.

"I wish I had a Regulator's glass."

Gage reaches into the front pocket of his coat and pulls one out.

"I took this off of the woman you killed before we buried her."

I take it from him and place it over the image on the top box. The figure solidifies into a bull with a red cape: the Tyre symbol.

"How'd they get a hold of those?" Gage asks, as I hand him back the glass.

"The same way the people in the Wasteland do. They steal them."

I close the back door of the carriage and head back to tell Braxton about the find. He suggests we take two of the Hostem carriages, partially for the equipment but mainly for camouflage if we encounter any Hostem on our way. As we transfer equipment,

Braxton removes a communications receiver from one of the carriages we aren't taking and installs it into our vehicle. I take note of the frequency numbers of the two vehicles we are taking and give them to Braxton so he can program them into our receiver.

Tobin and Lehen get into the first carriage, Braxton and I take the Morrigan vehicle, and Jagger and Gage follow at the end in the other carriage.

As we begin to move again, I turn on the receiver and call up Tobin and Gage's vehicles on the screen. I see their faces from the small camera housed in the screen, then move their images to one side to call up the main control insignia. By manipulating the controls, I'm able to block anyone from randomly locating our frequency. I enable the feature and advise Gage and Tobin to do the same as I try to locate other Hostems, so we can have a better idea of where they all are.

CHAPTER 28

We emerge onto the transport road an hour later and head north, descending the ridge. Snow begins to fall as we make our way down. There hasn't been much chatter over the receiver, so I haven't been able to discern anything. I keep the dial on search mode so it will continue to look for any transmissions.

It takes us several hours to reach the bottom of the range. We ride in silence, taking as few breaks as possible. The sun sets early, so we are forced to stop and make camp for the night. I want to push on, but Braxton advises it would be too dangerous to travel at night since we aren't driving on Acheron-made roads and it'll be hard to judge the terrain. We each take a turn patrolling while everyone else rests.

I have a hard time falling asleep on the hard ground, so I go into the Morrigan vehicle to see if I can locate any communications. Braxton is sitting on the driver's side, adjusting one of the controls on the screen. He looks up as I sit down on the passenger side, then goes back to his tasks.

"Find anything?"

"No," he responds in a frustrated tone.

"Why don't you try and get some sleep? I'll check the receiver."

He looks up at me, contemplating my offer, but declines, so the two of us stay awake all night, locating no transmissions.

"Jagger told me why you let me come along."

Braxton doesn't respond.

"Was any of it true?"

He hangs his head down, then looks out the window. "Yes," his responds in a remorseful tone. "I'm tired of the constant change in power. The High Ruler always threatening the people with persecution or death, even his own citizens, not just the Laics. It doesn't matter who's in power, they all act the same. I think the

Antaeans are more than soldiers to protect the cities. I've always hoped they were to protect the people."

We sit in silence the rest of the night. Our convoy leaves just as the sun rises.

After two hours, we come across an old set of shuttle rails running along the ground. We change direction and begin to head straight west, using the rails as a guide. I doze off periodically, my head hitting the doorframe every so often as we go over large divots in the ground. My eyes barely open as we come upon a brown, barren field. I notice rocks no bigger than five inches placed on the ground about two feet apart, spreading far back into the field.

"Stop," I yell to Braxton.

He radios Tobin to stop and places the Morrigan vehicle in park. I open my door, step down, and walk over the rusted tracks, my feet crunching on the hard dry ground. Grasses no taller than half an inch try their best to wave in the slight cold breeze that's blowing. I proceed down one aisle of rocks. The rows in front of me seem to go one for miles.

"What is this place?" I ask Braxton as he, Lehen, and Jagger join me.

"Asphodel."

"The tent city?" Lehen inquires.

"What remains of it."

I take a few steps away from the group, bend down, and touch one of the gray stones. The number 35 carved on top, barely visible from weathering, along with a symbol I haven't seen; a six-petaled flower, lines radiating from the center of each petal to the tip. I stand back up, surveying the land, mesmerized by the thousands of rocks littering the field.

"Each one symbolizes a person who was killed the night the tent city was destroyed," Jagger says, as he comes up behind me. "Thomas told me. He survived that night, and managed to escape being captured by the cities, only to be collected a few years later."

Braxton calls to us. "We need to get going."

Jagger turns and heads back to the vehicles while I stay a few seconds longer. I can see now how the Hostem came to be, and begin to question my intentions.

"Trea," Braxton yells, "we need to go now."

Who would massacre so many people? What was gained from their deaths?

Seeing this sickens me. My heart aches for those lost. Even though I never knew them, I feel connected to them.

We navigate the vehicles directly onto the shuttle rail in order to cross the large river that lies before us. It's been many hours since we left the ruins of Asphodel and we still have not located any Hostem frequencies. The bridge over the water appears to be rickety, so we cross slowly, one vehicle at a time. It takes over an hour with the sun almost set, but the bridge holds up.

Once it's too dark to continue, we make camp along the river's banks. Jagger takes the first watch after we eat a small meal. I decide to sleep in the Morrigan vehicle rather than on the cold hard ground.

My slumber is disturbed by a crackling from the receiver.

"Bevan...are you there?" A very young female voice asks. "Bevan...I need you to respond."

The line crackles for a few minutes. I turn the volume up just a bit, waiting for a response.

"Grainne, I thought we were on silence until tomorrow?"

"I know, but I haven't heard from Tak's group for days. I haven't been able to raise them in their vehicles and I can't locate their frequencies."

"Where were they supposed to be heading to after they picked up their supplies from the Trade Borough?"

"Towards one of Acheron's hatcheries, but that was several days ago."

I hesitate about whether to chime into the conversation or not, but Jagger knocks on my window so I discretely dial down the volume and open the door.

"Your turn," he says to me.

I step out of the vehicle, take the Beta rifle and Levin gun that Jagger is holding, and begin my patrol. He goes off and sleeps by the small fire we built earlier that is slowly dying.

As I walk on patrol, about a half mile in all directions away from the river, I think about the conversation I heard, wondering why the Hostem would be getting supplies from the Trade Borough.

I'm relieved four hours later by Gage where I return to the Morrigan vehicle, but the chatter has stopped. I try to locate other frequencies, but all is silent so I lean my head against the door and get some asleep.

I wake up mid-morning, hours away from the river. I ask Braxton if he's heard anything, but he says it's been quiet all morning.

"Speaking of quiet, you haven't had any nightmares in a while," he comments.

I don't know why they've suddenly stopped, but I've slept better since the night I recognized Terrance's face.

We ride in silence the remainder of the day.

As the sun begins to set on our third day, we notice thick plumes of smoke in the distance. Braxton indicates it's coming from the area of the Trade Borough. Ten minutes later we see the elevated rail lines of the defunct shuttle to Nuceira and turn north. Jagger radios us to see if Braxton wants to stop and check for survivors, but Braxton ignores his calls by turning off the receiver.

Since we're so close to where we think the Hostem are encamped, Braxton decides to push on through the night. Several hours later we all trade spots so that Braxton, Gage, and Tobin can get some rest. I turn the receiver back on, but don't hear anyone transmitting.

I drive through the night and into most of the morning. We switch again before the afternoon.

"We should reach Oasis One tonight," Braxton tells everyone over the receiver.

As evening falls around us, the receiver is hot with activity. The Hostem seem to have made Oasis One their base of operations, so we're forced to change direction, turning and heading west again. At our closest, we're about a mile from the nearest Hostem, from what I can tell on the receiver. We have to travel several hours out of our way to make sure we're far enough away from Oasis One to start heading north again.

As the sun begins to rise on our fifth day of travel, Duren transmits a message to the world through a Regulator channel the Hostem know about.

"Regulators, this is Captain Braxton of the Acheron High Ruler guard. We are planning an offensive strike against our enemies, the Hostem. All available units, please take a transport vehicle to the Dormitories where additional weaponry is stored. I will meet you there in two days' time."

We wait in hushed stillness for the Hostem to begin chattering, but all remains quiet.

"What day do you think it is?" I ask Braxton several hours after the message.

"I think it's sixty days after the Winter Solstice. Why?"

"I was born in the winter, so I must be nineteen now."

"You don't know when you were born?" he asks.

"Do you?" I respond.

"Laics are different. We aren't told the day of their births. It's to keep us from determining our age."

"Why would they not want you to know how old you are?"

"Control, I think."

I look out the window at the passing trees...snow changing to rain...the grass underneath our wheels coming out of its slumber. The seasons change, but the Laics have no marker to tell the passage of time for them. Somehow that makes their life seem even more dismal to me.

Hours seem to pass like days.

Even with the detour, we should reach the Dormitories by early morning at the latest, but the isolation and inactivity is making me anxious and agitated.

"I think I'm thirty-eight," Braxton whispers from a faraway daydream.

We stop for a final break when it's close to dark.

Our stomachs are growling, so we set up a small fire to heat up some of the provisions. Gage patrols, allowing the rest of us to eat. The food is only lukewarm, but we eat it all the same. We save Gage some, which he eats while Jagger drives.

The sun begins to rise as we find the transport road. We wind up and down several small hills before coming upon a shattered watchtower. Rusty metal pilings stick out from the earth; razor wire lays snarled across the entrance, as the fence it had been attached to has disintegrated. Lehen steps out and removes a swath of the razor wire so the vehicles can pass.

This place is very unpleasant for me. I can hear muffled screams and smell acrid smoke, though I know it's just my memories.

The road winds for another ten minutes before we stop at to the top of a rise overlooking the complex. I'm the first to step out of the vehicles, walk a few feet to my right, and look down into the gorge.

Blackened, cracked granite walls lie scattered across a blasted landscape. The concrete sidewalks are broken in large pieces, some with small trees breaking through, others with patches of grass peeking through the upturned edges. It's hard to tell how many buildings once stood, but I close my eyes and see the image from the tablet Devlan left me. The fountain in the center is the only discernable landmark; the manmade pool it sits in has long since dried up.

"It's amazing any of you survived," Braxton says, as he joins me.

The rest of the group stands along the ridge with us, surveying the destruction below.

"Let's prepare," I say and head back to the Morrigan vehicle.

CHAPTER 29

Once we reach the ruins, Lehen sets out to try and locate Vier, who I'm hoping is still close by. The rest of us remove the weapons from the vehicles and create a perimeter around the complex. Gage and Tobin plant detonators wherever they can find an open piece of land, synching them to a master control recovered from one of the Hostem carriages back at the hatchery. Jagger hides several conflagration cannons under the rubble of two of the housing buildings, leaving enough room for him and Keller to squeeze under so they can operate them. Keller and Braxton are working on our defensive and escape plans if something goes wrong.

I hunt through the remains, looking for anything, not even knowing what I'm looking for…but find nothing.

I crawl in and out of small dark spaces, my mind going back in time. I wander around the property, not quite going as far as the forest, my feet remaining on the cracked concrete. After some time, I head back to the pool in the center where Keller and Braxton are waiting. We're joined an hour later by Gage and Tobin as Jagger goes off to look for Lehen, who hasn't returned. I grow concerned and restless as another two hours pass before Jagger finally returns, Lehen trailing behind him.

"Did you find Vier?" I ask Lehen, as he sits down on the rim of the pool.

"Yes, but he won't come out. He's just on the other side of the tree line, but he won't move."

I strain my eyes to see if I can pick him out amongst the trees, but with the sun setting it's getting harder to see.

We eat a small meal, then make our preparations before the sun fully sets.

As Braxton walks Lehen back to the forest, Gage, Keller, and Tobin take off in the vehicles to hide them. Gage and Tobin are to remain by the vehicles and operate the detonators using the master control once the Hostem begin their approach. They're also to radio us at the first sign of movement. Keller walks back to us along the forest line, taking his place at his conflagration canon. Jagger mans the other one.

I voice my worries to Braxton about the possibility of the Hostem approaching from the forest.

"Lehen and Vier have it covered," he assures me.

The two of us lay low in the pool, which is only two feet deep. The pale blue tile is cracked, with tufts of grass peeking out from the deteriorated grout. We each have a Levin gun in hand, and lie in wait as the sun sets.

Hours tick by as the temperature slowly drops, the dampness from a light rain earlier seeping into our clothes. I lay on my back, looking up at the stars that have decided to grace the sky this evening, and think back to my favorite time of night out in the Wasteland, when the stars would start to sparkle before we had to hide inside our home.

Those moments of peace seem like centuries ago.

I roll back over and notice Braxton has nodded off, so I nudge him in the ribs with my elbow. He is startled awake, almost firing his Levin gun. I shake my head in amusement and survey the area, which is quiet, then roll back over.

"Why do we have to stay awake when you had Duren announce that the Regulators will be here in two days' time?" I ask some time later.

"Strategy. If the Hostem believe the Regulators will be here tomorrow, then wouldn't you want to arrive before they do, to prepare…like we did?"

"I hadn't thought of it that way."

I could sense the smile on his face without having to turn and look at him.

"Captain Braxton of Acheron?" A heavy voice blasts through the silence. "Captain Braxton, come out please."

Braxton raises his head above the rim of the pool, just enough to see who's calling his name.

"Looks like they've arrived. Stay here," he whispers to me, placing a hand on my shoulder.

I grab his right arm, just as he begins to stand.

"Be careful."

He smiles, stands, and climbs over the small lip of the pool. I turn over, prop myself up on my elbows, and strain my neck to see.

Braxton is cautiously walking to a group of men in odd Regulator uniforms, who have entered the complex from the main road. I begin to wonder why Gage and Tobin didn't signal to us that we had visitors, as they were supposed to.

The men are standing in front of a large armored vehicle with high-wattage spotlights attached to the front, casting shadows around Braxton.

"That's far enough, Captain," the man says.

"Who are you?" Braxton asks, hands fidgeting at his side.

"I'm Commander Caderyn of the Territorial Army of Tyre."

"Army? The cities don't have any armies."

"Acheron may not, but Tyre does," the man says, then snickers. He snaps his fingers and twenty additional Regulators climb out of the vehicle, all brandishing weapons I haven't seen before. "I need for you to come with me."

I hear movement behind me and turn my attention towards the sound. A small figure quietly jumps into the pool and crawls over to me. I pull out my knife from my back pocket, but I pause when she places her finger over her lips, making a shushing sound. I look quizzically at the young face streaked with dirt, filthy blond hair pulled back into a braid.

She can't be more than eleven years old.

I nod my head to show I understand and we both turn our attention back to the men.

"Why should I come with you?" Braxton asks, slowly backing away.

I notice Keller and Jagger stiffening; something doesn't seem right.

"It would be better if we spoke in private, Captain." Commander Caderyn takes a step closer to Braxton, his men readying their weapons.

"We can talk here just fine."

"Very well." Caderyn takes another step forward. "Captain Braxton, you're being detained for violations against Sirain."

"What the hell are you talking about?"

"Premier Vladim has ordered the detention of all those who have violated the laws of Sirain. You left your post as head guard to the High Ruler of Acheron, which allowed the city to be attacked by the Hostem. Therefore, Captain Braxton, you're to be remanded to the Reformatories until you're sentenced."

"High Ruler Vladim has declared himself as Premier? What about the Acheron High Ruler?"

"The High Ruler was assassinated several days ago. Premier Vladim has appointed a new leader to the city. Now, Captain, will you come willingly or forcibly?"

"Time to go," the girl next to me says.

She grabs my arm just as the evening sky lights up. Deflagration rounds scream across the atmosphere, landing only a few feet away, creating a series of concussions, and shrapnel flying everywhere. We run across to the far end of the pool, and jump the wall. Men and women pour out of the forest in front of us as the rounds continue to fly from the same direction. I prepare to defend against their blows, but they run past us.

I freeze in my tracks in confusion until the little girl tugs desperately at my arm.

"Come on!"

I look back in the direction we just came from. Braxton is fighting off three Regulators; Keller is firing his canon at the vehicles that are moving into the complex to no avail; Jagger is lying on the ground not moving and bleeding.

I shake the girl loose and run for Jagger as I hold out my Levin gun, firing at anything in a uniform. The Regulators seem to be shielded somehow, because the energy blasts aren't penetrating deeply enough to be fatal. But at least they're still causing substantial injuries.

Jagger is bleeding badly from his left shoulder, pieces of shrapnel poking out of his face. I look over to the cannon he was operating, but it's been utterly destroyed.

"Braxton," I shout out.

"I'm a little busy," he calls back, knocking a Regulator out.

"What do you need?" The girl asks, as she suddenly appears by my side.

"Here," I begin, grabbing her hands and placing them on Jagger's wound. "Keep pressure on it. I'll be right back."

I scramble over to Braxton. Two Hostem have joined in the fight, pulling a Regulator off of Braxton's back while he pounds the other one into the concrete. The man's head cracks and he stops moving. I help Braxton to his feet and we run to Jagger. From the satchel around Braxton's shoulders he removes one of the four remaining syringes and injects it into Jagger's bicep.

The two of us carefully pick him up, trying to balance his bulk between us.

"Grainne," a man shouts at us from a few meters away, "get them out of here."

"We have to go, now!" the girl shouts to us.

She leads the way past the pool, behind the building that was once the research lab to the outer rim of the complex.

I hear whirring sounds from above. The air begins to spin around, dried leaves and grass blow in our faces. I look up to see what's making the noise, but all I see is darkness.

We enter the forest, but don't stop right away. After a few minutes we come upon a large group of Hostem. Two men come over and relieve us of Jagger, laying him down next to another wounded man.

"I have to help Keller," Braxton wheezes, hunched over and panting from exhaustion.

"I've got him," someone shouts to our right. An elderly man sets Keller down on a fallen tree trunk. Braxton goes over to check on him while I make my way back to the tree line.

The whirring noise has increased, but I still can't find the source. I spot Commander Caderyn climbing into one of the vehicles, which then begin to retreat. Grainne appears next to me, the both of us crouching down, trying not to be noticed.

We see the bright blue flash before we hear it.

The shock wave hits us seconds later, throwing us several feet into the forest. I hit the trunk of a large tree, landing hard on the ground. I frantically look around for Grainne, calling out her name as I begin to heal from the cuts and the burns on my arms and face.

I hear her moan off to my right. Following the noise, I locate her buried under splinters of wood. I gingerly remove the debris, careful not to add to her injuries. She has suffered a deep gash just above her right brow, her cheeks blistering from the heat that was generated from the detonation.

"Lie still. You're badly hurt."

"I'll heal," she says, though with her injuries, I'm not sure she'll survive the next hour. I carefully uncover her legs and feet to get a better look at the extent of her injuries.

"That was a Quantum mortar," she says through shudders of pain. "It incinerates everything it hits."

I look behind us and see several feet of forest have been leveled. As the sun begins to rise I can better see the extent of the damage done.

All relics of the Dormitories are shattered; ash with tiny fragments of concrete and granite rain down from the sky, littering the earth. No one remains in the devastation, not even any body fragments. There's nothing left but bits of rubble and an indentation in the ground.

"Terrifying isn't it?" Grainne says.

I look down at her and am astonished at what I see.

The gash on her forehead is gone. There are no longer any burns on her face.

"Hi, Trea," she says. "We've been looking for you."

End of Book One